AMANUENSIS

Phil Egner

Copyright © 2020 Phil Egner

All rights reserved. No part of this publication may be reproduced, stored in a retrieval system, or transmitted in any form or by any means, mechanical, electronic, recording, photocopying or otherwise without the prior permission of the copyright owner.

This is a work of fiction. All characters, organisations and events portrayed in this novel are either products of the author's imagination or are used fictitiously.

Cover Design
SelfPubBookCovers.com /FrinaArt

For Sharon

'And what a long strange trip it's been.'

I closed my eyes and saw before me a hundred thousand tiny skiffs... all drifting helplessly with the tide... in each one a wee wrinkled corpse... hoisting its life story... and all its little lies... to catch the wind...

Death on the Instalment Plan
Louis-Ferdinand Céline

CONTENTS

Title Page
Copyright
PART ONE   1
1. Brian Maddox   3
2. Claudia   23
3. Jan de Keyser   45
4. Aidan   62
5. Sir Richard Milford   78
6. Kit   99
7. Barry Denham   122
PART TWO   135
1. Aidan   136
2. Kit   143
3. Claudia   150
4. Aidan   153
5. Kit   158
6. Claudia   164
7. Aidan   167
8. Kit   170
9. Claudia   174
10. Aidan   180

11. Claudia	184
12. Kit	188
13. Aidan	194
14. Kit	197
15. Claudia	200
16. Aidan	205
17. Claudia	207
18. Kit	212
19. Claudia	216
20. Aidan	222
21. Claudia	226
22. Aidan	229
23. Kit	234
24. Aidan	237
25. Claudia	240
26. Kit	242
27. Claudia	246
28. Kit	251
29. Aidan	254
30. Claudia	258
PART THREE	263
1. Spike	264
2. April 1970	278
3. Sy Johnson	299
4. May 1970	326
5. Amanda Palmer	353
6. July 1970	378
7. Reverend Warwick	392

8. August 1970	434
9. Declan McKelvey	459
10. September 1970	473
11. Sandy Beaumont	490
12. Kit	509
13. Tracey De Keyser	514
PART FOUR	529
Claudia	530
Afterword	543
About The Author	545

PART ONE

Preludes

1. Brian Maddox

Even in summer, Westerkirk casts a long shadow. By late afternoon the spire reaches across Prinsengracht, catching those tail end tourists scattered about the pavement cafes and hoping for the Anne Frankhuis line to shorten. Brian watched as a young backpacker at the next table gave a sudden shiver and then reached down into her bag to pull out a light sweater. Knotting the arms loosely around her neck to cover her bare shoulders, she turned her head once more to stare across the canal. The queue was as long as it had been an hour ago and Brian guessed she was starting to realise that there was no good time to get here.

Brian had been taught to read a street before this girl had even been born. *'Each one's got its own rhythm,'* his sergeant had told him on that first stakeout, *'and what we're waiting for here is a bum note'*. And that wouldn't simply be the same car cruising by once too often or an overly casual figure lingering at a shop window's reflection - your real antennae were the locals. Watch the postman and then watch the window cleaner and then watch the traffic warden, always register what catches their attention, what's making their heads turn. Or, reflected Brian as he placed his cup back down onto its saucer, the busker who sets himself up fifty yards down the road from the Anne Frankhuis entrance. Far enough away for its custodians to have no legitimate reason to move him along, but where he obviously believes he'll have a captive audience all day long.

Read the street.

Brian turned his attention back to their side of the

canal, where Bloemgracht took a ninety-degree turn to the left and gave him an unobstructed view of Gallery DeWit. When he'd telephoned yesterday, the girl he'd spoken to had said that unfortunately Mr Franklyn was away on business but would definitely be at the Gallery tomorrow afternoon.

Which had been good enough for Brian. He'd hung up before she'd a chance to press him further to the nature of his enquiry and then he'd checked the Eurostar timetable. This morning he'd paid cash for his ticket at Waterloo Station where, as he'd expected, no-one gave more than a cursory glance at his passport. He'd been in Brussels by mid-morning and arrived at Amsterdam Centraal just after one, where he'd exchanged five ten pound notes for guilders and bought a street map.

Gallery DeWit was a twenty-minute walk from the railway station and he'd paused for a moment on the pavement outside, looking for all the world as if his attention had suddenly been captured by the window display. He noted that the Gallery appeared to specialise in antiquarian books and prints, and that the interior gave the impression of several rooms knocked into one, the reception area on a slightly higher level from the others. He'd moved on, found a table at this cafe and ordered a late lunch.

Brian took his time with it, letting his instincts wash around Bloemgracht until he was as certain as he could be that he was the only one paying attention to the Gallery and that no-one was paying undue attention to him.

All he had to do now was wait.

At the next table, the girl with the backpack was signalling to the waitress for another coffee and Brian did the same.

* * *

The call had been four, no, five days ago now and just before lunch, Janice not yet home from the charity shop where she volunteered most mornings. And, since his retirement, for a couple of afternoons a week too - it seemed he wasn't the only one struggling to get a handle on this freshly minted life of leisure.

Picking up the phone, Brian found himself speaking to a Detective Inspector Amanda Palmer, who introduced herself as the head of a CCU in the Met.

"A Cold Case Unit," she added helpfully, as if he'd been ten years out of the job instead of three months.

"Right," said Brian, carefully.

"Thing is, something we're taking a look at seems to have led us to one of your former cases." She hesitated. "I was hoping we could have a chat, just for some background really. Wouldn't think it'd take up more than half an hour or so of your time."

The request wasn't that unusual, and God knows how many times he'd made it himself. Going over old ground looking for a fresh angle meant you were always interested in what hadn't gone into the files. Usually, it was the clutter around the fringes of an investigation - who'd got a free pass for the word on a firm putting one together or a DC's bit on the side stripper girlfriend earwigging what she shouldn't. Fragments which might not have seemed important at the time but twenty years down the line could prove the key part of a larger pattern.

"Sure," Brian told her. "When were you thinking?"

"Well, would today be possible?" asked Palmer. "Say two, two thirty?"

"No problem," said Brian. "I'll be waiting."

He slowly put the handset back onto its cradle, remembering the calls he used to make - sipping tea in the front parlour, polite smiles to old war stories until he had what he'd come for and then trying not to seem in too much of a hurry to leave. OTP visits they'd called them - Out To Pasture. Not that he thought for one minute he'd ever come across like that, but then again, who did?

So, he changed into a suit, his black brogues needed more of a dusting than a shine and Janice had been home in time to knot his tie properly for him.

"An old case of mine," he told her. "Seems they need a bit of help."

When Janice smiled, he realised that wasn't something he'd seen for a while and so he said look, as he was all dressed up why didn't they go out for a bite to eat tonight, seemed a shame to waste it and she told him that would be lovely. Then, leaving a pot of coffee percolating and a plate of biscuits on the kitchen table, she took herself off shopping for the afternoon with her sister.

But after Janice left Brian slipped into a reflective mood, the *frisson* of DI Palmer's impending visit generating a perhaps overdue wake-up call as to what life was becoming. He had to do *something*, he told himself, because if the last three months had taught anything then it was that it really wasn't in him to sit around all day doing bugger all. There was always private security... Investigative of course, not uniform. *Jesus!*

Or maybe even some kind of social work. It's not like he needed a salary, he had a bloody good pension and the mortgage was long paid off. Now the kids had flown the coop, they'd make a killing if they downsized to somewhere more sensible. Perhaps working with teenagers, crime prevention... Something to come in through the front door from and have a day to talk about.

And then she arrived.

* * *

DI Palmer came alone, which at first had reassured him. If this had been one of those *If he isn't telling us something that we already know then what else is he covering up?* fishing trips then there'd have been two of them - one asking all the questions, the other sitting off to one side, clocking reactions and body language.

She'd addressed him at first as Chief Superintendent, to which he'd felt obliged to say 'Please, Brian', while appreciating that was exactly the same technique he'd used to neutralise former rank when interviewing retired senior officers. They chatted in the kitchen while he made them both coffee, and the discovery that they had a couple of mutual acquaintances was something to stretch out until they sat themselves down in the living room, facing each other across the coffee table.

"Right," she began. "As I told you on the phone, I run a Cold Case Unit. Obviously, you'll know the sort of work that entails."

Brian nodded.

"What's less well known is that because of the skill sets we've acquired, we're occasionally seconded to current investigations. If a case takes on an historical aspect, then we might be asked to pursue that investigative line because we know from experience where to go looking."

Brian gave another nod.

"As a rule, we'll know which records have been computerised, which haven't and where to find them. We know how the old filing systems worked, how they were cross correlated and the manner in which they're likely to be, let's say, problematic. And also, that feeling you get when something's…"

She shrugged.

"Out of place," said Brian. "Or just plain wrong."

"Exactly." She gave him a quick smile. "And sometimes a current investigation drags up something from years ago - usually a confession, maybe re-examined physical evidence - which prompts a separate inquiry to be handled by us in its entirety."

Brian remained silent as she reached down into her briefcase, took out a thickish cardboard folder and laid it on the coffee table.

"Which is what we find ourselves with here." She tapped the folder with her fingers. "About a week ago, an enquiry being carried out by a partner agency came up with credible evidence of a homicide."

"Of who?"

"We don't know."

"Right. So, do you have any idea who the killer was?" Brian knew that cold case investigations were often arse about face - verifying a deathbed confession to a decades old crime could be just as difficult as solving the case would have been in the first place. Sometimes harder.

"No, but we do know when and we do know where." Palmer paused. "The when is nearly thirty years ago, in nineteen seventy. And the where is..." She flipped the folder open to reveal it was full of photographs. Palmer put a finger on the top one and pushed it across the table to him.

Brian hadn't been above using theatrics himself when he'd wanted to prompt a reaction and so he was careful to have his poker face well bedded in before he picked up the print. But it still took an awful lot to keep even a flicker of alarm out of his eyes.

"Well, there's a rave from the grave," he said softly and then looked up as if embarrassed by his *faux pas* - effective camouflage, he hoped, for whatever else might have been read into his expression. "Jesus, I'm sorry!"

She dismissed the apology with a wave of her hand.

"You obviously recognise it?"

"Three Pembridge Villas, Notting Hill Gate," said Brian quietly.

The photograph was of a five story Italianate town house, but with the grandeur it once possessed greatly diminished. It had been the middle property in a row of five, recalled Brian, although you couldn't tell that from the photograph. There was a small walled garden where overgrown shrubbery concealed the windows of a sunken basement and half a dozen stone steps ran up to a portico entrance. Full-length windows distinguished the floor above, opening onto wrought-iron balconies. The row of windows on the fourth floor, although less grand, sat under decorative hood mouldings. An ornate ledge ran the width of the building just below the top floor, where the mean little windows of the servants' quarters were set well back from the rest of the facade.

Brian put the photograph down, looked over at Palmer and said, "Go on."

"These photographs," she put her hand on the open folder and then slowly spread them across the coffee table, "are from a surveillance operation authorised by yourself, correct?"

"That's right," said Brian.

"Can we talk a bit about the background to that, Brian?" She picked up her cup. "Specifically, what prompted it?"

Brian considered for a few seconds as she sipped her coffee.

"The reason I ask," she continued, "is that according to the file, the target of this operation was a young man named Christopher Franklyn, wanted for jumping bail on drug offences - including intent to supply *and* trafficking." She studied Brian carefully. "Problem is, the only record we can find of a Christopher Franklyn being arrested was three years previous to this, in 1967, when he was subsequently sentenced to two years' probation on a *possession* of cannabis charge." Palmer put her cup down. "So, perhaps we could begin by clearing that up."

Brian came to a decision.

"It's probably best," he said slowly, "if we were to start from when I transferred to Special Branch, at the beginning of 1970."

"You were with the Met, I believe? Drug Squad, working out of West End Central?"

"Yes."

"Did you request the transfer or were you poached?"

"A bit of both." Brian hesitated. "There was a lot going on in the Met back then I wasn't comfortable with and the Branch were looking for someone who'd been undercover in the so-called counterculture - not exactly their usual beat."

"By 'not comfortable with' are we talking brown envelopes or funny handshakes?"

Brian gave her an even stare.

"Let's just leave it at not being comfortable, shall we?"

"Fair enough." Palmer picked her cup up. "I'm guessing the Special Branch interest was down to the credit claimed for the bombings over the previous year. And that attack on the American Embassy."

Brian gave an appreciative nod, she'd done her homework.

"That's right. They'd been passed off in the press as gas explosions, we had D-notices flying thick and fast. Residue from the bombs had been forensically identified as Nitrimite 19c, a French explosive known to be used by the First of May Group."

"Basque separatists?"

"Yes. Who'd been driven out of Spain a few years earlier and gone to ground in Britain. There'd been sporadic targeting of Spanish corporate business premises in London, but nothing had been taken too seriously until the Grosvenor Square attack."

"The communiques?"

"No one realised that the embassy had been machine-gunned until the Angry Brigade letter to the underground press." Brian smiled. "It wasn't until they stepped outside and took a good look at the wall that they found the bullet holes."

"And so you went undercover, infiltrating these groups?"

"Well, that had been the idea, but that's not what happened." He hesitated. "My boss was Chief Superintendent Jack Franklyn and yes, that had been his plan. Get someone hanging around the fringe political meetings or street selling left-wing magazines, maybe push a little dope. See how far they could work themselves in. So, that's what he'd had in mind for me, but as things worked out we found ourselves with another option."

He took a sip of his coffee before continuing, aware of

how dry his mouth had become.

"Jack Franklyn had a son, Christopher. It had always been a bit of a difficult relationship and when Jack's wife died, in sixty-five, it fractured completely. Chris ran away from home and spent some time living on the streets, eventually getting arrested for drugs. Jack called in a lot of favours and got him probation on condition that he went back to live at home. Or a Detention Centre if he didn't."

"Presumably he went home?"

"He did, and it turned out they had more in common than they'd thought. Once he'd got the whole teenage rebellion stuff out of his system, things between them became a lot better. Chris got his life back on an even keel."

"I'm guessing there's a 'but' here?"

"A week after I started at the Branch, Jack took me down the pub. That's when I heard the story about his son. Anyway, a few days earlier Chris had bumped into someone he'd known from 'his time away' as Jack put it. They'd gone off for a drink, where they'd been joined by two others, a bit cagey at first but once Chris's *bona fides* had been established they started to open up. And it soon became obvious that these people were into political agitation and had a lot more in mind than just stirring things up."

"It was Christopher Franklyn who went undercover?"

"Jack wasn't happy about it." Brian gave a slight smile. "Nor was I, really. But the credibility and the contacts Chris already had would have taken me months to build... Not something we could afford to pass by."

"So?"

"He left home and moved into the squat at..." Brian indicated the photograph on the table.

"Who handled him?"

"Only his father. Jack was adamant about that."

"And your role?"

"Well, I got a haircut and shaved off my quite fetching Zapata moustache."

Palmer gave a smile.

"No more undercover work?"

"At this point, the entire operation changed tack. One thing we learnt over the next few months was that this group was mostly being financed by fraud - stolen chequebooks from university halls of residence. Activists would move around the country giving talks at colleges, staying overnight and getting light-fingered before leaving. Once we knew that, things got a lot easier."

"Easier how?"

"Well, I'm sure they had no problem justifying theft as liberating funds from the bourgeoisie to finance the glorious revolution or some such bollocks, but in purely practical terms what it did was to make them criminals." Brian smiled. "Which became their Achilles heel."

"In what sense?"

"We might not have been that good at infiltrating underground urban guerrilla groups, not at first anyway, but we were bloody good at catching villains. So, we set up a parallel fraud investigation."

"Which you headed?"

"Yes. We liaised with banks, got them to immediately report chequebook thefts from students, the whole who, when and where from, together with where the stolen cheques had been passed. We correlated that information with who'd been giving talks at what meetings and came up with a target list pretty quickly."

"But you didn't arrest them straight away?"

"No. At that time the SDS was being created. The idea of a unit whose sole function was the long-term infiltration of extremist groups had been mooted for a while, but this operation really got everything shifting. So, the strategy then became to stop using Chris as an information source and instead use him to get SDS undercover officers into ultra-left political groups. Use his credibility to introduce them and then they could take things from there themselves. Plus, any intelligence they uncovered couldn't be directly attributable to Chris, which made Jack a lot happier."

"Right," said Palmer

"But then," said Brian, "in August 1970 Jack had a heart attack. At the time Chris was out of London and we had no bloody idea where."

"You had no other way to contact him?"

"No, he would always get in touch with Jack, they both felt it was more secure that way. Then two days later Jack had a second coronary and... Well, that was that." Brian shrugged. "With no way of contacting Chris, I put out an arrest warrant for him, supposedly for jumping bail. It seemed the safest means of bringing him in while preserving his cover." He indicated the photographs on the table. "Ditto. I needed to know what was going on at Pembridge Villas."

"They were obviously taken over several days," said Palmer. "What was it, a parked van?"

"GPO tent. There was actually a department within the Post Office staffed solely by Special Branch and MI5 - phone tapping and mail intercepts." He smiled. "And creating a fault on a telephone line can get you into pretty much anywhere."

"And then?"

"Eventually Chris was picked up in North London on the warrant. We talked, as you'd expect he was devastated about his father. I told him that if he wanted to quit then we understood, he'd already done more than enough. But a few nights earlier, the home of Sir John Waldron - the London Police Commissioner - had been bombed by the Angry Brigade. There'd been nothing in the media about it - yet one more D-notice - but it made him realise the stakes that were being played for. So, he agreed to carry on."

"For how long?"

"Two, maybe three years. Once we had the SDS properly up and running, it was something he could step away from."

"When were you last in contact with him?"

"It would be the summer of 1975, so twenty-four years

ago."

"And you've no idea where he might be now?"

Brian shook his head. "Sorry."

"Okay." With a smile and a nod, she began gathering the photographs back into the folder. "I think that just about covers it."

"So," asked Brian, "have I told you anything you didn't already know?"

"The Zapata moustache," said Palmer, "was a bit of a surprise."

Brian smiled.

"I'm sorry I can't be more forthcoming, Brian," she said, slipping the folder into her briefcase, "but you know how this works."

"I do but…" Brian shrugged. "It's not too much of a stretch that you believe your victim is either in those photographs and disappeared afterwards or be notable by their absence. The Pembridge Villas squat was pretty transient, so at the time someone suddenly disappearing wouldn't attract attention, but it might ring a few bells in retrospect." He gave a nod. "And Christopher Franklyn is definitely your best bet, he was the one person in the place actively noting the comings and goings."

"Well, it's almost certain that he's no longer living in this country," said Palmer. "No tax returns, utilities billings, phone records or bank accounts since the mid-eighties. His wife Karen applied for a copy of her degree certificate from the Central London Polytechnic about fifteen years ago, and that's about it."

Brian kept his expression inscrutable, but he'd been hoping for something of a head start here and she'd just handed him a giant one.

"And that," she said, with a smile that was tightening, "really is as much as I can tell you."

"It's okay," said Brian, "Like you say, I know how this works."

"Fortunately Christopher Franklyn isn't the only lead we have but you're right, he is our best shot." She took a business card from her pocket and handed it to him. "And if you think of anything else, then please get back to me."

She stood, and Brian walked with her to the front door.

"Thanks again for your time," she said. "At the very least, you've confirmed that we're moving in the right direction with this."

They shook hands, and he slowly closed the door behind her.

* * *

The waitress brought his coffee. Brian thanked her and then slipped his hand into his pocket, fingering the cassette tape.

After Palmer left, he'd gone into the garage and rummaged around in those old cardboard boxes. Lots of coppers spirited stuff away with them when they retired, occasionally for nostalgia, sometimes for insurance, but mainly it was an inexplicable sense of entitlement to things that once mattered and now didn't. This was a bit of all three, he guessed.

The trick was to leave enough bits and pieces behind to suggest that nothing had been tampered with, while removing the links that actually connected them. Brian reflected that he might have erred too much on the side of caution here. He should at least have moved those photographs to another case-file, suggesting cock-up rather than conspiracy in the eventuality of them ever seeing the light of day again.

Brian must have played the tape half a dozen times over the last few days, or enough to run it through his head word perfect. It had been the end of summer 1970 and he'd spent weeks scouring London for Christopher Franklyn. When confirmation finally came through that he'd been found in North London and was now under surveillance, Brian tried to arrange a safe house to have him taken to, but it was too short notice. So, he'd sent two DCs to lift him off the street using the warrant he'd told Palmer about, while he sorted out somewhere else.

In the end, it was a school in Hoxton. A retired copper was the caretaker, and he'd been decorating classrooms during the summer holidays. He didn't need an explanation, was just happy enough to be taken off down the pub for a few pints while they got on with whatever needed doing.

Brian found a classroom not overlooked by the street and sat on the edge of the teacher's desk to wait. He could remember the smell of fresh paint and the cartoon characters stencilled onto the walls. It must have been an infants' class, a giant Donald Duck was on the wall behind him. Then the incongruity of it all struck him and he'd stood up to find another room, but the door opened and Chris entered between the two DCs, each one holding him by the cuff of his sleeve. A trickle of blood ran down from his nose.

He stared sullenly at Brian and warily around the room.

Brian nodded at the two detectives.

"It's okay, I'll handle it from here."

On first listening to the tape he'd been surprised at how little his voice had changed over the years. Unlike most people he was used to hearing himself speak, police interviews endlessly replayed and analysed. The detectives left the room, Brian reached into his pocket and handed Chris a large white handkerchief.

"My name is Brian Maddox," he said. "Detective Sergeant Brian Maddox. I'm with Special Branch." He paused. "I believe your dad mentioned me to you - gave you my contact details in case you couldn't get through to him in an emergency?"

Chris had just continued to stare at him.

"We've been trying to find you for a while now," said Maddox. "Chief Superintendent Franklyn told us you would be away with your girlfriend, but he didn't know where."

"Right," said Chris slowly.

Brian pulled the chair out from behind the desk.

"I think you'd better have a seat," he said. As Chris sat down Brian took a deep breath.

"I'm afraid I've some really bad news." He reached forward and laid his hand on Chris's shoulder. "Your father suffered a heart attack at the beginning of August. He hung on for two days, but there was a second one which proved fatal. I'm very sorry."

"What?" Chris looked stunned.

"We put out a story about you being abroad," continued Maddox, "to explain why you weren't at the funeral. We've been doing everything we can to find you, but we couldn't risk blowing your cover." He paused. "So, we issued a warrant for your arrest and Holloway got back to us on the Visiting Order, which is how we had it staked out. Sorry," changing to a conciliatory tone, "if it got rough, but it had to look good - the two DCs who brought you here have no idea who you really are."

Chris had just sat there, staring at him.

"I know you and your father didn't have much chance to talk about what happened at Camden Town," continued Maddox, "but he wanted you to know that you did the right thing. There's absolutely no doubt they were behind the attacks and finding the *plastique* there will put them away where they belong for the rest of their lives." He paused. "Your father said you'd used old takeaway boxes out of the rubbish for the fingerprints, that was..."

Brian snapped out of his reverie as a blue Volvo estate car drew up outside of Gallery DeWit. The only occupant was the driver - white, male but Brian was too far away to see his features. He watched him move around the car to the tailgate. As he lifted it open, a young woman came out of the Gallery and helped him carefully take out a large picture frame.

Brian motioned to the waitress for the bill.

* * *

There were five people in the Gallery as Brian closed the door. The girl he'd noticed earlier was now sitting behind a glass-topped desk, a middle-aged American couple were discussing a small oil landscape on the wall and by the window a well-dressed woman in her sixties was examining a large photograph, turning it in her hands to better catch the light.

And standing next to her was Christopher Franklyn.

Brian would have passed him on the street without giving him a second glance, but not because the years had been unkind. The long curly hair he remembered was now trimmed stylishly short and a neat beard was little more than shaped stubble. What lines were on his face seemed to add character rather than age, and he was probably as slim as he'd been a quarter of a century ago. You could see the boy he'd once been if you were looking for it, reflected Brian, but you really did have to look.

"To me it is like magic." The woman was shaking her head and from her accent Brian guessed she was Dutch. "Does he put the pieces into his computer and then they fly back together again?"

Franklyn smiled.

"I think there's more to it than that." He gave a slight shrug. "But don't ask me to explain what any of that might be."

"Kit, that is a sure sign of growing old." The woman sighed, almost theatrically. "Not the aching bones or the fading sight, but the world beginning to change in ways you know you will never understand." She tilted the photograph back toward the light again. "And he is an art student, you say?"

"Yes," Franklyn nodded.

"So, computers for everything now. Even for artists. No brushes, no paints, just the computers."

"Would you like to meet him? Thank him yourself?"

She gave a snort. "Of course not. He's young, how could he be more pleased with himself than thinking he's done something clever? Do you really suppose he needs a crazy old lady muddying the waters, explaining to him that instead it is something wonderful that he has managed here?"

She paused as Franklyn smiled.

"But you will make sure I reward his efforts properly? Find out what it involved - I want to be generous."

"Of course."

Franklyn turned to walk away from the window. He gave Brian a cursory smile as he passed and then, almost involuntarily, seemed to hesitate.

"Can I help you?" he asked.

"Hello Chris," said Brian softly. "It's been a while."

* * *

"Okay - you can turn it off." Franklyn lifted his gaze from the tape player and gave Brian a tight smile. "I remember the rest."

They were in a small office at the back of the Gallery, Franklyn sitting opposite Brian at a desk. His smile faded and his expression hardened.

"So that's the deal, is it." A statement rather than a question as Brian leaned forward and pressed the Stop button. "Either I meet with these people or this," he gestured at the tape player, "finds its way to..."

"Bloody hell, Chris, no." Brian tried to keep the exasperation out of his voice. He took the cassette out of the machine and pushed it over to Franklyn. "As far as I know there's just the one copy and the only place it should find its way to is the bottom of a canal."

He returned Franklyn's stare.

"What I'm saying," Brian continued, "is that this is the kind of thing they're likely to turn up if they start *really* digging." He shook his head. "I tidied as much of it away as I could but..."

He made an empty gesture with his hand.

"Tidied away?" said Franklyn, but this time his smile had at least a touch of humour in it, which Brian acknowledged with a smile of his own.

"So how did you find me?" asked Franklyn, eventually.

"They have your wife's name on file as Karen," said Brian. "Not *Carin*. They didn't realise she was Dutch. So, as there's no record of either of you in the UK for the last fifteen years, I figured it was a good bet you'd moved over here." He shrugged. "I made some calls to old contacts who didn't know I'd retired and discovered Carin was at the University of Leiden and that - according to your tax returns - you're a writer."

"I ghost autobiographies," said Franklyn. "Sportsmen, actors, musicians." He gave a slight shake of his head and a smile. "It's a living."

"Which is why this address was a surprise."

"Well, it was Carin's father's business - he died last year. At first we intended to sell, but it turns out to be quite a little money spinner." He shrugged. "So, who knows?"

There was silence for a few seconds.

"Look," said Brian carefully, "I'm pretty certain that whatever they're looking into isn't anything to do with us."

"What makes you so sure about that?"

Brian hesitated.

"One of the other phone calls I made," he said, "was to an old friend still in the job. To ask about this DI Palmer."

"From the Cold Case Unit?"

"Well, not anymore, she's not." Brian was suddenly conscious of his fingers tapping on the desk and he steadied them. "She recently resigned to," Brian mimed quotation marks, "*'take up an opportunity in the private sector'*. But word is that she's with the Security Service now."

"MI5?"

Brian nodded.

"Apparently she'd been on secondment with them before. So - if it's the spooks looking at Pembridge Villas, circa nineteen seventy, there's only one person I'd imagine they have an interest in."

"Aidan McShane," said Franklyn quietly.

"Yes," said Brian. "And I'd guess that's their only concern. But that could change, particularly if they give up on finding you and start paying closer attention to some other names in the file." He paused for a second. "Barry Denham, for instance?"

"Barry?"

"Yes, your old mate Barry. He left the force under something of a cloud about ten years ago - nothing he'd ever be prosecuted for, if only because no-one could risk putting him into the witness box. Works as a private investigator now - husbands playing away from home, who's nicking the paper clips sort of thing and always cocky as hell whenever any of that spills over into actual police work."

"I'm not sure how..."

"Remind me how long that Brownlow woman's been dead?" Brian broke in, lowering his voice but hardening his tone. "Must be getting on for thirty years now."

Franklyn's expression froze.

"What exactly happened that day never came out," continued Brian, "mainly because of the trial collapsing. But Barry Denham is one of the few people who knows what really went down." His stare was unwavering. "And how long do you think he'll be keeping his mouth shut when he's got a couple of goons in a Thames House basement on his case, instead of a kid three months out of Hendon?"

"Jesus Christ!" Franklyn sat back in his chair, slowly shaking his head.

"Exactly, a real bloody mess," agreed Brian. He sighed. "Look, they're not saying much, not to me at least, but this is all about someone who they think was killed at Pembridge Villas. Do you know anything about that?"

Franklyn shook his head.

"Nothing at all? Maybe an overdose?"

"No."

"Do you keep in touch with anyone from back then?"

"I see Claudia Falcone a few times a year. Lee Munro's still a friend."

Brian raised an eyebrow.

"She's done alright for herself, hasn't she?"

"Yeah, but if either of them knew anything about something like this, they'd have said."

"Okay, so most likely over the years wires have gotten crossed. Answer their bloody questions, lead them away from where they don't need to be looking, and let's get this buried again."

Franklyn gave him a questioning look.

"Do you want me to contact them?"

Brian shook his head.

"It always plays best if they think they're doing the spade work themselves - I'll call Palmer, tell her I've asked around and word is you're running a bookshop in Amsterdam. Then we wait for them to find you."

Franklyn nodded.

"So, let's sort out exactly what you need to be saying to them," said Brian.

And for the first time in five days, he felt himself starting to relax.

2. Claudia

Years later, after Daddy and I were reconciled, he would put everything down to Mummy's drinking. I suppose that shouldn't have surprised me, even as a child I could always tell if she were tipsy when returning home from some function or other. 'A little bit gay' people would call it at the time, although not for much longer. But back in London after the divorce it somehow escaped me completely, with all the melodramas finally played out and the histrionics fused into a silent rage it manifested as something else entirely, something burrowed deep down inside and hidden.

Mummy returned from Rome in the February of 1964. I had been sent to London a month earlier, supposedly to begin St Catherine's at the very start of term, but I suspect the real reason was that the situation at home was now so bad that one of the few things my parents could still agree on was that I shouldn't have to bear witness to it.

For those first few weeks, I was to live with Uncle Alex and Aunt Anne. Alex was Mummy's twin brother, who worked in the civil service at Westminster. During the week I would stay at his flat in Pimlico (two stops on the bus from St Catherine's) and then on Friday afternoon we would travel by train down to the family home at Hawkhurst, in Kent.

During that first month, Alex met me from school almost every day and we'd take a taxi to view an apartment or maisonette. Alex would always ask what I thought and I would bite my lip and say that it was very nice, when all I really wanted to do was scream *'I hate it! I hate everything! I want to go home!'* I found it especially difficult because I'd been only three years old when Daddy had taken us to Italy and now all I could see through the grimy windows of the taxi taking us back to Alex's flat was a cold, wet, sooty city full of pasty-faced people in drab, ill-fitting clothes. It was only weeks ago that life had been the Via Veneto and Borghese Gardens. This was all just so *unfair!*

By the end of the month Alex had whittled the apartments down to a shortlist of three. He'd really wanted Mummy to fly to London and see them for herself, but she told him to make the decision, that she had enough on her plate. So, Alex took me to see each one again and then asked which of them I liked the most. Two were in South Kensington and the third was in Portman Square, behind Oxford Street. Portman Square was the most expensive and so I said that one - revenge on Daddy perhaps, because I knew he'd be paying for it. Alex said that if that was the one I wanted then that would be the one I should have - he'd tell Mummy he considered it the best option by far. He gave my hand a little squeeze, but now I just felt mean and petty.

Aunt Anne came up to London for a week, to organise the decoration and furnishings and left with contracts signed and assurances given. She also arranged a cleaning lady, a cook-housekeeper and - after much discussion with Alex - a live-in Companion. I believe the thinking behind it was that Mummy must not be allowed to *'dwell on matters'*. Returning to a city where she had few friends nearby - her coterie of fifteen years ago had mostly married and moved to the Home Counties - it would take time to establish a new circle of confidants.

Essentially a paid 'Companion' was someone on whom you could make all the demands you would feel entitled to burden a close friend with, whilst never feeling the need to reciprocate. Accompanying Mummy on shopping expeditions, visits to the theatre, sitting through charity lunches, she was to ease the unease of Mummy's newly single status. I also suspect that the choice of a pretty, chic French girl -

whom we referred to as Mam'selle, presumably a contrivance to avoid both the over familiarity of first-name terms and the awkwardness of something functionary - was no accident on Aunt Anne's part. Men would come flocking and that would do Mummy's confidence no harm at all.

Well, that was the idea.

* * *

Alex and Aunt Anne visited a lot during those first few months, Aunt Anne concerning herself solely with the arrangements of domestic trivia and leaving her sister-in-law's emotional wellbeing for Alex to tend. Alex and Mummy would talk at length, either retiring to her room or wrapping up for lengthy walks around the Serpentine. But at some point during the visit Alex would find an opportunity for the two of us to be alone and he would ask 'How are you?' or 'Are things alright?'

And I'd always reassure him. I'd give a nod and a smile because I knew his concern was both well-meant and genuine, but the truth was that I had absolutely no idea. It felt like my world had been knocked so far off kilter that I had no frame of reference to make those kinds of judgements anymore. School was alright, I supposed, I was the new girl and my slight Italian accent sometimes incurred amusement, but nothing that amounted to bullying or even bitchiness. At home I was generally left to my own devices, evenings and weekends Mummy and Mam'selle were at the theatre or some event or other to which I would occasionally be invited but usually declined, citing pressures of homework. I told myself that I didn't mind solitude, that I was someone who enjoyed her own company, but in retrospect I was being a lot more disingenuous than I'd care to admit.

I think more than anything else I was starting to miss Daddy. Who would always tell me I was as pretty as a picture or would become the belle of the ball, even though we both knew that neither were true. Now he was no longer there I realised I felt far closer to him than to Mummy, but that wasn't something I could ever admit - even to Alex - without it seeming that I was adding to the betrayal.

Self-absorbed as I undoubtedly was, my involvement with Mam'selle was minimal. In my head Mummy was her job in the same way that breakfast was the cook's and keeping the apartment spruce and tidy was the cleaner's. Her free time was Monday to Friday during the day, whilst I was at school. Occasionally when I returned home we'd be able to acknowledge each other's presence with a polite nod, but usually not.

So, one afternoon in early April, it wasn't unusual for the apartment to be silent and empty when I let myself in. Mummy would sometimes take an after-lunch nap and I assumed Mam'selle was out. It had been raining and so I slipped my shoes off in the hallway and walked in my stocking feet down the corridor to my room to get changed.

Mummy's bedroom door was slightly ajar and I've never been sure what caught my attention as I passed by - a trick of the light, a slight movement or maybe even just instinct. But I stopped, hesitated, and then pushed the door further open.

I stepped inside the doorway. Mummy was laying down on the bed fully clothed, snoring softly. Mam'selle was standing by the dressing table, she was facing away from me but her reflection in the mirror was taking two pound notes from Mummy's purse.

I started to back out of the room, but underneath my foot a floorboard creaked. Startled, she looked up and our eyes met in the looking glass. I turned and almost ran along the corridor, but within seconds she was behind me and I winced with pain as she grabbed my hair and pulled me around, pushing my head against the wall.

"You will say nothing," she hissed, her face a vicious mask. "Or it will be very bad for you. Understand?"

I nodded and then gasped as she gave my hair a twist. She pushed her face close to mine.

"I have friends - you think you are safe, the little rich

girl that nothing bad can ever happen to, but then one day you are walking home from school and that silly little face of yours gets cut, yes?"

I shook my head and she let go of my hair.

"Go to your room, but you remember what I say."

She turned away, gave a toss of her head and strutted back along the corridor to Mummy's bedroom. This time she closed the door behind her.

I walked slowly to my room, locked the door, sat on the edge of the bed and then burst into tears. It wasn't only the anger and impotent rage of that moment. Every single bottled up emotion of the last few months came pouring out as I buried my face in the pillow and just sobbed and sobbed and sobbed.

* * *

Of course I should have told someone and of course I didn't. There's little that's more unsettling for a teenage girl than to discover that in many ways she is still a child, and there's little that's more traumatising for a child than a fraught encounter with the adult world. I'm sure I came up with a dozen arguments to convince myself to remain silent, Mummy's fragile emotional state probably to the fore, but the fact that I can't remember any of them speaks volumes to their validity. The plain truth of it was that she had frightened me terribly and I remained scared of what anything I might say would lead to.

So, I kept out of her way.

Every day after our confrontation I stayed on at school for as long as I could. There were quite a few clubs and societies which I could have joined but I preferred the solitude of the library, which remained open until half-past five. When Mummy asked why I was getting home so late, I told her I'd started doing my homework in the library, which was true, because of the reference books, which wasn't. Mam'selle's half-smile which I caught from the corner of my eye was barely detectable.

But I wasn't the only one in there every day.

Although Emma Brownlow was in my form, I had registered little about her other than she was a scholarship girl, very pretty and who seemed studious without being - as it was called back then - a swot. And incidentally, there was very rarely any snobbishness toward the scholarship girls at St Catherine's and mostly - other than what was to happen in a few months' time - they were treated exactly the same as all the other girls, by pupils and staff alike. There was bitchiness aplenty, but that tended to be reserved for the minutiae of inter clique rivalries - who was off to Cannes for the summer, who wasn't whose best friend anymore.

Even though we were the only two in the library, we initially sat at separate tables. But after a few days she came over to ask if she could borrow a ruler. If that were the blatant ice breaker I took it for, then it was a welcome one and from then on whoever was the last to arrive would join the other at their table.

We didn't chat much in there - Miss Davenport, the librarian, had the hearing of a bat and enforced a zero-tolerance policy on whispered conversations - but we had a ten-minute walk to the same bus stop.

"You were living in Rome?" she asked that first evening.

"Until a couple of months ago," I nodded.

"Did you move here for school?"

I shook my head. "My parents have split up. They're getting divorced." I gave a shrug. "Mummy and I moved back to London and Daddy's in Rome with..." I let my voice trail off.

"I'm so sorry." We'd reached the bus stop and as we stopped walking, she turned to me, putting her hand on my arm. "Oh God, it must be horrible for you."

Nonchalance wasn't my strong suit at the best of times, but this unexpected kindness from a relative stranger was suddenly almost too much to bear. I felt the tears well up and reached in my pocket for a hanky.

She waited until I'd finished dabbing at my eyes and

then gave me a hug.

"Are you alright?" she asked, and I managed a weak smile.

"Look, I have to get back now," she said, nodding at an approaching bus. "But tomorrow, why don't we leave a bit earlier and go for a coffee."

"I'd really like that," I told her.

"Me too," she said and then added, almost sheepishly, "Sometimes it feels hard to fit in at St Catherine's." She gave a shrug. "You know?"

'*Of course I know,*' ran through my mind. '*I'm a chubby little Italian girl. At least you're pretty.*'

But I said nothing and just nodded back.

* * *

Our initial meeting outside of school was indicative of what a strange friendship this was going to be. We had decided to visit an Aubrey Beardsley exhibition at a gallery near Hanover Square and so arranged to meet at Oxford Circus tube station. I wore my normal 'day out in the West End' outfit of a cream silk blouse, camel skirt and Jaeger jacket. Emma appeared at the top of the escalator in baggy black corduroy trousers and a white T-shirt under an army greatcoat at least one size too large for her. It was the first time we had met not wearing school uniform. We stared at each other for about five seconds before simultaneously bursting into laughter.

Other aspects had more of an edge. 'Shall I call you?' I'd asked, prior to getting together for a coffee the next weekend. 'We don't have a telephone,' she'd replied, not quite meeting my eye. I didn't pursue the matter, but I supposed it was because her family couldn't afford one. From fragments of conversation, I knew her father had worked for many years as a docker but not anymore, for reasons Emma didn't go into and that I - for once - had the sense not to press her about.

She was more forthcoming about her mother, who lectured Politics at a polytechnic.

"Mum used to be a seamstress, but she studied at evening classes to qualify as a teacher," she told me with obvious pride. "What does your mum do?"

Good question. And coincidentally, I'd recently tried using 'Mum' at home, a term which struck me as being more grown-up than Mummy whilst remaining just as affectionate. 'Would you please never again address me as though you were a parlour maid,' was her response after a long, frozen stare, bringing to an end that little experiment in egalitarianism.

"She's still sorting things out," I said lamely. "After moving back here."

"Of course," said Emma. "Must be lots to do."

We instinctively knew to keep our larger worlds apart. We certainly never visited each other at home. In my head the 'East End' was a jumble of foggy alleyways, populated by Fagin's child pickpockets or Pearly Kings and Queens eating jellied eels. I was well aware of how ludicrous a caricature that must be, but then again I had no eagerness to correct it through experience. And Lord knows what Emma would have made of a household employing three staff to take care of a perfectly fit mother and daughter.

Once it became obvious that Emma was unlikely ever to visit me at home, I created the fiction that Mummy received free tickets to exhibitions and concerts, because of her involvement in sponsoring the arts. I knew that Emma would never accept anything which could be interpreted as charity, so I would buy the tickets to events I wanted to attend and then tell Emma that if we didn't use them they would just go to waste.

It didn't strike me until years later how much a case of like mother like daughter this actually was.

* * *

Two weeks before the summer half-term break, Miss Foster, our English teacher, made an announcement.

"As you will be aware," she said, "this year is the fiftieth anniversary of the beginning of the Great War - World War One - and the school has decided to publish a special commemorative edition of *Invicta*."

Invicta was our school magazine, a monthly mimeographed collection of essays, poems and unlikely holiday experiences.

"All of you will have relatives who served their country," Miss Foster continued, "and I would like each of you to select one of them to be the subject of your essay. Please regard this as the homework project for the weekend and the best ones will be published in *Invicta*."

I broached the matter with Mummy at dinner that evening.

"Well... Your great uncle Charles was in the Royal Flying Corps," she mused, "until he was invalided out after a crash." She took a sip of wine. "He would always claim to have been shot down by the Red Baron, but then there was this tremendous to-do years later at some reunion, when it emerged that he'd become lost in the fog."

"Did he parachute out?" I asked, wondering if I might salvage some drama from the story.

"Oh, the Flying Corps didn't have parachutes, darling," she said. "They regarded them as terribly bad for morale. Can't have chaps bailing out over the side at the first hint of trouble."

Eventually I managed five hundred words based on Mummy's increasingly hazy reminisces and half an hour skimming a copy of *Biggles of the Camel Squadron*, which I found in Alex's bookcase. I didn't imagine fact checking was likely to be too rigorous, provided no over the top heroics were involved.

The following Monday Miss Foster collected the essays from us. We all stood at our desks and, as she walked by, we each gave a brief description of whom we'd written about and how they'd served, before handing them over and sitting down.

"My great uncle," I said. "He was a fighter pilot."

Miss Foster paused. "In the *Italian* air force?"

"No, Miss." I shook my head. "He was in the Royal Flying Corps."

"Oh." She gave a sharp nod. "Well done, Falcone."

"Thank you, Miss," I said sitting down, ignoring the giggles behind me.

"My grandfather, Miss," said Emma. "He was a stretcher bearer at the Battle of the Somme."

Miss Foster stared at her.

"He was in the Army Medical Corps?"

"No, Miss." She hesitated. "He was a conscientious objector. Becoming a stretcher bearer was a way of remaining true to his beliefs in wartime."

Miss Foster was actually glaring at her, completely ignoring the essay that Emma was holding out.

"Sit down, Brownlow," she hissed. "The subject of these essays are those who served this country, not disgraced it."

Emma blushed scarlet. A few girls tittered, but nervously, whilst the rest of us just looked down at our desks. She seemed as if she were struggling to say something.

"Sit down," barked Miss Foster.

It was the last lesson of the day. When the bell rang Emma was the first out of the classroom, her expression inscrutable. I went to the library as usual and I'm ashamed to admit that I was relieved not to find her there. I simply wouldn't have known what to say to her - not least because I wasn't even sure what being a conscientious objector was, let alone what sort of opinion I should have about it.

* * *

Emma was absent from school on the Tuesday and also the following day. Word of her altercation with Miss Foster began to spread and, the nature of rumour being what it is, by Wednesday afternoon their terse exchange had been blown up into a full-scale row, her absence even fuelling rumours of an expulsion.

On the Thursday morning, a few of us were waiting to go into Assembly when one of the girls in our form came rushing up with a newspaper in her hand.

"Have any of you seen this?" she asked, breathlessly.

She was holding a copy of the *Shoreditch Observer*. I'd never even heard of it and judging by the blank expressions on the faces of the other girls, I wasn't the only one. She shook her head at us in exasperation.

"On the bus, this woman kept staring at my uniform. Then she asked if I was at St Catherine's. When I told her I was, she gave me her paper and said that I might want to read it. Then she got off before I could ask what she meant."

She opened the newspaper up.

"Just take a look at this!"

We formed a semi-circle behind her and I found myself looking over her shoulder at a double page spread. Emma's photo was on the left-hand side, a picture of an elderly man addressing an outdoor meeting on the other.

'*What a Disgrace*', ran the headline.

I carried on reading down.

'*Most of our regular readers will remember Joe Brownlow,*' the article began. '*As a councillor in this district for many years, Joe battled tirelessly on behalf of the under-privileged, winning respect across the entire political spectrum for his commitment and integrity.*

'*Sadly, four years ago Joe finally lost what had been a lengthy battle with cancer and some of you will recall the last interview he gave to this newspaper. He spoke of the advancements that had been made in our community during his lifetime, particularly in those areas of health and education which had concerned him the most.*

'*But one thing Joe talked about that day was of a more personal nature. His granddaughter Emma had recently won a prestigious scholarship to St Catherine's School for Girls, in Westminster. Joe reflected on opportunities that would have been un-*

thinkable only a few years ago and predicted that soon there would be as many girls taking up University places as boys.

'However, Joe's optimism regarding the changing nature of our society would appear to have been sadly premature. Last week, St Catherine's asked its pupils to write an essay for inclusion in their School Magazine. The subject was to be a relative who had taken part in the First World War, and Emma chose to tell of Joe's experiences on the Western Front.

'Joe, as he made no secret of, was a conscientious objector and spent three years as a stretcher bearer, frequently under intense enemy fire. However, Emma's essay was rejected by the school and Joe Brownlow was described by one teacher as "a disgrace to his country".

'Well Emma, we knew Joe and we'll publish your essay, and our readers can judge for themselves where the real disgrace in this matter lies.'

"My God, she is in so much trouble for this," said one girl quietly.

I turned to Emma's essay on the opposite page. Emma had chosen just one event and - although she related it simply and without frills - it was a remarkably powerful and evocative piece from a fourteen-year-old girl.

She told of how a German attack had been repelled and the British troops dropped back down into their trenches. A German machine gun was still firing overhead. Screaming was coming from No-man's-land.

Joe Brownlow climbed back up a ladder, ignoring a sergeant who told him to come back down. On reaching the top, he took a white handkerchief from his pocket and waved it over the ridge.

Machine gun fire kicked up earth and Joe snatched his hand down. When the firing ceased, he raised the handkerchief again. The sergeant was telling him that if he didn't come back down, right now, then he would kick the ladder away. The machine gun started up again, but this time slightly to the left, and there seemed something more hesitant about it. Then it stopped completely.

Still holding the handkerchief above his head, Joe climbed up into No-man's-land. With his free hand he pointed to the screaming man on the ground, then slowly made his way over to him. The German machine gun stayed silent. The soldier had been shot in the leg, blood spurting from a wound in his thigh. As Joe slipped a tourniquet around the leg, he heard a low moaning coming from about ten feet away. Turning his head he saw that a German soldier also lay wounded.

Joe stood up, faced the opposite trenches and pointing at the German soldier called out '*Helfen*', one of the few German words most British soldiers knew. There was a pause and then two figures climbed up from the German trenches, scurried over to where their comrade lay and knelt to tend to him. Joe finished tightening the tourniquet, rose, and as he struggled to raise the soldier from the ground, one of the Germans came over and lifted him up onto Joe's shoulder. The two men exchanged small nods, then Joe turned and carried the wounded man back to the British trenches.

'*The sergeant said that my grandfather deserved a medal for what he did,*' concluded Emma, '*but that never happened. It seems that any act of bravery on a battlefield must be witnessed by an officer to be considered for an award, and this one wasn't. But I don't think that would have bothered my grandfather, he always said that it was what you did that mattered, not what other people thought about it.*'

We all stared at each other. It was as though no one wanted to be the first to say anything.

"What are you girls still doing here, you should be in Assembly?" Mrs Featherstone, the headmistress, seemed to have materialised out of nowhere. "And what is it you have there?"

She reached out her hand for the newspaper. Wordlessly, it was handed over.

"Now you girls get along. You're already..."

She froze, staring at the open page.

And she continued to stand there, rigid as a statue while silently, almost conspiratorially, we slipped past her into Assembly.

* * *

By lunchtime I doubt there was a girl in the school who didn't know what had happened, which, combined with an edginess about the teaching staff, ensured that by the final bell the entire building felt permeated with unease.

Our first lesson on Friday should have been English, but Miss Foster never arrived. After about ten minutes Mrs Curtis, the school secretary, came into the room.

"Girls, this morning's English lesson has been cancelled. In fact," she raised her hand to quiet the low buzz of muttering that began spreading around the room, "all of your lessons for this morning are cancelled. Mrs Featherstone would like to speak to each one of you concerning the incident earlier this week, of which I'm sure you're all aware." She gave a sad shake of the head. "Whilst you're waiting to be called, please occupy your time constructively. Do you have a course book to read, perhaps?"

"*All Quiet on the Western Front*, Miss," said Charlotte King, totally deadpan. Mrs Curtis just stared at her. How the rest of us kept straight faces I'll never know. After a few seconds she simply nodded.

"You will be called in Register order," she said. She must have heard the gales of laughter as the door closed behind her, but I think we all knew that this was no time to be reading the Riot Act.

It didn't take long to reach the Fs, but I had the sense that Mrs Featherstone was already only going through the motions.

"What *exactly* did Miss Foster say to Emma?" she asked, but before I could reply there was a knock on her door from the outer office. With a sigh of exasperation, she stood up and walked over to open it. At first the conversation was too low for me to hear, but then I caught the word 'guardian'.

"I'm far too busy to deal with any guardian or parent right now," snapped Mrs Featherstone. "You'll have to get...-"

"No, not *a* guardian!" Mrs Curtis sounded on the edge of tears. "*The* Guardian. The newspaper."

There was silence for a few seconds.

"Would you take their name and telephone number?" asked Mrs Featherstone. "And tell them I will return their call in thirty minutes."

She closed the door and then came over to sit down behind her desk. She was looking at me but not really seeing me, it was quite scary in a way. Then she seemed to get back in control.

"I'm sorry, Claudia - Miss Foster?"

I told her what happened. She nodded at each point - she'd probably heard the same story half a dozen times by now - and only queried the words Miss Foster had used.

"'A disgrace to his country.' Are you sure that's *exactly* what she said?" Her tone was challenging, but there was a weary resignation about her.

"Yes, Miss."

"Very well." She gave a curt nod. "Thank you, Claudia."

It was the last day before the half term holiday and with that went any chance of St Catherine's being able to manage the story.

* * *

We were to spend the holiday at Lyme Regis in Dorset, where one of Mummy's old school-friends now owned a hotel. I'd not been looking forward to it and the journey down there didn't exactly whet my appetite - slow train to Dorchester and a rustic taxi the rest of the way - but when we arrived, it seemed to possess a sense of wilderness that I really hadn't expected from an English seaside resort.

I spent the Saturday and Sunday scampering around on the rocks looking for fossils, a local pastime whose novelty quickly wore thin, but it had occupied me enough not to have seen the weekend newspapers. So, it was quite a shock to suddenly catch up with how fast things had been moving.

On Monday, the *Daily Telegraph* published a letter from a retired Colonel, who had borne witness to Joe Brownlow's excursion into No-man's-land.

'It's simply not true that it wasn't witnessed by an officer,' he wrote. *'I was a young lieutenant at the time, and I sent a full report up to HQ with a recommendation for gallantry. A few days later, word came quietly back down the line that there were no circumstances in which the General would ever consider putting a "conchie" forward for a medal, and that it would be of no advantage to myself if I continued to press the matter.'*

By Tuesday retired army officers were writing to *The Times* offering to give their medals to Emma. An editorial in the *Daily Mirror* discussed the illusionary nature of our new so-called classless society. *'The same hypocrisy which robbed a brave man of his due recognition fifty years ago still does its best to bury it today, this time by attacking a fourteen-year-old schoolgirl.'*

By Wednesday it was on the BBC evening news. With other guests, we gathered around a television set in the hotel lounge. After some background to the story from the newscaster, there was a brief interview with Mrs Featherstone. She was looking older than the last time I'd seen her.

"The actual subject of the essays was to be a family member who had *enlisted* in the military," she told the reporter, "which I think is what's led to this misunderstanding."

"A teacher at your school apparently referred to Mr Brownlow as a disgrace to his country," continued the reporter.

"Remarks taken out of context," said Mrs Featherstone. "They reflected a general viewpoint, rather than the actions of Mr Brownlow in particular, the details of which - at the time - she was unaware of."

"Unaware because she refused to read Emma's essay!"

"Well, they were very unfortunate remarks," said Mrs Featherstone "and she will be apologising to Emma for them at the first opportunity."

The picture cut back to the studio.

"Earlier today," said the newscaster, "we put these comments to Emma herself."

The screen cut to Emma, looking very young and demure. And also, I noticed, possibly the only schoolgirl in the country wearing her school uniform in the middle of the half-term holiday.

"We were told," she said, "to write about a member of our family who had *served* during World War One." She gave a slight shrug. "I know that one girl wrote about her grandmother, who had travelled to France at her own expense and volunteered as a nurse at a field hospital there. Nobody said anything about having to be in the military when *she* handed her essay in."

Emma paused.

"My grandfather wasn't prepared to kill for his country, but he was prepared to die for it and I'm learning that's what people have difficulty accepting. That courage can take many forms."

The screen returned to the studio.

"A remarkable young lady," said the newscaster.

"A friend of yours, you say?" asked a genial red-faced man, sitting on the other side of the room.

"Yes," I told him. "We're in the same class."

"Well, I'd stick to her like glue from now on, m'dear," he said, with an appreciative nod toward the TV set. "That little minx is bulletproof after this."

"Gerald!" exclaimed his wife, giving him a sharp dig in his ribs with her elbow.

But he was right. By the end of the week Miss Foster had taken early retirement.

And I'd come to a decision too.

* * *

We arrived back in London on the Friday afternoon. That evening Mummy and Mam'selle were at Covent Garden, so I knew that there would be plenty of time for what I had in mind.

Letting myself into Mummy's room, I went straight over to the dressing table. Her best jewellery was in a lacquered, antique Chinese box which she kept in the bottom left-hand drawer; I wasn't sure what I would do if it were locked, but it slid open. I took out a brooch I knew had belonged to her mother and always sat on the top of the other jewellery. I also took a string of pearls I'd seen her handle carefully enough to suggest it meant a lot to her. I didn't know how valuable they were, but I was confident both would be missed quite quickly. I left everything else as I'd found it.

Mam'selle's room was small, but she kept it neat. A single bed, small dressing table, chest of drawers and a wardrobe were the only furniture. I started with the chest of drawers. At the back of her underwear drawer was a roll of one-pound notes held fast with an elastic band. I took the bottom drawer out completely, lay the brooch and pearls in the space and slid the drawer back in, checking I could pull it in and out with nothing catching.

Then I went to bed before they returned home.

* * *

If I were at last starting to warm to London, it was because of the museums. All the major ones were within walking distance of Portman Square - the National Gallery and British Museum I discovered first, but my favourites were the ones in South Kensington.

The Victoria and Albert, the Science and the Natural History museums were all only a stone's throw from each other and there was something so cosmopolitan about the entire area - almost a central European elegance and grandeur. Most Saturdays, if I weren't meeting Emma, I'd cross Oxford Street and stroll down through Hyde Park to Exhibition

Road, where I'd spend at least a couple of hours and sometimes a lot longer.

So, it wasn't out of the ordinary for me to be gone for the entire day.

Arriving back home at teatime, I opened our front door to find Alex in the hallway talking to a uniformed policeman.

"Hello Claudia," he smiled, a little wearily.

"Is everything alright?" I asked.

"Nothing for you to worry about," he said. "We're just sorting something out, but it would be better if you stayed in your room for a while."

As I passed the living room, the door was slightly ajar, and I heard Mam'selle's fraught voice. "These I have never seen before." I hurried by, not wanting her to realise that I was home. "And the money," a stern male voice was saying. "Are you telling us we wouldn't find your fingerprints on these notes?"

I closed my door to shut it all out. I wasn't sorry about what I'd done, but I realised I didn't want to be any part of the consequences. 'You're such a coward, Claudia,' I told myself as I dropped onto my bed, 'you're not like Emma at all. She faced everyone down.'

It was about an hour later that there was a soft knock on my door. I opened it and Alex gave me a smile.

"We're going out for a bite to eat," he said.

Mummy was in the living room, sitting on the sofa, her coat folded on her lap. She didn't look in a hurry to go anywhere.

"Your mother's a little distraught," said Alex, moving to stand beside her. "It turns out that Mam'selle was… Well, she's betrayed our trust quite badly."

"That little bitch has been stealing from us for months." Mummy almost spat the words out, I hadn't seen her so upset since the divorce.

"Yes, well, that's all done with now." Alex put a hand onto her shoulder. "You have your jewellery back. And probably most of the money."

"I don't care about the money." She shook her head. "I knew the money was going from my purse, I'm not that much of a..." She looked despairingly at Alex.

"But if you knew money was being taken," Alex was shaking his head, "why didn't you say something?"

"Because I thought it was Claudia."

She stifled a sob and looked across the room at me.

"I thought it was you," she said, and then she did start crying. "I thought you were stealing from me, trying to punish me for... Oh, I don't know!"

She reached up and pulled Alex's hand away from her shoulder. "I trusted a complete stranger before my own daughter. What kind of mother does that make me?"

I crossed over to the sofa, sat down and took her hand. I had no idea what to say to her, no idea at all.

"I am so sorry, darling." She let go of my hand and gave me a tight embrace. "I'm so, so sorry."

"It's alright Mummy," was all I could manage.

"Go and fix your face, Sandra," said Alex, after what seemed an awfully long time but probably wasn't. "Then let's go out and cheer ourselves up."

Mummy gave a weak smile and a small nod.

"She really does love you very much, you know," said Alex, when the door had closed behind her.

"I know," I said quietly.

"This divorce business." He hesitated. "It's affected her very, very badly. And often when we've been hurt, it's the people closest to us that we make suffer rather than those more deserving of our anger. Sometimes it's hard - particularly hard for a child - to understand that."

I just nodded.

"So, if ever you feel that you want to talk to someone - even if it's only for a bit of company out of the house then give me or Anne a ring, alright?" He reached down and squeezed my hand. "We've always got time for our favourite niece."

"I'm your only niece," I said weakly, and he gave a laugh.

"Well," he said, "you must be our smartest niece, too."

He stood up and held my coat open for me to slip my arms into.

"What about school?" he asked. "Have you made any friends there yet?"

"Yes," I told him. "One."

* * *

But Emma never returned to St Catherine's.

The first day back at school - with her absence giving her a prominence that her presence never had - the rumours were flying thick and fast, the staff constantly breaking up gaggles of wide-eyed girls exchanging wild speculation about what Emma had been driven to by rage or remorse. Eventually one girl, whose mother sang in the same church choir as Mrs Curtis, gathered us around her in the playground.

Mrs Featherstone, in consultation with Emma's parents, had concluded that it wouldn't have been in either Emma or the school's best interests for her to return. She had 'put out feelers to determine the best way forward' and the result was that a foundation - originally established during the First World War to provide financial support for the education of children of British army officers killed in combat - was persuaded that under the circumstances they could widen their purview to embrace Emma. And with that pesky detail taken care of, she was now a boarder, we learnt, at a Ladies' College in Kent.

Meanwhile, whatever the Latin might be for 'Least said, soonest mended' could well have served as St Catherine's new school motto. Miss Foster had been excised from the display of school paraphernalia in the main lobby every bit as efficiently as Trotsky from a May Day Parade Podium photograph. Emma I never heard referred to by a member of staff ever again.

And a few days later, the school noticeboard invited essay submissions for *Invicta* on the subject of '*My Favourite Pet*'.

3. Jan De Keyser

There was an eclectic collection of artwork cluttering the walls of Carin Franklyn's office. A scribbled figure in charcoal, rumoured to be a Bacon preparatory sketch, hung next to the reproduction of a Renaissance crucifixion and Impressionist posters from the Belle Époque overlapped delicate lithographs of eighteenth-century Venice. But today, as always, what drew Jan's eye was the canvas of a bizarrely misshapen dwarf, a grotesque fantasy of gigantic lips, hands and genitalia.

At first Jan had thought it an example of German expressionist art - he'd once come across a paper on the *Lustmord* paintings of the Weimar Republic and the style was strikingly similar. But on mentioning it to a colleague, he'd been directed to the catalogue of an exhibition entitled '*Unintentional Art*'. The piece, he learnt, was originally from a medical school, a schematic of the human body re-proportioned to represent the sensitivity of the nervous system.

'*Our lives lived so far might prove equally disturbing if viewed solely through the mind's eye,*' Carin had written in the accompanying notes. '*Long stretches atrophied by humdrum indifference and then the days - perhaps only hours or minutes - endlessly stretched by pain or passion which decades later we still revisit, sometimes enraged and often baffled by what we allowed to happen or let slip away.*'

Jan had been impressed.

He guessed it was because he was the new boy that he'd drawn the short straw with Carin Franklyn's biography of Caravaggio, but he didn't mind. She'd contacted the Psychology Department, she told him, because she felt that a professional appraisal of her take on the dichotomy between this wondrous art and its murderous creator would be essential at some point - getting it done now would hopefully save rewrites down the line.

And then, hesitantly, added that in the past she'd seen assessments from his department which seemed so chock full of terminology as to seem intent on definition at the expense of clarity.

"No disrespect," she'd said to him, "and I'm not trying to tell you how to do your job here, but could you keep it simple?"

He'd nodded, given her a smile and taken the manuscript from her.

"*Okay, forget your dilettante, aristocratic poets,*" began his email back to her a week later. "*This is where mad, bad and dangerous to know is really at.*"

There weren't many interdepartmental friendships at the university, he reflected, but theirs was fast becoming one.

Then the door opened.

"Hi Jan," she said, breathlessly coming into the room. "Sorry for keeping you waiting, got a bit sidetracked."

She sat down behind the desk, caught her breath and then looked across at him with a smile.

"Any plans for tonight?" she asked.

* * *

"So, it's like a club?" mused Tracey as they backed out of their driveway. "For buying stocks?"

"Kind of," replied Jan. "As Carin said, it's about as much to do with investing in the stock market as your average Book Club concerns itself with literature." He shrugged. "The idea is just for a group of interesting people to meet up regularly, for a meal and good conversation."

At any given point, Carin had explained, there were twenty-four members and - as twelve was deemed the optimum number for a dinner table - it was the first dozen respondents to the invitation who were sent the time and place of this week's venue. It was an arrangement that caused less friction than might be imagined, she'd told him. Most members had careers in business or academia that frequently saw them otherwise socially committed, and those same careers could be surprisingly transient.

"There's no formal membership?" Jan had asked.

Not as such, Carin had said, and no set policy for enrolling newcomers. The secretary of the Share Club was rotated on a monthly basis, and as the actual share trading was left to Manfred - who was a big shot at Euronext - the duties amounted to little more than sending out an email detailing the current week's venue and responding to the initial dozen RSVPs. As secretary for August, Carin had dibs on who to invite tonight in place of Ray and Diane - recently relocated to Dublin - and so had thought of Jan and Tracey.

There were no selection meetings - certainly nothing like a black ball in a bag - she'd explained, just a consensus reached afterwards through casual discussion. It was usually fairly obvious who'd be a good fit and who wouldn't.

"But don't feel you have to jump through any hoops tonight," Carin had smiled. "It'll be fine."

Tracey hadn't been so sure.

"I know nothing about the stock market," she'd said when he'd arrived home. "And isn't everyone going to be old?"

Probably, Jan had told her with a shrug, but this was how things were done, this was how you got on. Invitations to meet influential people and making new friends who could lend a decisive hand to your career.

"Okay, baby," she'd shrugged. "You know best, I guess, but don't blame me if everyone thinks I'm a dummy."

* * *

Jan had first been a student at Leiden, but then moved to the States to work for his PhD at Princeton. Where his doctoral thesis had so impressed that on qualification he'd been offered a faculty position. That was eight years ago, and with talk of tenure there'd been little thought of moving back to the Netherlands.

Little thought until Tracey, that is.

As with most universities, relationships between teaching staff and students were strictly verboten, and so Jan and Tracey were ultra-careful. They would never meet at his apartment. For their weekends away Tracey even took a cab over to Plainsboro and Jan would pick her up from there.

So how word got out neither of them knew.

Tracey's family had raised hell, first taking her back home to South Carolina and then demanding Jan's dismissal. The University balked at that, probably because of legal advice Jan's lawyer told him. But eventually a deal was brokered, which gave him both a generous severance package and references glowing enough to have Leiden rubbing their hands.

And then, one crisp fall morning, Tracey left the house with an overnight bag and - telling Mom and Dad she was staying over with her friend Denise - caught a cab all the way to Columbia Metropolitan, where she'd boarded a flight to Schiphol with the ticket Jan had arranged to be collected from the KLM desk.

And a week later they were married at a civil ceremony in Leiden.

So, screw you Princeton and screw you twice over Mom and Dad.

* * *

They were early arriving at the restaurant and so Jan suggested driving around the block, in case they appeared too eager.

"I need to pee," Tracey told him, "so kind of eager, okay?"

But then he'd spotted Carin's Saab in the car park.

"Okay," he said, turning in and pulling up alongside it.

"Thanks honey," she said. "I'm kinda nervous."

"You'll be fine," he reassured her.

Carin was sitting on a high stool at the bar by herself, and she turned toward the door as they entered.

Jan knew that when he told people he and his wife had been at Princeton together, it was a bit disingenuous to let them assume that she'd been a faculty member rather than a student and so he was used to the double take when colleagues met her for the first time.

But Carin didn't even blink.

"So nice to finally meet you," she smiled, kissing her on the cheek. Jan ordered a round of drinks and when Tracey returned from the restroom they moved over to a table by the window.

"Kit got caught up at the Gallery," said Carin. "He sends his apologies and shouldn't be too long."

"Jan says he's a writer?"

"That's right," Carin nodded. "Mainly as a collaborator on autobiographies."

"Anyone interesting?" asked Jan.

"Usually, it's part of the contract that his involvement stays confidential." Carin gave a slight shrug. "So it's not really something he can go into detail about."

"Is that what they call a ghost-writer?" asked Tracey.

"Or an amanuensis," said Carin. "If you want to get fancy about it."

"I've not heard that expression before," said Jan.

"It's a Latin term for a secretary or scribe," Carin smiled, "but one of its translated meanings is *'partner in crime'*. Which is why I think Kit likes it."

* * *

The remaining members of the Share Club arrived in quick succession and Carin made the introductions - Peter was something to do with computers at Shell in Den Haag and his wife Carol was a graphic designer. Bernard and Helen were from Seattle and both worked for Microsoft, Henri and Clémence ran a PR company representing French businesses in the Netherlands. The last to arrive were Rudy and Truda from Munich, who were in *'import and export'*.

The last apart from Carin's husband, that is.

"Look everyone," she said eventually, staring at her watch, "you all go through. I've no idea what's kept him, but I'm going to ring the Gallery and find…"

She broke off as, if almost on cue, the street door opened.

"I don't know," smiled Clémence, "some people just can't resist making an entrance."

There was good natured amusement as Kit made his apologies.

"Sorry - something came up at the last minute," he said.

"Was it about Peter Mathews?" asked Carin, a bit pointedly, thought Jan and Kit seemed surprised.

"No," shaking his head. "Why would you think that?"

"You haven't heard - he died today."

"Peter Mathews, the children's author?" asked Rudy.

Carin nodded.

"Apparently he'd been ill for a while." She turned to Kit. "Did you know that?"

"I didn't," he told her and looked over to Rudy. "We share the same publisher and had a couple of meetings recently, about an official biography."

"Knowing your publisher," said Carin dryly, "that's a project likely to get a fire lit under it now."

"I'll email them in the morning," said Kit. "Feels like the end of an era, though."

"For your English childhood?" smiled Truda.

"Well, for a childhood I'd like to have had." Kit smiled back at her. "Summers of adventure exploring Scottish mountains, Cornish beaches or Welsh valleys - exciting yet somehow never too fanciful." He shrugged. "I liked him too, from what little I knew of him."

"So, what kept you?" asked Carin.

"I'll explain later," he said and then turned to Jan. "Hi,

you must be Jan - nice to meet you at last."

"You too," said Jan. "And this is my wife, Tracey."

"Shall we go in?" suggested Carin.

The restaurant was busy, but Carin led them through to where an archway opened into a room only large enough for a single table set for twelve.

"By the way, did Dorothea come over to see the photograph?" Jan heard Carin ask Kit as they sat down, but before Kit could respond Bernard turned toward him.

"Oh yes, how did that work out?" he asked.

"It was pretty amazing," began Kit and then hesitated, as Carin laid her hand on his arm.

"We had quite the drama recently," she said, turning to Jan. "I'd better explain before we discover the outcome."

* * *

A couple of weeks previously, Carin had been getting ready for bed when there'd been a phone call. Few people rang that late at night, Kit was in London for a meeting with his publisher and they'd already spoken earlier that evening.

It was a female voice, distressed and asking for her father.

"Pappa had died the year before," Carin said. "So naturally I asked who it was."

Dorothea Bauman and her father had been friends since childhood, so she more than anyone must have known...

At that point, the call was taken over by a man who introduced himself as Hoofdagent Schenke from the Amsterdam police, asking who he was speaking to.

Carin identified herself and asked what had happened.

Dorothea, it transpired, had arrived home that night to disturb three burglars. As they fled the apartment, Dorothea had been pushed over. She was shaken but not injured, Schenke told Carin, and the paramedics said she wouldn't need to go to hospital if there were someone to stay with her. Her daughter lived in Paris, apparently, and so she'd called her friend Henrick.

Carin explained about her father. Dorothea obviously still had the number on speed dial and in her confused state…

No problem, Schenke said, it's probably better that she spends the night in hospital, just to make sure. Carin sighed and told him she needed to pack an overnight bag - about thirty minutes, she guessed, if she could get a cab straightaway. Schenke told her he'd have someone stay with Dorothea until she got there.

When Carin arrived, Dorothea - on the sofa in the wreckage of her living room and staring blankly around her - seemed barely aware of her presence. Carin had expected disarray, but not this level of wilful vandalism.

"Junkies probably," said the young policewoman who led Carin into the kitchen on the pretext of making coffee, and Carin didn't bother to enquire as to the likelihood of them being caught.

"If you're worried about Dorothea at any point, then call an ambulance. Better to be safe than sorry, but the paramedics said they weren't too concerned. The main thing is to keep her occupied, start tidying up now rather than in the morning, keep talking to her, keep her mind grounded in the here and now and not letting her dwell."

Carin nodded, and they took the coffee back into the living room.

"Well, at least you're insured," said the policewoman, looking around at the smashed TV, upturned furniture and broken picture frames.

"Only for the things that don't matter," said Dorothea quietly, which the policewoman at least had the grace to acknowledge with a small nod before leaving.

A few hours later they had most of the damage swept away and were making an inventory of what they could repair and what needed to be replaced.

"Bring the pictures to the Gallery," Carin told her. "We'll get them re-framed."

Carin stayed until Dorothea's daughter arrived from Paris the following afternoon. A few days later a huge bouquet of flowers was delivered with a thank you note and a message to say that she'd bring the prints along to the Gallery on Saturday.

"The prints weren't a problem," said Kit, taking up the story. "When she brought them in, I explained that they were easy enough to re-frame."

But then Dorothea reached into her bag and took out a large, padded envelope. Unsealing the top, she poured torn fragments of a photograph out onto the counter.

'If it's possible to mend this," she said, "then I don't care what it costs.'

Kit told her that photographic restoration wasn't their speciality, but he'd ask around and if it could be repaired, it would be.

Dorothea gave a sad little nod and left.

While Kit was taking the prints through to the storage room, Jaclyn, the receptionist, returned from lunch with her boyfriend Mirko, an art student. As Jaclyn took off her coat and sat down behind her desk, Mirko began sorting through the fragments on the counter and then looked at Carin quizzically. She was explaining what happened when Kit came back in.

"Okay," Mirko said. "Well, I might be able to fix this."

Carin and Kit must both have been looking at him like he was insane, because he suddenly gave a big grin and shook his head.

"Then he started talking about Macs and scanning and vectors and jpegs," said Carin, "and I knew from the way Kit was nodding sagely at all of this that he had even less of a clue what Mirko was talking about than I did."

"So," Kit grinned, "everything went back into the envelope, we handed it over and told him to knock himself out."

"And two days ago," said Carin, "Jaclyn arrives at the Gallery bursting with pride that her boyfriend has put back together what all the king's horses and all the king's men could not."

* * *

"What was the photograph?" asked Jan.

"A couple in their twenties," said Kit. "I'd guess it was taken between the wars."

"It was her mother and father," said Carin. Everyone turned to look at her.

"I hadn't realised she'd spoken to you about it?" queried Kit.

"She didn't," Carin said.

"Well," said Kit, "it's probably a good guess.".

"I heard my parents talking about Dorothea once," said Carin. "When I was a little girl. I think my mother may have been jealous of my father's friendship with her, although I didn't understand that at the time. He told her that during the war Dorothea had been smuggled out of the city, to a farm near Breda."

"She's Jewish?" asked Jan.

Carin nodded.

"My grandfather and her father were friends, and my father - Henrik - and Dorothea spent a lot of time together as children. After the Occupation and the round-up of the Jews began, my grandfather bought her father's business. The idea was they would buy passage on a ship to America, but the family were taken the day before they were due to sail - most likely betrayed by the person arranging the passage, which happened a lot. All the family except Dorothea - she had been playing outside in the street when the Gestapo arrived. She ran to my grandfather's house, who took her in and hid her."

"No small thing," said Jan quietly.

"He would have been shot had she been discovered," said Carin. "Or sent to a camp." She shrugged. "But she wasn't. And after the war he looked out for her - he found a family for her to lodge with - eventually she married their son. They had a daughter, but her husband died of cancer quite young, in the early seventies I believe."

There was a silence.

"The thing is," said Kit, "I was talking to Mirko about how he reconstructed the photograph and what he did is even more impressive than I thought. Because he couldn't salvage all the image, he used a stock photograph of a period drawing room to construct the background, soft focused it and then superimposed fragments of the figures onto it, blending the edges together."

"And you can't tell that?" asked Carin.

"I never saw the original photograph," said Kit, "so I've no idea how much of a facsimile it is, but you wouldn't know it's not an original just by looking at it."

"And Dorothea said nothing?"

"No."

"You know, maybe the photograph isn't the one she originally had," said Jan carefully, 'but that doesn't mean that it's not the one she will remember."

"I don't understand," said Carin.

"Freud believed in a process called memory re-consolidation." Jan smiled. "He claimed that every time we remember something, we alter it slightly."

"How would that be possible?"

"Exactly. We've learnt since Freud that memories are physically hard-wired into the brain - that they are collections of neurons arranged in certain patterns. And we believed that recollection was - to use a simplistic analogy – like shining a light on those patterns to highlight them. That they were solid and permanent."

"But...?" Kit with a quizzical smile.

"There's now neurological evidence - quite strong evidence really - that the act of recollection breaks up those clusters of neurons. Physically dissolves them, in fact. And when we've finished with a particular memory, it's rewritten using a different collection of neurones and possibly - but probably - in a slightly different pattern."

"So?"

"Let's take this evening," said Jan. "Tomorrow morning we'll all have pretty much identical recollections of tonight's shared events. But in five years' time, with those recollections rebuilt perhaps hundreds of times during the course of shifting relationships, divided loyalties, wilful self-interest, maybe changing perceptions of love and betrayal - tonight will be a very different reality in each of our minds."

"If only you could guarantee my life was about to become that interesting," said Bernard, and everyone laughed.

Jan turned to Kit.

"When you interview the friends of your subjects," he asked, "how often do you get exactly the same recollections?"

"Time and place usually match up," Kit nodded, "But the 'he said she said' is always a bit of a free for all."

"You know," said Carin, "there's this theory in physics, I don't know what it's called, but it says the world keeps splitting off into different dimensions, to cover all possible outcomes."

"The Many Worlds Theory," nodded Bernard. "Postulated by Hugh Everett in 1957."

"Do you seriously believe," asked Henri, "you've just made yourself seem more interesting?"

Bernard tossed a bread stick at him.

"I thought that was kind of fanciful, you know. A bit of a glib answer to the mysteries of the universe - if it can happen, then it will somewhere. Where's the drama in that? But this." Carin turned her head toward Jan. "The past curating itself in my wake to establish I've always been right. I'm on board for that."

She paused until the laughter subsided.

"Because let me tell you something."

She put her glass down.

"About a week after Kit and I first met," said Carin, "he took me back to where he was living, a rundown house in Notting Hill. Dilapidated grandeur probably describes it best, not what you'd really find in central London anymore."

She hesitated, realising Kit was staring.

"Hey," she said, after a couple of seconds, "it's okay, I'm not going to spill any family secrets." She grinned. "Well, none you need to worry about."

"S'okay," said Kit. "Just weird you mentioning that tonight."

"Anyway, we were in Lee Munro's room," continued Carin, "because Kit..."

"*Lee Munro!*" Jan was staring. "What, the actress Lee Munro?"

"She was making a TV series in London at the time," said Kit. "But we'd met a few years before."

"Shit, I'm impressed." Jan shook his head. "Are you guys still in touch?"

"Yes." He and Carin exchanged smiles. "In fact, I'm seeing her next week."

"Really? Here in Amsterdam?"

"England." He gave a shrug. "Long story."

"Wow." Jan turned back to Carin. "I'm sorry, that was rude. I didn't mean to get sidetracked."

"That's alright," Carin smiled. "Anyway, Kit and Lee were talking about some benefit at the Roundhouse they were helping to organise, so I just sat myself down on the sofa and picked up a magazine to read." She took a sip of wine. "*Oz* magazine."

"It was a counterculture monthly," Kit said, glancing over to Jan. "A bit like *Rolling Stone* but less music oriented." He gave Carin a slightly quizzical look. "I wrote a few pieces for it myself."

"Not for this one, you didn't," said Carin dryly. "So, I was sitting there flicking through pages that were basically an explosion of multi-coloured inks and then I came onto this double page photograph of a woman, a twenties flapper I thought at first, wearing nothing but a Gatsby turban and a brazen stare. Fairly typical period erotica was my reaction, a bit of an oddity to find in some hippie rag, and I'd almost flipped the page over when it registered." Carin took another sip of wine. "*She* had a penis."

Carin gave a wry smile and shook her head slowly.

"It was a total shock, no, more than that, a total *erotic* shock - sex was no mystery to me but sex only as a physical manifestation of love." Then, with a grin, she shrugged. "Or desire. But this was dark and dangerous and it came as an ambush that was frightening, but yet in its own way thrilling. I couldn't understand what kind of world I'd just entered... '*Blew my mind*', that's what everyone used to say about everything back then, a record, a film, a book. '*Oh man, it blew my mind*'. Well, this really did." She clasped her hands to each side of her head and then made them fly outward in imitation of an explosion. "*Poouff!*"

Carin reached for a cigarette.

"I closed the magazine. You and Lee were still talking and I think by the time you noticed me again, my expression was neutral. But that photograph has always stayed with me in every detail. A twenties salon, the figure reclining on a leather chaise longue, large vases with ostrich feathers, a massive ornate mirror on the wall behind, a crystal chandelier hanging low."

She looked over at Kit, who slowly smiled. Everyone else was staring at her.

"This afternoon I was in Waterlooplein with some time to kill, and so I went over to the flea market. There was a stall selling sixties memorabilia, and they had a complete collection of old OZ magazines - so, you can guess what I found there, can't you?"

"The magazine?" asked Rudy.

"Eventually." Carin smiled. "Kit and I met in May 1970, so I started looking at issues back from there."

"And you found it?"

"Well, I certainly found the magazine - it was the February edition - but that photograph was not what has been in my head for all these years. It was one of the transvestites from Andy Warhol's Factory, Candy Darling. Bold and brash, a stark background, nothing like I remembered. And then the second total shock from this image - I realised the room in my head was Lee Munro's. That I'd transposed the two into a symbolic fantasy creation."

She drew on her cigarette and blew smoke out slowly.

"And you know what the spooky thing is?" she asked.

"That when you think of the photograph," said Jan smiling, "even now, knowing what it actually looks like, you still see the image you've carried in your head for all those years."

Carin nodded. "Yeah."

"So, did you buy the magazine?" asked Kit.

"I had to buy all of them," said Carin. "They wouldn't split the collection."

"If they're in good condition, that could be a nice investment."

"They're like new."

"How much?"

Carin hesitated only slightly.

"Five hundred guilders."

Kit smiled at her.

"Maybe," he said, "you should be out on the road doing the buying."

* * *

After the meal they'd moved into a private bar at the back of the restaurant and Jan found himself chatting to Kit.

"You're in England next week?" he asked. "Is that for the eclipse?"

"Actually, it is," said Kit. "Lee Munro's coming over for the opening of an art gallery in Cornwall, scheduled to coincide with the eclipse - so that's where we're meeting up."

"Are you planning a biography?"

"No." Kit shook his head. "At least I don't think so – to be honest with you, it's all a bit of a mystery."

"In what way?"

"About five years ago, I wrote a script for a one-off TV drama. I sent it to the usual agencies and to a couple of friends I knew in the business." He shrugged. "Including Lee. She liked it, passed it on to some people she thought might be able to help, but nothing ever came of it. In fact, I'd almost forgotten about it."

He hesitated.

"Then about two weeks ago I got a phone call from Lee asking if we'll still be seeing each other in Cornwall, because she and her American agent wanted a meeting about my screenplay. That they have a project in mind."

"Wow!"

"Trust me, movie people and their projects aren't anything to get excited about. At least not until the contract's signed and there's money in the bank."

"But even so," Jan was smiling. "What's the script about?"

"Have you heard of the novelist John Cowper Powys?" asked Kit.

Jan shook his head.

"He wrote historical novels during the first half of the twentieth century. But his best-known work is *A Glastonbury Romance*, which was set in Somerset during the nineteen twenties, making it a contemporary piece."

"That's where the music festival is, right?" asked Jan.

"Well, close enough to lend its name to it," said Kit. "But one character Powys created, Philip Crow, was the fictitious owner of the very real Wookey Hole, a series of caves that are a tourist attraction about ten miles from Glastonbury. The actual owner of the caves, Gerard Hodgkinson, claimed that he'd been libelled and took legal action, which he won. The damages almost bankrupted Powys."

"So, the idea was to write a script about the legal case." Kit shrugged. "And intertwine it with events from the novel."

"Which," added Carin, joining them and picking up the

thread of the conversation, "is longer than *War and Peace* and has way more protagonists."

"Are you both going over there?" Jan asked.

Carin shook her head.

"I'd like to, as much for the exhibition as the eclipse, but I can't get away." She shrugged. "I'm in London for a college reunion at the end of the month, so I may try to go down to St Hannahs for a few days then."

"What's the exhibition?"

"Aidan McShane - his *Cradle of Thorns* series. The paintings are now all in private collections and so it's the first time they've ever been displayed together."

"I know the name but not his work." Jan looked around the room. "Can you see Tracey anywhere?"

And with a sudden start, Jan realised he couldn't recall Tracey speaking a single word all night long.

4. Aidan

With a sense of entitlement being the one guaranteed attribute a first-born child never lacks, I'd be hard pressed to tell you when it first came to me that I was being treated differently from the other children of the village. A pat on the head in O'Donnell's grocery store - and a penny gobstopper to walk out the door with - seemed as normal a state of affairs as my grandmother being ushered to the front of the queue by the gossiping old biddies waiting to be served in that and every other store we visited.

Also, a child raised by grandparents marches to a different beat of the drum than other children. Young families can be fraught endeavours, beset by anxieties financial and emotional, everything untried and untested with the stakes seemingly so high and the world so judgemental. Twenty years down the line, with a marriage well bedded in and a bit tucked away under the mattress, there's slack to be cut the second time around.

On the downside, from the child's point of view at least, is a tendency for everything to feel a touch old-fashioned. We were one of the last houses in the village to own a television set, although that might have been down to sheltering my innocent ears from the frequent references made to my grandfather during the evening news. *'Prominent republican'* was a euphemism everyone caught the drift of at an early age in fifties Ireland.

I have no memories at all of my father. *'He gave himself for the Cause'* was a mantra repeated throughout my childhood to justify an absence never actually explained. A faulty timer on three sticks of dynamite he was attaching to the east coast railway line, I later discovered, but only by looking through the newspaper records of the day. Ours was a Cause with enough fallen to be selective with its roll call of martyrdom.

My mother exists as nothing but a miasma of softness and sweet perfume, the most fleeting of wisps. I once heard my grandmother, believing me to be out of earshot, describe her as someone who was *'no better than she ought to be'* an expression I couldn't really make sense of at the time, but which stayed with me because of the uncharacteristic bitterness with which it was delivered. My grandfather possessed a more forgiving nature, at least toward what he probably regarded as both the weaker and fairer sex. The only occasion he ever mentioned her to me was when I must have been around six or seven years old and we were in his van, driving back from Dublin. I don't recall the circumstances which had made her a topic of conversation.

"Aidan lad, there are some people in this life," he said and even at that age I recognised the sadness in both his voice and his eyes, "who'll always be paying more for the things that they want than they'll ever pay for anything that they get."

Our family was ostensibly in the meat trade, involved in all aspects from half a dozen farms to a chain of butchers' shops throughout the Republic, my grandfather and his brothers each nominally owning a separate division. My grandfather's was a Dublin slaughterhouse, and he also had a share in several boarding houses my uncle Shaun managed in the Pentonville area of London, together with a property development firm in Holloway.

And if at the time I gave little thought to any of this, then it's because the very nature of small children is to take things as they find them. So, if you were being sent out to play, or off up to bed early, when the Garda made one of their regular visits, then well, wasn't that just the way of the world?

* * *

The initial rumblings of a different order of things arrived on my first day at the village school. At morning break we lined up in the playground where the milk monitors were dispensing tiny bottles from a stack of crates and selling cellophane packets of two large digestive biscuits for a penny apiece. I took my bottle of milk, handed over the coin and was walking away peeling off the tinfoil top when I realised my path was being blocked.

He was an older boy, a head taller than myself, twice as wide and with a shock of red hair that appeared to have been cut with the aid of a pudding basin. His expression of belligerent stupidity I regarded more with interest than alarm until he gestured at the packet of biscuits I was holding.

"I'll be having those."

This took me so much by surprise that I simply stared at him. He suddenly attempted to grab them, but I pulled my hand back away from his grasp. He took a step forward and pushed me hard in the chest, I went backwards off balance and dropped the biscuits onto the ground. He gave a smirk and reached down for them. Without a second's thought, I made a fist and smashed it into his face. By luck rather than skill it landed squarely on the tip of his nose, which exploded into founts of blood. He howled and straightened up. For a moment we both stared, each of us incredulously enraged at how the natural order of our worlds had been violated, and then we sprang toward each other.

We fought with that savage viciousness which comes naturally only to small children and the deranged, unmindful of cause or consequence. We must have been at it for seconds rather than minutes before being pulled apart, but in that time we'd both done a fair bit of damage. I could feel my left eye closing and there was a wobbly tooth where there hadn't been one before. His nose was really gushing now and his upper lip was already starting to swell.

"What in the name of all that's holy is happening here?" screeched Sister Bernadette, pulling me backward by my collar with a strength her scrawny frame belied. My opponent had his arms pinned to his sides from behind by a red face priest but was still squirming violently.

"Ritchie O'Mulley," bellowed the priest, "I'm giving you this one warning only - cease your struggles or you'll not be sitting down for a week."

He slowly became still. A circle of children had surrounded us while we were scrapping but as the priest turned his glare on them they scuttled away, whilst looking furtively over their shoulders.

Sister Bernadette - Bernie as I'd already learnt she was called behind her back - took me off to the staff room where, after checking that my wounds required nothing more than a bit of on the spot first aid, she began to harangue me about what I had waiting in store once Father Patrick had finished with Ritchie O'Mulley.

"Ye little heathens," shaking her head, "ye'll both be feeling the buckle end of Father Patrick's belt."

But she was wiping my face with a tender touch. And when she next spoke, her voice had softened too.

"If Father Patrick asks you..." she began but broke off as the door opened and the priest came into the room. But he didn't look angry, or even annoyed.

He looked worried.

"Are you alright, Aidan lad?" he asked, in a tone soft enough for Bernie to give him a sharp, quizzical look.

I nodded.

"Was it the bullying again?" He shook his head. "The trouble we've had with that Ritchie O'Mulley. Well, next year he's off to the Brothers and there's surely no-one here who'll be sorry to see the back of him." He hesitated. "One of the girls said that he tried to take your snack away from you. Is that what happened?"

It's almost encoded in my family's DNA that silence is

the default response to any form of interrogation and so I just bit my lip. After a few seconds, a hesitant Bernie put her hand on my shoulder and said, "He's still very upset."

"Well, Ritchie's been sent home for the day." He hesitated again. "Would you like to go home too, Aidan? I could take you in the motor car."

I shook my head.

"Good lad," he said, nodding. He looked across to Bernie. "When Mrs McShane arrives to collect him, would you tell her that I'd like a word? Just to explain what happened."

I was taken back to the classroom where I enjoyed being the centre of attention for the rest of the day. When the final bell rang, Bernie had me wait by my desk and ten minutes or so later returned with my grandmother.

"Oh, dear lord," she said, staring at me. I had a real shiner by then. "I'm so sorry, Sister Bernadette," shaking her head. "On his first day too."

She gripped my hand tightly on the walk home and barely spoke to me. On arrival, she sent me straight up to my room.

"It's bread and dripping for you tonight," she told me, "shaming us like this. And just wait until your grandfather gets home."

I spent the next couple of hours sitting in my room, flicking through comics without really looking at them, until I heard the front door open and close. A few minutes later my grandfather called out from the hallway.

"Aidan! Bring yourself down here!"

By the time I got to the bottom of the stairs, my grandfather had gone back into the kitchen. He was standing next to my grandmother by the window, looking out over the garden. He turned around and stared at me, his face expressionless.

"So," he said slowly, "what does the other fella look like?"

"Oh Conell!" said my grandmother, angrily. "For goodness' sake!"

The front doorbell rang. None of us moved for a few seconds and then my grandmother, still bristling, brushed past me. My grandfather seemed as if he were about to speak, but my grandmother called out "Conell! Aidan!"

I walked out into the hallway, my grandfather following.

At the front door was Ritchie O'Mulley, being lifted by the scruff of the neck up onto tiptoe by a man who could only be his father, so strong was the resemblance.

"Good evening to you, Michael," said my grandfather from behind me.

"And to yourselves," said Mr O'Mulley. He paused. "It's about the trouble at the school that I'm here."

"Would you come inside, Michael?" asked my grandmother, but Mr O'Mulley shook his head.

"Thank you, Nessa, but no, this will barely take a moment." He stared at me. "Are you alright, son?"

I nodded. "Yes."

"This one will have me in my grave, he will." He shook Ritchie by the neck and gave a groan that struck me as almost theatrical. "The lazy good for nothing learns from neither kindness nor the belt. His mother down to the school every week..."

He paused, his anger seeming to rob him of words. Then I noticed a trickle of sweat run from his forehead down the side of his face and I realised it wasn't rage he was trying to control but fear. Michael O'Mulley was really frightened.

"Oh, Michael," said my grandfather softly and with a smile, "it's two kids having a bit of a scrap. Did you and our Patrick ever go a school week without one of you laying into the other, and didn't you both stand up at each other's weddings?" He nodded towards Ritchie. "And I'd say that your lad there got as good as he gave, from the look of him."

I'd been staring at Ritchie too, and he looked a lot worse than when I'd last seen him. There was a particularly nasty weal around his left wrist that hadn't been there before.

The relief that suddenly came off Michael O'Mulley was almost physical. With his free hand he raised a small canvas sack and offered it to my grandfather.

"Kathleen's been all day curing ham," he said, "and that's the finest piece."

My grandfather shook his head, but Mr O'Mulley insisted and in the end my grandfather took it from him.

"And now let's have you two be shaking hands," he said and Ritchie sullenly stuck out a paw that was twice the size of mine. But as we stared at each other over the handshake and my grandfather lent forward to rustle Ritchie's hair, I remember thinking that I knew what was really happening here and he didn't.

Revisiting a childhood memory is like putting a sketch scribbled on the fly up onto the easel and getting the watercolours box out - the light and the shade of it begs for the brushes and who can leave well alone? But while I already understood that my grandfather was a man greatly respected, the realisation on our doorstep that day that he was also a man to be greatly feared is not something filled in by hindsight - trust me when I tell you that the sweat on Michael O'Mulley's furrowed brow was glistening in the evening light just as brightly back then as it does in my mind today.

* * *

It was the weekend after my seventh birthday that I first held a paintbrush in my hand, during a characteristically tardy visit from my Aunt Brianna. Bree was the youngest of my grandparents' children and would have been in her late twenties at that time. I learnt in later life that it was she who had introduced my mother to my father, doubtless after their paths had crossed at the same *being no better than they ought to be* classes.

Considering that she lived not much more than a spit and a stone's throw away, Bree's visits had been a rarity, something which made me treasure them all the more. She was an impossibly glamorous creature in the eyes of a child old enough for her musky scents and tender hugs to stir responses as disturbing as they were intoxicating, and yet too young to truly understand why.

Home to Bree was a grand Georgian house off Merrion Square in Dublin, in what she described as a 'studio' and my grandmother always referred to as 'that poky old room'. I remember my first visit there well, I'd never before seen a bed and a sofa together in the same room, let alone a gas ring and that juxtaposition made far more of an impression on me than the exotic fabrics draping the wall or the floor length Hunter's Green velvet curtains. My grandmother didn't remove her coat during our entire visit.

Bree rotated through a variety of jobs that seemed wilfully selected to provoke disapproval - barmaid, usherette, a demonstrator in the Beauty and Fragrance Hall at Arnotts Department Store and most *risqué* of all as an artist's model. There was actually a painting above her fireplace of Bree posing soulfully in the clinging robes of a medieval maiden, although each time we visited I also noticed that a couple of canvases would be stacked on the floor and turned to face the wall, on which could be discerned two faint squares. I'd give a lot now to be able to take a look at them.

My belated seventh birthday present from Bree was a 'painting by numbers' set, which to everyone's surprise she had actually wrapped in gift paper and tied with red ribbon. I opened it up to find a canvas divided by thin lines into small, numbered areas, a paintbrush and six pots of paint also numbered. Bree explained that if I coloured in an area on the painting with the same number paint, I'd create a picture identical to the one on the lid of the box, a fishing boat leaving a small harbour.

"Isn't that a bit old for the lad?" my grandmother asked of Bree, who shook her head.

"No, he'll manage it fine," she said, giving me a smile. "Won't you, Aidan?"

I nodded and so my grandmother fetched some newspapers to cover the kitchen table and a jam jar half filled with water to clean the brush. Bree got me started, filling in a couple of the 3's, which were green and a 4, which was blue.

"You can either do all the same numbers at once," she said, "or do all the colours in one part and then move on to another, which is what I think I'd do."

And she left me to it.

There was a certain degree of consternation when they returned an hour later, from my grandmother at least.

"Oh Aidan," she said. "You've completely spoilt it."

"I thought it was a bit boring," I told her.

At first, I'd done what Bree had suggested and coloured in the houses and the harbour walls, but then I decided to strike out on my own. I replaced the fishing boat with a submarine, which I attacked with a Spitfire. I'd been adding tracer shells from the aircraft's wings down to the conning tower, when they'd come back.

I looked up at Bree.

"Sorry," I said, contritely.

She picked the canvas up and stared at it.

"Well, it's a scene I'm sure has never been witnessed in Dún Mór," she said slowly, "but your execution is faultless."

She handed it over to my grandmother.

"It seems we have an artist in the family."

And returned next week with a sketchbook, charcoal and a tin of watercolours.

* * *

I've always believed that if you've a knack for something, then it's better to be shown than taught, at the outset at least. You'll pick it up fast enough and at a pace which suits you.

In our garden Bree set up an easel and sketched out the guidelines of perspective with a soft pencil, and I understood what she was doing without the need of a single word of explanation. Watercolour washes were applied and our shrubbery recreated by the blending of colour rather than the outlining of shapes.

Bree was a more than competent amateur artist, she'd hung around enough professional ones to pick up the tricks and techniques needed to make a composition work. She got me to start with charcoal, that most forgiving of materials, and over the next few weeks I doubt there was a single visitor to our house whose likeness I didn't capture.

It would be easy to say that all of this was a watershed event, a light on the road to Damascus moment when I discovered my life's true destiny, but that really wasn't how it seemed at the time. Of course, I welcomed the attention that being apparently exceptional at something brought, both at home and at school, and I derived satisfaction from the work itself, but mostly it was Bree's company I cherished.

With no children of her own - and seemingly little prospect of that situation changing - the fact was that I seemed to be filling a void in her life, particularly now that we had something other than family to bond over. Most Sundays she'd drive to our house in her Baby Austin, my grandmother would make us sandwiches and a flask of tea and then the two of us would head off into the countryside. Watercolour is a medium the Irish landscape lends itself to wonderfully, and we'd drive until we came across a stone bridge or a ruined manor house and create our separate visions. I can't think of a time of my life that I look back on more fondly.

I didn't begin working with oils until I started at the Christian Brothers School in Dublin. They had a fully-fledged art department, a competitive Head Brother, and in my first year I won the Caltex Children's Art Competition, a nationwide event.

Bree was in tears when the result was announced at the awards ceremony, and I think even my grandfather's lower lip quivered slightly. Afterwards I saw him deep in discussion with Brother Murphy, my art teacher.

About a week later, my grandfather called me into the

front parlour. He closed the door behind us and asked me to take a seat.

"Aidan," he said, "what is it that you have in mind for your life?"

I was silent, a little thrown by the question.

"I ask," he continued, "because it seems you have an exceptional talent. Your teacher believes so, he says he's never had a pupil like you in thirty years. He also tells me one of the judges on the panel at first refused to believe your painting was the work of a child."

He hesitated.

"My concern is that there's a tendency in this world," he said, "for people to champion their own enthusiasms through the efforts of others. And very often others whose wellbeing, present and future, they hold no responsibility for. Do you understand what I'm saying?"

"I think so," I nodded.

"We've always assumed you would come into the business," he continued. "Perhaps first go to college, where you'd learn something of accountancy and management, and then either help Kienan out with the shops or me with the abattoir."

I'd also been assuming along those lines.

"But is this a dream of yours?" he asked. "The painting?"

Although no-one had asked me that before, I found myself answering without having to think.

"I couldn't imagine ever not being able to do it" I told him.

He nodded slowly.

"We'd better be on the lookout for an accountant then," he said.

* * *

Six years later I was accepted to the Slade in London. It was Bree who drove me to the ferry, and we stopped for a pub lunch outside Dublin.

"I do worry for you over there," she said, as we finished

our meal. "We're a gregarious people and in return tend to be universally loved by just about everyone except the bloody English. I can't help but wish that it was America you were off to." She stared at me. "Do your drinking with your own and even then be keeping your wits about you."

"I'll be fine, Bree," I told her, perhaps a little too dismissively.

"Oh, you think I'm going all Mother Hen on you, hey?" she said archly. "Well, keep this in your pocket for whenever you should find yourself in a tight corner."

Under the table, she slipped something into my hand. I looked down and saw that it was a six-inch leather sap.

"A souvenir from Mulvany's Farm," she told me. "And the closest you'll ever get to a family heirloom."

"Jesus, Bree!" I said. "Where the hell did this come from?"

"Da gave it to me when I went off to live by myself. And I'll tell you what he told me, if you always keep it with you then it's odds on that you'll never need it, but if you do, crack them on the nose or bring it down on their shoulder - if you go for the top of the head they'll not be getting up again." She shrugged. "Personally, I've found that stroking it across the bollocks works wonders too, but Da was probably being too gentlemanly to mention that one to me."

"*Bree!*"

"Aye, so much for odds on." She stood up. "I'm off to powder my nose and then we'll be on our way."

I'd never actually held a weapon in my hand before, at least nothing that had been manufactured with the sole intent to maim or kill. What struck me most was the artistry that had gone into it, thin brown leather strips tightly braided over what must have been a spring-loaded lead weight. *'You wouldn't get workmanship like that these days'* was my first reaction to it. Although heavy for its size, the slightest motion activated the spring, which, together with the leather quickly warming from the heat of my hand, created the sensation of something alive.

And needy.

There's nothing as evocative as the physical presence of the past, and with her family heirloom crack Bree knew that she had handed me much more than a way out of a drunken Saturday night brawl. Mulvany's Farm sat on the edge of our village and the events that unfolded there over four decades previously had passed into the family folklore that I'd been listening to for almost my entire life. Or at least some form of it - like so many of my family's stories, it was one that could be served up in a good few flavours.

When told in earshot of women and children it became a tale noticeably fuzzy around the detail, a broad strokes yarn of ambush and treachery and bodies spirited away in the night by warriors with the souls of poets. It was at weddings and wakes that the story took on its darker hue. The women busy in the kitchen, the men in the parlour passing along the whiskey bottle and more often than not a young cousin or nephew deemed ready for the mantle of his heritage. The ebb and flow of the tale would depend on who was doing the telling, but it was unspoken that it be related without interruption or contradiction.

The bones of it are this:

In 1921 the Black and Tans snatched Donal McShane, my grandfather's younger brother, off the Dublin streets. They suspected, correctly, that he was a member of Fianna Éireann and that he'd been involved in the plot that led to the killing a week earlier of five members of British Intelligence known as the 'Cairo Gang'. They took him off to Dublin Castle for questioning and while it's uncertain if he told them anything it was deemed unlikely, because three days later his lifeless, broken body was found back at the same spot where they'd picked him up.

Given that the assassinations had already brought about the Croke Park massacre, this - tragic as it was - seemed reprisal on a small scale, but my family counted their loss dearly. They buried him in the churchyard of our village, mourned him for a week and then held counsel.

It was a few days after this that two Black and Tans in an armoured car were making what had become a carelessly regular evening patrol along the narrow lanes that bordered what was known as Mulvany's Farm. Mulvany's line had ceased without issue toward the end of the nineteenth century, but a succession of failed tenancies since had served to emphasise that in this part of the world it's tenacity which sticks in people's minds.

At the gateway to the farm, a young woman knelt by a dogcart harnessed to a small pony. The cart sagged down to the ground, where a wheel had buckled and splintered.

The armoured car came to a halt behind it, the girl rising with a nervous air as the soldiers got out. There was a brief exchange, an offer of assistance eliciting her cautious gratitude followed by a suggestion of quid pro quo. When it became apparent that the quo was expected to precede the quid, the girl turned and fled into the farm. The Tans gave her twenty paces to make at least the appearance of a sport of it and then went after her.

She ran clumsily, one hand lifting her skirts above her ankles while her other arm flailed wildly to keep her balance and the soldiers quickly closed her down. A small barn stood alongside the derelict farmhouse and she was barely an arm's reach ahead of them when she went through the door, slamming it shut behind her and sliding the bolt home.

The soldiers laughed and then kicked, rotten wood splintering below the handle. A second kick and the door flew open. The girl was stood facing them against the far wall and their smiles widened as they moved towards her.

Then something strange happened.

She smiled back at them.

That, together with the changing of the light as the door closed behind them, stopped them dead, but it was already too late. Dark figures slipped out of the shadows, all the more deadly for their silence. One of the Tans went down to a rifle butt in the kidneys, the other was grabbed by the arms, lifted by his legs and lowered onto his back.

They continued to struggle as they were stripped - army uniforms there was always a use for - but froze as they saw one of their attackers hand the girl a bone handled straight razor. Caitlin Ryan - Donal McShane's fiancée - didn't flinch as she knelt down and though they'd never admit it, not one of Donal's kinsfolk watched as she gelded them both, their eyes fixed on each other as the terrified screams were followed by gurgled sobs.

Caitlin rose, stood over the soldiers, and spat down on each of them. She handed back the bloodied razor and without a glance around her, left the barn.

"For pity's sake, would you put the bastards out of their misery," someone said.

The bodies were dumped on the same spot in the Dublin street where my great uncle's body had been found. The armoured car was stripped down and scrapped. And the next day Caitlin was on a boat to America, the last time she was ever seen in these parts.

The teller of the tale always left a pause here.

"And lovely girl that she was," he'd continue, "and fine bride that she would have made, you'd still have to say that there wasn't a man in the village not secretly relieved to see her gone."

Then the laughter would ring out through the room, a dark spell broken, the youngster slapped on the back as bottles were cracked, pipes and cheroots lit and Mulvany's Barn settled itself down again into the shadows.

* * *

At the docks I really had no idea of what to say to Bree - everything that was about to happen I owed to her, but the words just wouldn't come.

"I'll write to you and let you know how I'm getting on," I eventually managed.

"Oh, a week in the big city and there'll be a cute dolly bird twisting you around her little finger and we'll all be gone like a will-o'-the-wisp," she smiled.

But I wasn't the one gone.

Three months later Bree had been crossing Henry Street when, to the consternation of the traffic, she'd paused and then turned her head, as if looking for something in the far distance. The horns had barely a chance to begin their cacophony when she'd dropped to the ground, *'as sudden as a stone and just as hard'* one witness declared.

A brain aneurysm was the conclusion of the post-mortem, undetectable and unpreventable was the medical verdict and if, as the priest assured us at the funeral, she was now in a far better place then it was at the expense of leaving the rest of us in a much poorer one.

5. Sir Richard Milford

Receptions at 10 Downing Street were occasions Sir Richard mostly contrived to avoid, but in this instance it would have been rather difficult. His wife Sarah was the patron of a charity devoted to establishing clean water sources for villages in sub-Saharan Africa, and he'd been left in no doubt that his presence was mandatory.

"You only have to walk downstairs," she'd complained at his initial reticence. "Not exactly an effort, is it?"

It wasn't so much the distance as the precedent. If he attended Sarah's function and refused similar invitations, then it could be construed that he was either favouring his wife's charity or snubbing others, neither of which would be acceptable. They eventually compromised on his skipping the buffet lunch but joining her afterwards for drinks.

He arrived to discover Sarah in conversation with Eifion Griffin, Minister Without Portfolio. Whenever occasion required smiles and congratulations, it was usual to find the Prime Minister presiding. But when engagement of the arm-twisting variety was necessitated, well, there was Eifion Griffin.

When Sir Richard's granddaughter, Emily, had been a child one of her favourite toys was a cuddly teddy bear which, with a tug to pull its head inside out, transformed into a fanged monster. Eifion Griffin always brought that to mind, a tubby little Welshman whose cheerful bonhomie could turn in a second and his sing-song accent suddenly be dripping with menace.

"Indeed, Lady Sarah," Eifion Griffin was saying as Sir

Richard joined them. "We do rather tend to regard Sir Richard as Head Prefect."

"Do you?" asked Sarah. "Not that good an analogy though, is it? Not when you think about it. After all, it's you lot who come and go, whilst Richard and his colleagues are the constant factor at Westminster."

Griffin's smile tightened, and Sarah appeared to study him carefully.

"No, I'd say that the role of Cabinet Secretary," she seemed to consider for a moment, "is more akin to that of a Madam in a brothel. You know, taking care of the recent arrivals, who think they're the bee's knees, while reassuring the old hands they've still got what it takes to keep the punters happy. And *forever* dealing with all those bitchy little cat fights, that always seem to take up far more of their time than the function which they're actually there to perform."

By this point, more than a few neighbouring heads had turned to stare at them.

"Perhaps, Lady Sarah," Griffin's smile now seemed almost rictus, "you could remind us who said that a little knowledge is a dangerous thing?"

"I've no idea," smiled Sarah. "Possibly the same sage who observed that all political careers end in failure."

"Always a pleasure, Mr Griffin," said Sir Richard, taking Sarah by the arm and steering her across the room.

"Loathsome little toad," said Sarah when they were - Sir Richard hoped - out of Eifion Griffin's earshot.

"And not one you'd want to cross," said Sir Richard. "Although that ship seems to have sailed."

Sarah snorted.

"He may not be the sharpest tool in the box, but even he's not stupid enough to fuck with the mandarin mafia."

Sir Richard winced at her choice of words, but he knew she was right. Sand in the wheels of departmental machinations was extremely effective and almost impossible to quantify. During Sir Richard's tenure, more than one complex piece of legislation had been brought to a grinding halt as the result of a Permanent Secretary being rubbed up the wrong way.

"Sir Richard?"

He turned to see his secretary, Naomi. She leaned forward, whispered in his ear, and Sir Richard suddenly stiffened.

"Seriously?" said Sarah with raised eyebrows.

"I'm sorry, Lady Sarah," said Naomi, contritely.

"If I find out that you two have cooked this up..." she began and then caught Sir Richard's expression. She gave a brief nod.

"Go on," she said. "But don't worry, I will find a way for you to make this up to me."

"The car's by the Horse Guards Road gate," Naomi told him.

Sir Richard nodded, started to move away and then turned.

"Naomi?"

"Yes, Sir Richard?"

"Stay with Lady Sarah, would you? Try to see she stays out of trouble?"

* * *

Fifteen years as Cabinet Secretary had left Sir Richard blasé about quite a few things, but never the intelligence services. Technically, his duties included overseeing the Joint Intelligence Committee, which theoretically gave him control of the various agencies responsible for the nation's security. But in the same way that Lady Sarah had succinctly outlined the realities of the relationship between politicians and the civil service, similar realities existed in their relationship with the intelligence community.

You didn't fuck with the spooks.

Which to all practical purposes reduced Sir Richard's role to one of assessing and maintaining ministerial plausible deniability and acting as arbiter in the frequent turf wars that flared up between rival agencies. The cessation of the Cold War a decade earlier had left both MI5 and MI6 in rare unison as their *raison d'être* - and consequently their budgets - came under closer and closer scrutiny. At the same time, Special Branch, often regarded as a distant poor cousin in the intelligence family, utilised its century long experience of dealing with domestic unrest to grab an increasingly sizeable portion of the burgeoning terrorist threat.

So, the phrase *'multi-agency investigation'* that Naomi had whispered into his ear was always one to give him pause. And when the car sent to collect him headed not south towards the river and Thames House, but north into Kings Cross and then into the underground parking garage of a seedy-looking office block, his heart really did start to sink. A task force hidden away behind a commercial facade usually meant either a serious internal inquiry was in progress or a security breach had been uncovered.

Keith Venables, MI5's Assistant Director General, was waiting for him by the lift.

"I'm sorry to break into your schedule at such short notice, Sir Richard," he said as the doors closed, "but we've a developing situation here which I felt needed to be brought to your attention." He hesitated. "And with which you may wish to brief the Prime Minister, before we take it before the JIC."

Well, that did nothing to reassure Sir Richard's concerns. The lift doors opened and Venables led him along a corridor and into a small boardroom, whose centrepiece was a round table at which three figures were seated. On the end wall was mounted a large TV screen.

Venables was brisk with the introductions.

"Chief Superintendent Kendall from NCIS, who I think you already know."

Sir Richard had attended several briefings with Jim Kendall and liked him. You'd have taken him more for an academic than a copper, Sir Richard always thought, but in his time he'd headed up the Flying Squad, Counter-Terrorism and had been involved with the National Criminal Intelligence Service since its inception.

"Good to see you again, Sir Richard," said Kendall as they shook hands. "Let me introduce DS Sule," he indicated a young Indian woman with an open laptop on the table in front of her, "one of our star analysts."

Sir Richard and DS Sule exchanged smiles.

"And this is Amanda Palmer," said Venables, "who until recently ran a Cold Case Unit in the Met and whom we're trying to tempt to join us on a full-time basis."

"Sir Richard."

Sir Richard would have taken Palmer for a middle ranking civil servant or businesswoman. Fortyish, he guessed, almost his own height and trim in a trouser suit that managed to be both stylish and functional. Her handshake was brief but firm.

Venables took a seat midway along the table and Sir Richard sat beside him.

"Okay, let's not waste time on preambles," said Venables. "Jim, perhaps you could kick us off?"

"Right." Kendall lent back in his chair. "Two weeks ago, the RUC arrested a twenty-five-year-old man in Antrim for a double murder. Probably not what you're thinking - it was his wife and her golf coach, who he'd found in bed together when he returned home from a business trip a day early. A barrel each from a 12 bore."

"Indeed, *crime passionnel* not what one usually associates with the Ulster temperament," said Venables dryly, and Kendall shrugged.

"Anyway, it was the husband who called it in. He comes quietly so all pretty cut and dried thought the Antrim police." Kendall paused. "Twelve hours later they get a visitor at the station, where he's still being held while they tidy up the paperwork. The lad's father."

"If Superintendent Kendall were to tell you this individual's name," said Venables softly, "you'd recognise it from any number of Security Service briefings to the JIC, but in the light of what you're about to hear it's probably best..."

Venables gestured with his hand, and Sir Richard nodded. The legalities of off-the-record briefings were frequently something of a tightrope walk.

"So, let's be singularly unimaginative," said Venables, "and call him Paddy."

Sir Richard gave a slight smile.

"After seeing his son," Kendall continued, "Paddy asks to speak with not only the most senior Special Branch officer in the six counties, but also with the current highest ranked Security Service officer and what really gets everyone's attention is that he asks for them by *name*. The local force might not know who Paddy is, but when they all sit down together at a hotel in Coleraine, it transpires that MI5 have a file on him a yard thick and Paddy knows it. He's been the IRA's top money man for twenty-five years, and the short of it is that he wants to cut a deal.

"Well, it's a bit late for that, he gets told. What with the Good Friday Agreement signed, sealed and delivered *plus* amnesty letters from our new Prime Minister to show that all is if not forgotten then at least forgiven, anything Paddy might have to offer is basically just dotting the I's and crossing the T's. Sorry pal, you've missed the boat with this one.

"But Paddy's anticipated this. It's not us he wants to make the deal with - it's the Yanks."

Kendall smiled as he caught the flicker of surprise that crossed Sir Richard's face.

"Like I said, Paddy's been their money man. And that means weapons deals in Libya and money laundering in the Middle East. Interesting bedfellows indeed, Sir Richard, and he has stories to tell aplenty."

"Al-Qaeda," said Sir Richard quietly, referring to the organisation behind the simultaneous bombing of US embassies in Dar es Salaam and Nairobi, leaving hundreds dead and thousands wounded.

Venables nodded.

"We've spoken to the CIA's London station chief," he said. "And they want him. Badly."

"So?"

"He and his family are going into the US Witness Protection Program." Venables hesitated. "We obviously can't go into the details of how that will be facilitated..."

Sir Richard raised a hand.

"Please, spare me," he said dryly.

"But we have at least another four or five days before we can get all the pieces in play for that to happen. So, for the moment Paddy is carrying on with his life as normal and last week we had him in London for a few days. A debriefing of our own. The Americans have been quite generous in return for our cooperation, but we'd still like to squeeze as much out of this as we're able."

"Something came up during one of our chats with him," said Kendall, and looked over at Venables.

"We've prepared a draft JIC briefing document," Venables tapped a folder on the desk in front of him, "which you're welcome to read, but I'm afraid it can't leave this room. Or we could just run through the salient points?"

Sir Richard nodded. "Please."

"I'll make it as concise as I can." Kendall leaned forward and rested his elbows on the table. "As a young lad back in the late sixties, early seventies, Paddy'd been over in London, working on the building sites. One night in 1970 - we've got it down to just after the August Bank Holiday weekend because he remembers it being his mother's birthday and earlier that night he'd phoned home - he and a mate get pulled out of the pub by a couple of Belfast heavies. They're put in the back of a Transit van, which drives over to Notting Hill and pulls up outside of a house. They're sitting there for a while when Paddy hears a terse discussion, moving closer. Someone was saying that this is from Conell himself, so let that be an end to it.

"Things go quiet for a minute or two after that. Then the back doors are opened and a couple of men are standing there, carrying a rolled-up carpet. A carpet with a foot sticking out of the end of it. They help get the bundle into the van and before the doors close, one of the men says that there was no choice, this is the only way if they want a man on the inside. Then the doors shut, but Paddy hears the same voice saying that he'll clean the room up. They just need to worry about their end.

"They drive up to Kilburn and onto the building site where they've been working. Foundations have been dug and the cement's ready to go in the next morning. They dig a deeper hole, in he goes, carpet and all, they fill it in and that's the end of it. A fistful of tenners each, no need to tell them to keep their mouths shut and then it's back to the pub."

"Do we know whereabouts in Kilburn this was?"

Venables shook his head.

"He was driven all around there, but the area's changed beyond recognition. He thought it was a small office block being built on the side of a warehouse, but we can't find anything like that. A lot of industrial units came down in the eighties, to make way for residential redevelopments."

He shrugged.

"Anyway," said Kendall. "At the house in Notting Hill? The men with the carpet?"

Sir Richard waited.

"Paddy's certain the one who told them that they just needed to worry about their end was Aidan McShane."

Sir Richard stared at him.

"Oh, bloody hell!" he said.

* * *

"We've had more luck with the house in Notting Hill."

A tray with coffee and biscuits had been brought in, although Sir Richard was untempted by either.

"Despite the massive amount of gentrification over the

last thirty years," continued Venables, "the area itself has hardly changed at all."

"Quite," said Sir Richard, and then added dryly, "I live in Ladbrook Grove."

"Well, not too far away from Pembridge Villas then," said Venables. "Number three. Paddy found the place in about ten minutes. It was a rundown slum back then, must be worth over a million these days."

"Do we know who owns it?"

Kendall gave a tight smile.

"Well, we do now. Initially, all we had was what looked like a shell company in the Cayman Islands - Maybe Enterprises. We weren't sure whether or not that was dodgy but..."

"Look, we're getting a bit ahead of ourselves," interrupted Venables. "Perhaps Ms Palmer could step in here."

Kendall nodded.

"One of the first things we discovered," said Palmer, "was that around the time this killing was supposed to have taken place, 3 Pembridge Villas was already the target of a Special Branch operation." She turned to DS Sule. "Shall we take a look, Shravasti?"

DS Sule tapped the keyboard of her laptop, and the large screen filled with thumbnails of what were obviously surveillance photographs of the house in question. Sir Richard listened, as Palmer explained what she'd learnt from ex-Chief Superintendent Maddox about Christopher Franklyn.

"He'd been proving surprisingly elusive," she said, "but after my visit, Brian Maddox got back to me. He'd done a bit of digging of his own for us and heard that Franklyn was now running a bookshop in Amsterdam."

"How very salubrious," said Sir Richard, dryly.

"Once we had that information," said Kendall, "he became quite easy to track down."

"You've spoken to him?" asked Sir Richard.

"Oh yes," said Venables, with that tight smile again. "We've certainly spoken to him. Or rather Ms Palmer has." He sat back in his chair. "We're presenting this to all persons of interest as a straightforward cold case murder inquiry, and as such we thought it best that Ms Palmer conducts any initial interviews." He smiled. "She 'talks the talk' you might say."

Sir Richard nodded.

"We initially spoke on the phone," said Palmer, "and he agreed to be interviewed in person. We offered to pay his expenses for a trip to London, but he was already coming over to England for the eclipse - he's staying with friends in Cornwall."

"Fortuitous," said Sir Richard. "For the taxpayer."

"Quite," said Venables.

"Shravasti took him through these photographs," said Palmer.

"What we did," said DS Sule, "was to draw a plan of each floor of the house, and then Mr Franklyn identified who'd been living in which room at that time." She shrugged. "As best he could. It is almost thirty years ago. We gave each name a unique ID and where we found them in the photographs, we wrote the number against them, in green if he was sure they were still around after our supposed cut-off date, and red if he wasn't."

"How many 'not sures'?" asked Sir Richard.

"That's where it gets tricky." She paused. "Of the people who lived there, only one. But we're not certain that our victim was a resident and there were a lot of visitors, some of whom he remembered but others he didn't."

"Or so he claims," said Kendall.

"Well." DS Sule shrugged. "What I did next was to go through the visitors, also giving them a unique ID and checking that they were in an even number of photographs."

"Arriving *and* leaving," said Sir Richard.

She nodded.

"While Shravasti was getting on with that, I interviewed Franklyn myself." Palmer nodded to DS Sule, who typed on her keyboard. A video image of an interview room appeared on the screen and Sir Richard got his first look at Christopher Franklyn.

Sir Richard expected someone a little, well, *seedier*. But Franklyn's appearance was well groomed and his clothes, if casual, were expensive. And there was something about his bearing too - Sir Richard had seen recordings of more than a few interviews and had always been struck by the polarity of demeanour, either nervous and cagey or bristling with faux belligerence, rarely anything in between. But Franklyn was, well, not languid exactly, but... To tell the truth, he seemed politely bored. Sir Richard knew that the recording would have been analysed by experts in body language and vocal inflection, and he wondered what they'd made of that.

"What exactly did you tell him?" asked Sir Richard.

"We're sticking to the same story with everyone," said Venables. "That an unrelated investigation has provided credible intelligence of a murder, committed at that address around the August Bank Holiday in 1970. We've additionally told Franklyn that the body was wrapped in a carpet and removed in a Transit van."

"To say Franklyn was sceptical is an understatement," said Palmer. She turned her head to DS Sule. "Can we have some sound?"

The first voice from the speaker belonged to Jim Kendall.

"We don't seem to be getting anywhere fast here, Amanda. Let's rattle his cage a bit, see what that does, shall we?"

On the screen, Palmer gave an almost imperceptible nod. Sir Richard realised that she must be wearing an earpiece and that the playback also included those communications.

He settled back to watch.

* * *

"Okay, Mr Franklyn," said Palmer, "so could we now

move on to talk about the *background* to your involvement?"

"Involvement in what, exactly?"

"Sorry, that was carelessly phrased." Palmer smiled. "What I'm trying to do here is build a picture of how you became... *caught up* in this scenario." She looked down at an open file on the table. "It says here that your father - Detective Chief Inspector Franklyn, as he was then - filed a report in 1967 stating that you were working as an undercover informant. But that wasn't true, was it?"

"No." Franklyn shook his head. "I'd been arrested for possession of cannabis. It was only half an ounce, but enough to get me six months in a Detention Centre."

"I've read about those. The short, sharp shock."

"It was a pretty grim prospect."

"I gather you and your father hadn't been getting on up to that point. With you becoming increasingly something of a handful."

"I wouldn't disagree with that."

"Indeed. Shoplifting, truancy - and of course the drugs." Palmer sat back in her chair. "When we spoke to Brian Maddox, he passed it off as just the usual teenage rebellion stuff."

Franklyn shrugged

"And was it?" she pursued. "'The usual teenage rebellion stuff'?"

"It didn't feel that way at the time," Franklyn said slowly. "But looking back... Yes, probably."

"Okay, so you ran away from boarding school and then -"

"I *left* boarding school," Franklyn interrupted. "I was sixteen, I wasn't exactly skipping off down the road with a bundle on a stick."

"But you were technically a minor, and you were reported missing." She glanced down at the file again. "Until your arrest in April 1967." She looked back up at him. "So, what were you up to during that period?"

Franklyn gave another shrug.

"This and that."

"Presumably with people you befriended and then subsequently betrayed?"

Franklyn shook his head.

"Not really, the arrangement was that I'd only inform on anyone who was dealing." He paused. "Look, although pretty much every force had its own drug squad by then, all of them were next to useless. Most coppers wouldn't have known a bag of grass from birdseed and as far as infiltration went, a police cadet in a combat jacket was deep cover. As long as I was giving them a network of dealers to play whack-a-mole with, no-one was interested in my friends' ten bob deals."

"And you had no problem with that?"

"I wasn't happy, but I wasn't losing any sleep."

"But it was different in 1970, wasn't it? In Notting Hill?"

"Damn right it was different - people were setting off bombs and firing machine guns at the American embassy."

"But you still had no problem gaining the trust of friends with the intention-"

"Look," Franklyn broke in, with a note of weariness, "have I wandered into some bizarre *Alice Through the Looking Glass* world here? I was *asked* to infiltrate extremist groups by Special Branch and I was thanked for doing it by the Home Secretary, so please, spare me the retrospective moralistic hand-wringing."

"Mr Franklyn!" Palmer's tone became terse and then increasingly monotonously formal. "We have credible intelligence that at least one murder was committed at Pembridge Villas during the time you were living at the squat there. No, we are not sure of exactly what happened and nor were we able to gain access. But today we finally obtained a warrant to search the property and that search will be immediate and forensic - cadaver dogs in the grounds and in the house we'll be going behind walls and under floorboards."

She paused.

"What I need you to be perfectly clear about is that if we were to uncover evidence which suggests that you have, either by intent or omission, hampered the course of our investigation, then I can assure you the consequences will be very serious indeed."

Franklyn seemed to reflect for a few seconds.

Kendall's voice cut in again.

"Well, that seems to have given him food for thought. Maybe let him have a chance to digest it."

Franklyn looked at Palmer with a quizzical expression.

"I'm not exactly sure," he said slowly, "what would constitute 'hampering by omission'."

Palmer stared at him.

"It would be withholding information which you knew to be pertinent to our investigation, whether directly asked for it or not."

"Right, got it," nodded Franklyn. "Well, I'm not sure how pertinent this is to the investigation itself, but you do seem to be under the impression that Pembridge Villas was an actual *squat*."

"I'm sorry?" Palmer couldn't keep the surprise off her face.

"It wasn't - the house was being managed by Lee Munro and everyone living there paid rent."

"Managed?" Palmer was shaking her head. "Managed for who?"

Franklyn began to smile.

"Don Mayberry."

"The actor?"

"Yeah, he bought it as an investment, when he first went over to Hollywood." Franklyn sat back in his chair. "Lord Mayberry now, of course. You know, the Queen's favourite thesp and long-term polo playing chum of the Duke of Edinburgh. And you've obviously checked that he doesn't still own it, haven't you? Because that would be a really interesting conversation the next time he was round at the palace for lunch or having a chat between chukkas - Special Branch ripping his home apart. Be a fair bet that whatever clown put a fiasco like that together would be spending the rest of their career checking ferry passenger lists at Immingham Docks."

"*Shit!!*" Kendall's voice.

Palmer was staring at Franklyn speechlessly.

He stared back at her and then tapped his ear with a finger.

"Cat got your tongue?" he smiled.

* * *

"It was a close thing," said Venables. "The search team were almost at the front gate."

"We didn't learn an awful lot more," said Kendall, except that..."

"Actually," interrupted Venables, "would you play the last five minutes of the interview, DS Sule?" He turned to Sir Richard. "I did find it rather - *insightful*."

The video ran in jerky fast forward mode for a few seconds before resuming normal play.

"In fact, she's over here this week," Franklyn was saying. "For the eclipse."

"In Devon?"

"Cornwall," said Franklyn. "St Hannahs. She's got a place there." He smiled. "Of sorts."

"Of sorts?"

"Lee's a silent partner in one of those businesses where companies send along their middle management for a few days of military style training exercises. You know, to supposedly determine leadership qualities, staying cool under pressure, that kind of thing."

"I've heard of them."

"I wouldn't imagine they get a lot of factory managers or engineers, but they probably do well out of Covent Garden ad agencies and Soho PR firms." Franklyn shrugged. "Carpenter, squeaky gate."

"And she's there this week?"

"Flying into Newquay from Los Angeles the day before the eclipse."

Palmer smiled and shook her head.

"I holiday a lot in the West Country," she said, "and I can tell you that there are definitely no direct flights to Newquay from Los Angeles. Or from any other North American city."

"There are when you travel by private jet," said Franklyn.

"Well," said Kendall softly, "isn't that just the conversation stopper?"

Sir Richard smiled.

"So, she'll be in Cornwall this week?" asked Palmer. "If I wanted to talk to her?"

"Lee's over here for the eclipse and to open the Aidan McShane exhibition in St Hannahs," Franklyn told her. "I'm not sure how long she's staying, though."

"I was thinking of visiting that myself," admitted Palmer, "if I could get down there this summer. I've always liked his work."

"Well, there you are," said Franklyn. "A treat on expenses."

Palmer smiled.

"Look," Franklyn sat back and studied her. "I think I've been about as much help as I can be, and I have other business today."

"Of course, Mr Franklyn." Palmer folded the file closed. "We appreciate your help and I'm sorry if things appeared to get a bit - *fractious* earlier."

She made as if to stand up.

"DI Palmer..." began Franklyn and then hesitated.

"Yes," she said, sitting back down.

"I know I don't have all the facts here," he said and then raised his hand as she seemed about to speak, "and I get why that has to be. But could I just talk for a minute? And ask you to bear with me?"

She nodded.

"A couple of years ago, for my birthday, my wife bought me '*The World At War*' on VHS. I don't know if you remember it, twenty-six hours of Second World War newsreel footage cut with interviews and narrated by Laurence Olivier. It was a big TV event at the time, back in the seventies."

"Yes," Palmer said slowly. "I was only a teenager, but I do recall it."

"And it's still pretty good. I was worried that twenty-odd years later it wouldn't stand up. Lots of things don't but this actually did. Anyway, episode ten is '*Wolf Pack, War in the Atlantic*'. You probably don't remember, it was about the U-boat attacks on the merchant fleet."

Palmer shook her head, her expression becoming one of bemusement.

"I must have seen it but, no, nothing specific comes to mind."

"Well, exactly. But the thing is, we all know now that the reason the Germans were beaten at sea was because Alan Turing's team at Bletchley had cracked the Enigma code - British Intelligence knew everything that German Naval Command was about to do. But when the series was being made, that information was still classified. Which gave the Ministry of Defence the interesting challenge of coming up with a plausible explanation of how a handful of rusty old frigates, and a squadron of Swordfish torpedo biplanes, managed to almost annihilate a fleet of four hundred U-Boats that were spending most of their time submerged in the middle of the Atlantic."

Franklyn paused.

"And do you know what their solution was?"

Palmer gave another shake of her head.

"Johnny Walker."

"I'm sorry."

"Captain John Walker RN." Franklyn grinned. "Every time I think about what must have happened, it puts a smile on my face. It's late at night, the top brass are sitting around a table at the Admiralty, scratching their heads over what the hell can they come up with here. The whisky bottle's being passed along, glasses are being refilled, then someone looks at the label and slowly says 'What if...?'

"And so that was the story they spun. Captain Walker, terror of the high seas, scourge of the Kriegsmarine. U-Boat captains only had to see his frigate on the horizon puffing its way towards them and they might as well scupper the boat there and then and have done with it. *'Captain Walker's tactics in submarine warfare'* - and this was a really nice touch - *'were so revolutionary that aspects of them are still classified today'*. And unfortunately, he couldn't be interviewed - he died of natural causes just before the war ended.

"And no-one batted a bloody eyelid." Franklyn leaned back in his chair. "Look, I lived undercover for years and the first lesson you learn is that people will believe pretty much anything until you give them reason not to. That the most effective deceptions are about managing expectation by manipulating context." He shrugged. "And if you don't have the correct context, then any 'intelligence' can be made to seem credible."

He paused and seemed to be choosing his words carefully.

"I think you're being spun a line," he said. "I think you've been convinced that Johnny Walker sank all the submarines. And I think that what you really should be doing here is finding out why."

Franklyn gave DI Palmer a smile, stood up, shook hands and left the room.

She turned, stared into the camera, and the screen went blank.

"Well," said Venables, "he's definitely wasted in that bookshop."

* * *

"I have to admit," Sir Richard spoke slowly, "that at this point my inclination is to agree with Mr Franklyn." He turned to Venables. "Although I assume my presence here means you have reason to disagree."

Venables nodded.

"Actually," he said, "that *was* the conclusion we were coming to, particularly in the absence of a victim. Disinformation not exactly the Provos' usual M.O. but never underestimate their capacity for mischief." He shrugged. "Because all that's required to give the story credibility is the knowledge that Aidan McShane was living at the sqa… Pembridge Villas," he corrected himself. "And we can assume that if Conell McShane's grandson were living in London in the early seventies, then someone would be keeping an eye out for him - word, I'm sure, would have got around."

"But?" asked Sir Richard, quietly.

"Shravasti," said Kendall.

One of the surveillance photographs expanded to fill the entire screen.

"This is the resident Mr Franklyn couldn't be certain was still living at Pembridge Villas, after that August Bank Holiday weekend," said DS Sule. "He recalls him as 'Pete' but can't remember his surname."

"I don't see how that helps much," said Sir Richard.

"That was my reaction too," said DS Sule. "At first. But take a good look at it, because we can narrow things down quite a bit. He's white, in his late teens, early twenties, brown hair, around five ten." She paused. "The police missing persons reports from thirty years ago are an absolute shambles, but DI Palmer reminded me that back then the police weren't the only option for finding a lost relative - the Salvation Army also ran a missing persons service for families."

"Their records from the seventies aren't computerised," said Palmer, "but they're about as cross-referenced as you can get outside a database."

"DI Palmer gave me the name of her contact there," said DS Sule. "Who checked out their files of that period for me."

She began to tap at her keyboard.

"A Peter Marshall was reported missing by his sister in October 1971. She didn't have an address for him but believed that he was living in West London, before she lost touch. He was twenty-two years old, brown hair, blue eyes, five eleven. The girl I spoke to at the Salvation Army scanned his file and emailed it over to me. Including the photograph his sister gave to them." The photograph on the screen shrank to half size and moved to the left. A second photograph, a head and shoulders shot, appeared on the right-hand side of the screen. Then the first image zoomed in on the face until it reached the same scale as the other.

"Good lord," said Sir Richard, his eyes flicking back and forth between the two images.

"We have his actual date of birth so... He's never had a passport, a driving licence, been given a National Insurance number, got married, paid income tax or served in the armed services. No death certificate's ever been issued for him."

"His sister?" asked Sir Richard. "Has she been contacted?"

"Not yet," said Palmer.

"But this is where it gets really interesting," said DS Sule. "When she filed the missing person report, guess where she was living?"

Sir Richard shook his head.

"In Cornwall," said DS Sule. "St Hannahs. And still is."

"That's where Lee Munro has a home."

"I'll tell you something else it is," said Kendall. "It's where Christopher Franklyn was arrested in April 1967."

Sir Richard considered.

If there were anything to this, it would not only end the career of the Secretary of State for Northern Ireland, who Sir Richard both liked and admired, but also create a crisis of a magnitude not seen in British politics since the Profumo affair.

"The key factor here," said Sir Richard carefully, "would seem to be one of *habeas corpus.* Without a body this is little more than gossip and hearsay - correct?"

Both Venables and Kendall nodded.

"So, first," said Venables, "we need to find out what the sister of this Peter Marshall has to say. And secondly," he turned to Kendall, "it can't be impossible to discover what construction sites were underway in Kilburn during August 1970. Planning applications would have been submitted - the utilities companies will have records of new commercial customers for electricity, gas and water."

"Whatever resources you need," said Sir Richard, "let me know and I'll make sure you're unhindered."

"Thank you, Sir Richard," said Kendall.

"I'll speak to the Prime Minister," he said quietly. "And for the moment we'll treat this as an 'eyes only' matter until he's decided on an immediate line of action. Are we clear on that?" he added.

They all nodded.

"And you'll keep me updated?" he asked Venables.

"Of course, Sir Richard."

"Good work everyone." He shrugged. "Not an ideal situation but at least we know where we are."

He rose from the table.

6. Kit

You wake in the Daily Express building on Fleet Street. Like all major newspapers it houses a small dormitory, a room with a row of camp beds where reporters working on a fast-breaking story can catch a few hours' sleep. The previous day, in the Welsh mining village of Aberfan, half a million tons of coal slag poured down a hillside and buried a school full of children. So, you figured the newsroom would be chaotic enough for you to make your way up the back stairs and get your head down for the night without attracting too much attention.

You quickly dress and slip out quietly. Having done this a few times now, there are even a few friendly nods of recognition as you cross the newsroom, the hacks assuming you're a cub reporter drafted in from one of the affiliate rags to help cover the phones.

Outside you turn right and head toward the Strand. At Charing Cross Station, you collect your holdall from the left luggage locker and walk down the steps, through the Gents and into the Wash and Brush Up. Stripping to the waist you brush your teeth, wash your face and shave. Removing the rest of your clothes, while coyly watched by the attendant, you change into a fresh set of underwear, a clean shirt and then you put your old clothes into a large plastic carrier bag in the holdall. Once a week you hand this over to Connie, a chambermaid along the road at the Savoy, who for ten bob puts it all through the hotel laundry for you. But the suit, you notice as you slip the jacket back on, has lost a little of its crispness and so you'll need to do something about that.

To glide easily between the many worlds of London's West End - Mayfair clubs, Soho dives, bohemian Fitzrovia and Tin Pan Alley - requires a chameleon presence and just about the only place in the world where a suit won't blend you into the background is on a beach. You've learnt that a dark suit, with a light grey or blue shirt - white can look grubby very quickly - and a knitted wool tie in the pocket for when things turn formal, will get you in through the door of most places that you need to be and settle an air of anonymity around you once inside.

"Thanks, ducky," says the attendant as you tip him a shilling and leave. "You're always the highlight of my day."

You put the holdall back in a locker, the key in your pocket and mingle with the early morning commuters entering the Lyons Tea Rooms across the road. Finding an empty table, you sip Russian tea from a glass cup and map out the rest of today.

* * *

You've never been keen on South London, it always feels like travelling through endless identikit provincial town centres, linked by stretches of shitty post-war suburbia. And you take almost an hour to get to the Somerleyton Road in Brixton.

Bunny's Cafe is probably the cheapest place in London to buy hashish and the reason it's your first call of the day is that it can be the most dangerous. Whenever you've scored here before it's been with Vic, a Jamaican poet who's become a familiar face at counterculture venues from Notting Hill to the Roundhouse and you've formed a tentative friendship. But you haven't seen him for a while and with this being your first solo visit, daylight hours seems a smart move.

There're about a dozen guys in the cafe when you enter, all West Indian, and the buzz of conversation dies as you walk up to the counter. You try to sound confident as you order a coffee.

"Is Vic around?" you ask the guy serving and who you

recognise from your previous visits. He stares at you and then points, clicking his fingers.

"Hey, I know you," he says, and you've rarely been as relieved to see a smile break out on someone's face as you are at that moment. "You here with Vic before, yeah?"

You nod and hope your tone conveys confidence rather than relief. "Yes."

"You a poet too." He reaches for a cup. "You called Kit."

He's half right, but you don't contradict him.

"Vic's in Kingston, mon," he says, pouring the coffee. Conversation behind you starts up again, with almost a physical sense of tension dissipating. "Seeing family. He back next month."

"That's a shame." You pay for the coffee and make a gesture for him to keep the change. "I was hoping to catch up with him."

He acknowledges the tip with a nod.

"When I see him, I'll tell him you came looking."

"Thanks."

You sit at a table by the window. A couple of minutes later a tall, skinny guy comes over and takes the seat opposite you.

"You lookin' for resin, mon?"

You nod.

"How much?"

"An ounce."

"Seven pound," he says. "That okay?"

"Sure," you tell him.

"Let's take a walk," he says, standing up.

You finish your coffee in one gulp, follow him outside and along the road. He stops at the gate of a narrow alleyway between two houses and says, "In here."

As you step in after him he turns, in his hand is a flick knife and the blade springs open. Before you can react, he stabs the knife into the wooden gatepost, lets go of the handle and reaches into his pocket. He takes out a block of hash the size of a small paperback book.

He looks at your expression and gives a broad smile.

"Nearly wet yourself there, hey Kit Kat?"

He sizes off a piece of the block with his finger, about an inch down from the top.

"An ounce, okay?"

You nod. He pulls the knife out of the gatepost and with the blade scores the hash along the edge of his finger. You count out seven one pound notes, as he saws the piece away. You make the exchange silently and then step back out into the street.

"Any morning between ten and twelve you find me here, mon," he says as you separate by the cafe. "But if not, then ask for Wilfred, they'll know where to send to."

"Okay," you say. "Thanks."

As you cross the road, a bus comes to a halt at a zebra crossing. Before it moves off, you grab the rail and pull yourself up onto the platform. You have no idea of its destination, but at this moment away from here is good enough.

* * *

But the bus takes you to almost exactly where you want to be and you get off at Oxford Circus. You walk along Oxford Street toward Marble Arch and then turn into Selfridges. You head upstairs to the Gents and in front of the mirror fasten your collar and put on your tie. You go into a cubicle, sit down and examine the hash.

It's good quality paki black, still wet and sticky. With your penknife you cut off around a sixth, wrap it in a Rizla and slip it into your breast pocket. You score the rest of the block into a dozen equal parts and slice each into a twist of silver paper, which goes into an empty Players packet.

When you've finished you leave, take the stairs up to the next floor and carefully judge your pace over to a door marked '*No Admittance*' so you go through it immediately behind a group of junior sales staff. Together you climb another short flight of stairs to arrive at the staff canteen.

Most London department stores have a subsidised canteen. Saturday is the best day to use them because the high turnover of part-time staff means that you're unlikely to be challenged. During the working week, large company headquarters - Unilever, Shell, Lloyds Bank - are a better bet. Any questions and you're up from Manchester or Bristol for a meeting. Some canteens operate a voucher system, but most opt for keeping things simple and charge a nominal amount – today, mushroom soup, steak and kidney pie and a rum baba for dessert, costs you ninepence.

You take your tray back and walk down to the menswear department. You slowly drift over to the racks of off the peg suits, all the while scoping where the store staff are and what they're doing. As you'd expect for a busy Saturday, all are occupied with customers - you check the size of a suit almost the exact colour as the one you're wearing and carry it into the changing room. You undress, try it on and it's pretty much a perfect fit. You carefully remove the sales tags, just as carefully attach them to your old suit, and then transfer the contents of the pockets. You put the old suit onto the hanger and confidently stride back out into the store. You hang it on the rack from where you took the other one and casually examine a couple more. You don't seem to be the focus of anyone's attention and so make your way over to the exit.

There's always a moment, stepping out through the door into the street, when you expect the dead weight of the hand of authority to come clamping down onto your shoulder, followed by a rush of euphoria as you realise that's not going to happen.

You head towards Oxford Circus.

* * *

You plan to spend the afternoon turning the quid deals into cash. There're half a dozen or so pubs in Fitzrovia and Soho you can drift through, and you'll be unlucky not to have it all unloaded by teatime.

Your first call is at the *Duke of York* in Rathborne Place.

A couple of familiar faces catch your eye and you follow them into the Gents. Two swift handovers, a good start, but as you leave Tony, the barman beckons you over.

"Have you seen Nikki?" he asks. "She's been in here looking for you, last night and then again about half an hour ago."

"No, I haven't." You shake your head. "I thought she was in Amsterdam?"

"I don't know about that - if she was, then she's back now." He shrugs. "I got the impression it was important."

If Nikki's checking out your usual haunts there's a good chance your paths will cross in the next few hours, but you tell Tony that you'll pop in about sixish if they haven't.

"If she comes in again, I'll tell her," he nods.

You head off down the road to *The Wheatsheaf*, but just as you push at the door you're grabbed by the elbow and a deep voice says, "One moment please, sir".

Your heart leaps into your mouth, your instinctive reaction is to break free and run, ditch the hash round the next corner. Then the grip loosens and you hear soft laughter.

You whirl around.

"Jesus! For fuck's sake, Mick!"

Mick grins and shakes his head, thick curls bobbing up and down.

"Jesus Kit, I really thought you were literally going to shit yourself then."

He's been a friend for longer than anyone else you still know. You met about eighteen months earlier at the poetry reading organised by Allen Ginsberg at the Albert Hall, which was also your first day alone on the streets of London.

Mick operates on the literary fringe, flitting between magazines like *Peace News* and the poetry rags which surface for a few issues before sinking forever. About six months ago you'd both contributed to a magazine called the *Long Hair Times*, an attempt to set up something along the lines of New York's *East Village Other*, a blend of reviews, original essays and event listings. It only made one issue, but last week it had been revived under the rather more ambitious title of *International Times* and you've heard whispers there's serious money behind it from the music world. Rumours reinforced by a benefit concert at the Roundhouse, with Paul McCartney in the audience.

"Do you want a drink?" you ask him, and he nods.

You find an empty table and try to pump him about the new magazine, without trying to sound too eager. He suggests you do a piece on spec, *'anything that takes your fancy'* and he'll make sure Hoppy or Miles get a look at it. He gives a shrug, indicating that's the best he can do, but you're okay with that.

"Have you seen Nikki today?" you ask him. "Word is she's looking for me."

The smile leaves his face.

"You didn't hear what happened?"

"No."

"She and Baz got busted." He grimaces. "With a shit load of acid in Amsterdam. Or at least Baz did, he's in jail over there waiting for a judge to throw away the bloody key."

You've known Nikki almost as long as you've known Mick, would-be actress, part-time model and occasional 'escort' when the straight work dries up. She also isn't shy about pushing the odd pill or spliffing up for her showbiz pals who want to get down with the kids, but an international drug bust...

"What happened?"

"Baz had this deal set up with a Dutch chemist for crystalline LSD - you know, ten thousand trips in a test tube." He takes a sip of his drink. "My guess is that he had Nikki along to bring it back through customs packed in her fanny." He shakes his head. "How bloody stupid is she, you never get involved with a junkie, they always fuck up."

It's widely known Baz has a serious heroin habit.

"Look man, any chance you could..." Mick draws on an imaginary spliff. "I'm a bit skint at the moment," he adds apologetically.

You take the Players packet out of your pocket and slide it across the table to him. With a quick glance to make sure no-one is watching, he filches out a quid deal.

"Thanks, I'll let you have it back or square up with you next week." He stands up. "And when you see Nikki say hi from me, okay? Tell her I'm sorry about the way things worked out for her."

You smile and nod, but you're starting to get more than a little worried about why she's trying to find you so urgently.

* * *

You see Nikki before she sees you, standing outside *Finches* on Goodge Street, knee bent back with the sole of her boot flat against the wall as she cups her hands around one of her foul-smelling French cigarettes. She thanks the punter who's just given her a light with a sharp nod, causing her loose chignon to flick from side to side.

As she inhales, you're tempted to turn away before she notices you and maybe that hesitancy registers in her peripheral vision because she suddenly whips her head around, sees you and then raises both hands to heaven in a theatrical pantomime of a supplicant's thanks for prayers answered.

She pushes herself off the wall and strides towards you.

"*Hallelujah!*" She puts a hand on your shoulder and plants a kiss on both cheeks. "Darling, I have been searching for you forever!"

"Okay." You gesture at the pub door. "Shall we go in and sit down?"

She grimaces.

"Actually," she says, "I'm sort of persona non grata at the moment." Giving an apologetic little shrug, she slips her arm through yours and leads you off down the street. "A bit of a misunderstanding, but it'll get sorted out soon," she tells you, as you stroll towards Tottenham Court Road.

You've never been sure of Nikki's age, it's tricky to reconcile her appearance with her reminiscences and so despite looking a decade younger you'd guess late twenties, early thirties. She has a gamin prettiness, a slim but shapely figure which she emphasises by dressing a size too small, and she does sweet coyness to perfection. But if that doesn't get her what she wants, then watch out...

"It was pure bad luck really," she says, as you settle down in a cafe by London University. "The cops raided Espen's - the chemist - place while Baz was picking the stuff up." She shakes her head. "I was back at the hotel, thank fuck. Got a phone call from one of the Dutch guys who set the deal up and two hours later I was on a flight out of Schiphol."

"Tough," you sympathise. "But what did you want to see me for?"

She hesitates, before reaching into her bag and taking out a British passport.

"Baz left all his stuff at the hotel," she says. "He thought it would be safer. So, I brought it back with me."

"You want me to sell his passport?" You're puzzled, Nikki has more than enough contacts of her own to sort that out for her.

She hands it over.

"Open it," she says.

You flick through and study the photograph.

"No one would mistake you for twins in the flesh," she says, "but as passport photos go, you could pass for him."

You stare at her.

"Baz is registered. He's got a weekly scrip due today." She gives a tight smile. "That's twenty-eight grains of H, about the same of coke and fourteen amps of meth."

You sit back in your chair and think this through. Baz is a registered addict, so as far as the law is concerned he's a patient, not a criminal. The Home Office has a list of drugs that doctors are allowed to prescribe for treatment and that list includes heroin, methedrine and cocaine.

This isn't available as a free NHS service, only by a private consultation with a doctor who issues the prescription

- a 'scrip'. The usual consultation fee is around three quid. Then the prescription needs to be paid for at the pharmacy. You're up enough on the junk scene to know that over the counter it will be two to three quid. The street price is around twenty times that.

"You pay for the doctor and the pharmacy," she says, "and we split it fifty fifty."

"There isn't going to be a surgery open now," you tell her. "We'll have to wait until Monday and…"

"He's registered with Krasner," she interrupts, and that shuts you up.

Doctor Krasner has recently been exposed by a Sunday newspaper for registering pretty much anyone who'll pay for a prescription. He's lost his practice, he's being investigated by the cops and he's almost certain to be struck off in the very near future. But right now he remains a doctor and can be found most evenings, via word of mouth, in West End pubs and cafes where he still - for a fee - writes scrips for his registered addicts.

"I know he'll be at Lyons in Leicester Square tonight," she says, and so you make your mind up.

"Okay," you tell her. "But I'll need a couple of hours to get the bread together."

"I'll see you in Lyons at seven," she says, picking up the passport. "And in the meantime, I'll keep hold of this."

She smiles, stands up and leaves.

* * *

Leaving the cafe, you walk back to Goodge Street.

Finches is a pub in transition, once a favourite of the post-war bohemian crowd, some of whom still hang around to bore you stupid with their recollections of Dylan Thomas or Augustus John, until you finally buy them a drink just to be rid of them. But most have moved on now, south into the Soho drinking clubs, replaced by a motley collection of teenage would-be poets and artists, weekend ravers and the inevitable dead eyed, dissolute middle-aged predators doing their best to draw them into conversation.

Being a Saturday, there's a fair sprinkling of musicians here too. *Les Cousins* on Greek Street has an all-nighter after the evening headline gig, and while you might get one or two names - Bert Jansch or Roy Harper perhaps - trying out new material, it's mainly an opportunity for the bedsit Donovans and street buskers to show what they can do. And for more than a few in here, it's a night off the streets in the warm.

And maybe tonight yourself included.

As your eyes adjust to the light, you see one of the *Les Cousins* regulars sitting at a table, talking to a young couple. Judith is in her forties, had arrived in Britain as a refugee during the war - probably from Germany, but her accent is almost impossible to place - and she keeps an open house at her Cable Street flat in the East End. Word is Paul Simon stayed there for a while, but it's mainly bedraggled strays emerging into a Soho Sunday morning sunrise who get an invitation back for breakfast and a bath.

Seeing you, she gives a wave and so you go over and sit down. The girl is in her late teens and although she's kept her coat on, you notice a nurse's uniform underneath. The guy looks older, but not by much.

"Hello Kit," greets Judith. "This is Jack and Alexandra."

We all nod at each other and you turn back to Judith.

"Have you seen Coochie?" you ask.

She looked around.

"Well, he was in here earlier," she says and immediately appears distracted. You follow her gaze across the bar, to where a student looking blond girl in a duffel coat has been joined at her table by a middle-aged man and doesn't seem too happy about it.

Judith rises from her chair and zeroes in on them, just as a guy you've sold to before comes over and whispers in your ear that he's after a quid deal.

"I'll be back in a second," you say to the couple and head to the Gents. It's a move picked up on by a few people, and you do a brisk trade by the urinals for the next few minutes. When you return to the table, you've only the piece you put aside for yourself and two quid deals left.

Judith is still at the other table, deep in conversation with the girl and the older man.

"Are you dealing?" asks Jack. He's American, not that unusual in London, but it is in this scene. When you nod, he asks what you're holding.

"Hash," you tell him. "But I've only got a couple of quid deals left."

"Okay, man." He reaches into his pocket, but Alexandra catches his hand. "Wait a sec."

Two burly figures have come in through the door and they walk up to the bar. One of them turns around and leans back with his elbows on the counter, surveying the room. With a fixed smile, the barman sticks a glass under the whiskey optic and squirts a double into it. He puts the glass down and repeats the process.

"See," says Alexandra *sotto voce* to Jack, "*that's* what real cops look like."

Each plainclothes empties his glass with a single gulp and having marked their territory, they slowly swagger out.

Alexandra turns to you.

"A couple of days ago," she says, "we're in Soho Square and a friend was skinning up. Suddenly Jack here hisses, 'There's a cop coming'." She sighs. "Everything flies into the bushes - papers, tobacco, the shit, the lot. And then around the corner comes an AA man."

Jack shakes his head ruefully.

"Sure as hell looked like a cop to me."

That's the first thing to put a smile on your face all day.

Alexandra stands up. "Shall we go outside?"

You follow them out. As you pass the table where Judith is sitting, you hear the girl calling the older man 'Dad'. You mentally wish her good luck with that.

You walk down the street together, then step into a

doorway. You hand the silver wraps over and Jack gives you two pound notes. Alexandra smiles and says thanks. As they walk away, you recognise a figure on the other side of the road and so cross over, quickening your pace to catch up.

* * *

"Coochie!"

He turns and seems to take a second to register you.

"Kit." He smiles. "Good to see you."

"You're looking well," you say, falling into step alongside him.

"A week in Tangier," he says. "Courtesy of Thomas Cocks Tours."

In all honesty, like an urchin scrubbed up for a family wedding, a suntan doesn't really sit right with Coochie. From a distance he registers as your typical Soho mod, but up close there's something freeze dried about the boyishness and a look in his eyes which tells you that he's been around the block a few times more than once. But you're always careful to keep on his good side, the general notion of queer might be Julian and Sandy from *Round the Horne* and while Coochie can camp it up with the best of them, there's a streak of viciousness underneath it all that's truly frightening. He got his nickname when a drunk in an East End pub had minced "Coochie coo" as he'd walked in with a boyfriend and then made the mistake of turning to his mates to laugh, missing the smashed glass that took half his face off.

"You too, ducky." He gives you a smile. "So, what are you selling?"

Ask Coochie what he does for a living and he tells you PR. He genuinely does draw a small salary from one of the film production companies on Wardour Street but that's little more than a cover for brokering his discreet services out to showbiz and establishment types, whose personal appetites are greatly at variance with their public image.

"Coke and meth." You know Coochie isn't interested in H. On the queer scene, it's all about prime grade speed. Tactility and staying up all night long...

"How much?"

"At least seven amps of meth and around fifteen grains of coke." You hesitate. "Maybe half as much again of both. I'll have an idea in a couple of hours."

He studies you carefully.

"Are you looking for a stake here?"

You shake your head. If something goes wrong, the last thing you need is Coochie thinking you've ripped him off.

"I've got the bread," you tell him. "It's just how things might work out."

He seems to relax.

"Right," he says, "I'll take whatever you can get."

Major problem solved.

"I'm putting a scene together tonight," he tells you. "You okay to deliver? You remember the place on Wigmore Street?"

You nod.

"Sure."

He pats you on the shoulder.

"Stay lucky," he smiles, then turns and walks away.

With the coke and meth sorted, you need to think about the H.

Heroin is much more of a recreational drug than its reputation might suggest. London is one of the few places in the world where the supply is a hundred percent pure, entirely the surplus from registered addicts. It usually sells by the grain, with the street price of a quid. A grain is six small pills, called a jack, and two of those are all a weekend raver needs to get off on. Any tolerance built up gets dissipated by the time next Friday rolls around and the purity makes overdoses - among none addicts at least - virtually unknown.

You know a couple of regulars at the *Marquee* and *Flamingo* clubs who smoke it to take the edge off a Purple Heart comedown, and you can probably get five bob a jack from them. You run other options through your mind, as you head down to Leicester Square to meet Nikki.

* * *

As you enter the Lyons Tea Rooms, you see Nikki sitting by the window, she's with a silver-haired banker type in an expensive suit and whose conversation she seems to be pointedly ignoring. Seeing you, she gives a wave. The man turns his head and clocking you making your way purposefully towards the table promptly gets up and moves away.

"Very distinguished," you tell her.

"The really dirty buggers always are," she says. "Everything okay?"

"Yeah." You nod. "And I've got a buyer for all the meth and coke at street price, if you want me to shift your half for you."

"I'll hang onto the meth," she says. "I can get a better price from Danny's chorus boys at the Whitehall. But you can have half my share of the coke - I'm seeing a friend later and promised him a scene."

"A friend?"

"This sweet guy I've met, who's really into me. I've turned him on a couple of times and now he wants to get more into it." She shrugs. "He'd been expecting a trip after I got back from Amsterdam - since that's all gone tits up, I feel I owe him."

She slips the passport across the table to you and nods towards a figure seated about ten feet away.

"When he's done with the girl, there's the guy in the herringbone jacket and then it's you," she says.

Krasner is middle-aged, balding, bespectacled, wearing a suit and tie but still shabby enough to have the air of a refugee about him. The girl sitting at the table across from him is in her early twenties and although her clothes look expensive, her skin is sallow and her hair lank.

"Watch how it's done," says Nikki.

The girl puts three pound notes under a napkin and slides it across to his side of the table. Krasner casually glances around him, takes a pad from his inside pocket, uncaps a fountain pen and begins to scribble. Tearing the sheet off, he lifts the napkin, exchanges the scrip for the notes and slides it back across to her. She puts it into her pocket, rises and leaves. Almost immediately her place at the table is taken by the young guy in the herringbone jacket.

Through the window, you watch the girl walk around an MGB GT sports car to the passenger door. For a second you think the driver is a man, with short cropped hair and open-necked shirt, but then you see the outline of her breasts as she leans across and unlocks the door. She gives the girl a smile as she slips in beside her, but as the car pulls away the girl looks blankly ahead.

Then you're up.

You sit down in front of him, and he stares at you curiously.

"I don't remember you," he says, with the trace of a German accent. "And I'm not registering any new patients at the moment."

"My name's Barry Foulds," you tell him. "I'm already registered with you."

From inside his jacket, he takes out a slim leather-bound notebook about the size of a pocket diary and begins to turn through the pages, licking the tip of his finger each time. Eventually he stops.

"When did you last see me?" he asks, looking up.

"About a week ago," you tell him. It seems a safe bet.

As he hesitates, you take the passport out.

"If you want proof of who..."

"Put that away," he interrupts. He appears to reflect and gives a nod. "I'll keep you on the same dosage, alright?"

For the second time that day, you try to hide the relief in your voice.

"Okay."

Checking his notebook, he writes out the prescription. You run the Find the Lady routine with the napkin and stand up.

"Next time," he says quietly, "the consultation will be five pounds."

You hesitate and then nod. As you leave, a middle-aged woman who looks like a librarian takes your place at the table.

"What was all that about?" asks Nikki as she gets up.

"We've been rumbled."

You tell her what he said.

"Next time!" she snorts as we step out onto the pavement. "This time next week he'll be in Wormwood bloody Scrubs."

"Where do you want to go?" you ask her.

There are only a few pharmacies in London that dispense heroin and coke. The closest is the 24-hour Boots in Piccadilly Circus, but on a Saturday night you won't get out of the door without being surrounded by people looking to score, and a good few of them probably drug squad. After that, it was a branch of John Bell and Croyden behind Debenhams. Which is almost on the doorstep of where Coochie's scene is being set up.

"We can make Bells before it closes," you suggest.

Nikki nods, following your unspoken reasoning. Then she hesitates.

"Actually, why don't you pick the stuff up?" she says. "Do the deal you've sorted out and then let's meet at Julian's place?"

"Julian?"

"The guy I was telling you about. I'm thinking of going around there now - like I said, I feel I ought to make things up to him." She sighed. "You know?"

You smile.

She scribbles the address with an eyebrow pencil on your Players packet, begins to walk away and then looks back over her shoulder.

"Don't feel you have to rush."

* * *

You remember it being a Georgian house, squeezed between an art gallery and the embassy of a new African republic with a name bringing to mind an Edgar Rice Burroughs tale. There's no bell, only an ornate brass knocker, but the door was opened immediately by a skinny kid with bleached hair and eyes like piss holes in the snow.

"I'm Kit," you tell him. "Coochie's expecting me."

He stands back to let you in and indicates a wide curving staircase with a nod.

"First floor," he says, in a flat South London accent.

Climbing the stairs, you come to an open door and stick your head inside. It's a small room, about ten feet by ten and empty of all furniture except for a couple of clothes rails on wheels, the kind you see being used to deliver suits and jackets to department stores. There were about a dozen hangers on each rail. Another door to the right is half open.

"Hello!" you call out.

You hear footsteps, and Coochie appears in the doorway.

"Hi man," he says. "Come on through."

You follow him into a much larger space, which you guess must once have been a reception room or library, running the entire width of the building. The windows overlooking the street are covered by floor length crimson curtains and there's a lot of artwork on the walls, most of it from the Victorian school of suppressed homoeroticism, muscled youths in various David and Jonathan type scenarios. Others have a Weimar Berlin touch to them and are more explicit.

Quite a bit more.

Incense is burning, *chaise longues* and sofas are positioned along three of the walls, and a sideboard supporting a ten-foot square movie screen sits against the fourth. Coochie picks his way through cushions scattered across the floor to a small table where a cine projector has a reel of 16mm film half threaded and half a dozen silver canisters are stacked on top of each other. Next to that is a 35mm slide projector and another skinny blond kid, a clone of the one downstairs, is filling the carousel from an open box of what are unlikely to be anyone's holiday slides.

"Everything went okay?" he asks.

"Yeah," you tell him and pass over the boxes of meth. He opens one up, checks the contents and stacks them on the table. With the coke he is more cautious, rubbing a dusting into his gums.

"The other week some little shit tried to sell me crushed mothballs," he says and then catches your look. "No offence man, but you could have been ripped off too, right?"

As he takes out a wad of notes from his pocket and starts to count out what he owes you, the blond kid who let you in walks into the room.

"Hey," says Coochie, "you need to get changed. Now." Then to you, "Just a sec."

There're a couple of holdalls on the floor by the projector. Coochie picks one up and empties it out onto the nearest sofa, a tangled heap of studded leather and chains. He starts pulling it all apart and you make out collars and cuffs, a riding crop, handcuffs, and a harness with a phallus attached. Coochie hands the kid a hood with zippers on the eyes and mouth, plus a few other items you don't look too closely at.

"Get a move on," Coochie tells him and goes back to counting out the notes.

"Thanks, man," he said. "You okay to see yourself out?"

"Yeah."

"You're welcome to stick around." He gives a shrug. "Just don't tread on my toes."

In other words, no dealing on my turf. But Coochie's scenes are as much voyeuristic as participatory and right now it's looking a better option than risking another night at the *Express*, or nodding off at a *Les Cousins* all-nighter.

"Perhaps later." You smile at him. "I've a few other

people to see first."

"Okay, make sure the door's locked behind you," he says, turning back to the projector.

* * *

You're not that surprised at the West End address Nikki gave you, there's a surprising amount of council housing hidden away behind the grand facades. The aristocracy of Britain's glory days needed a lot of looking after and they liked to keep the help close to hand - you know quite a few pads where the rent book has been handed down through the generations. But the mansion block just off South Audley Street doesn't even remotely fall into that category, it's prime Mayfair real estate.

Nikki buzzes you in through the front door and tells you to come up to the third floor. Naturally, there's a lift, but it's one of those ornate wrought-iron deathtraps, so you figure the stairs are a safer option. Nikki has left the door to the flat slightly ajar. You tap on it and let yourself in.

"Kit Julian, Julian Kit," says Nikki, and you exchange brief nods, both way too cool to acknowledge each other with anything as *gauche* as a handshake. If you've not interrupted them it's by a whisker, Julian is in a Kimono style dressing gown while Nikki wears only a man's shirt, mostly unbuttoned.

Julian is a surprise. You'd expected someone older, in their thirties and a worldly sophisticate for all their narcotic naivety. But he's about twenty, tall and thin with that floppy haired, dissolute public schoolboy thing going. And while he emanates all the self-confidence which comes with that, you still pick up a vibe that he could get skittish pretty quickly.

You sit down in an armchair and start emptying your pockets out onto a low coffee table. Nikki and Julian sit side by side on a sofa opposite.

"You made the deal?" asks Nikki and you nod. You put her boxes of meth to one side, split the H in two and count out her share of the money for the coke.

"Did you get any works?"

Syringes and needles come with the scrip. You reach into your inside pocket and place them on the table.

"So, there's just the H to sort out, fourteen grains each," you say. "I can't be bothered selling it a jack at a time, so if you want my share you can have it for a tenner."

Nikki turns to Julian and whispers in his ear. After a few seconds, he gives a nod.

"Okay," he says, getting up and leaving the room.

"Thanks," Nikki says to you. "And hang on to the passport. If Krasner is still around next weekend, I'll leave details in the *Duke of York*." She shrugs. "It's a sweet deal as long as it lasts."

"Sure," you tell her.

Julian comes back, passes over two fivers and then sits down next to Nikki.

"We're going to shoot up now," Nikki tells you. "Speedballs. You okay to stick around for the night, ride shotgun?"

You nod nonchalantly, as if that's not a major problem solved, and then take out the piece of hash you've saved for yourself. You pull three Rizlas out of a packet and ask Nikki for a cigarette. She tosses one over.

"Kit," says Julian languidly. "So, what's that short for?"

You shrug.

"Just a childhood nickname that seemed to stick - you know what it's like."

"Afraid not." He leant back into the sofa. "Not really the kind of childhood I had."

Nikki has fitted a needle into the syringe and is breaking the top off an ampule of meth.

"Can I use your bathroom?" you ask Julian.

"Down the hall, last door on the right."

It's so luxurious that you're tempted to take an actual bath but think that would probably be pushing it. Instead, you wash your face and brush your teeth with your finger.

Back in the living room, Julian is now sitting in the

armchair, Nikki kneeling beside him. You sit down on the sofa and start to roll the joint. Julian's dressing gown sleeve is rolled up and as Nikki stands, a thin trickle of blood appears in the crook of his elbow. She slips the belt she's used as a tourniquet from his arm and picks up the syringe.

"I'm going to rinse this out." She looks over to you. "Keep an eye on him, okay?"

Julian is rigid, mouth open and gripping the arms of the chair with white knuckles. He reminds you of nothing so much as one of Francis Bacon's screaming popes.

You've almost finished building the joint when Nikki comes back into the room.

"Some pad," you say to her, looking around. "What does he do?"

"He has rich parents is what he does," she says, kneeling by the table and fitting the syringe with a new needle. She unscrews the top of the barrel and drops three jacks into it, followed by a small piece of coke. She screws the top back on and presses the plunger down. She puts it on the table and breaks the neck off an ampule of meth, puts the needle in the amp and draws the liquid up into the syringe. She shakes it until the H and coke dissolve, turns the syringe upwards and with her brow furrowed in concentration slowly presses the plunger until a trickle of liquid appears at the tip of the needle. She gets the rest of the air out by tapping the barrel next to any remaining bubbles. Satisfied, she puts the syringe down and stands up.

Nikki unbuttons her shirt all the way down and opens it wide. Picking up the syringe, she moves her legs apart and slips two fingers into the crease between the top of her thigh and her vulva. She widens her fingers to stretch the skin taut and with her other hand carefully slides the needle into the femoral vein. She eases the plunger back a fraction with her thumb until the liquid blooms red and then steadily depresses it.

She has time to pull the needle out before it hits, but

only just. She flops down beside you on the sofa, staring blankly. You lean over, take the works from her fingers and put it on the table. You watch her carefully for a few minutes to make sure she keeps breathing - if someone's going to OD this is when it happens - and then you light the joint.

There's a TV set in the corner of the room, and you switch it on. A BBC news bulletin is saying that over a hundred children and five teachers are now believed to have died in Aberfan.

"The twenty-first of October nineteen sixty-six will be a day of infamy in British history," says a reporter, and you give a sudden start.

This has been day four hundred and eighty-nine of the six hundred and seventeen days you will eventually spend on the streets of London, and the only thing that distinguishes it from any other is that it has been your eighteenth birthday.

7. Barry Denham

On those social occasions when the nature of his profession delivered him, if not a captive audience then at least an intrigued one, Barry Denham had a few party pieces to trot out. The one which always went down best was his observation that errant husbands generally fall into two categories, those who seek solace and those who crave excitement.

The former, declared Barry, would typically drift into an affair with a colleague who's been led to believe that a rosy future awaits, despite themselves being *prima facie* evidence of how unlikely that actually was. The second were those spouses whose occupations took them far from home, the travelling salesmen and long-distance lorry drivers, who perhaps discovered opportunities for infidelity as they first presented themselves or - and much more likely in Barry's opinion - had chosen their occupation in anticipation of exactly such opportunities.

"And what about wives?" he was often asked at this point. "What leads them astray?"

In mixed company, Barry's response was genial.

"What mere male," he'd respond to great amusement, "would dare claim to have unravelled the mysteries of the female psyche?"

Down the pub or at one of the drinking clubs he frequented, it was rather more brutal.

"Who the hell ever knows what's really going on in any of their fucking heads?" he'd tell them. "I mean, seriously."

But whoever the audience, Barry would always be pressed for more detail and always with a fascination for sordid minutiae rather than motivation. Which was a shame in a way, reflected Barry, because by far the most intriguing thing he could have told them was that while men were invariably shocked by the discovery they were being cheated on, women rarely were.

Unless...

Barry studied Anne Meadows, sitting on the other side of his desk. Unravelling these webs of romantic deception seldom proved a challenge. Love comes at a price and one usually reflected in credit card statements, hotel booking records and florist receipts. At times it seemed the only unpredictable factor in the whole sorry scenario would be the wife's reaction as she viewed the photographs, read the report, or listened to Barry's gentle summation.

He kept a box of tissues on top of the desk, a bottle of Courvoisier in the bottom drawer and made sure there was nothing breakable within arm's reach of the chair opposite. No matter how often you'd been here before, at this point you were always winging it.

Especially when you found yourself not only under the outer edges of the bell curve, but also with Barry's little party piece batted right out of the park...

"Do you have someone you can talk to?" he asked. "A relative, maybe a friend."

"*Talk to!*" Anne Meadows tore her eyes away from the photographs scattered across the desk between them and stared at him incredulously. "Talk to! Who the fuck can I talk to about *this*?"

"You know," said Barry, "men are really, really good at compartmentalising."

"Compartmentalising!!?" She grabbed one of the prints and for a second Barry thought she would tear it apart. "These aren't *compartments,*" she hissed at him, "these are padded cells and cages."

Barry stared down at the remaining photos. The original two sets were now jumbled together, as she'd clawed her way through them with increasing disbelief. One set had been taken with a buttonhole camera in a Gents public toilet, a well-known 'cottage' off the Holloway Road. The other was from Hampstead Heath a week ago.

Usually when presenting evidence, Barry would choose the images carefully. A selection intended to leave no doubt of the husband's indiscretions, while shielding the wife from the full extent of his indulgences. But here he'd used no filters at all - in their first two meetings Barry thought he'd read something in Mrs Meadows, and he was about to see if his intuition played out.

To their mutual benefit.

Anne Meadows took a deep breath.

"Do you think…? Is it possible this has only just started?" she asked. "That it's something he's trying…?"

Barry shook his head.

"In my experience, that's unlikely."

"So this," she tossed the photographs back down onto the desk, "has been… *Jesus Christ!* All these years."

"And also, in my experience, it doesn't stop. In fact, the only thing that's different about things now," said Barry carefully, "is that you know what's going on."

She stared at him. Barry opened his desk drawer and took out the bottle of brandy and a glass.

"Most relationships," he said, "are about what we've decided we can live with."

"*No!*" she almost spat the word at him. "We are *done!* We are fucking *finished!*"

"And so where does that leave you?" Barry poured a stiff measure into the glass. "Emotionally? Financially? Socially?"

He passed the glass across the desk and studied her. He knew exactly what was going through her mind - the fifty something widows and divorcees already in her social circle, whose single status had edged them incrementally out to the circumference. A spare for dinner parties when the numbers needed making up, a target for wayward husbands if still attractive and an object of pity for their wives if not. A role that alimony or a pension, however generous, would never take the sting out of.

Barry took out his pen and scribbled onto a blank card.

"I'm giving you the number of someone I'd like you to talk to," he said.

"Counselling, I suppose," she said disparagingly, "or a solicitor. Something you'll be getting a kickback from, I'm sure."

Barry shook his head.

"Actually, it's a client who a couple of years ago was sitting where you are now and in almost the exact same circumstances." Barry paused. "And, also like yourself, an exceptionally strong-willed woman, seething with the injustice of a situation not of her own making."

"And why should I want to speak to her?" Still aggressive, but curious.

"Because she asked my advice." Barry paused again. "And I suggested that she disappear for a few days before confronting her husband. Invent some family emergency or a friend with a crisis. Just leave straight away."

"And did she?"

"Yes, she went to visit a cousin," Barry nodded. "And matters did actually resolve themselves. You see, all of this," he gestured towards the photographs, "this cruising and cottaging is fraught with risk." He shrugged. "Muggings, queer bashing, drugged up rent boys. I sometimes think that for a lot of them danger is part of the attraction. So, while she was away, her husband was attacked in a park in South London. Stabbed to death for a wallet with only thirty pounds in it. The police never found out who did it, but under the circumstances it's difficult to believe they looked that hard." He reached forward and topped up her drink. "They certainly never did in my day."

Anne Meadows had him fixed with an even stare.

"Well, the inquest was quite distressing, as you might

imagine. But she got through it, took back her maiden name, made a fresh start for herself. She moved to the Algarve, in fact, and with London property prices being what they are these days, together with the insurance money, she's doing very nicely out there, I hear. As I said, fresh fields and pastures new."

Still staring at him, Anne Meadows gulped her drink down in one.

"Give her a call," said Barry, nodding at the card he'd written the phone number on. "Probably best from a phone box. And after you've compared notes, come back and let's talk again."

* * *

After she'd left, Barry was tempted to take a quick snort of brandy himself but resisted. It was still early, and he'd never gone with the whole *'sun over the yardarm somewhere in the world'* ethos - he'd watched entire squad rooms of detectives switch their perspective to one viewed through the bottom of a glass and it rarely ended well. Barry knew he had his faults, but that wasn't one of them. He did his drinking after the office door closed behind him for the day.

He returned the bottle to the desk drawer, slid it shut and took her glass into the small kitchenette out back. That she'd phone Maggie Clarke he had no doubt, then probably she'd reflect for a few days. As he'd told her, it was all about what you could live with and he was still convinced of his initial assessment.

Anne Meadows was not the forgiving kind.

He and Maggie Clarke had agreed on fifty thousand to have her 'affairs reconciled' as she'd put it, settled monthly in bulky envelopes after probate on the late Mr Clarke's estate had been granted. He didn't think that would be a figure the potential Widow Meadows would balk at - bank managers had heavily subsidised mortgages, and the family home in Highbury had to be worth at least ten times that.

Barry'd started to rinse the glass when the buzzer

sounded, warning him someone had entered through the street door - the nature of his business lent itself toward caution. As he stepped back into his office, there was a perfunctory knock at the door. He crossed the room and put his eye to the spyhole.

He didn't recognise the man standing there, which given the fisheye distortion of the lens, wasn't surprising, but he was alone and there was nothing belligerent or threatening about the body language. Barry opened the door and stepped back.

The man looked at him and then smiled.

"Hello Barry," he said.

Recognition dawned slowly, but when it did Barry couldn't conceal his surprise.

"Bloody hell," he said. "Kit Franklyn."

"Long time, no see." Kit stuck out his hand and Barry shook it. "How are you doing?"

Barry gestured him into the room and indicated the chair at his desk.

"You know, getting by." Barry hesitated. "You're looking well, Kit. I heard you live abroad these days?"

"The Netherlands." Kit sat down and Barry moved around to the other side of the desk. "We're in Amsterdam."

"You and Carin?" asked Barry.

Kit nodded.

"Carin's a professor at Leiden University. I'm still doing freelance work, but I've also taken over her father's business. He died last year."

He smiled at Barry's quizzical look.

"Rare books and antique prints," he said.

"Well," said Barry, cautiously, "it is good to see you again, Kit. But I'm really not someone in the market for a Dickens first edition."

Kit laughed, and Barry found himself laughing too.

"The thing is," said Kit, "a couple of days ago I had a visit from Brian Maddox."

"Oh, yeah?" said Barry, careful again now. "In Amsterdam?"

"He came to the Gallery. Told me that a DI from a Cold Case Unit had been to see him. That they wanted to talk about Pembridge Villas and were trying to find me." Kit hesitated. "Have you had anyone around, asking questions?"

Barry matched his stare and then shook his head.

"No," he said. "But that's because they know I'd only tell them to piss off."

Barry reached down, pulled open his desk drawer, reached for the bottle of Courvoisier and placed it on the desk. Sometimes rules were just there to be broken. He lifted two glasses out of the drawer and tilted one towards Kit, who nodded.

"I didn't leave the job under the best of circumstances," said Barry, as he half-filled each glass. "And what I do for a living now hasn't exactly poured oil on troubled waters."

He put one of the glasses in front of Kit.

"The thing about the Met these days," he continued, almost reflectively, "as you may well be discovering, is that some things which were a crime thirty years ago aren't any longer. And other things, which weren't a crime thirty years ago, near as dammit are now. Which means that anything from back then that's being given a second look at now, can get you stitched up every which way from here to Sunday." He raised his glass. "Cheers."

"Cheers." Kit raised his glass and took a sip.

"So," continued Barry, "on the rare occasions when I've had some snarky dyke fast-tracked to DI knocking on my door, asking if I could clarify some arrest report from nineteen fucking sixty-seven, my reaction has been only if you get a court order and present it to my solicitor. It's an approach I'd advise you to take."

Kit gave a slow shake of his head.

"Well, I've already been to see them," he said, "and it's pretty much sorted. They were trying to identify one of the kids who'd been living there. Supposedly killed in the house."

"They're investigating the death of some hippie, thirty bloody years ago?" Barry stared across the desk with an expression between mirth and incredulity. "And you actually believe that?"

"They were cagey as hell." Kit slowly shook his head. "But it was obvious they thought Aidan McShane was implicated."

"Right." Barry gave a conciliatory nod. "Yeah, well, I can see them getting their knickers all in a twist over that." He lifted the bottle and topped up Kit's glass. "Anything to it?"

"Unlikely." Kit shook his head. "Probably just the Micks stirring the shit." He gave a shrug. "And I've steered them away from anything we'd have to worry about. But I thought if they'd been on to Maddox about this, then they might have had you in too. I just wanted to let you know that it had been taken care of."

"Well, I appreciate that," said Barry carefully. "But like I said, no one's been around here about it."

"At least, that's part of the reason I wanted to see you," said Kit quietly, and Barry's antennae started twitching again.

"*Part* of the reason?"

"When Maddox came to see me, he told me what you were doing these days." Kit seemed to choose his words carefully. "And that's the other part."

"The other part?" asked Barry softly.

"It's best if you just listen to this first." Kit reached into his jacket pocket, took out a tape cassette and placed it down on the desk. "Got anything to play it on?"

"Sure." Barry pulled open a drawer, retrieved a battered-looking portable cassette player, and pushed it across the desk to him. Kit slotted the cassette into the tape compartment.

"My home answerphone," he said to Barry's quizzical expression and pressed down the chunky Play key.

"Hello," Carin's voice came through the speaker. "*You're through to the Franklyns. I'm afraid we can't take your call at the moment, but if you'd like to leave a message after the tone, then one of us will get back to you as soon as we can.*"

There was a beep and then: "*Hello! Carin!? It's Jenny - pick up if you're there.*" A few seconds' silence. "*Okay darling, I was just calling to say that...*"

"*Hi Jenny.*" Carin breathless. "*Sorry, I was in the bathroom. How are you?*"

"*I'm fine.*"

"*Everything still on for London?*"

Kit reached out and pressed the Pause key.

"I'm not sure whether it's a fault or a feature," he said, "but if you pick up while a message is being left, it carries on recording right through to the end of the call."

"I think I'd definitely regard that as a fault," said Barry.

"So, what you need to know." Kit leant back in his chair. "Carin and Jenny are old friends, were at University together. Every summer there's a reunion dinner in London, apparently half a dozen of them are regulars with the occasional ex-pat or two back in town to make up the numbers."

"Apparently?"

"Really not my thing." Kit shrugged. "I've never gotten my head around how women manage to stay friends with other women who they don't actually like." He gave a tight smile. "Plus, Carin had it tagged as a girls only night. Nothing I should get bothered about."

"Midnight feast in the dorm at St Hilda's?"

"Well, not the image I had in mind, but yeah, close enough."

Kit started the tape playing again.

"*When does your flight get in?*" asked Jenny.

"*The Friday morning, around eleven thirty.*"

"*You'll be the last one getting here, I think. Belinda's coming up from Bath on the Wednesday and Charlotte's been in London since the beginning of August, although Jamel's still out in*

Saudi."

"Is she staying with you again?"

"Oh God, no - Mike put his foot down after last year. Swanning around like Lady Muck, expecting to be waited on hand and bloody foot." She paused. "The final straw was when I wouldn't take a few days off from the agency to go to Glyndebourne. 'Oh, Jamel would never allow me to work.' I could have throttled her."

"Yes, well, Jamel would also never allow her to have her own bank account or even drive a car."

Jenny laughed. "That's pretty much what Mike said. Plus a few cruder scenarios. In some ways I do feel sorry for her, I'm not sure that she had any idea of what she was getting into there. But she doesn't make things easy for herself."

"How's Belinda now? Didn't she have a couple of health scares?"

"Yes, the dreaded lumps. She's had two biopsies, clear on both so fingers crossed."

"Good. I'm so looking forward to catching up with everyone."

"Well, the main reason I'm ringing is that Mike's booked a restaurant for that night. He thought this year he'd get the husbands, partners, significant others etcetera together for a bit of a bash of their own. I know you and Kit always prefer to stay at Kit's uncle's place when you're in London, but we thought that later everyone could meet up for drinks. Maybe instead of Kit picking you up afterwards as usual, you could stay over at the hotel this time, with the rest of us."

There was silence on the tape. Kit was staring down at the cassette player.

"Like I said, I've never been on one of these reunion weekends with her." He shook his head slowly. "And I don't have an uncle. In London or anywhere else."

"Okay, well, I'll mention it to Kit," said Carin hesitantly. "Hopefully, we'll be able to work something out for the evening."

"Great," said Jenny. "Look, email me a couple of days before you leave and we'll sort out all the details. Okay"

"*Sure,*" said Carin. "*Bye.*"

"*Take care. Bye.*"

Kit switched the machine off and took the tape out. He put one finger on it and slid it across to Barry's side of the desk.

"I want to know who it is," he said. "I want to know who's been picking her up afterwards. As usual."

*   *   *

Never, Barry had promised himself when he'd first gotten into this business, take on a friend as a client. Dispense advice, be a shoulder to cry on but when all else fails don't be the one shining a light into the murky shadows of lives part shared. Secrets will out and - like toothpaste or genies - they won't be going back in again. Because however things may eventually go down, they will never be the same.

So, it was with mixed feelings that Barry stared at the door that had just closed behind Kit Franklyn. Was someone you hadn't seen for twenty-odd years still a friend? And it wasn't like he'd be delivering bad news - the guy already knew that his wife was screwing around, all he was asking Barry to do was discover who with.

Barry glanced down at the notepad he'd filled over the last hour - phone numbers, email addresses, bank and credit card accounts, which he knew would be enough to come up with the information Kit wanted. The digital pads and spores of modern life, laying a trail for a keyboard tracker exactly as blood on the tracks of wounded prey did for the hunters of old. And hunters, reflected Barry, was probably something of a Freudian slip here, because he'd already decided to use Spike for this.

Controlling Spike was always a carrot and stick exercise, ironic in that the stick was the threat of exposing his peccadilloes and the carrot was allowing him to indulge them. 'Moral equivalence' was an expression used a lot by Barry's former boss in his Flying Squad days, when they'd give some old lag *carte blanche* for B&E in return for grassing up a wages heist. 'For the greater good' was Barry's interpretation, and it was something he'd had no problem with at all, back then. But the greater good these days was no more than Barry's bank account.

Barry looked at the bottle on the desk and then poured himself another drink. Maybe he finally should kick it in, he thought. He'd let Spike have a good run, time to bring the twisted little sod's fun to an end. Get one last payoff, courtesy of Anne Meadows' dirty bastard of a husband, and then bugger off to the Costa Brava. Start hobnobbing with all those villains he'd spent years putting away. He had a fair bit in the bank and a lot more in a couple of safety deposit boxes.

Enjoy it while he still could.

PART TWO

Coalescence

1. Aidan

"An advertising agency!!?" Frank Bishop's face was a pantomime of disbelief. "A fucking bastard son of a poxed whore advertising agency!!!"

Barbara stared at Frank in stunned silence. We'd found ourselves subjected to his tirades on a regular basis since the previous September and I daresay we all thought we'd gotten used to them by now, but this was pretty explosive even for Frank. With the rest of the class also sitting there shell-shocked, I let a couple of seconds pass before casually raising my arm.

"Should we be taking that to mean it's not an option you'd fully endorse?" I asked, and he turned his glare full on in my direction.

"It's expected that we find gainful employment during the holidays," I reminded him.

"Don't you get fucking smart with me, you bog trotting Mick," he snarled. "If it's honest work that you're looking for, get yourself a pickaxe and spend three weeks on one of your uncle's building sites. Where, if you're lucky, you'll get a crossbeam dropped on your head and some fucking sense knocked into it."

I could see Barbara biting her lip, trying not to cry, and I didn't blame her. The first time she'd burst into tears - at his criticism of her effort at a still life *'It's supposed to be still, not fucking dead'* - he'd made her go stand in the corner, wearing a dunce's cap fashioned from cartridge paper.

That was one side of Frank. The other was half an hour later, when he led her back from the corner, stood her in front of her painting and picked up her palette. He worked furiously, as we all cautiously drifted across the studio and gathered behind him. After several minutes, he stopped and stood back.

The transformation was astounding. Swirling brush strokes had animated the piece to make a mockery of the term 'still life' and he'd blurred the finely defined edges of objects into each other, until the composition had become one of texture rather than form. The effect made you believe that you could reach in and pluck a grape straight from the bowl.

Without a word he'd put the brush down, turned to stare at us and walked away.

That had been a watershed moment. Those in the class who were here expecting direction, who'd assumed that there were rules to be learnt which once mastered would leave them competent artists, began to fall away. Sometimes Frank would arrive and bellow a theme at us - *'Marriage' 'Pain' 'Delight'* and we'd spend the rest of the day working on a composition, while he sat at his desk thumbing through *Tit-Bits* or reading a Penguin paperback. He'd sporadically get up and take a walk around the studio, shaking his head sadly or giving the occasional chuckle and *sotto voce* obscenity. After six months of this we were down to twelve from the twenty-five who'd started, brothers in arms under a banner of unspoken faith in osmosis.

Finished glowering at me, Frank turned back to Barbara.

"Look love, I get it. I really do. Hobnobbing around the West End, rubbing shoulders and whatever else with swinging fucking London." He softened his tone. "Had a girl here, two or three years ago, just like you. Laura, her name was, did I ever tell you about her?"

Barbara bit her lip and shook her head.

"Right." Frank stared at her. "Well, like I said, she was just like you, one of the best students I ever had. Know what happened to her?"

Barbara stared at him with understandable, open-mouthed shock. I took it as a compliment if Frank didn't whitewash over one of my acrylics while I was in the lavatory - seriously, twice - and to suddenly find yourself the object of his praise was surely as disturbing as being subjected to his wrath.

"Well," said Frank. "She got herself a job for the summer holidays at an advertising agency. 'Where's the harm?' she probably thought to herself. 'Six weeks putting layouts together for *Dobbin Dog Food* or *Fanny Fresh*. What's the worst that can happen?'

"And at first that's all it was, just cutting and pasting Letraset. Fucking Letraset." Frank shook his head, disbelievingly. "Anyway, after a few weeks she gets to work on a couple of storyboards, gives the artwork a bit of a flourish which gets noticed and commented on in the presentation. So, she's taken out to lunch by the art director. Off to somewhere in Mayfair with no prices on the menu, and one of those actors off the telly, whose name no-one can ever remember, is at the next table, giving her the eye. Very heady stuff.

"'What are you wasting your time at college for?' asks the art director. 'Do you know how much money you could make working for us?'

"They're starting a new TV campaign next month, he tells her, for an insurance company. For each commercial they'll be taking a famous painting, not sure which ones yet, could be up to her but depends on the rights and the rest of that legal shit. But the idea is to have the characters in the painting narrate the copy."

Frank paused and fixed his eyes on Barbara.

"Because that's what they do," he said, holding his gaze steady. "They take something that's meaningful, that's special, that's genuinely fucking profound and then they rebuild it out of stinking wet dog turds. An exact replica, in steaming brown shit, and do you know what they want you there for?"

Barbara shook her head.

"To cover it all in pretty pink icing sugar. To squeeze out a cascade of sparkling whorls and snowflakes and diamonds until no-one can see that underneath it's just shit.

"But Laura, what with being young and stupid and all, doesn't see this. Maybe she tells herself that she can work for the agency and still do her own painting. Or perhaps she starts to weigh off just how few artists actually succeed against what she's being offered here.

"But whatever, she only comes back to tell me what's happened, that she's decided to take this opportunity she's been offered, and how grateful she is for everything I've done for her."

He shrugged.

"The thing is," he said, "I'm not here for your fucking gratitude."

He pushed himself up off of his desk.

"Go on," he said. "Have yourselves a good break and I'll see you all next term."

"And you," Frank pointed a finger at me. "You just hang about for a bit."

* * *

We waited while everyone filed out of the room and there were several curious glances in our direction. When it was just the two of us, he pulled out a packet of Woodbines and offered me one. He flicked a match alight with his thumbnail - a trick that continues to impress me to this very day and something I've never been able to master - lit us both up and motioned for me to take a seat.

"So, what plans do you have for Easter?" he asked. "If any."

"None, really," I told him. "My uncle has the car ferry to Dublin booked, so I've a lift home if I want one." I shrugged. "It would be good to catch up with family and friends, but nothing definite."

He looked at me carefully.

"Joyce Kelly is having an exhibition this Easter. Her first

for five years."

"Right," I said, not sure what he expected my reaction to be. Joyce Kelly was one of Britain's leading abstract expressionists, and over the last decade had also established a reputation as a sculptress. She'd given a talk at the Slade a few months back that I'd been dragged along to by a third year Bardot lookalike, an affair which came to nothing but at the time had been distracting to the exclusion of anything else.

Frank gave one of his rare smiles, always something which lent him a sinister air. "*Pulse* are doing a piece about it. An entire show, apparently."

Pulse was a weekly arts program from the BBC. Frank appeared on it perhaps half a dozen times a year in his role as irascible elder statesman of the British *avant garde*. Which, to his credit, wasn't as contrived a persona as some contributors concocted, although still nothing like the full-blown Captain Bligh experience we got, after his studio door closed behind us and land was sinking below the horizon.

"They interviewed me a couple of days ago," he continued. "I fed them the usual guff, leading light of her generation, works bordering on true genius." He flicked ash into an empty coffee cup on his desk. "Anyway, she rang me last night. She's looking for some help in putting the exhibition together. Lugging stuff around, hanging paintings." He took a deep drag. "A student, someone promising, she said. Asked me if I knew of anyone."

A number of thoughts started running through my mind at this, but before I could bring any of them to a standstill, Frank was off again.

"What she obviously intends," somewhat tersely now, "is playing to the camera as some fucking mentor, succouring the talent of tomorrow at her withered old tit. Having some fawning eager beaver following her around, telling her - and the audience - how truly fucking inspirational she's been." The ash went into the cup again, this time a little more viciously. "So, I immediately thought of you."

"I'm not sure that..." I started out slowly, but Frank cut me off.

"Listen," he said, "this is an *opportunity*. At some point they will want to talk to you and if you are as much of a fucking gobshite to Tony," Anthony Drydon was *Pulse's* presenter, "as you are with me, well..." He gave a small shake of his head. "Look, the bloke just loves bolshie talent - maybe I can even get him to look at some of your work, when you're both back in London."

"Well," I began, and then his last sentence registered with me. "*Back* in London?"

"She lives in Cornwall," said Frank.

"*Cornwall?*"

"Oh, you'll love it," said Frank encouragingly. "It's even more desolate and primitive than that shithole you're from. You'll be right at home there." He stared at me. "So, I can tell her yes, then?"

Most of what he'd said made sense, and so I nodded.

"Good." He passed me a piece of card with an address scribbled on it. "Because she's expecting you the day after tomorrow, so don't you go letting me down here."

"Right," I said. "You mean, not like Laura the Letraset Whore."

He narrowed his eyes at me.

"Or was it Amanda?" I stared straight back at him. "Because a couple of months ago I was in the pub with Shaun Brody." Shaun had been one of Frank's students and was now back at the Slade taking a life class. We knew each other because he was from Dublin and had taken me under his wing for my first few weeks here. "Shaun was telling me about this girl he'd been sweet on a few years back, who got a real dressing down from you when she temped a few weeks at Collet Dickenson Pearce. She and the whole class heard about Amanda, one of your star students, who'd also been lured away into the temple of Mammon and now lives in Virginia Water with her advertising executive husband, spending her time doing paintings of her W.I. friends' kids on their ponies at gymkhanas and..."

"The essence of art," interrupted Frank, "is to portray the world in ways it is not, in order that we may grasp its underlying reality. Know who said that?"

I shook my head.

"I did, just then," said Frank, letting his cigarette stub fall into the cup with a sizzle. "Now fuck off."

There'd always been a lot of down the pub speculation as to why Frank taught, ranging from the Slade having really serious dirt on him to some weird form of twisted redemption on his part. But years later I read an article about George Gurdjieff, the Russian mystic and cult leader who'd had a commune of sorts outside Paris in the nineteen twenties. Apparently, someone once asked him why - if he'd achieved the level of enlightenment that he claimed to have done - did he still feel it necessary to surround himself with followers and acolytes. *'Need rats for experiment'* was the guttural response. I think he and Frank would have gotten on like a house on fire.

2. Kit

By the Easter of 1967, Julian and Nikki were very much an item. He'd taken to speedballs like a duck to water and whenever they shot up I'd stay over to keep an eye on them. Which made me a frequent enough visitor to have a change of clothes in a drawer of my own.

So, it wasn't unusual to get a message from Nikki asking me to come around the following evening, that they needed to score. But as I turned the corner from South Audley Street, the sight that greeted me was the flashing lights of two police cars and an ambulance parked outside of his building. Without changing my pace, I crossed the road whilst feigning the casual interest any passer-by would most likely display and walked on by.

Suddenly, I felt my elbow gripped from behind.

"S'okay," said Nikki softly, letting go her hand and then slipping her arm through mine. "Just smile at me and keep on walking."

Once around the corner at the end of the road, I stopped and turned to face her.

"What's happened?" I asked.

"Julian's dead." A small tear formed in her eye and moved down her cheek.

"What?"

"He OD'd."

"When?"

"Probably last night." She gave a shake of the head. "When I got there this morning, he was already cold."

I stared in disbelief and shock.

"Okay, I need to get my stuff out of there," I said, but she shook her head again. Reaching into her pocket, she took out a key and handed it to me.

"It's in a locker at Paddington station," she told me. "At least, anything I could find of yours. I moved my stuff out too."

I was still staring at her, and now she stared back.

"Do you know who Julian was?" she asked evenly.

"Who he was?" The question didn't seem to make any sense.

"His father is the Duke of Cleveland. His uncle used to be Foreign Secretary." She nodded her head towards the corner. "You think you get that kind of turnout for just any dead junkie?"

Slowly, what she was saying began to register.

"The cops will go through his flat with a toothcomb," she continued. "And you can bet that his family will be looking for anything other than their own self-centred indifference to blame this on. You get that, right?"

Numbly, I nodded.

"And it won't be just the police digging around here. There'll be reporters too because, my God, nothing sells the Sunday papers like gilded youth getting its comeuppance. And probably private investigators hired by the family, if only to keep a lid on things."

Nikki took a deep breath.

"So, we need to disappear, Kit. We have to get out of London." She put her hand on my arm. "At least until after the inquest. Once there's a coroner's verdict there's nothing much anyone can do, but until then who knows what kind of shit we could find ourselves dragged into." She reached into her handbag. "I've some friends in Paris, I'm going to stay there for a while." She pulled out a bundle of ten pound notes. "When I was putting our stuff together, I found five hundred in a drawer." She shrugged. "Well, Julian doesn't need it anymore so fifty fifty, okay?"

I took the notes from her and slipped them into my jacket pocket.

"Good while it lasted, hey, babe?" She gave me a sad smile and then leaned forward to kiss my cheek.

"Remember, get out of London. Today."

She turned and walked away.

It was the last time I ever saw her.

And it was a long, long time before I got to the bottom of what had really happened here. And why she had wanted me out of London so quickly.

It was in the mid-nineties - and purely by chance - that I came across the obituary of Julian's father in one of the broadsheets. It detailed his decorated war record and his family's lengthy history of government service, but it was the paragraph that dealt with what was described as the greatest tragedy of his life, that really grabbed my attention. *'His son Julian, unbeknown to the family, had formed an addiction to opiates and in 1967 had died, aged nineteen, from a heroin overdose. Distressingly, Julian's body had lain undiscovered for three days in a Mayfair apartment, which had been stripped bare of family antiques and heirlooms, probably having been sold for a pittance to feed his addiction.'*

Well, not the last time I'd been in there, they hadn't.

I'm sure that Julian's death was an accidental overdose, I find it impossible to believe that Nikki would have harboured any malice toward him. My guess is that she'd arrived at the flat forty-eight hours before she claimed she had, and when she couldn't find a pulse on that cold body she'd stood up, looked around and thought those same words she'd spoken to me. *'Well, Julian doesn't need it anymore.'*

It had probably taken her a couple of days to clear the flat out. She would have done it herself, not trusting any co-conspirator to stay quiet. I'd been the only problem - she couldn't have me going back inside, but Nikki handled that beautifully. From the distance of three decades, I was as full of admiration as at the time I would have been of outrage, two hundred and fifty quid in my pocket or not. It was more money than I'd ever had before in my life, and I've no doubt that she'd guessed that too.

Years later, Lee Munro told me Nikki had been killed in a car crash in the South of France but couldn't remember who she'd heard it from or any other details. She asked if I wanted her to try to find out more, but I said to forget it.

As closure went, it was enough.

* * *

I watched Nikki disappear around the street corner, stuck my hands into my pockets and hunching my back I headed towards Paddington Station. Collect my stuff, head down to Charing Cross and pick up my holdall ... And then what? My instinct was to jump onto a train as soon as I'd got everything together, but where to was the question.

As I reached Marble Arch it began to rain, a real downpour, and so I slipped into the nearest pub, which was *The Quebec*. The only other time I'd been there was about a year before, when Coochie had given me a guided tour of queer London and I remembered it as being quite subdued compared to some venues we'd visited that night.

"Now let's go and chat up some thespian old queens," Coochie said as we left a basement club just off the Bayswater Road, where I'd been fascinated by a TV newsreader - pretty much part of the furniture in every living room in the country - in full drag, smooching with a stalwart from the *Carry On* films.

But when we arrived at *The Quebec*, they were either having a quiet night or in my naivety I was missing something. Possibly a bit of both, we'd had a couple of drinks sent over by a silver-haired guy at the bar who acknowledged our thanks with a foppish wave of the hand, but that was about it.

And it was slow tonight too, only a dozen or so in. I took my drink over to a table near the door, sat down and considered my options.

Leaving the country was no problem, if that's what I decided to do. Baz's passport was in my bag and he wouldn't be needing it back anytime soon, even with time off for good behaviour. And with Amsterdam in mind, I had contacts in the Provo anarchist movement there - I'd written a feature about the White Bicycle Plan a couple of months earlier. Which also reminded me that Mick had said if I wanted to hitch down to Morocco and do a piece on the changing scene there - it had recently become something of a haven for American soldiers going AWOL prior to a Vietnam tour of duty - *IT* would cover the expenses. So maybe both. Get the train to the Netherlands and check out the Provo scene first-hand. Then try to hook up with some chick who fancied hitching down to Tangier. It would be a damn sight easier getting lifts with a leggy...

"A penny for them."

"Sorry!!?"

Startled, I turned to the next table where an elderly but stylishly dressed man was smiling at me.

"Your thoughts," he said. "You appeared miles away."

"I suppose I was." I gave him a cursory smile back. "Just running a few things through my head."

I lifted my drink and finished it. He seemed pleasant enough, but I really wasn't up for this right now - time to make a move.

"May I get you another?"

"Thanks, but I should be going."

"It's still pouring down out there - you'll be drenched. And sometimes," he flashed a smile again, "actually talking things through rather than simply 'running them through your head' can bring a degree of clarity."

What the hell - I thanked him and asked for a half of bitter. He rose and walked over to the bar, returning with two pint glasses, and he joined me at my table.

"I'm Roy," he said, extending a hand.

"Kit," I said.

"Well, Kit, are we mulling a problem or weighing options?" He took a sip of his beer. "Not that the two are mutually exclusive?"

"I need to be out of London for a while," I told him. "I was just trying to work out the best way to… manage that, I suppose you'd say."

"Are you in some kind of trouble?"

"No." I shook my head. "At least not at the moment. But if I don't leave, there's a chance I could get caught up in something that might create a few problems."

"You'd probably be well out of it then - where are you thinking of going?"

"Amsterdam."

"A delightful city. Do you have friends there? Somewhere to stay?"

"Yes." I nodded but didn't feel inclined to go into details.

"Far be it from me to pry, but are you in financial difficulties?"

"No - at least I've enough cash to get me there and live for a month or so. After that, I'd have to find a way to make a living."

"Never easy in a foreign country, pitfalls aplenty for the unwary."

And you sometimes needed to stay sharp on your own turf, was on the tip of my tongue, but he had bought the drinks.

"You know, there might be a solution to your problems closer to home."

"Oh, yeah?" I said, perhaps a little too warily because he gave a soft chuckle.

"No, not in the way I'm sure you think I'm implying." He nodded towards the TV set behind the bar, which was showing film of an oil tanker caught on a rocky outcrop. "There's a situation full of opportunity."

"What's happened?"

"You haven't heard?" He took another sip of beer. "An oil tanker called the *Torrey Canyon* has run aground off the Scilly

Isles. Tons of crude oil are leaking out and already washing ashore - it's a major disaster."

As he spoke, the scene moved to a sandy cove that I realised I knew, even though the beach had been covered with a thick black liquid.

"That's Cornwall," I said. "Bloody hell!"

The picture cut to a closeup of a herring gull, wings coated with oil, and it was vainly trying to take flight.

"They're saying there's over two hundred miles of coastline at risk of further pollution. The idea is to cover the beaches with detergent before it arrives." Roy paused. "They'll need every man they can get to help spray that stuff, and they'll be paying through the nose for them. Or rather, the government will."

I was silent.

"I was thinking of driving down there myself," he said. "My daughter and her husband farm just outside of Helston and she's forever nagging me to visit - that part of the country is every bit as tiresome as one might imagine, but this could prove an interesting scenario to find one's self embroiled in."

"Cornwall..." I said softly.

"About as far away as you could get from London without having to show a passport," said Roy. "And it will certainly be frantic enough for no-one to care who you are or why you're there."

"When were you thinking of leaving?" I asked.

"No time like the present," he told me. "Particularly with convivial company to while away the journey."

He finished his beer, placed the empty glass down on the table and looked at his wristwatch.

"An hour to pack a bag," he said, "and we could be crossing the Tamar by breakfast."

3. Claudia

We ugly ducklings tend to be wary creatures in later years. Having spent so long outside the party, with our faces pressed against the glass, it's a disconcerting experience to be unexpectedly taken by the hand and led inside. What other surprises, we wonder, might life have tucked away up its sleeve, as we stand fascinated by this stranger mimicking our every movement in the bathroom mirror.

I grew six inches in eighteen months, a spurt seemingly fuelled by puppy fat, as cheekbones emerged and a waistline appeared. Mummy actually took me to a Harley Street clinician, fearing I'd contracted some form of wasting disease. Though I was pronounced to be in good health, I still sometimes caught her looking in my direction wearing an expression which suggested that she wasn't quite sure what to make of me. I wasn't quite sure what to make of me either, particularly as I increasingly found myself an object of attention by the opposite sex. Brazen stares on the Underground or catcalls as I walked by a building site would turn my face crimson. Even a visit to a schoolfriend could be a trial, if their brother - or, on one especially disturbing occasion, father - were home.

But, like most things in life which become the norm, you gradually learn to cope, or in this case emulate those of your sisters - and yes, the very same ones previously dismissed as brainless little moppets - who know exactly when it's a winsome smile or a withering look which a situation requires. But occasionally, although less and less as time moved on, I would still catch a glimpse of little Claudia Falcone peeking back out of the looking glass.

There were other changes in my life too. It was in the spring of 1967 that I began to realise how much of a problem Mummy's drinking had become, initially during a conversation about our holiday home in Cornwall. *Cam Ryr* had been in the family for generations, I still don't know who bought it originally, but Mummy and Alex were forever talking about their childhood holidays there - scrambling up cliffs or crabbing in rock pools before making their exhausted way home for a cream tea.

It all sounded far too Famous Fiveish for my taste and so when Alex and Aunt Anne told me they were going down there for Easter, to 'open it up for the year' and that I was to accompany them, I put up an uncharacteristic amount of resistance. Then Anne went into the kitchen to make a pot of tea and Alex leant forward and gently laid his hand on my wrist.

Mummy was to go away, he explained, for her nerves. Hopefully, only for a short while, but it would be best if he and Anne took care of me in the meantime.

I knew that Mummy did drink an awful lot, but I hadn't thought it was a problem because it never seemed to affect her, that it was something she managed.

"We'll have a smashing time down there," Alex smiled reassuringly, "just you wait and see."

Easter in 1967 was about as early in the year as it could be. With Good Friday falling on the 24th of March, St Catherine's had extended the usual two weeks break, allowing families to arrive at holiday destinations in advance of the weekend. Last day of term was to be the Tuesday and Alex intended to leave on the Wednesday morning, to avoid the Bank Holiday traffic jams.

And then the whole trip was almost cancelled.

The week before Easter, an oil tanker called the *Torrey Canyon* ran aground off the Cornish Coast and suddenly all the world was watching as the first major environmental disaster unfolded. Crude oil began washing up on beaches and the TV news bulletins were full of seabirds being gently soaped with detergent.

"I'm not sure it's fitting to be holidaying there at the moment," Alex had said, and for a few days it looked like that was going to be that. But Aunt Anne had spoken on the telephone to friends in St Hannahs, who told her that everyone there was worried sick that this would devastate the tourist industry and they were desperate for holidaymakers to still come down at Easter.

And so we began to pack.

4. Aidan

I'm not sure how one would describe nostalgia for a period one's never experienced, although I daresay the Germans have a word for it, ten syllables clattering into each other like goods wagons in a siding. But elegant travel is a notion I've always had a romanticised yearning for, especially those great transatlantic ocean liners that took the pithy aphorism of it being *'better to journey than to arrive'* and made it an actuality. I may have been a little late for that world, but the sleeper train isn't a too shabby second place.

And, given the opportunity, it's still an option I'll take over a flight any day of the week. Where airports have all the ambiance of a suburban shopping mall, there are few European cities which don't host a railway station bearing architectural comparison with its cathedral, and even a North American terminus can be an Art Deco wonder.

It's not that I'm a nervous flier, it's the *freedom* I crave. To stretch my legs with a stroll to a leisurely three course meal in the dining car and then a cigar and nightcap, as the world rolls deceptively slowly by in a panoramic window. And to engage with a fellow passenger whilst looking them in the eye - rather than the strained sideways exchanges that air travel always makes feel so furtive - has made for some memorable engagements, and not all of them in the sense I imagine you're assuming. There's a tendency to become remarkably candid in convivial company which you're sure will never be encountered again - exchanged confidences can be surprisingly pertinent when not burdened with emotional investment or confessional dogma. Some mornings

I've woken up a lot further away than the five hundred miles from where I went to sleep.

All of which lay far in the future from that first sleeper I travelled on, the *Night Riviera* which ran overnight from Paddington to Penzance. My station was Truro, and the scribbled instructions on the card Frank had given me were to take a local bus service to St Hannahs. But it only took one look at the queues of harassed parents - carrying large suitcases and dragging small children - to see me heading over to the taxi rank.

It was a half hour journey to St Hannahs, made interesting by the driver's tendency to turn his head toward me whenever he spoke, usually as we were entering a bend on a series of lanes which I seriously doubted were wide enough for two cars to pass. So, by the time we arrived at Joyce Kelly's studio, any nervousness I might have felt about fulfilling her expectations had been washed away by a wave of relief at finding myself still in one piece.

"Well, don't expect me to be paying for that," boomed a voice behind me, as the driver lifted my bag out of the boot.

* * *

I always liked Joyce Kelly, but she didn't make it easy. I've generally regarded the battle of the sexes being for the most part guerrilla skirmishes against rank-and-file troops and whilst I can't recall a single instance in military history where partisans didn't eventually wear the occupying force down, it's wise to pick your battles... It's probably fair to say that Joyce was no strategist.

I'd only ever seen her the once before, at that lecture she gave at the Slade and where a stage or lectern usually creates a larger-than-life persona, the opposite seemed true here - she'd looked almost a diminutive figure then, half turned toward a backdrop of projected slides, as she spoke.

But face to face she was anything but.

Joyce was my height and the sort of woman you'd think of as bony rather than slim. Her face and hair were usually flecked with paint or plaster, as was her studio attire of corduroy trousers and a man's check shirt. For outdoor wear she favoured a blue fisherman's smock, the *de rigueur* fashion item not only for St Hannahs artistic community but also adopted by the owners of the gift and craft shops hidden away in the back streets. The fishermen themselves wore boilersuits or oilskins.

"That's alright," I told her as I paid the driver. "I'd assumed that I'd be covering my own expenses, as small recompense for the opportunity afforded." Which was flannel of the highest order, but I wasn't looking to pick a fight at the outset, at least not if I could avoid it.

And she did seem to soften at that.

"Well," she said, leading me inside. "I had intended for you to stay here at the gallery, I keep a small apartment upstairs for whenever I need to stop over. But Fiona - a student at Plymouth - will be working with us on the exhibition and I thought it more appropriate that she has her privacy." Joyce hesitated slightly before adding, "She is quite young."

"That's no problem at all," I told her. "If you can recommend a good hotel or guest house, then I'm happy to…"

"You'll never find anything now," she broke in. "Easter's completely booked up. But a friend of mine owns Petroc, a local holiday park and campsite, and so I've managed to get you into one of the chalets there."

"Oh, right," I said.

"I've booked it for two weeks," she told me. "It shouldn't take more than three or four days to get the gallery ready and once Tony Drydon's finished, your time will be your own. But I thought you might want to stay on for a while. St Hannahs can be truly inspirational and you'll find the light quite unlike anywhere else in the country." She shrugged and waved a hand around the gallery. "You're welcome to help yourself to any materials you may need."

"Thanks," I said. "I haven't any other plans. Who do I owe for the chalet?"

"It's taken care of," she said. "Do you want to go over there now and freshen up, or should we make a start?"

"I'm fine," I told her. "Why don't you explain what you'd like me to do?"

* * *

Curating an exhibition is harder work than you'd imagine, particularly if the actual artist is involved in the process. It's not only a question of how a piece might best catch the light, which at least has some degree of objectivity. The real problems start with sequencing the pieces to minimise the emotional resonance carried forward. Sometimes that's achieved by stark contrast and other times by a gradual correlative and you can argue until the cows come home which works most effectively in the here and now.

Not that my opinion or that of anyone else was needed to set up a conflict, Joyce being more than adept at second guessing herself. One painting Fiona and I must have hung in half a dozen different locations before finding ourselves back where we'd started, but it was the bronze casts that especially took it out of you. Even the smaller pieces were heavy lifting.

"Alright," she said, at the end of the day. "That's given me something to sleep on."

Which was really what you wanted to hear.

"I'll run you over to Petroc," she told me, "while Fi cleans up. After you've unpacked, if you fancy a meal - and you've earned one - we'll be in the *Harbour Lights* down by the quay, it's only a fifteen-minute walk if you take the footpath."

I thanked her and said I'd see how I felt after I'd showered. I appreciated the offer, but thought that once I'd sat down I was unlikely to be getting up again.

The chalet was basic but clean and functional, a sofa bed in the living room, off which was a small shower room and lavatory. As well as a sink, there was an ancient Baby Belling cooker hooked up to a Calor gas cylinder, probably best left alone unless I wished to tempt the same fate as my father, I reflected. So, after a shower and weary as I was, I decided to take Joyce up on her offer.

In the site office I was asking for directions to the *Harbour Lights* from the receptionist, when a couple in their fifties interrupted to say that they had a barbecue about to start and that I was welcome to join them.

"That's very gracious of you," I said. "Thank you."

"I'm Wilf," said the man, in what I'd recently learnt to identify as a cockney accent, "and this is my wife, Frieda."

5. Kit

It was only seconds after Roy dropped me off down by the harbour in St Hannahs that the first army truck appeared. Even then, I didn't get it. An exercise, I assumed - they'd been using the Burrows for mock battles as far back as the build-up to D-Day. Not until the arrival of a second lorry, containing large drums of detergent which the soldiers began unloading, did I finally understand - the government must have declared a national emergency and drafted in the troops.

Well, so much for making some easy money, I reflected, but it didn't really change anything. There was no point going back to London, and I should be able to make the cash I'd had from Nikki last awhile.

The priority at the moment was to lie low.

I had a few options. Like St Ives, there was a strong Beat community in St Hannahs during the summer. They either camped out on the dunes or moved into old army pillboxes, scattered along the coast. The problem with that was they were hassled a lot by the local cops, and until I knew whether my name had been connected to Julian's death, I couldn't afford to get picked up.

So...

Time for some pragmatism, I thought, and more than a little compromise.

* * *

The chalet wasn't one of the best, to call it tired would be flattering but, as I expected, it was clean and came with that sense of freshness you always get when sea salt's in the air.

I didn't have much to unpack and once finished I debated whether to try to sleep. I'd only dozed fitfully on the drive down, so I knew that if I risked a nap, the chances were that I'd be waking up in the middle of the night, totally out of sync.

I was still deciding what to do when there was a knock at the door.

"Hi," said the figure standing there. "I noticed you'd just arrived, thought I'd come over and introduce myself."

He was about my age, shoulder length hair, denim shirt and jeans, and he was smoking a liquorice paper roll up. A harmonica was poking out of his top pocket.

"I'm called Jake," he said, offering his hand. "And I'm staying over in the Barns."

"Kit," I told him. "Barns?"

"The camping barns." He turned and pointed to the other side of the campsite where two old outbuildings stood. "New this year - five bob a night to put a sleeping bag down, there's a sink and cooker in there and you can use the shower block." He flicked the ash off the end of his cigarette. "Main thing though, it keeps the pigs off your back - they can't touch you here, not like down on the dunes or in the pillboxes."

"Sounds cool," I said, trying not to be obvious about studying him. Because there was definitely something familiar about...

"And I was wondering if you were still dealing," he said, staring straight at me. "It is you, right - Coochie's mate from *Finches*?"

Opening the door fully, I gestured with my head for him to come inside.

"I figured if you were renting a place like this then you were probably trying to keep your head down," he was saying as I closed the door. "I used to see you on the scene a lot, *Cousins, UFO Club* - even scored from you a few times, but I suppose you don't remember."

"Sorry."

"S'okay man. Nice pad," he said, looking around. "Compared to the Barns."

I guessed it was safe to take him at face value. The middle-class accent and at least twelve months' growth of hair suggested it was unlikely that he was an undercover cop, but it never hurt to be cautious.

"So, you down for the summer?" I asked.

"Yeah," he gave a nod. "Had it with the Smoke for a while, too much of a bad vibe these days. You?"

"I'm not sure yet," I told him. "I'll see how things go."

"Been down here before?"

I nodded.

"I thought I'd come down early this year," he said, "and get myself set up, before the bloody weekend ravers start arriving."

"Set up?" I asked.

"Dope and acid," he said. "St Hannahs is so far off the beaten track that people really pay through the nose for it." He gave me that frank stare again. "You'll do well down here."

So that was the reason for this insistent curiosity. He had me pegged as competition and was checking me out. With that, I relaxed and gave him a smile as I shook my head.

"I'm not dealing," I told him. "There's stuff going down in London I'm waiting to blow over before I head back. But in the meantime, I'm not looking to attract attention."

"Hassles with the fuzz?" he asked.

"Could be," I said, "but unlikely."

"Just a bad scene?"

"Yeah."

"Bummer," he said sympathetically, but probably with as much a measure of relief as mine. "Fancy a smoke?" he asked, fishing a short stubby joint out of his pocket.

"Sure," I smiled, but I didn't want the chalet stinking like a shebeen ten minutes after arriving here. "Let's take a walk."

* * *

It was a two mile journey from Petroc to St Hannahs following the road around the headland, but a public footpath over the hill behind the campsite - despite being a steep climb - reduced that to a fifteen-minute walk. On the crest of the hill were two wooden benches, giving uninterrupted views both out to sea across St Hannahs and down into the valley below. You could see anyone approaching from half a mile away.

We sat down, and Jake lit the joint.

"If you're thinking of going into town tonight for something to eat," he said, "don't bother. You won't get served in any of the cafes or pubs."

"Things are that bad?"

Jake nodded.

"You can still buy stuff in the shops, though. Most nights there's a beach party on the Burrows, anyone's welcome who turns up with a loaf of bread or a packet of sausages to chip in."

"The cops leave it alone?"

"The only way to reach it is over the sands, which they're too bloody lazy to walk across."

I wouldn't get too cocky about it, I thought, or one of these nights they'll surprise you with a couple of Land Rovers and let the Alsatians loose.

"Or there's always Wilf and Frieda, back at Petroc," said Jake, handing me the joint.

"Wilf and Frieda?"

"You'll find out soon enough." He gave a wry smile. "There're about a dozen of them altogether, Wilf does the talking but you get the feeling that it's his wife Frieda who wears the trousers. Apparently, they've been coming down here every Easter for donkey's years. They spend all day in little groups working out how to put the world to rights and then get together around a campfire at night, for a fry up and singsong." He shook his head. "Everyone's welcome, but it's not exactly a laugh a minute."

I passed him the joint back.

"I'm going down into town," he said, standing up. "See if I can do a bit of business."

"Thanks for the smoke," I told him. "Catch you later."

He nodded and headed off down the hill.

* * *

I'd been asleep when the second knock on my door that day came. I'd only taken a couple of hits off Jake's spliff, but either it had been powerful stuff or I was more bushed than I'd realised - as soon as I got back to the chalet and sat down, I was gone.

And had been for quite a while, I guessed. The moon hung low in the night sky but was bright enough to cast shadows through the windows. Then another sharp knock at the door. I pushed myself up onto my feet and stepped across the room to open it.

A girl of about my own age was standing there. One of the Beats was my first thought, probably looking for Jake to score had been my second and how to get rid of her my third.

"Hello," she said. "We noticed you'd just arrived and wondered if you'd like to join us for supper."

As my eyes adjusted to the light, I realised that my initial assessment was mistaken. Her clothes were more utilitarian than bohemian and although she wasn't wearing make-up, the effect was scrubbed clean rather than shabby.

With her hand she indicated a largish campfire about fifty yards away. A dozen or so people were gathered around it.

"We?" I asked.

"My mum and dad and some friends - if you've been travelling today, we thought it would save you cooking or finding somewhere in town to eat."

I didn't need two years' worth of street smarts to understand that no-one got something for nothing, but the aroma of bacon being barbecued came wafting over and I hadn't eaten all day.

"Thanks, I appreciate it," I said.

It only took a few seconds to grab my jacket and lock the front door.

"Have you come far?" she asked, as we walked over to the campfire.

"London."

"Oh, whereabouts?"

"I've moved around a fair bit," I told her.

6. Claudia

In those far off, pre-motorway days it was a two-day expedition from London to Cornwall. On the Wednesday night we stayed with Aunt Anne's sister at Dunster in Somerset having, as Alex put it, 'broken the back' of the journey, an expression I've always thought casts a grim light over any enterprise. Under overcast skies we set out again the next morning to follow the coast road down to Cornwall, a slow and winding route, but Alex was keen from previous experience to avoid the apparently infamous Exeter bypass.

This was my first visit to the West Country, and I had to admit that the scenery at times was spectacular. Through leafy Devon we drove along the tops of wooded sea cliffs and then into Cornwall, where the road weaved between rocky coastline and sparse moorland, desolation with a beauty all of its own.

Occasionally we passed high, narrow stone towers that seemed as ancient as the moor they rose from.

"Are they castles?" I asked Alex.

"No, they're winding shafts for tin mines," he said, and explained that in the distant past the moorlands of southwestern Britain had been an industrial heartland. Tin, copper, even silver and gold had been mined and smelted here. He told how centuries ago miners had come from the Germanic regions to work on Exmoor, and before that the Phoenicians sailed up to Cornwall from the Mediterranean of the Roman Empire, to trade for tin.

"Do they still mine here?" I asked.

Alex shook his head. "There hasn't been much profit

in it for a long time, and it became increasingly dangerous when they had to dig seams out under the sea. It was cheaper to import from abroad, and so the miners moved out there. To Canada, South Africa, Australia. Look around the churchyards of mining communities in any of those countries and you'll find plenty of Trelawnys, Pengellys and their like. 'Cousin Jacks' they called them, although nobody seems sure of why."

Alex's explanation seemed to lay a sombre sadness across the already stark landscape, and we journeyed on in silence. But finally the sun broke through and with that our mood lifted - by the time we drove down the hill into St Hannahs we were chatting brightly.

I'd expected it to be busy, if not chaotic, but the only sign of anything out of the ordinary were stacks of large drums on the quayside, which I recognised from the television news as detergent.

We turned into a small, cobbled street, passing several stone-built cottages, and then Alex pulled up in front of a row of narrow weather-boarded houses, each a bleached shade of pastel.

"So here we are," said Alex.

Initially, I was rather disappointed. *Cam Ryr* seemed tiny and poky and was stuck out of the way up this side street. But once inside, whatever the house lacked in width was more than made up for with depth, room after room branching off a long corridor which ended at a large conservatory, opening out onto a sandy beach complete with breaking surf.

"Oh, wow!" I found myself saying.

"Yes dear, quite," smiled Aunt Anne.

We went back outside to where Alex was still unpacking the car.

"We're the first ones here this year," Aunt Anne said, "so there's a fair bit to get ready and all the rooms will need a good airing."

"Can I help?" I asked.

"That's very sweet of you darling, but Alex and I know where everything is and to be honest, you'd probably just be under our feet. Why don't you explore the town for a while, find your way around and be home for tea at half-past five?"

"Are you sure, Aunt Anne?"

"Half-past five prompt," smiled Alex.

I walked back along the road we'd just driven up.

7. Aidan

If the arrival of *Pulse* at the gallery seemed a bit of an anti-climax, it was because I'd been expecting something along the lines of an outside broadcast vehicle the size of a furniture lorry, childhood memories of visiting London and watching *'In Town Tonight'*. The reality was an estate car belonging to a BBC News team already in the area to cover the Torrey Canyon disaster and complete with a cameraman and a sound engineer, commandeered by Tony Drydon and his producer, who'd travelled down by train the previous day.

"BBC management is ever conscious of its responsibility to the license payer," I overheard Tony say to Joyce as they started a sound check, "until lunchtime rolls around."

The exhibition was finalised by then. The walls of the main gallery held a collection of new paintings, but the centrepiece was a cast bronze of a bull, a front hoof raised and a steady gaze you could imagine taking the measure of a toreador. Two other tables offered different studies of what was obviously the same animal, some cast in bronze but most in plaster.

Joyce's ceramic collections were displayed in three smaller rooms which led off the gallery, and I was more impressed by these than I'd expected to be. Less by the designs, I'd have to say - there's little you can do with a vase or a plate that hasn't been done before - but by the effects she'd created with the glazing, subtle variations of pastel colouring, suggestive of desert vistas or oceanic expanses without specifically defining them. It wasn't an art form I'd ever really taken seriously, but over the last few days the more I'd studied them, the more intrigued I'd become.

It was certainly educational watching them put the documentary together. Joyce took Tony through the exhibition, giving him background to the various pieces while he scribbled in a notebook and the cameraman moved through the gallery and the ceramic rooms to get a record of everything.

"What I have in mind," I heard him say, "is to start with a five-minute voice-over, showing a montage of some of your earlier work, together with footage that we'll shoot today of the new collection. After that, I'll interview you about the exhibition as a concept, before we feature two or three specific pieces. Is that okay with you?"

Joyce nodded.

"And I thought we'd finish off," Tony continued, "with a section about St Hannahs, why you've based yourself here and what this place means to you, maybe end with some shots of you out and about in the town, part of the local community." He paused. "Do you want to know the questions I'll be asking, or would you prefer to wing it? In all honesty it comes across better if it's spontaneous, it can all seem a bit stagey when it's rehearsed, but we'll go with whatever you're most comfortable with."

"No, let's just go ahead with it," said Joyce.

And that was pretty much the way it went. A couple of hours in the gallery and then they departed, with Fiona, to shoot the footage around the town. I was left to reposition two of the paintings which Joyce had decided needed a different light, tidy everything away and then lock up for the night.

Well, thanks a bunch Frank, I thought to myself as I gave the floor a sweep, so much for 'they'll want to talk to you' and 'this is an opportunity'. But then again, it had been good practical experience of putting an exhibition together, I admitted to myself as I locked the main doors and stepped out onto the street, because who knew how soon...

I came to a halt. Across the road the BBC camera car was parked at the kerb, Tony Dryden half perched on the bonnet, arms folded and grinning at me.

"Hello Aidan," he said. "Would you care for a glass of the black stuff?"

8. Kit

Sitting by the campfire that first night at Petroc, I was expecting some form of evangelism, I just wasn't sure which brand. During my time on the streets of London I'd been targeted by everyone from the Sally Army to The Process (a Scientology splinter group) but until then my only real contact with the political left had been in folk clubs.

Throughout the early sixties, quite a few of those clubs had been run by the Communist Party of Great Britain, who'd formed links with CND during the Aldermaston marches and then gradually began infiltrating what they perceived to be potential youth recruitment venues. But lately, as singer songwriters found these clubs useful launch platforms to build a fan base, it was all starting to fragment as - with true Stalinist resolve - the purists insisted they should perform only traditional material.

But what they hadn't seen coming was a two-way street.

Society in flux, times in transition, the mix always throws up strange bedfellows. The Socialist Workers Party were pretty much what you'd expect from an ultra left-wing political group in the mid-sixties - those members by the campfire that night were all short back and sides haircuts, NHS specs and dressed by the Co-op, the occasional peacock flaunting a corduroy jacket with leather elbow patches. They called each other 'comrade' without the slightest trace of irony, smoked nothing more exotic than Park Drive or Players No.6 and were passing around bottles of brown ale.

If you'd told them that within eighteen months a huge

chunk of their membership would have splintered off into the International Marxist Group - where 'man' was the usual form of address, fashion lent toward suede and flares, and at meetings there was usually a spliff making its way around the table - they would have thought you insane.

Both groups were hard core Trotskyist, but the IMG believed the SWP to be hopelessly out of touch and irrelevant to the modern world, while the SWP declared the IMG to be middle class dilettantes with no genuine commitment to the core concept of continual revolution. I found it difficult to disagree with either assessment, although towards the end of the decade it was an entertainment watching them go for each other. I once saw a mini riot break out in Trafalgar Square when the IMG leader, Tariq Ali, walked out onto the platform at a demo and the SWP faction in the crowd began chanting *'IMG, IMG, Idle sons of the bourgeoisie'*.

All a little way off at that point though, but I bring it up because that evening was the first time I witnessed seeds of future conflicts being sown.

Rather unsteadily - the lingering effects of Jake's joint - I rose to my feet and walked over to a trestle table, stacked with paper plates, cooked meats and loaves of bread.

"Okay, but what I don't get," a long-haired Beat in a combat jacket and bell-bottom jeans was saying to an earnest looking woman in her forties, "is that if it's there to actually keep people out, then why is everyone being shot crossing it going in the opposite direction?"

The woman pursed her lips at him, as he cumbersomely constructed a sausage and bacon sandwich.

"You shouldn't believe everything that you read in the bourgeois press," she said sternly. "There're a lot of things they don't want you to know."

"Look, I get that the Russian peasants are a lot better off now..." he began.

"*Russian peasants!!!*" she spluttered and then fixed him with an evil stare. "There are no peasants in the Soviet Union, comrade, but there are plenty in America."

With that, she turned her back on him and stormed away.

"Think you've blown your chances there, mate," I said to him softly, buttering a slice of bread. He grinned at me and slowly shook his head.

Turning to head back to the campfire, I found my way blocked by the girl who'd invited me here. Her arms were folded and her expression stern.

"You think that's funny, do you? Mocking people," her eyes dropped to the sandwich in my hand, "while eating the food they've offered you."

"Look, ah…" I began, racking my memory.

"Forgotten already, have you? Reassuring to learn that I create such a lasting impression."

I didn't know if it was the dope, the lack of sleep, maybe a combination of the two, but I'd had enough.

"Okay," I said. "Thanks for the food but I've sung for my supper before and whether it's eternal salvation or an Orwellian nightmare masquerading as…"

"*Orwell?* Oh right, no surprise you'd be siding with the fascists, is it?"

I took a deep breath.

"I'm sorry I can't remember your name - it's been a long day but still, I apologise for that," I told her. "But if that's your opinion of George Orwell, then you really are talking out of your arse."

Her mouth dropped open, and - before she could gather herself to speak - I moved past her. And I didn't need to look around to know that her eyes were following me all the way back to the chalet.

* * *

The next morning, after a good night's sleep, I was feeling a little more conciliatory. I took a stroll into town where I knew there was a second-hand bookshop, hoping to find a copy of Orwell's *Homage to Catalonia*. The owner was apologetic, but he did have a dogeared *Road to Wigan Pier*.

That would do.

Back at Petroc, I sellotaped the book into a brown paper bag and went over to the site office. I explained who I wanted it delivered to, and the receptionist had no problem knowing which pigeonhole to slip it into.

Walking to my chalet and reflecting on the previous night, it seemed that the girl had been more combative than angry, the confrontation almost a pretence. But for what?

An air of mystery is always intriguing when you're young, but in later years you've generally cottoned on that anything going down which you don't understand is usually bad news, even if at the time you have little sense of foreboding.

9. Claudia

For such a small place St Hannahs made it surprisingly easy for one to lose one's bearings. Other than the church spire - which looked very much the same from every viewpoint - there were no tall landmarks and the narrow streets restricted viewing to almost directly overhead. I'd walked down to the harbour and taken a side road which led to the town square. I had a look in the few shops there and headed off in a direction which I thought would take me further inland. Five minutes later I was back at the harbour. I decided to sit on the sea wall for a while and then try again.

A couple of things I'd noticed. A lot of the houses - once fishermen's cottages, I supposed - had been converted to either craft shops or galleries. I knew St Ives had an artist colony, even its own school of painting, I recalled, but I hadn't realised that St Hannahs had followed suit.

The other thing was that quite a few shops I'd passed, and every pub, had a notice on the door saying *'No Beatniks'*. Some were neatly typed cards, others scribbled on pieces of cardboard, but it was a message that struck me as rather incongruous for such a rurally idyllic spot.

I was deciding whether to have another walk through the town or perhaps go back to *Cam Ryr* and sit in the conservatory until teatime, when a tentative voice said, "Excuse me".

I turned around.

The boy looked to be about my age. He was wearing an old suit waistcoat over a white T-shirt, scruffy bell-bottom jeans and plimsolls. His hair hung down to his shoulders from a centre parting and he had the beginnings of a wispy beard.

'Oh goodness,' I remember thinking.

"I wonder if you could help us?" His voice was soft and with no discernible accent, which was unusual back then. People tended to speak either RP or with a regional dialect.

With a turn of his head, he indicated across the road at a girl, pointedly disinterested behind wraparound sunglasses.

'He's going to ask me for money,' I thought, and instinctively grasped my bag tighter. Whether he noticed the gesture or simply picked up on my general unease, I don't know, but he smiled and stepped back slightly.

"It's okay," he said. He reached into the pocket of his waistcoat and pulled out a handful of coins. Then he offered them to me in his open palm.

"Would you buy us some bread?" he asked.

"I'm sorry?" I must have been staring at him like an idiot.

"From the grocers," he said. "Around the corner. They won't serve us because..." He gave a shrug.

"Yes, of course," I almost stammered. "Just bread?"

"Yeah," he smiled as I took the money out of his hand. "We'll wait in there." He nodded towards a small shelter, further along the harbour wall. "Out of sight."

No shoplifter ever entered a store with greater trepidation than I carried into that grocers. *'What are you doing Claudia?'* one half of my mind was screaming while the other half replied, *'Buying a loaf of bread, for Heaven's sake!'* And suddenly how confusing that was proving to be - sliced, unsliced, white, brown. I could hardly go back outside and ask, so I picked up one large white farmhouse and a sliced Hovis. I slipped the coins that he'd given me into my pocket and took out my purse, paying at the till with a half-crown. The grocer put them into a paper carrier bag and gave me a genial goodbye as I left the store. I walked over to the shelter, half expecting him to come running after me.

"I wasn't sure what sort you wanted," I told the boy, as he opened the bag and looked up at me. The girl was sitting on one of the benches, studiously rolling a cigarette with a liquorice paper.

"And..." I said, reaching into my pocket and pulling out the coins he'd given me.

"No," he shook his head. "I didn't expect you to pay."

"It's fine," I told him. "Honestly."

He hesitated and then took them out of my hand

"Well," he smiled. "You're really cool."

In the corner of my eye, I registered the girl give a wry smile and a slight shake of her head. I could feel myself blushing and I started backing out of the shelter. All I wanted now was to go home.

"Okay. *Ciao!*" Without waiting for any acknowledgement, I turned and began to walk away. But I'd only taken about four brisk steps when:

"Claudia!!!?"

I turned around. The girl was walking towards me and then she stopped, took off her sunglasses and stared incredulously.

"Claudia Falcone?"

It was Emma Brownlow.

* * *

"Well, nothing they promised actually materialised," said Emma. "After the summer term ended, they said there'd been a problem with the school fees arrangement. That the trustees weren't happy with the circumstances. So, I never went back for the following year - it had all been a cover-up because of the publicity I might cause."

The three of us were sitting down on the beach. Although intent on catching up after the initial mutual shock of our reunion, I couldn't help but register that while the boy she'd introduced as Jake was obviously keen on her, she was treating him with almost blasé indifference.

"The journalist who wrote the story in the *Shoreditch*

Observer was a friend of my mum's, and one thing she discovered was that back in the thirties, Miss Foster's brother had been a leading figure in Oswald Mosley's Blackshirts. So, she started going through the paper's archives and came up with a photograph of Miss Foster on the platform at a British Union of Fascists meeting. *That* was the reason everything got taken care of so quickly."

"Couldn't you have gone back to the press?" Jake looked at her quizzically, and I realised that Emma's story was all new to him. "Reignited it with the whole Miss Jean Brodie angle?"

"Mum wanted to." She shook her head. "But I thought it might end up sounding like sour grapes - I didn't want it to seem that I was someone who had problems fitting in anywhere." She shrugged. "And I was never comfortable at St Catherine's - you remember that, right?"

I nodded.

"Well, Kent was a lot worse - I was a boarder there, so there was no real escape from it. In a way, I was glad to be out of it all."

"Where are you now?"

"At a local Grammar - I'm doing A'levels this summer. What about you, still at St Catherine's?"

"Yes, and the same - A'levels in June."

"Have you got a university place yet?"

"I've applied to Oxbridge, Bristol and a few others, but I've not heard back. What about you?"

"Magdalen Oxford made an offer, but only if I get the grades - so we'll see."

I didn't think there'd be much doubt about that, and I couldn't help a small flash of envy. *Dreaming spires.*

"Anyway, Claudia," she said, "what on earth are you doing here?"

"I'm on holiday," I told her. "My family have a house here and... Oh, good grief!"

I looked at my watch, and then almost leapt to my feet.

It was five thirty.

"Sorry," I said. "I'm supposed to be back by now."

"Where do you need to get to?"

It occurred to me I didn't know the address.

"Over there," I told her, pointing. "The other side of the harbour."

"I'll walk part of the way with you," said Emma, and then raised her hand as Jake also began to rise.

"It's okay," she told him. "I'll see you back at Petroc. Claudia and I still have some catching up to do."

Without waiting for a response, she slid her arm through mine and led me away.

"Petroc?" I asked.

"It's a campsite outside of town," she told me. "We've been coming down here for years."

"Who's we?"

"SWP - the Socialist Workers Party. Mum and dad run the Whitechapel branch and we've been having a fortnight's national workshop at Petroc since I was little."

"Was that your boyfriend?" I asked.

Emma's laugh was more like a bark.

"Jake?" She shook her head emphatically. "He's just staying at the campsite. Quite a few of the Beats are this year."

"Beats?"

"Or Beatniks - you've probably seen the signs outside the shops and pubs."

I nodded.

"Which is why your friend wanted me to...?"

"Oh, good heavens no - Jake just fancied you. He was hoping you'd fall for his sweet little bohemian act and probably thought it might make me jealous. Men!" She gave another shake of her head. "But it is why I was a bit standoffish until I realised who you were."

"So how...?" I let my voice trail off.

"It was just the way you said *'Ciao'*. I mean, I wouldn't have recognised you in a million years, but voices never change, do they? As soon as you said it, I saw you giving me a smile and a wave at the top of the escalator at Oxford Circus tube station. Couldn't have been anyone else. But," she stopped walking, took my hand to turn me to face her and staring, slowly shook her head, "*wow!*"

I laughed, probably blushing a bit too.

"I turn off here," she said. "But we're having a barbecue on the Burrows tonight - why don't you come down and we can have a really long chat, we've so much to catch up on."

"I'll try to get away," I told her.

"If not, come over to Petroc in the morning. We'll spend the day together."

10. Aidan

"We understand that the struggle of our comrades in Ireland has been a long and bitter one," said Wilf, in a monotone as casual as if he were enquiring after the traffic on the Exeter bypass. "And I tell you from my heart, that everyone you will meet here stands shoulder to shoulder with all who would rise up to overthrow the yoke of capitalist oppression."

And I'm sure there'll be dancing in the streets of the Bogside when that gets back to them, were my thoughts, but I kept my expression solemn as I filled my plate.

I've heard it said that the gift of a skilled orator is being able to address a crowd whilst making every single member of it feel as though they're being spoken to personally. Wilf Brownlow had the gift of making you feel that you were at the back of a large auditorium when you were the only two people in the room.

That first night Wilf and Frieda had led me from the site office over to the campfire where a barbecue of sorts had been built. As a couple they seemed ill matched in every way except in their commitment to the triumph of the proletariat. Physically, they couldn't have been further apart. Wilf was about six feet tall and although still muscular, you could tell he wouldn't be for much longer. He had short dark brown hair, starting to grey at the temples, and a thick moustache that continued just far enough down past the corners of his mouth to create a somewhat doleful expression. He wore rough black corduroy trousers, held up with wide leather braces over a collarless shirt which on me would have been fashionable, but on him conjured up the ghosts of Jarrow.

His movements were slow and deliberate and whatever you might think of any opinion he offered, it did come with a sense of being carefully mulled over.

Frieda was about a foot shorter, thin and sharp featured. The initial impression was one of nervousness, her hands were constantly moving, either gesturing to emphasise a point she was making or tapping on her thighs as she listened, but I think that was just the way she was wired - her gaze was always steady when it met yours.

"Have you lost family to the Troubles?" asked Frieda.

"I have," I told her. "But I doubt you'd find a family in all thirty-two counties without a sacrifice of one sort or another, and there's many bearing a greater loss than mine."

Which in its way was a bit rich, but experience had shown that stoic reticence was always a solid pivot to swing the conversation away from my family background and so it proved. We'd soon moved on to Frieda telling me about a Claimants Union, that she and her daughter were setting up in the area of London where they lived.

"Sorry?" It wasn't an expression I'd heard before. "A claims...?"

"Claimants Union. The state intentionally makes claiming benefits and payments to which the underprivileged are entitled ridiculously complicated. A Claimants Union is a group of volunteer solicitors, social workers and others who process their claims through the proper channels, while explaining to them the inequities of the system and encouraging them to become politically engaged."

"Oh, I see," I said, thinking a bit like a Salvation Army soup kitchen - you get your supper eventually, but first you have to get your hands together.

"Here's Emma now," said Wilf, and I looked up to see a girl of about seventeen and one of the long-haired Beatnik types walking towards us.

"Mum, dad," said Emma, sitting down with a slight toss of her head to one side, doubtless to better let me admire her profile. Which, I had to admit, was worth looking at.

"This is Aidan," said Wilf. "He's an art student and working at..."

He looked at me questioningly.

"I'm at Joyce Kelly's gallery for a few days," I told them. The boy stuck his hand out.

"Jake," he said.

He seemed uncertain whether or not to sit, until Wilf passed him a bottle of beer and motioned him down with his hand.

"Which college are you at?" asked Jake.

"The Slade, in London," I said, as Emma continued to look politely bored and then - with the snap realisation that they weren't actually a couple, that she was just a wilful little madam leading the poor sap around by the dick - I suddenly felt a rush of empathy for him. "The BBC are making a documentary about Joyce's new exhibition and I was asked down here to help."

That turned Emma's head, and she seemed to be about to speak when I pushed myself up onto my feet.

"It's been a long day," I said, "and I really need to get some sleep. Thanks for the hospitality," I nodded down at Wilf and Frieda, "and good to meet you, Jake."

"Goodnight Aidan," said Wilf, and Frieda added, "Maybe see you tomorrow night."

I gave her a nod and headed off back to the chalet.

* * *

I didn't see them the next night, or on any of the days I was working at the gallery, because each evening Joyce took Fiona and I out to a restaurant down by the harbour. So, it was five nights later that I came out of my chalet with half a mind to discover whether there was a barbecue going, or if not to take a walk into St Hannahs.

The only person who seemed to be around was Jake, who told me Wilf and Frieda had gone to Penzance for a fishermen's union meeting.

"If you want a barbecue," he said, "there's one on the Burrows tonight. We could pick up some sausages and booze in town and head over."

"Who's likely to be there?" I asked.

"Beats mainly," he said. "Local chicks, perhaps."

If I hesitated it was because I'd gathered - from overheard conversations between Joyce and her friends - that there had been a lot of ill feeling in the town the previous summer towards the Beatniks. The gist of it was that the long-established artists' colony in St Hannahs meant there'd always been a fairly tolerant attitude to the summer influx, but now that 'live and let live' ethos was being stretched to the limit by petty theft, street begging and blatant drug dealing.

Still, it was only one night and when all was said and done, I'd never actually been to a beach party before.

"Okay," I told him. "Lead the way."

11. Claudia

I didn't get back to *Cam Ryr* until well after six o'clock and I was expecting a bit of a ticking off for that. Alex was relaxed about most things, but he did have a bee in his bonnet about punctuality - 'the politeness of kings' as he would refer to it.

But I was in for a surprise. As I let myself in, I could hear laughter and the sound of more than two voices coming from down the hall. Curiously, I walked along to the kitchen and pushed open the door.

Alex was pouring wine from a decanter and, seeing me, he broke off from chatting to a rather good-looking man, aged about thirty. Aunt Anne was sitting at the kitchen table with a teenage boy.

Alex gave a big smile.

"This is our niece, Claudia," he said. "Back from exploring the village. And these," turning his head to me, "are our new neighbours."

"Well, for the next two weeks at least," the man smiled, extending his hand. "Don Mayberry," he said as we shook. There was definitely something familiar about him, and how he said his name seemed to imply that I should know it. "And this is my young friend Lee," he said and gave another smile. "I'm in *loco parentis* for her over the next couple of weeks."

"More loco than parentis," said Lee dryly, and everyone laughed. She raised a languid arm and gave me a slow wave. I nodded back, trying to match her detached sangfroid. Her short hair, T-shirt, jeans and - to be blunt - flat chest had all made equal contributions to my false impression and 'Lee' didn't exactly help. Even with her girlish voice, I might still have been guessing if Don hadn't said 'her'.

"We're opening at the National at the end of next month," Don said to me, and then I knew him, he was an actor. And not just any actor, he played a doctor in a TV series that Aunt Anne watched religiously every week. I turned to see her reaction to this real life little drama unfolding in her very own kitchen and then realised that she was sitting there like a glassy-eyed rabbit caught in a headlight beam.

"It's pretty much a two hander," continued Don, reaching for a glass of wine, "so Lee thought it would be a good idea for both of us to get away and work on the script with no distractions."

"This is Don's first time in Cornwall," said Lee. "As a child I used to come down here most summers with my parents, when I wasn't working."

Working!?

"Do you remember Lee from *The Hendersons*?" asked Alex, and when I stared at him blankly, he gestured apologetically toward me. "Claudia was living in Rome until a few years ago," he told her.

"Oh, lucky you!" she said. "I did a screen test at Cinecitta last year, I absolutely loved it over there."

"How was your walk?" asked Alex.

"Actually, I bumped into an old schoolfriend," I told him. "We've arranged to meet later on for something to eat, if that's alright?"

"Is it someone whom we know?" asked Aunt Anne, abruptly snapped out of her trance by proxy parental responsibility.

"Well, it's someone you know of," I said. "Emma Brownlow?"

Alex looked blank for a second and then nodded in recognition of the name.

"Of course. Yes, I remember that very well."

He gave a brief recap to our guests, both of whom also recalled the media storm that had briefly swirled around

Emma.

"And she's a friend of yours?" asked Lee.

"Well, today's the first time I've seen her since she had to leave St Catherine's," I told her, "but we were close for a few months, when I started at the school."

"And she's on holiday here with her parents?" asked Aunt Anne.

Probably not exactly how Aunt Anne might assume, but close enough for me to nod my head and say yes, without feeling deceitful.

"Well, we've decided to go out for a meal," said Alex. He hesitated. "But I know it must be exciting to see your friend again. And you say you'll be dining with her?"

Fish and chips or sausages blackened over a driftwood bonfire, I imagined, but again dutifully nodded.

"Very well," said Aunt Anne. "But on condition you join us at the restaurant before it closes. We'll all come back together."

"Thank you, Aunt Anne." I started to back out of the room. "I'll just get changed and..."

"I'm with Claudia," said Lee, pushing herself up out of her chair.

"Oh really, sweetie," said Don, "I'm sure that Claudia and Emma..."

"Come on, how often do you get to hang out with an actual *enfant terrible*," interrupted Lee and then looked at me. "If that's okay with Claudia?"

"Yes, of course," I said, but not sure at all what I really felt about this.

"Give me twenty minutes to freshen up?"

I nodded and Don stood up, saying that he needed to get his jacket and would be back in two ticks.

"You will be careful, darling," said Aunt Anne after they left, but Alex shushed her.

"She's just made a new friend and she's off to meet an old one, for heaven's sake let the girl have some fun," he said, as I slipped away upstairs to get changed.

* * *

I rang the doorbell next door, and when it opened I realised that I'd assumed only Don and Lee were staying there. However, it seemed Don also had a lady friend with him and as I started to introduce myself to the smooth young *ingénue* standing there - obviously another actress - and explain that I was calling for Lee, she stepped out and closed the door behind her.

"After you," an amused drawl at catching my expression.

Because I couldn't take my eyes away from her. These days the whole world is *au fait* with Lee Munro's chameleon talents on the cinema screen, but close up and unheralded the effect was truly astonishing. There wasn't a single aspect of her features any different from earlier, yet, with none of the accoutrements you'd believe essential to bring about such a transformation – make-up, a wig - she had metamorphosed from street urchin to starlet.

So, it took a while to notice that the black silk dress which clung to her was tight enough to suggest she may be wearing nothing underneath and short enough to possibly confirm that, were she to simply lean forward.

It was, I thought as she slipped her arm through mine and we stepped out into the night, going to be an interesting evening.

12. Kit

A couple of nights after I'd left the Orwell book at the site office, there was a knock at my door.

"Hi there."

She had the paperback in her right hand and held it out to me.

"Apparently," she continued, "you're absolutely correct. Informed opinion is now unanimous that I was, in fact, talking out of my arse."

"Keep it," I told her.

"Thank you," she said, and then gave me a smile. "Can we start over - I'm Emma."

"Kit," I smiled back at her.

"There's a barbecue down on the Burrows tonight," she said. "Do you fancy going - we could get some bacon and sausages on the way over?"

"I'll get my coat."

* * *

The trouble at the grocery store started as soon as we entered.

"Out!"

The woman behind the counter was pointing at the door.

"Why?" asked Emma.

"Because I'm not serving you."

"All we want," I told her, picking up a loaf of bread, "is to buy this."

"Put that down," she said, "or I'm calling the police."

"For what reason?" said Emma, shaking her head disbelievingly.

"Because I said I won't serve you - so, if you don't put it down then it's theft."

Emma turned to me.

"Leave it," she said. "Come on, let's go."

I wanted to argue, but Emma was tugging at my arm. As we left the shop, I saw the woman reaching for the telephone.

"We should get away from here," I told her. "Let's head for the beach."

But we'd only made it to the end of the street and into the Square when, with a squeal of brakes, a Panda car pulled up alongside by the kerb. Two cops got out, a burly middle-aged sergeant and a spotty-faced cadet.

"You stay right there," said the older one, moving toward us. "Don't you bloody move."

Emma and I backed against the wall.

"What's the problem, officer?" I asked, trying to play it cool.

"What's the problem? You're the bloody problem, sunshine." He stood about a foot in front of us, breathing heavily. "Two people fitting your description have been reported trying to steal a loaf of bread from the grocery store."

"She's lying," said Emma defiantly. "We wanted to buy it, but she wouldn't take the money."

"So, you admit you were in there?" said the cadet triumphantly.

"Yes, but we weren't trying to steal anything," I said.

The sergeant shook his head.

"Get in the car," he said. "We'll sort this out down the station."

"We're not going anywhere," I told him, starting to move forward, but the sergeant took me by the shoulders and slammed me back against the wall. Emma cried out and tried to push him away, but the cadet grabbed her from behind, pinning her arms to her side. As she struggled, one of his hands cupped her breast and he gave a smug smile.

"What's going on here then?"

A soldier was standing there, taking in the scene with a quizzical, almost amused air about him. The sergeant twisted his head to give him a contemptuous stare.

"Piss off, squaddie," he grunted. "This is fuck all to do with you."

Dismissively, he turned back to me.

"You can get in that car yourself," he said, "or I can put you in it."

"Oh, I don't think so," said the soldier, and from around the corner he was swiftly joined by a dozen others. The sergeant hesitated, then released me and turned to face them, while Emma still struggled to free herself.

"Look lads," he said, taking a placating tone, "we're just…"

"If you don't get your hands off that girl right now," interrupted one of the soldiers, pointing a finger at the cadet, "I'm going to break your arm off and shove it up your fucking arsehole." Then almost apologetically, "Excuse my French, miss."

The cadet stared at him and then let Emma go. The soldier who'd first appeared, a corporal I noticed, made a sharp upward nod of his head indicating us to move towards them. As we did so, they surged forward and suddenly Emma and I were surrounded by khaki, and it was the cops now backed up against the wall.

"You listen to me," blustered the sergeant, "I'm ordering you to move on here."

The corporal gave an indifferent shake of his head.

"Do you know the first thing the army teaches an officer in cadet school?" he asked. "Never issue a command that you're not one hundred percent certain will be obeyed." He smiled. "Because when it's obvious that you're no longer in control, things can get very nasty, very quickly."

"You want 'em," said another voice, "then come and get 'em."

The corporal and the sergeant stared at each other for a few seconds, and then the corporal turned away.

"Let's go," he said and turning to Emma, "You'd better stick with us for a while."

"Thanks," said Emma, giving him a big smile, and that was the first time it registered how good looking he was. And not the current trendy, long-haired, pretty boy good looks, but in the classical sense - the strong jaw, high cheekbones and even features straight from the cover of every adventure novel that I'd lost myself in since I was eight years old. *Great*, I thought as Emma fell in alongside him, her expression a picture of gratitude.

"So, what was all that about?" he asked as we walked along.

"We'd tried to buy a loaf of bread," said Emma. "The woman in the shop wouldn't sell it to us - and when we argued, she called the police and said we'd tried to steal it."

"Fag mate?" asked the squaddie next to me, offering an open packet of Capstan Full Strength.

"Thanks," I said. He offered one to Emma, and we stopped walking while he lit them for us.

"Because of the way you look?" asked the corporal.

"Yes." I dragged deep on the cigarette. It tasted so good after roll ups.

"We're trying to get a pint," he told us. "In two of the pubs they said there were private functions on tonight, the landlord at the last one suggested we might be more comfortable out in the courtyard."

"We've been cleaning up their bloody beaches all day long," said the squaddie who'd handed out his cigarettes, "but we ain't good enough to sit in their soddin' pubs."

"I'm Kit." I held my hand out to the corporal. "And I haven't thanked you yet, for helping us out back there."

"Paul," said the corporal, and there were handshakes and introductions all round, nicknames along the lines of Dusty, Bonzo and Buzz. The squaddie with the cigarettes was

Torchy, and he asked where we were staying.

"We're at a campsite along the coast," Emma told him. "But we were on our way to meet some friends for a barbecue on the Burrows." She shrugged. "You can't get to it by road and the cops know we can see them coming from half a mile away, so they haven't bothered us there yet."

"We could do that." Torchy gave a shrug and looked at the others. "Get some brews and bangers, head to the beach and build a fire."

Paul nodded.

"Okay."

"Why don't you come with us?" said Emma.

"You sure?" asked Paul

It was a strange moment, everyone aware that two very different worlds were coming together here, except that it seemed completely natural. Other than for that flash of jealousy again – *of course she wants him to come with us.*

* * *

The soldiers might not have been popular in the pubs, but they didn't have any problem getting served in the shop. They came out carrying two crates of beer, packets of sausages, loaves of bread, and we headed off to the Burrows.

The bonfire was enormous and about twenty or thirty people were milling around holding drinks. Some girls were dancing at the water's edge, to a strummed guitar. As we approached, heads turned and the music stopped. I saw Jake stand up and walk toward us, followed by another guy I'd seen at Petroc. I sensed a sudden hesitation by Paul and the other soldiers. So did Emma, because she said, 'It's okay' and strode forward to meet Jake.

"We're late because the cops pulled me and Kit outside the store," she told him, loud enough for the others to hear. "They were giving us a hard time and things were getting really heavy, when these guys came along and stopped it."

"Are you alright?" asked Jake.

Emma nodded and explained what had happened,

while everyone gathered in a circle around us. As she finished, she looked at the soldiers and grinned.

"*'If you want 'em then come and get 'em'*, right? That's what you said?" She laughed and turned back to Jake. "God, you should have seen their faces."

Jake leaned forward and shook Paul's hand.

"Good to meet you," he said and indicating the figure beside him, "this is Aidan."

After shaking hands with Paul, Aidan turned to me. "You're staying at Petroc, right?"

I nodded.

"I'm Kit."

Torchy dropped a crate down onto the sand.

"Anyone for a beer?"

A guitar started up again and a couple of people came over and took a bottle. Paul gestured toward the bonfire.

"Okay if we start cooking?" he asked. "We're famished."

"Sure."

One of the girls who'd been dancing by the water's edge had shimmied her way over to us. As she transitioned from a darkened silhouette against the setting sun to a real-life girl in the light of the fire, Torchy's mouth dropped open in astonishment.

"Strewth!" he said.

She was completely naked. Laughing, she reached out to take the bottle from him and raise it to her lips, still swaying to the music. Then, smiling, she grabbed him by the hand.

"Come and dance."

"I don't know how to."

"Oh, we can fix that."

Paul watched her lead him away, a bemused expression on his face.

"Bloody hell!" he said softly.

13. Aidan

I'm not sure why the young corporal and I gravitated toward each other, but possibly because we'd both noticed the hesitancy with which we each handled the joint that was being passed around. Not that I was averse to trying something I'd heard so much about, only that I'd have preferred a more private venue, first crack out of the box.

"Someone's coming," said Kit, seemingly from some distance away, even though he was sitting alongside me. While puzzling that out, I turned to see two figures walking across the sands toward us.

"It's Claudia," said Emma. "With someone else."

"Claudia?" The name sounded familiar. In fact, I had the sensation of it swirling around in my head and then joining hands with every other thought entering my mind, in a choreography of colour and light.

"Emma's schoolfriend, who we met earlier," said Jake.

"I hardly recognised her," said Emma. "She wasn't *fat* exactly, back then, but she was short and a bit chubby."

"Well, not anymore," said Jake emphatically and, as I watched Emma walk over to hug her, I couldn't help but agree. Claudia was tall and lithe, with curly jet-black hair tumbling over her shoulders and either dark complexioned or well-tanned, it was difficult to tell in this light. I began to push myself upright, a feat surprisingly harder than expected and I decided to rest halfway.

"Hello," said Claudia, looking around, slightly bemused at the mingling soldiers and Beats, before turning to Emma. "Er, this is Lee - she's staying next door to us and," with a slight shrug, "she really wanted to meet you."

Lee held her hand out and when Emma hesitantly took it, pulled her close and gave her a hug.

"Oh wow," said Lee. "This is such a pleasure."

She stepped back and looked right into Emma's eyes.

"When all that shit was going down, you know, about your school and the essay and your grandad, I just thought 'Wow, what an inspiration this girl is'."

"Well, er, thank you," said Emma, somewhat nonplussed. "All a long time ago now, though." She retrieved her hand. "You met Jake earlier, this is Kit and this is Aidan."

Finally upright, I realised how small and slight Lee was. Sitting down and trying not to be obvious about taking advantage of the perspective that position offered, she'd seemed to tower above me, but standing she was only up to my shoulder. I stuck out an unsteady hand. "Nice to meet you," I said.

As we shook hands, one soldier who'd been staring at her moved closer. Then he shook his head in mock disbelief.

"Jenny Henderson," he said slowly. "Jenny... Fucking... Henderson."

Lee smiled and raised her hands in a gesture of surrender.

"Oh," said Emma. "You're an actress?"

Lee nodded. The young soldier bent down and whispered into her ear. As he finished, she laughed and putting her hand on his shoulder, leant forward and kissed him on the cheek. As he backed away smiling, I heard a noise behind me and turned around. The corporal was having as much trouble getting to his feet as I had. He'd arrived at a half crouching position but now seemed frozen, staring at Lee.

"What did he say to you?" Claudia asked Lee.

"That all the time they were posted out in Aden he had a photograph of me, ripped from a magazine and pinned to the wall by his bunk."

"Oh, that's sweet," said Emma.

"And that he used to wank off to it every night."

Emma's mouth dropped open.

"The thing you learn about adulation, darling," Lee said to her with a smile, "is that any is better than none."

The corporal burst into laughter. He stayed down on the ground, his head moving from side to side as he continued shaking with apparent disbelief. Lee reached out and took the joint from me.

"I think this was his first time," I told her.

"Really?" said Lee, raising the joint to her lips. "Bless him."

14. Kit

Emma, Jake and I walked back together from the Burrows, moonlight bright enough to guide us over the hilltop and down into Petroc. I was light-headed from the dope we'd been smoking, but it didn't make the climb seem an exertion and I guessed from the easy silence that we were all of a similar mind.

Although, it seemed with Emma that you could never be really sure what was going through her head.

"They were okay, weren't they?" said Jake eventually, as we approached the campsite. "The soldiers, I mean."

"They were," I nodded.

Emma remained silent.

"Goodnight," I said to them as we reached my chalet.

"See you in the morning, man," said Jake.

"'Night," said Emma.

I watched them walk on for a few seconds and then unlocked my door and went inside.

I hung up my jacket and slipped off my shoes. I was feeling nicely mellow and not ready for sleep at all, but it was too late to be putting the radio on for some music. The chalet walls were almost paper thin.

There was a soft knock at the door.

"Mum and Dad aren't home from Penzance," said Emma, stepping inside, "and I forgot my key." She gave a shrug. "I'm locked out."

We stared at each other and then with her foot she pushed the door shut behind her, clamped her hands around the back of my head and her tongue was pushing into my mouth. Tumbling backward onto the bed we were tearing at each other's clothes, her jumper pulled over her head, her skirt around her waist, my jeans kicked off my ankles and I was rolling across on top of her.

And then hesitated.

"What's the matter?" she asked, breathless.

"I don't have a..." I broke off.

"I'm on the pill," she said, and the next few minutes were fast and savage. She almost screamed when I entered her, muffling the sound by sinking her teeth into my shoulder, releasing them when she sensed my slowing.

"No, it's alright," she gasped. "Don't stop."

I tried to make it last, but I was being grasped tighter than I'd ever been before and it was with a groan I exploded into her.

"It's okay," she said, "it's okay, stay inside me."

I lay there, unable to speak through a succession of quick gasps.

"Although," she added, "you might take a little of your weight on your elbows."

I managed a laugh, but as I raised myself up, I slipped out of her.

"Sorry," I said, rolling over onto my back.

"It's fine," she said, "everything's fine."

The bedclothes had become tangled around us and I pulled them free. It took a second to register that what I thought had been a small dark shadow on the bottom sheet was actually moving with the sheet. That and the tightness...

I turned to her.

"This was your first time?"

She bit her lip and nodded.

"Are you okay?" I shook my head. "I don't understand - your first time but you're on the pill?"

She rose and laid a finger across my mouth to silence me.

"Is this something you want?" she asked, the hint of a

smile playing on her lips.

I knew better than to hesitate - or at least thought I did.

"Yes," I said.

"Then no-one can know." A slight shake of her head. "I don't mean only my parents, I mean *anyone*. Do you understand?"

I nodded.

"No drunken confidences with the boys, no sly innuendos." She was staring hard now, any trace of a smile gone. "Because while this is just between the two of us, you can do anything you want. But if word gets around, it's over."

"Look, Emma, I began..." but she raised her finger to my lips again.

"No questions, no pillow talk, only this - yes or no?"

I nodded again.

"Say it."

I took a breath.

"This is something we do, not something we talk about and we keep it between the two of us. If anyone finds out, it stops."

"Good." Her tone softened. "I will try to explain - it's only... there's stuff I have to go through in my head, first."

"That's okay," I told her thinking, *'You and me both'*.

15. Claudia

Lee and I went down to the Burrows most nights after that. The Beats may have looked like a bunch of scruffs, but most of them - the ones we met, at least - were really interesting, with a slant on life genuinely fresh and unconventional. They'd share battered copies of novels by Herman Hesse or Sartre, and around the campfire you'd hear anything from old English folk songs to Dave Brubeck fingerpicked on a twelve-string guitar. And sometimes an original composition, although I have to admit they were usually quite dire.

At first the soldiers made me nervous, but once we got to know them we realised the occasional rowdiness was born from a camaraderie formed under great pressure. Some of their stories about what it had been like stationed out in Aden were pretty hair-raising, and we guessed we weren't being told the half of it.

And the other thing was, we felt safe with them around. Coincidentally or not, since Kit and Emma's clash with the local police there'd been no repeat instances and I gathered from Jake that before then they'd been almost a daily occurrence.

It was fun getting reacquainted with Emma all over again, even if I sort of resented having to share her with Lee. Who had that trait which I've since noticed in other actors - and a few writers - of attaching themselves to someone they find fascinating until they've absorbed everything of interest and then falling away like... Well, a blood-filled tick comes to mind, but that's just being bitchy. I suppose it is part of their job, but I hadn't really grasped that at the time and occasionally found myself a tad jealous.

Not that Emma couldn't take care of herself. In some ways she'd seemed to have become more worldly, more *purposeful* might be the word I'm searching for - as if she'd set herself a goal in life the rest of us weren't able to discern and deep down was single-mindedly in pursuit of it.

The person who made the greatest impression was Aidan, forever in the background with his sketchbook and obviously so talented. I still have two of his pencil drawings from that time, a study of Lee walking through the surf and the other of Kit curled up asleep by a bonfire. We all knew he was shortly to be on television in a documentary about one of the local artists, and because there was no TV at Petroc I'd been thinking of inviting him and Emma to *Cam Ryr* to watch it.

I was still reflecting on how I might do that when my aunt solved the problem for me.

* * *

It had been a chance remark overheard by Aunt Anne in the greengrocers, between two townswomen discussing the soldiers.

"Charles at the *White Lion* won't even have them in the Snooker Room," one of them had said, "let alone the Lounge."

"Well, if ever they try to get a table at the *Harbour Lights*," the other replied, "Stella tells them they're fully booked for the entire evening."

Aunt Anne had been so incensed by this that she was still shaking at dinner.

"Those boys are working all day long on the beaches," she said, "and really hard too, I've watched them and..."

"Oh, yes?" said Alex with a smile. "Stripped to the waist, muscles rippling as they lift drums of detergent off the lorries."

"Oh, for goodness' sake!" Aunt Anne gave an exasperated shake of the head. "It's not funny Alex. It's the sheer petty-minded snobbishness of these people that really gets my goat - their businesses are being saved from rack and ruin at no cost to themselves, and they won't even serve the lads who are doing it in their pubs and restaurants."

Alex and I were both taken aback by her anger, it was uncharacteristic to say the least. Seeing us both staring at her, she gave a sigh.

"I'm sorry, it's only that I thought I knew these people and now I realise I don't." She bit her lip. "I know the soldiers may be a little rough and ready but... When I came out of the butchers yesterday, there was this old lady struggling with her shopping bags. Two of them went over to see if she needed any help and then said they'd carry them for her. I stood and watched them going off together, laughing and joking and... Oh, I don't know." Aunt Anne lifted her hand to her face, and I realised she was brushing away a tear. "It was just so kind. And the sort of thing one used to see all the time years ago, but hardly ever these days."

Alex reached out and put his hand on her arm. "I'm sorry," he said, "I didn't mean to be facetious."

"I'm not sure I want to stay here any longer." Aunt Anne raised her head and stared at him. "And I'm really not sure that I want to come back again."

"Look - if you feel that strongly," said Alex, "then do something about it."

"What do you mean?"

Alex leant back in his chair.

"Well, you could offer our hospitality, by way of thanks for what they're doing here - an invitation to dinner, perhaps." He shrugged. "I guarantee word of that would go around the town like wildfire."

"And how would we manage that?" Aunt Anne shook her head. "Walk up to them on the beach - for heaven's sake Alex, what on earth would they make of such a thing." She raised her hands. "We don't even know any of them."

"I do."

Both of them turned to stare at me.

I shrugged.

"My friend Emma - you know, who I was at school with?"

Wordlessly, Alex nodded.

"Yes, of course," said Aunt Anne. "And please stop using 'you know' as punctuation, it's very unbecoming."

"I'm sorry, Aunt Anne. Well, the other night Emma was being bothered by some locals. She said that things were getting a bit scary." Stretching the boundaries of truth here, but definitely not breaking them. "Then some soldiers came along and they stood up for her."

"Oh, I'm sure they did," said Alex with that same smile.

"No, it wasn't like that at all." I shook my head. "It's as Aunt Anne says, they can't get served in the pubs or restaurants and so they were just taking a walk down to the seafront. Emma brought them to meet us and we just chatted."

"Us?" asked Alex.

"Me, Lee - and some friends of Emma from the campsite where she's staying."

"And you've become friends with them?"

I nodded.

Alex considered this.

"I'm not exactly sure how I feel about you and Lee spending the evenings in the company of squaddies," he said.

"Well, judging by Emma's experience, I'd say that she's a lot safer than not spending her evenings with them," said Aunt Anne briskly, "but why don't we take this opportunity to create an informed opinion?" She turned to me. "We'll say dinner tomorrow night, dear. And let's invite Don and Lee."

"Actually," I said hesitantly, "could we make it the night after next?" In for a penny, I thought as they both stared at me. "One of our friends, an art student, is on television that evening - in a program featuring a local artist."

"Joyce Kelly?" Alex nodded his head. "Yes, I saw that in the *Radio Times*, there's a feature about her new exhibition on *Pulse* this week."

"That's right," I said. "Aidan - our friend - is at the Slade, and she asked for him to come down and help. He's staying at Petroc, which is how Emma met him. There's no television over there, so I thought perhaps he and Emma could come around after the meal and watch it with us. Just for half an hour."

"Of course," said Alex, turning his head to Anne. "A bit of a bore, if one's on television and one misses it."

Aunt Anne nodded.

"And," she said, "we'll finally get to meet some of these new friends of yours."

16. Aidan

I'd spent the day down by the harbour, sketching the soldiers working on the beach. I noticed it was mostly the civilian volunteers who were soaping down seabirds covered in crude oil, while it was the squaddies hauling around huge drums of detergent.

"Well, you've certainly got a better job than I have today," said a voice behind me. I turned to find the corporal, Paul, standing there. He offered me a cigarette, as we lit up he indicated my sketch pad.

"Are these intended to be studies for paintings," he asked, "or are they finished works by themselves?"

"To be honest, it's mostly about keeping my hand in - one of them might spark a bigger idea or I could come back to them when I'm home and thinking of perhaps doing something in oils. But mostly..."

I shrugged.

"Chops?" he said.

"Sorry?"

"Like a musician - a practise piece?"

"Indeed." I gestured towards another lorry packed with oil drums entering the harbour. "I imagine you'll be glad to be out of here, just for the rest."

He was silent for a few seconds.

"It's possible we'll be gone within the week," he said eventually.

"Really!" My surprise was genuine, this crisis didn't have the feel of something likely to be solved anytime soon.

"There're all kinds of rumours," he said. "None of them

good."

I stared at him, uncertain of what to say.

"The worse is that they could ship us back out to Aden." He shook his head.

"Jesus!"

"The problem is," his voice dropped lower, "not everything was done by the book the last time around." He shrugged. "In a combat zone, things rarely are. But I've a mate out there who's got word to me that a lot of questions are being asked about…"

"Hello!"

He broke off as Claudia and Emma appeared.

"We've been looking for you two," said Claudia.

"Lucky us," said Paul, and perhaps I was the only one who noticed his smile was a little forced.

"More than you realise," Claudia told him.

"Guess," smiled Emma, "who's coming to dinner?"

17. Claudia

We were all sitting in the conservatory when the doorbell rang. Don and Lee had arrived about ten minutes before and Don was teaching Aunt Anne how to mix 'the perfect Martini', explaining it was one of the few experiences that the longer you took to get it right, the more fun you actually had. Even to a teenage girl it had the feel of a well-polished pickup line, but Alex didn't seem to mind - I guessed because her nervous giggles were infinitely preferable to her blue mood of the other evening.

I rose half out of my seat but Lee, already on her feet, headed for the door.

"Don't worry, I'll get it," she said and was gone.

A few seconds later I heard muffled voices coming back down the corridor and then Lee breaking out into laughter. I felt a sudden twang of not jealousy exactly, but...

"A stranger bearing gifts," announced Lee, cutting off my thoughts as she opened the door.

Paul entered the room behind her. I'd been half expecting him to arrive in civvies, which I knew would have disappointed my aunt, but the battledress he wore was in much better repair than anything I'd seen him wearing before, almost starched in appearance. He was carrying a bunch of roses and a bottle.

"Good evening, everyone," he said, an easy smile on his face. "You must be Aunt Anne," holding the flowers out towards her. "Probably best to get these in water quite quickly."

"Oh, they're lovely!" exclaimed Aunt Anne, her expression one of total surprise. "You shouldn't have." She took them from him. "I'll just get a vase and take them through to the dining room."

"Hello, it's Paul, isn't it?" said my uncle, extending his hand. "I'm Alex, Claudia's uncle."

"I'm pleased to meet you, sir," said Paul as they shook, and Alex pooh-poohed him and said there were no formalities here. Paul smiled and handed him the bottle he'd brought.

"I wasn't exactly sure what would go with the meal," he said, "but in my experience, after the coffees you rarely go wrong with a single malt."

"Damn right you don't," said Don, stepping forward and shaking Paul's hand. "Don Mayberry."

He took the bottle from Alex and stared at the label.

"Bloody hell!" he exclaimed. "A Dimple Haig."

"The best the Officers Mess has to offer," said Paul, and gave a slight shrug. "The military term is 'foraged'."

Alex and Don stared at him and then both burst into laughter. Don put an arm around his shoulder and led him over to where he'd been mixing cocktails.

"You know," he said, "You and I are going to get along. Come and try one of my pre-dinner Martinis."

* * *

I think it would be true to say that the evening confounded everyone's expectations, including my own.

"Shall I say grace?" grinned Lee as we sat down at the table.

"That would be lovely dear," said Aunt Anne, intentionally or not delightfully wrong footing her, and we sat with heads bowed as Lee stumbled through thanking the Good Lord for what we were about to receive. That slowed her down, at least for the first course, leaving Aunt Anne and Alex to question Paul about the clean-up operation. Paul remained polite, respectful but in no way deferential - with hindsight I'd call it the manner of someone who had learnt how to make his opinion known from within a structured chain of command. It was noticeable how Alex and Don's attitude changed towards him as the meal progressed.

Aunt Anne and Lee were cleaning the dinner plates away when Alex said that he understood the regiment had been in Aden before coming here.

Paul gave a quiet nod.

"I've heard things were quite dicey out there," said Don.

"However bad you may have been told things were," said Paul, with a softness that actually emphasised his meaning, "they were a lot worse."

Don seemed about to pursue the point, but Alex cut in before he could speak. "What say we crack open that single malt, hey?"

"Absolutely," said Don, turning around to the sideboard to reach for it, and I saw Paul give my uncle a slight nod of the head.

"Claudia told us that the other night you rescued her friend Emma from some local yobbos," said Alex, folding up his napkin and laying it on the table. "What were they, teddy boys or something?"

Paul met my eyes with a smile.

"Something like that," he said.

"Bring back National Service is what I say." Don was shaking his head. "Didn't do me any harm, and that'd sort the young thugs out."

Aunt Anne came back from the kitchen and sat down beside Alex.

"Which service were you in?" Paul asked Don.

"The RAF," said Don. He pronounced it 'Wraf'.

"Were did you serve?" asked Alex.

"Coningsby in Lincolnshire at first and then Berlin." He sighed with theatrical contentment. "A lot less bloody dangerous than RADA, I can tell you."

We all laughed.

"What mob were you in?" he asked Alex.

"Oh, Alex isn't allowed to talk about his war service,"

said Aunt Anne, rolling her eyes. The theatrics were certainly catching on this evening. "All very hush-hush."

Alex gave a self-deprecating shake of his head. "I can assure you it was nowhere near as dramatic as that might imply." He shrugged. "But technically, it is still covered by the Official Secrets Act, so..."

"Oh my God!" Lee had her hand to her mouth. "You were a spy."

Aunt Anne burst out laughing and rested her hand on Alex's arm. "I'm sorry, dear," she said to him and turned to Lee, shaking her head. "I'm afraid no one will ever be torturing Alex for his secrets."

"Don't you be so sure of that," smiled Alex good naturedly. Then he grew serious and stared across the table at Paul.

"Look, I know that you've not had the warmest of welcomes in this town," he said, "but believe me, that's only a noisy minority. The rest of us thank you, not just for what you're doing here but for all of your service - we understand the sacrifices which come with that." He lifted his glass a few inches from the table, tilted it towards Paul and then drained it. It seemed to strike the perfect note, an easy acknowledgement rather than a formal toast.

"Well, thank you," said Paul. "And for your hospitality." Then he smiled and gave an almost apologetic shrug. "But you know, we're really used to things *much* worse than this."

"Oh, I can imagine," said Don, leaning back in his chair. "How does it go?" And closing his eyes, he let the words roll off his tongue with an actor's cadence.

"For it's Tommy this and Tommy that and 'Tommy wait outside',

But it's 'thin red line of heroes' when the troopship's on the tide."

"Ah," smiled Alex. "Kipling."

"Not very fashionable these days," Don opened his eyes, "but you have to admit the man knew how to make a point."

"Indeed," said Alex, and turned back to Paul.

"How long have you been in the army?" he asked him.

"Three years," said Paul.

"You must have been very young when you joined," said Anne.

"I was sixteen," Paul told her, and she shook her head slowly.

"Is military service a family tradition?" asked Alex, slightly hesitantly because, of course, that was what had become the elephant in the room. I think what Alex, Don and Aunt Anne were all wondering was why, from his manner and demeanour, wasn't this a young First Lieutenant or even a Captain who they were entertaining tonight and if not, why not?

None of them were snobs - well, not by the standards of the day - but this encounter was definitely not what they'd been expecting, not by a long shot. So, *'What,'* we all knew was Alex's real question, *'is your story?'*

And then the doorbell rang.

18. Kit

"Could I tempt you with the offer of a drink?" asked Aidan, as we arrived on the outskirts of the town. "Seems a pity to waste the opportunity."

I knew what he meant - in deference to Claudia's family, all three of us had smartened ourselves up a bit and so could probably slip under the *'No Beatniks'* radar most pubs operated. The most stringent of those was at *The Barque,* down by the harbour, and so it was in for a penny, in for a pound as we stepped inside the door. But tonight, as we made our way through the lounge and up to the bar, we didn't even raise a second glance.

"Claudia won't mind," Emma had said, as we'd disentangled ourselves from each other late that afternoon. "And she's hardly likely to turn you away from her door, especially if you arrive with me and Aidan."

After all the talk of the TV program, I'd been if not eager then curious to watch it but finding somewhere to do so was proving surprisingly difficult. Few, if any, of the pubs had TV sets in the bar and Petroc certainly took the view that you weren't down in Cornwall to spend all your time in front of the goggle box.

"You're not worried that...?" I'd let my voice trail off and Emma had shrugged, a complicated gesture with both hands behind her, fastening her bra. Is a woman ever as desirable as when she's slowly getting dressed after sex, the urge to reach out and pull her back down is almost irresistible?

"You were interested, I offered to bring you along - nothing unusual about that is there?" she'd said and that had been that.

"So how did you and Claudia become friends?" Aidan asked Emma as we settled ourselves down at a table. "I know you were at school together an' all but it strikes me you're an odd match, if you'll forgive my saying so."

"I suppose we were both outsiders at St Catherine's, in our different ways," said Emma. "I was a scholarship girl and while you didn't exactly get looked down on..." She hesitated. "People were cautious about becoming friends - probably because they worried about putting you in a position where you might be embarrassed at not being able to afford to mix with them socially."

"I think we have different definitions of what construes 'not getting looked down on'," said Aidan dryly.

"No, a lot of the girls had very extravagant lifestyles," Emma told him. "Off to country estates at the weekend, flying away to the South of France for holidays. Trying to fit in with any of that would have been uncomfortable, to say the least."

"And would that have been the crucible of your radicalism?" smiled Aidan, mocking but not in an unkindly fashion.

"Jesus, of course not." With faux perplexity, she slowly shook her head. "You have met my family, right?"

"I have that," Aidan grinned.

"No," she continued. "And most of the girls were actually very nice. Just..."

She gave a shrug.

"Misguided?" I suggested.

"Yes," she said, fixing me with a stare. "As are many people."

"And Claudia?" prompted Aidan.

"Well, she arrived at St Catherine's midway through the year, which is never easy - all the little cliques and coteries have become established by then. Her parents were in the middle of a divorce and I gathered that her mother was taking that very badly. But, for whatever reason, she used to stay on at school every day to do her homework in the library and so did I, it could be a bit of a madhouse at home. So that's how we got to know each other."

"Just at school?" I asked.

"No, her mother was involved with a lot of charities, mainly to do with the arts - homes for retired actors, that sort of thing. She'd be sent complimentary tickets for events and exhibitions, which she didn't have much interest in going to, and so Claudia and I went instead." Emma took a sip of her drink. "That's really how we became friends."

"I get the impression that the family's very well to do," said Aidan.

"I never actually visited her at home," said Emma "but I know it was one of those mansion block apartments behind Oxford Street."

"Bloody hell," said Aidan. "They're not exactly ten-a-penny, are they."

"Didn't you think it odd that she never invited you around there?" I asked.

"Not really - like I said, I got the impression things weren't that good at home." She shrugged. "If she was delaying going back there herself after school, then she wasn't likely to be inviting visitors along. To be honest, she seemed to be a lot closer to her aunt and uncle."

"And that's who she's down here with?" I asked Emma, and she nodded. "And what do they do?"

"Alex is in the Civil Service, which branch I'm not sure. When Claudia first came back from Rome, she'd stay with him during the week - over in Chelsea, I think it was."

"During the week?"

"They had a house down in Kent, where they'd go for the weekend."

"I'd guess they're not short of a few bob, either," said Aidan. "When you throw a Cornish holiday home into the mix."

"Claudia's alright," said Emma, with that sudden flash

of the eyes I was finding myself getting entranced by. "I don't think life has been as straightforward for her as you might assume, and she's certainly not the kind of person that it would have been really easy for her to become."

"It's okay," said Aidan softly. "I think she's alright too."

He drained his glass.

"We should probably get going," he said. "I'd hate to miss myself."

19. Claudia

I made the introductions and Kit helped Alex carry some extra chairs through into the sitting room. Alex then had to fiddle with the TV set to adjust the picture. I remembered that we sometimes had a problem with the signal here, but a blizzard of static on the screen was quickly replaced by the announcer.

"Would you switch off the lights, Claudia?" asked Alex, and we settled down to watch the program.

I found myself more engrossed than I'd expected to be. I knew nothing about Joyce Kelly, but the first five minutes were a recap of her work over the last thirty years, snippets from old interviews being played over photographs and film of her paintings and sculptures. It was cleverly done, I thought, creating both an introduction for the casual viewer like me and a testament of sorts for her aficionados.

The next section began with her walking with Anthony, the presenter, through the current exhibition. She explained the inspiration for some of her pieces and the techniques she'd had to develop to realise her changing artistic vision. At one point a young girl and Aidan moved across the background, carrying a large painting between them, and she turned to Anthony.

"Young people are very important to me," she said. "Particularly art students - I try to encourage as much as possible, while listening to what they have to say. After all, they are the future."

A brief interview with the girl, an art student named Fiona, followed. She explained how she'd always wanted to paint and had long been inspired by Joyce's work, first encountering it on a childhood trip to St Hannahs with her parents. She was now at Plymouth College of Art and working with Joyce, bringing her latest work to public view, was both an honour and a dream come true.

The film cut to Anthony, standing alone outside the gallery.

"Another student helping Joyce with her current exhibition is nineteen-year-old Aidan McShane. Originally from Dublin, Aidan is now studying at the Slade in London under the tutelage of Frank Bishop, one of this country's most distinguished postwar artists. And Aidan, Frank assures me, is the most outstanding talent he's encountered throughout his entire twenty-year tenure."

The screen cut to the inside of a pub. Aidan was sitting at a table, smoking a cigarette with a pint glass in front of him.

"First, I have to ask," Anthony off camera, "do you come from an artistic background."

"No, not at all." Smiling, Aidan gave a shake of his head. "Although my aunt was a gifted amateur artist, and she gave me my first set of watercolours."

"You won the Caltex, I believe, Ireland's national art competition for children."

"I did, which helped to convince my family that I possessed enough talent to make a career in the arts a realistic goal." He shrugged. "If not for that, I'd probably have been taken into the family business."

"Which is?"

Aidan looked into the camera and gave a soft smile.

"Oh," he said, "we're butchers."

For a while they discussed the artists who had influenced Aidan the most – none of whom I'd ever heard of - when Anthony's tone seemed to shift.

"Frank tells me," he said, "that you're working on a series of pieces depicting biblical scenes transposed to Ireland during the Troubles. I have to say that surprises me."

"Really? It's not that unusual - Renaissance artists frequently depicted both old and new testament events in a contemporary setting. In the Rijksmuseum, they must have..."

"What I meant," interrupted Anthony, "is using religion as a subject at all, when its grip on society seems to be rapidly loosening."

"Well, not in Ireland it isn't." Aidan took a sip of his drink. "Although, that's probably down to the grip being mainly around the throat."

"What I think I'm trying to say," Anthony gave the appearance of choosing his words carefully, "is that while many people I know do experience a spiritual longing, they no longer feel that organised religion can satisfy that need. In fact, a lot of them are turning toward the spirituality of the East, rather than the dogma of Rome. Could it be that perhaps one is out of step with the times here?"

"If what *one* is trying to create with *one's* work," said Aidan, with equal care and a definite sardonic edge, "is emotional resonance, then while *dogma*," his emphasis on the word was pointed, "that's been imprinted throughout childhood - and then hung as a backcloth to the unfolding dramas of life thereafter - might not be fashionable right now, it nevertheless does persist as a tangible entity."

He drew on his cigarette and exhaled slowly.

"Which, I'd suggest, is more than *one* could say for vacuous twaddle cobbled together from half-baked notions of eastern mysticism."

Anthony's chuckle was off camera. There was further... good natured banter I suppose you'd call it, rather than an argument, about what the artist's role should actually be. And all of it way over my head, so much so that my mind began to wander a little.

But then, a sudden sharpness in Aidan's tone brought me back again.

"No matter if you're a painter or a musician or a writer,"

Aidan was saying, leaning forward and his eyes intense, "and whether genius is something possessed or something channelled, I don't think there can be any dispute that it's fleeting - right?"

Anthony acknowledged Aidan's point with a nod and a smile.

"It's here and then it's gone and all that's left behind may be a few novels or a stack of canvasses or a collection of shellac 78s. And it's odds on that - the essence of genius implying that it's going to be ahead of its time - no-one has a clue what you've been all about. Not the wife you've driven crazy with your obsessions or the manager in despair that you've given him nothing remotely commercial and certainly not a public who have no idea what they need, while being adamant about what they like."

Aidan sat back, picked up his glass and seemed to study it.

"But," he continued, "if you're lucky enough to keep on hanging in there, then things just might turn around. Twenty, thirty years down the line who knows, people might even start to get it. Not the wife, she's long gone and wouldn't have cared anymore anyway, and you've lost count of how many managers you've driven to despair. But the fickleness of the public will never let you down."

The camera cut to Anthony, smiling but silent.

"And here's the thing of it, Anthony - if you're a novelist, you'll never need to write another sentence to finally reap your just rewards. The royalties from those twenty-year-old tomes - from which you probably can't recall a single word you wrote - will begin rolling in. As a musician, even if you were robbed blind by the record company back then and which of them wasn't, there'll be a new deal to be cut and you'll find yourself on stage again."

"But an artist." Aidan shook his head. "Do you know how many artists traded their best work for a bloody meal? Or a bed for the night? And that's it, once that painting's gone, then it's gone for good. No royalty cheques for Modigliani or Vincent, little in the way of acclaim and barely a residue of morbid curiosity whether it'll be the absinthe or syphilis which puts them into the ground first."

"It's not an original observation that the public can't recognise genius in its own lifetime," Anthony's voice off camera.

"That's not what I'm saying." With his thumb, Aidan flicked open the top of a packet of Players, slowly slid out a cigarette and tapped the end on the tabletop.

"Sorry?" Anthony still off camera.

"The public *never* recognises genius." Aidan stuck the cigarette into the corner of his mouth and lit it. "Genius for them is no more than an article of faith," he blew a smoke ring, "and one which they're gathered in droves to worship by shepherds like you."

The camera was back on Anthony, who stared for a few seconds and then shook his head with a wry smile.

The camera cut to a small gallery, but rather than being hung on the wall, the paintings were lined up along the floor against it, resting back at an angle as the camera slowly panned across them. Even on a small black-and-white TV screen, most of the images were very striking.

"Back at the Slade," Anthony's voice-over, "it's hard to disagree with Frank Bishop's assessment. While Aidan's work has the power to outrage, there's rarely the feeling that shock is the prime aim here, rather one simply senses artistic vision unleashed."

The camera stopped at the canvas of an old man, sitting in an armchair at some kind of social gathering - surrounded by merriment it seemed at first that the subject was sleeping. But then, as your eyes took in all the painting, you caught the expression of a woman entering the room - perhaps his wife - and the scene took on a much more sombre tone. It was a remarkably compelling piece, and I was aware of everyone staring at it.

"Those of us growing fearful of the vacuum seeming to form behind the emergence of talents such as Francis Bacon and Lucien Freud, can perhaps rest easy again. And while the name Aidan McShane may not yet be mentioned in such illustrious company, one has the sense that time may not be far off."

The screen cut to the credits.

20. Aidan

Of course the whole thing was as elaborate a confection as a six-tier wedding cake. Essentially, Tony had taken me off down to the pub where we'd tanked up on Guinness whilst putting the world to rights, any notion of a formal interview evaporating after the first pint.

I'd assumed that Tony, having gotten the footage he'd needed of Joyce and the Gallery, was just winding down at the end of an assignment, and that Frank's expectations of any interest in me or my work had been overambitious.

"We'll let the camera roll and I'll stitch something together back in London," Tony told me as we sat down in the bar, creating the impression that I might get a two-minute segment tacked on at the end. Which just goes to show my naivety in those days. You wouldn't think you'd need to explain to an artist that context was as equally important as content, but this was my first outing in the media and it was a lesson I never forgot.

At my Tate retrospective a while back, they had that *Pulse* interview on a continuous loop in a side room. When I saw what they were doing, I contacted the BBC to see if they had Tony's original footage which, I figured, would make far more insightful viewing. But if it did still exist, they couldn't find it. The researcher I spoke to told me that lots of producers squirrelled stuff away when they left the Beeb, optimistic for a golden pension pot but then - as in Tony's case - pegging out before the nostalgia gravy train came pulling into the station. Apparently, Bob Dylan in a *Wednesday Play* is probably decomposing in someone's garden shed.

When you watch the interview, the real giveaway is that you rarely see Tony ask a question on camera. There are reaction shots aplenty, those I recall were done in a five-minute session afterwards, where he pantomimed various degrees of surprise, thoughtfulness, disbelief, amusement and acquiescence, until the producer said 'Yeah, okay Tony, we're pretty much covered now'.

At the time it seemed a bit overkill, but watching the dissected, re-cut and then reassembled version is to understand that these snippets are the glue holding in place a seamless mosaic. The part about emotional resonance had nothing to do with Catholic dogma but was me speaking of my childhood, and the eastern mysticism comments had been a reflection on the vapidity of current London trends. So, he'd stitched together two unrelated statements to create an answer to a question I'd never been asked.

Which is why, two minutes into watching the interview, I found myself with as little idea as anyone else in the room what the fella on the screen doing all the talking was about to say next. I was also growing conscious of the curious sideways glances in my direction, especially disconcerting because I had no idea where Tony Dryden was going with this. But what I was really waiting for was the piece where I'd spoken about the artist rarely receiving his full due.

Because it had been spurred by Tony launching an all-out attack on Joyce's ceramic works, comparing her quite literally to some *Ye Olde Gift Shoppe* owner, using her reputation to peddle bric-à-brac for financial security. I wasn't having any of it and that was the only time the discussion got heated. And, although I'd been defending Joyce, I'd just seen enough on screen to understand how my words could be turned inside out to serve Tony Dryden's agenda.

But he'd cut it. He led into my lamenting the artist's lot with a comment along the lines of *'Do the public ever really respond to raw artistic vision'* and then tagged on my diatribe as a response to that.

I've never been able to quantify my feelings during the last sixty seconds of the program, where he reviewed some of my latest pieces. I suppose it should have been relief or elation or surprise, but because we'd arrived at what was obviously a career defining moment through such a weird, tortuous route, I recall nothing other than a strange numbness. I remember Claudia turning the lights back on, Kit slowly shaking his head and smiling while Lee almost skipped up to me, said, 'Oh wow!' and planted a kiss on my cheek.

The actor, Don, came over and with a smile shook my hand and began telling me he was a collector, only in a small way but he'd been looking to acquire pieces from fresh new talent and that he'd love to come and see some of my work when we were back in London. But the figure who really had my attention, albeit at the edge of my peripheral vision, was Claudia's uncle Alex.

There's a certain English stereotype which we're all familiar with - languid, self-deprecating and with a sense of innate decency that will always triumph over adversity. It plays well in the pages of fiction or on a cinema screen, but anyone with an Amritsar or Croke Park in their DNA needs nothing about velvet gloves and iron fists explained to them. When the colonial bully boys are wading through the crowds with billy clubs or chambering the next round, these are the characters sending in reinforcements or back at the embassy encoding a telegram that the situation's now in hand.

Alex was in his late forties I guessed, still boyish looking, medium height and with a lean build. Sandy haired - probably cut by the same Jermyn Street barber for the last twenty years - and the absence of a tie was about as casual as he was ever likely to get. A civil servant, Claudia had said, but didn't that cover a multitude of sins.

"Well done," he said to me, offering his hand. "That's quite a favour he did you there."

He had a smile on his face, but there was an uncertainty about it.

"Thanks," I said, careful to look him in the eye.

"You're from Dublin?" he asked, as we shook hands.

I nodded, but before he could say anything further Don asked if anyone would like a drink. I just wanted to be out of there, for a variety of reasons and not least to collect my thoughts, and so was glad when Emma and Kit shook their heads, saying that we had to be going.

"Thank you for your hospitality," Emma said to Claudia's aunt. There were smiles all around and then thankfully we were on the street outside, with the door closed behind us.

21. Claudia

"I'm afraid I need to be going too," said Paul, glancing at his watch.

"Time for another, surely?" said Don.

"Eleven o'clock curfew," Paul told him, and rose from his chair.

"One more," said Don, "and I'll run you back."

"I'll keep you company," said Alex.

"If we make it a quick one," smiled Paul.

"And it's time Claudia was in bed too," said Aunt Anne, and I blushed as I felt one of the very few flashes of annoyance I'd ever had toward her - treating me like a child in front of Paul who I...

Who I what?

My thoughts, doubtless confused by the wine, which I really wasn't used to all, seem to tumble around in my head but it was Lee who, intentionally or not, now spared my embarrassment.

"It's past my bedtime too," she said, standing up. "Thank you Alex and thank you Anne, it's been a lovely evening."

She gave each of them a peck on the cheek, more daughterly than showbizzy I have to admit, and with a casual "See you in the morning" wave to Don was gone.

"Goodnight everyone," I said, and with deliberate intent made my way to the door, before finding myself caught up in a flurry of hugs and kisses which, I was sure, would reveal my inner confusion when it came to Paul's turn.

"Goodnight dear," came Anne's voice, as I shut the door

behind me.

* * *

Up in my room I discovered exactly how unused I was to drinking wine. Every time I lay back and closed my eyes the room span around and around, and so I sat up and read for a while. After half an hour or so I felt a little better, but then the other effect of too much wine manifested itself and so I put on my dressing gown and made my way downstairs to the lavatory.

Walking back to the staircase, I heard voices coming from the dining room. Alex must have returned, I thought, and wondering if Don had come back with him - Aunt Anne rarely stayed up late - I stood outside the door and listened.

At first, I could only make out low muffled conversation, but then Aunt Anne - *wrong again, Claudia* - raised her voice.

"Is that what he told you?" she asked, sounding upset.

"No," said Alex, and for some reason the sound was a lot clearer now. "He doesn't know. None of them do."

"But when?"

"As soon as they've finished here. Perhaps as early as next week." There was a slight pause. "There's talk of bringing in American troops to take over the clean-up operation - they've already offered."

"Americans?"

"A goodwill gesture." From his tone, I could picture Alex's expression of distaste. "And presumably an assumption that newsreels of GIs cleaning up Cornish beaches will provide at least some counterpoint to what we're seeing coming out of Saigon."

"You're certain?"

"About Aden? Yes." The sound of a glass being filled. "And from what I gather, things are likely to be much worse than they were on their last posting." His voice suddenly sounded closer. "I'm going to get some ice from the kitchen."

I shot along the hallway in my bare feet and turned onto

the staircase, hopefully out of sight. I waited until I heard the kitchen door open and then climbed up to my room. It wasn't until I closed the door behind me I realised I'd been holding my breath and exhaled slowly.

It didn't have much of a calming effect.

Paul and all the others being sent back to Aden was terrible news. But - and this really was a huge but - how was it that no-one else knew about it except my uncle?

22. Aidan

The reason I always gave for staying on in St Hannahs after the opening of Joyce's exhibition, was that I wanted to work on the Cradle of Thorns paintings with no distractions, and in its way that was true enough. I'd called home a few days after the *Pulse* interview and my aunt told me that the phone hadn't stopped ringing, friends wishing me well and journalists wanting to speak to me. It was the latter which gave cause for concern, I could do without the press digging into my background and I guessed that went double for my family. Give it a week or two, I reassured myself, and they'll have moved on to someone else.

As for *Cradle of Thorns*, it had been less a definite project than a concept I'd bandied about whilst having a few drinks with Frank down the pub. So, suddenly finding it under the national gaze gave it a substance it didn't really warrant, but staying on in Cornwall needed a justification and that seemed as good as any.

And, as with any project which you've had bubbling away on the back burner for a while, you discover that when it becomes the focus of your attention again, it's actually a lot more fully formed than you realised. Most of the biblical scenarios found natural counterparts in the Troubles, and I sketched out most of the themes in a couple of days. Using the people who were around me at the time as models was born of necessity, I needed bodies and I needed faces and there they were. But what that gave me was a technique for figure study that's lasted a lifetime.

Guerrilla portraiture, some critic dubbed it back then,

and it was an expression which seemed to stick, if only because it bestowed a sense of excitement onto a fairly mundane process. The customary practice of having your subject sitting immobile in your studio for hours on end, while you made small talk masquerading as insightful character exploration, had always struck me as absurd and - in this day and age - also archaic, so I tried something a tad different.

The technique of following someone about their daily business – 'shadowing' I believe is the expression these days - while shooting off a couple of rolls of 35mm film and filling an A4 cartridge pad with thumbnail sketches, had been in my mind for a while. The combination of the two, I was convinced, would give me everything I needed back in the studio.

I was also careful not to let anyone know which role I intended for them. In truth, for most studies I would wait until I got back to the studio and see what shook out. But not all - Don Mayberry assumed he'd have the Christ role, but I'd had him pegged for Pontius Pilate. He was way too imperious for a crown of thorns. It was Kit who I thought could embody that. He had a way about him of being physically unassuming and yet your eye was always drawn to him. A challenge to capture on canvas but if I could pull it off, I believed it would work well. I had toyed with using Lee. That androgynous quality she projected would make a striking figure, but the project was likely to prove controversial by its concept alone - particularly when now heralded by the *Pulse* interview - without the addition of gender ambiguity.

And using her for all the central female characters became contentious enough. But it's not a decision I regret. If you didn't know that she was the model for both Mary Magdalene *and* the Virgin Mary, it's doubtful you'd spot it, but once you did you'd wonder how you'd missed it. And the same with all the other roles I cast her in - I always took satisfaction in pre-empting Hollywood with her on that score.

My initial subjects were Don and Lee, they were spending a lot of time rehearsing together, so it was two birds with one stone. I sat in the corner clicking away as they worked through the script, fascinated as they slipped in and out of character, first enacting a scene and then pausing to analyse it.

"Not spoiling the magic, are we?" asked Don dryly, after a couple of hours. He'd meant it as a joke - at least I think he did - but as someone who destroyed his preparatory sketches after finishing a composition, I took his point. I made some comment about it being always rewarding to study people doing what they did best and then - deciding I now had everything I needed - thanked them and said I'd be on my way.

"We could do with a break ourselves, I fancy," said Don, and Lee nodded. "Care for a spot of lunch?"

* * *

Don slipped on a pair of Ray Bans for the walk down to the restaurant.

I'd always assumed celebrities wearing sunglasses was an affectation, it being ludicrous that alone would spare them recognition. But walking through the streets alongside him brought the realisation that wasn't the purpose at all - their function was to prevent eye contact, the initial precursor to unwelcome attention.

Don was obviously a regular now at the restaurant and the owner shepherded us to a table on a terrace overlooking the harbour. The only other diners were a middle-aged couple seated at the far end. As I recall, we talked mainly about art, Don had two recent acquisitions he thought I might like to take a look at - an early Francis Bacon and a John Minton self-portrait. And to his credit, in my eyes anyway, he explained that he'd bought them less as an investment than for memories of times spent in a Soho drinking den, where both men had shown a broke drama student more small kindnesses than they had any reason to, or their reputations belied.

The meal passed quickly. I was constantly aware that the couple we were sharing the terrace with had not only recognised Don but were obviously dying to speak. As we finished dessert the husband, doubtless seeing this opportunity about to disappear forever, finally summoned the courage to come over, brandishing the menu and a ballpoint pen.

"I only wanted to say," he smiled, "how much Joan and I enjoy your television series. We think you're such a talented actor."

Over the years I was to learn that actors and women seldom receive a compliment they can't perceive at least a grain of truth in.

"Why thank you," said Don magnanimously, reaching out for the pen. "Are you on holiday here?"

"No," the man told him. "My good lady wife and I have lived here all our lives."

"Well, it's a beautiful part of the world," said Don, scribbling away. "I always think that..."

He broke off as a raucous peal of female laughter came from further along the terrace. A party of half a dozen or so women were being seated at a large table, but I had the impression, from their noisy confidence, that they'd been inside at the bar for a while. One of them, I realised, was Joyce Kelly and I also noticed that over on the other table the good lady wife had pursed her lips distastefully and pointedly turned her head away.

Her husband, conspiratorially, leant down to us.

"Lesbians," he whispered.

"Golly," said Lee breezily, and turned to Don with a bright smile. "What are lesbians, Daddy?"

The man blushed scarlet. "I'm sorry, I..."

He grabbed his pen and menu and almost stumbled away from the table.

"You," whispered Don, "are incorrigible."

The couple rapidly gathered their belongings and left.

"Would you like another drink?" asked Don.

I shook my head.

"I'm fine," I told him, but then became aware of Don and Lee staring over my shoulder. I turned to see Joyce Kelly standing there.

"Hello," she said dryly. "I just wanted to say how much I enjoyed your show the other night."

I hesitated.

"I honestly didn't..." I began, but she cut me off with a shake of her head.

"Don't worry - I've known Tony Dryden long enough to understand that no-one gets a free ride where he's concerned." She paused. "I also have friends at the BBC," she said carefully, "and I know what was left unsaid in that transmission." She hesitated again. "So, thank you for that, Aidan."

"Would you like to join us?" asked Don, indicating a seat and I sensed something passing between them, doubtless some subtle exchange only intelligible within the freemasonry of fame.

But Joyce shook her head.

"I'm with friends," she told him, "and I wouldn't want to intrude. But thank you."

She turned back to me again.

"I think life might get very hectic for you over the next few years," she said. "But should you ever need a bolt-hole, you're always welcome in St Hannahs."

"I may well take you up on that," I told her.

"Good luck, Aidan," she smiled and returned to her friends. Both Don and Lee were looking at me quizzically.

"You had to be there," I said.

23. Kit

It took a second to register Paul. This was the first time I'd seen him out of uniform, it was surprising how jeans and a sweatshirt played with the mind's preconceptions.

"Hello," he said. "Do you have a minute?"

"Sure," I told him, standing aside to let him pass by me into the chalet and closing the door behind us.

"Coffee?" I asked, and he nodded. I indicated for him to sit in the only armchair and then I filled the kettle, lit the stove and sat down on the edge of the bed.

"What can I do for you?" I asked, aware of his uncharacteristic hesitancy.

"I gather," he said softly, "that you might be the person to talk to about how to disappear."

"Disappear?"

Paul seemed to consider.

"It seems likely," he said, "we're about to be sent back to Aden. You're better off not knowing who told me that, but I believe them." He paused again. "I can't go back there - in fact, I probably can't even stay here for much longer."

"You're going AWOL?"

He nodded.

"And I could use some advice on how best to do that."

He had, I guessed, been talking to Emma or more likely Claudia, who always seemed to be gazing at him with doe-eyed devotion whenever the two of them were around each other. In bits and pieces, Emma had wheedled out of me the life that I'd been living over the last couple of years, and probably hadn't been shy about sharing it during girly heart to hearts, if glossing over the circumstances by which she'd gained it.

"Will they be coming after you?" I asked and when he hesitated, "There's a difference between living under the radar and being hunted."

"Yes," he said. "They will."

I was tempted to pry but figured that if he intended to tell me, then he would and if not, it probably was genuinely one of those 'best if you don't know' situations. Real ignorance or surprise is hard to fake under questioning.

"So, you need to become someone else," I told him, "rather than yourself on the run."

"So, what's the easiest way to…?" he began but broke off when I stood up and walked over to the wardrobe. I rummaged around in my holdall until I found what I was looking for and sat back down on the bed.

"He's serving five years in a Dutch jail, on drug charges," I said, handing him Baz's passport, "but it should pass - I doubt the name's on any international watch list."

Paul flicked the passport open.

"Thanks," he said. "I appreciate this. But it doesn't really look much like me."

"Not yet," I told him. "I need to pop out for a minute."

* * *

I outlined the situation to Aidan as we walked across the campsite to my chalet.

"Good morning," he greeted Paul brightly, holding out his hand for the passport.

He studied it carefully, his eyes flicking back and forth to Paul.

"The photograph's not a problem," he said eventually. "I've a Polaroid camera with me but we will need to change the entries for eye colour and height, which can be fiddly - you only get one shot at getting it right."

"How soon," I asked, "are you planning on leaving?"

"I think," Paul said, "I may have a lift to London in a

couple of days. I don't want to leave it any later than that."

"Is this to do with what we were talking about down at the harbour?" asked Aidan. "About what happened when you were serving abroad?"

Paul nodded.

"Do you have anywhere to stay in London?" I asked. "And what about money?"

"Maybe the first night or two," he said. "And I've been taking my savings out of the Post Office over the last few weeks – around three hundred."

"It's more than enough to set you up," I told him. "Look for a bedsit in West London - Earls Court or South Kensington, they're transient areas which means very few nosey parker neighbours. Stay smartly dressed when you're out and about. There's casual work in pubs and restaurants, who won't ask for a National Insurance card."

I spoke for about ten minutes, where to go, what to avoid, last resort places to spend the night like the *Daily Express* and all-nighters, essentially the ABC of keeping your head down in a big city.

"I can't tell you both," Paul said eventually, "how much I appreciate this."

"I won't ask what your trouble is," said Aidan, "because that's your business and I'm glad to help. But one thing I'm curious about is how you ever ended up a squaddie. No disrespect," he raised a hand, "but you strike me as being cut out for more than that."

Paul smiled.

"How long do you have?"

"Oh, we're not going anywhere," said Aidan.

24. Aidan

This wasn't idle curiosity. If anyone could help Paul disappear in London, then it was me - or rather my family. They'd been spiriting away wanted men for decades and had it off to a fine art, either hidden in plain sight throughout the metropolis or off out of the country, beyond the reach of colonialist retribution. But the fly in the ointment here was that by no stretch of historical circumstance had a single one of them been a member of Her Majesty's armed forces.

So, you might say that it was a loophole I was looking for here. And maybe something of a miracle.

* * *

Laying out your life for strangers is rarely a coherent process, hows and whys long tendrils tightly gripping distant when and wheres.

One thing which Paul and I had in common was that we never knew our fathers - Paul's had been a Major in the British army and seconded to the King's African Rifles. In 1952, at the outbreak of the Mau Mau uprising in Kenya, he'd been one of the first officers killed.

A war widow's pension didn't amount to much back then, and Paul's mother received little by way of support or consolation from her husband's family. They'd always believed he'd married beneath him and channelled that resentment into excluding her - and their grandson - from their grief.

She quickly remarried, more - Paul, in retrospect, believed - for financial security than love. Moving from London to Nottingham, Paul found his new home dark and dismal.

His stepfather was a cold, indifferent figure, at least until Paul's stepbrother and stepsister arrived, emphasising how little emotional attachment he had to raising another man's child.

"About the only place I was doing well was at school," Paul told us. "One teacher had taken me under his wing - I think he had an idea of what things were like at home. After the eleven plus, I was awarded a scholarship to the Blue Coat School."

He paused.

"My stepfather wouldn't let me go. He said that we couldn't afford it, bus fares across the city, the uniform, but..." He shrugged. "So, I started at the local secondary modern." A wry smile. "And fell in with the wrong crowd - all that rage, resentment and teenage hormones were a heady mix. And eventually it all went bad." He shook his head slowly. "Really bad. I'll spare you the details - and me the embarrassment - of exactly what happened, but I found myself in juvenile court. Where my old schoolteacher turned up to speak for me - no-one else did - and so they offered me a choice. Two years in Borstal or enlist in the army."

"Jesus," said Kit.

"I'd emphasise," said Paul, "this wasn't a unique situation. Getting rid of National Service created something of a recruitment problem for the forces."

"And the local juvenile courts are doing their bit, are they?" asked Kit dryly

Paul shook his head.

"The thing is," he said, "if I'd taken the two years, I'd be a free man now. With none of this shit in my life."

"What happened in Aden...?" Kit began, but Paul cut him off.

"It's not that I don't trust you," he said. "Either of you. But if you knew and were ever to let it slip, there's a chance they could have you under the Defence of the Realm Act."

"They?" asked Kit.

"That's right," I said, exchanging glances with Paul. "Them."

25. Claudia

I thought long and hard about telling Paul what I'd overheard that night of the dinner party. But it wasn't as if this were information entrusted to me, a trust which I'd be betraying. And I could only assume that if Alex knew about it - presumably from his contacts in Westminster - then how much of a secret was it likely to be?

I found him down at the harbour. A new scheme to protect the beach involved floating a large boom across the harbour mouth, made of some chemical composition intended to both absorb the oil and create a barrier. This had been the lead story on the local TV news the previous night, and a sizeable crowd had gathered to watch. The boom comprised of several sections, which were being unloaded from lorries and joined together on the beach. When that was completed, presumably it would be floated out to the end of the quay and fastened in place.

I slipped through to the front of the crowd where I hoped I could attract Paul's attention. After a few minutes he noticed me and gave a wave - rather than returning it I nodded my head sideways towards the shelter on the harbour wall. As he stared, I nodded again and then turned to walk toward it.

He joined me a few moments later.

"Claudia - is everything alright?"

I shook my head.

"No, it's not." I took a deep breath. "You're all going to be sent back to Aden. I-"

"Claudia!" His tone was so sharp, it startled me. Seeing

my reaction, he reached out and placed his hand against my arm.

"Claudia." Much more gently. "You can't tell me that, alright? You could get into real trouble."

"But..."

"Claudia, this is serious," he said. "You can't tell anyone about this."

I just stared at him.

"Promise me!"

Numbly, I nodded.

"I don't want you to go," I said weakly. "I'll really miss you."

"Claudia, listen. You don't have to worry - trust me."

"Will you write? So that I'll know you're okay. God, I must sound so stupid."

"No, you're not stupid. And of course I'll write."

I reached into my pocket and gave him a sheet of paper with my address written on it.

"If we don't see each other before you go."

"We will see each other again, Claudia - I promise you." He smiled, squeezed my arm with his hand, and I felt my knees go weak.

I didn't trust myself to say anything else, I just turned and walked away.

26. Kit

It had been a lazy afternoon so far. Jake, for once, had offered a joint rather than try to sell us one, and so we headed out to the Burrows to smoke it. We were listening to a pirate radio ship on someone's transistor radio and Aidan was sketching Lee in a thoughtful pose atop of a dune. We'd been there about an hour when I noticed Claudia walk over to Emma and kneel beside her, whispering something initially too low for me to catch.

Emma nodded and stood up.

"Aunt Anne and Alex have gone shopping in Truro," Claudia told her, handing Emma a door key. "My room's the first on the right, at the top of the stairs."

"Okay," said Emma, "I won't be long."

As she passed by, Emma caught my eye and gave an almost imperceptible tilt of her head. I waited a minute and then casually rose to my feet and followed her.

She was waiting just on the other side of the dune.

"I thought," she smiled, "that you might want to give your legs a stretch."

"Where are we going?" I asked, as we started out toward the town.

"Claudia's house," she said.

"What for?"

"To get something."

"What?"

She stopped and turned to me.

"A *girl* something."

"Oh. Okay." I nodded. "Right."

* * *

The thing about St Hannahs was that you were never far from anywhere. It only took about ten minutes to reach Claudia's place, but when Emma tried the key in the front door, it turned but wouldn't open.

"That's strange," she said. "Maybe it's for the other door."

We made our way down to the harbour and back along the beach to the house. Emma slipped the key into the conservatory door, but it wouldn't turn at all.

"This is odd," she said.

"Look." I pointed to a window. The stay fastener at the bottom was missing, the only thing keeping it closed was the catch on the side. "Have you got a nail file?"

She raised an eyebrow.

"What do you think?"

I looked around. Over by the wall was a plastic bucket, full of rusty old tools. I rummaged inside and found a hacksaw blade. Slipping it between the jamb and the frame, I managed to slide the catch up and the window swung open.

"After you," I said. The wall below the window was only about three feet high. She pivoted over it easily. I followed, and we went into the house.

"Back down in a sec," she said, as we reached the stairs.

I wandered further along, looking at a selection of watercolours decorating the hallway. Then from one of the rooms I thought I heard a muffled sound. And another, almost like a cry this time. It was coming from a room where the door was slightly ajar. Curiosity drew me towards it. Standing outside, I pressed with my fingertips, widening the gap only a few inches more, but enough to see inside.

And froze, my breath caught in my throat and my heart thumping.

Alex was bent forward over a dining table, and Paul was attacking him from behind. He held a leather belt in a loop around Alex's neck, while Alex writhed frantically to free himself.

They were naked.

Alex became still.

"Tighter!" he said.

They began moving again, not *grappling*, I realised, but *thrusting*. Then, in the corner of the mirror hung over the mantelpiece, I caught further movement. Don Mayberry was sitting back in an armchair, also naked, his body glistening with sweat and one hand holding a glass tumbler to his lips, while the other rested down between his splayed legs. For a second I thought he might have seen me, but his focus was on the two figures in the centre of the room.

Emma was coming back down the stairs, how could they not hear her every creaking step. Alex grimaced as the belt tightened, but Paul's expression was strangely inscrutable as he reached around Alex with his free hand.

As carefully as possible, I eased the door to the position I'd found it, turned, and arrived at the foot of the stairs at the same time as Emma.

"Okay?" I asked, or almost croaked, my mouth as dry as ashes. She nodded, staring at me, and I forced a smile as I led her back down to the conservatory.

"Is everything alright?" She sat on the windowsill and lifted her legs over.

"Yeah, just felt a bit dizzy," I said as casually as I could manage, following her out through the window. "Probably the dope."

"Do you need to sit down?"

"No, I'll be fine. It's okay, leave that," I told her, as she started fiddling with the catch. I just wanted to be away from there.

"Done now," she said, turning back to me. "Come on, let's go."

* * *

As we walked along the beach, I became increasingly certain we'd been heard. That behind us, the door was opening and eyes were watching us moving away. After about a hundred yards, I could stand it no longer.

"Maybe I should sit down," I told Emma and without waiting for a response lowered myself down onto the sand. As surreptitiously as possible, I turned my head and glanced back the way we'd come.

Nothing.

"Hey," said Emma, sitting down beside me. Edging closer, she reached her arm around my shoulders. I could smell her hair, a hint of musk and then I was suddenly overwhelmed by her femininity, wanting nothing more than to be completely enveloped by her melting softness.

"Feeling better now?" she asked, after a few seconds. I took a deep breath, nodded, and managed a reassuring smile.

"Come on then," she said.

We stood up and carried on walking.

27. Claudia

"So how did it start?" I asked Lee. "The acting?"

We were sitting at a table in *The Barque*. Earlier we'd walked over to the Burrows to discover it deserted, almost eerily so. But neither of us had felt like giving up on the evening and so we'd found ourselves here in the lounge bar, Lee sipping a gin and tonic whilst I nursed a glass of cider.

She had seemed unusually subdued on the walk back, and for once I was the one making conversation to break the silence. But I was genuinely interested.

"Well, my father has always been in the theatre," she said. "Even during the war, he was with ENSA - you know, entertaining the troops."

I nodded.

"When the war finished he went into repertory, which is where he met my mother, who was an actress. They got married and then mum fell pregnant with my sister, so she stopped working. And then I came along."

"Did your mother go back to acting?"

She shook her head.

"Dad started to have a bit of a rough time of it - he was getting some parts, you often see his face in Ealing comedies and the odd TV episode from back then. But the only regular work was in provincial rep, which would have meant being away from home for weeks on end. They didn't want that, so Mum was the breadwinner mostly, working in department stores, demonstrating make-up and perfume."

She sipped her drink.

"But in the end, he gave it up. Not the theatre, professional acting - he's the stage manager at a playhouse in the East Midlands. But he does a lot of amateur dramatic productions, and he got quite a few names that you'd recognised started. He's kept his contacts from the early days and if he thinks someone has genuine talent, they listen to him."

"Like you?" I smiled.

Lee's expression was hard to read.

"My sister and I grew up smelling greasepaint," she said, "and before she was ten, Helen had been in half a dozen television commercials - 'Mummy, why are your hands so soft?'" Lee shook her head. "So, when the casting sheet for *The Hendersons* went out, Dad got her an audition."

Lee let a smile play around her lips.

"Helen's the pretty one," she said. "Daddy's little princess."

She took another sip of her drink.

"So, we go down to the audition as a family - later we plan to go shopping in the West End and one of Dad's friends is in a play at the Old Vic, which he's sent us tickets for and an invitation to come backstage afterwards. Then the last train home.

"There're a dozen or so kids up for the role, all there with their parents. But Dad knows the producer from way back and he's making a big thing out of chatting away to him throughout - auditions are full of low-level psychological gamesmanship.

"One after the other, all the kids go up and read. But through it all I notice that one man, sitting with the production team, keeps staring at me. The auditions finish, the producer starts to thank everyone for coming, but the man who'd been staring stands up and says, 'Just a sec'. He walks over and asks me my name, I tell him. He smiles at Mum and Dad and hands me the script.

"'Want to give it a shot?' he asks.

"I didn't really have time to be nervous, but I still didn't think I'd made a good job of it. But he thanks me, the producer thanks all of us, we'll hear shortly, and that's it.

"We spend the rest of the day as planned, my party piece goes entirely unmentioned. It's like I'd farted in church or something and that night we're back home.

"Three days later Dad gets a call from the producer. They want me for a screen test. I'm down to London again, just with Mum this time - the Playhouse can't spare Dad, but I think everyone knows that wouldn't have been a problem if it had been Helen who'd had the callback.

"This time we're at a huge TV studio complex next to Wembley Stadium. It's down to three of us now and they put us up overnight at a West End hotel and ferry us back and forth by taxi. A week later, I find out I've got the part."

"Wow!"

"To cover my education the TV company enrol me at a stage school in Islington, and I move in with Mum's sister and her brood, who still live in London."

"Do you see much of your family?" I asked her.

"I'm close to my Mum," she said. "Dad and I get on, mostly."

She finished her drink and placed the empty glass down on the table.

"But I don't think that Helen's ever forgiven me."

* * *

"You must have made a fair amount of money from it?" I suggested, as we slowly walked back home.

"I certainly *earned* a lot," she said. "But I never really got more than pocket money. Legally, I was a child - for God's sake, *legally* I still am a child - which means that I wasn't regarded as being competent to handle my affairs."

"So?"

"There was a trust fund to manage expenses - school fees, cost of living, but I doubt there's much left in it now."

"You doubt?"

She shrugged.

"It was set up by Dad's accountant, and the two of them

administered it together. I'd occasionally be told that an investment wasn't working out as well as they'd hoped. And that they were using funds for Helen's school fees, they were sure I wouldn't object to *that*."

"Literally cashing in on the guilt?" I smiled.

She nodded.

"I've never pushed to see the accounts, but when I'm twenty-one I'll get an accountant of my own and see what he says."

We'd reached *Cam Ryr*.

"Look," she said hesitantly, "I don't want it to seem that I'm interfering, but..."

She shook her head.

"Interfering? In what?" I asked.

She seemed to consider me, as if trying to come to a decision.

"You really like Paul, don't you?"

"Paul?" I didn't know whether to feel embarrassed or angry. *God, was it that obvious!* But her tone sounded well meaning...

I nodded.

"Yes, I do."

"And as more than a friend?"

Again, I nodded.

She took my hand and squeezed it, staring into my eyes.

"I can't betray a confidence," she said carefully, "but I can't let a friend get hurt, either. And if you let your feelings carry you away here, then believe me - you are going to get really hurt."

"Betray a confidence." I shook my head. "I don't understand?"

Then one tiny glimmer of comprehension began to shine through.

"Do you mean he's married?" I asked.

Lee looked at me as if she had a decision to make, but then simply pulled me close and gave me a hug.

"No," she said. "But trust me on this, okay?"

We drew apart, and she started to walk away. After a few steps, she turned to see me still standing there, staring after her.

"Goodnight Claudia," she said. "I'll see you in the morning."

* * *

As I let myself in the front door, my head was swirling. I thought I'd say a quick goodnight to Alex and Aunt Anne and then disappear up to my room to collect my thoughts.

I didn't hear any voices as I walked down the corridor. Usually at this time of night they were having supper, but when I pushed the kitchen door open Aunt Anne was sitting alone at the table.

"Hello dear," she said. "Did you have a nice evening?"

I looked around the room.

"Is Uncle Alex out?"

"He's had to go back up to London."

"London?" I stared at her.

"It seems there's some kind of flap on at the Ministry." She sighed. "Whenever isn't there is what I'd like to know, but apparently they can't manage without him, so that's that." She gave me a smile. "He wanted to say goodbye, but he has to be there by the morning and so he couldn't wait - he'll be driving throughout the night, as it is."

I tried to digest this.

"So," I asked, "does this mean we must go home by train?"

"No, that's one small mercy," she said, shaking her head. "Alex had a word and we'll be getting a lift back to Town with Don and Lee."

Aunt Anne gave a sigh.

"Cup of cocoa, dear?"

28. Kit

I don't know why it had gotten to me – I'd faded into the background at enough of Coochie's scenes over the last couple of years to consider myself pretty much unshockable. Then again, perhaps it wasn't what I'd seen that had touched a nerve, but what had spurred it. Maybe, I reflected, it resonated at that same fraught, compulsive sexual pitch as the savage coupling that Emma and I had just brought to its conclusion.

Or had I just had enough of bloody secrets?

"What's the matter?" asked Emma as we lay in the dark, her leg thrown over mine, alabaster white in the moonlight.

"Back in London," I tried to keep my tone neutral, "are we going to keep seeing each other?"

She pulled back her leg and sat up. After staring at me for a few seconds, she gave a shrug.

"I don't know," she said. "Probably not."

"So, I should... What? Just make the most of it?"

"Isn't that what you've been doing?"

"And what is it you've been doing?"

She was silent.

"Don't you think it's time to talk?" I asked.

She rolled away from me.

"I've got a boyfriend - back home," she said, eventually.

"Okay."

"He's a student at mum's college."

"Right," I said.

"He's doing politics."

"I'd sort of assumed he wouldn't be on a Business Studies course."

"He - he said he didn't want to do it until we were married. That we should wait."

"And you didn't want to?"

She rolled back over, ferocious.

"Women aren't men's playthings anymore - or their skivvies."

"So, you...?"

"Women have needs too," she interrupted angrily. "That deserve more than a drunken wedding night when..."

She broke off, shaking her head. Sitting upright, she drew her knees towards her and wrapped her arms around them, turning to stare at me.

"I wanted it out of the way," she said and tossed her head, almost petulantly, to one side.

"I'm guessing you thought a bit of practice wouldn't go amiss, either," I said, quietly.

She whirled her head back around to glare at me.

I sighed.

"Whatever," I told her. "So why me? Not that I don't feel flattered... But I am curious."

"Because I didn't think you'd care," she snapped. "I assumed..."

She seemed to struggle with her thoughts.

"That I'm a heartless bastard."

"Yes." She shook her head. "No, I meant - I thought you'd be the one person who wouldn't get hurt. That to you I'd just be..."

She trailed off.

"Another notch on my bedpost."

"Well, there must be a good few on there."

I lay back and closed my eyes as she started to get dressed.

The few fleeting encounters I'd had over the previous couple of years, which didn't have a quid pro quo undercurrent, had seemed little more than reaching out in the night for bonds of mutual comfort. With no assumptions leading to regrets or recriminations. But if sometimes I wilfully misread signals suggesting things might be otherwise, then I was getting my payback here. Were decades, if not centuries, of society's courtship rites now being thrown into the mix? One tiny pill and shotgun weddings about to go the way of the dowry?

I knew that in her heart and soul, Emma was a 'good girl'. I understood this was about emancipation rather than hedonism. I was yet to grasp that over the next few years the universities would become full of her, but I did have a real premonition that some angels should be fearful of where they chose to tread, the ground beneath their feet perhaps more treacherous than their expectations had the experience to imagine.

I also had the sense to keep that thought to myself.

"For the record," I told her, pivoting around and sitting up on the edge of the bed as she finished dressing, "you were right. I'm not hurt. My ego may be a little bruised, but my heart remains unbroken."

She smiled, and after fastening her blouse came over and sat down alongside me.

"Shipboard romance," she said. "Okay?"

"Okay."

She kissed me on the cheek, stood up and left.

29. Aidan

I woke to a knocking on the chalet door which, while insistent, didn't carry that authoritarian resonance which you can never define but also never mistake. So, I was more irritated than apprehensive as I dragged myself out of bed and across the room to answer it.

I hardly had the door open before Lee was in through it like Yosemite Sam, her head turning this way and that.

"Is Paul here?" she asked.

"Paul? No." I shook my head. "Why would he be?"

"The Military Police are after him. They were next door at Claudia's earlier, they knew he'd been there for a dinner party. They turned the place inside out looking for him."

"The military doesn't have that kind of jurisdiction here."

"Yeah, well, it was the local police waving the warrant around, but it was definitely the army pulling their strings."

I sat back down on the bed and tried to think this through, all the time conscious of Lee's eyes on me.

"Have you seen Kit?" she asked. "This morning?"

"This morning? No, of course not - I've only seen you. Why?"

"He's not in his chalet."

"Lee, would you please tell me what's going on?"

She was suddenly deflated, her entire body seeming to sag. Slowly she sat down on the edge of the bed.

"The soldiers left last night - a fleet of lorries turned up outside the Town Hall, and half an hour later they were gone."

"They could be working further up the coast."

"With all their gear?" She shook her head. "I went by there an hour ago. Council workmen are inside putting the place back to normal. Rumour is that American troops are taking over, and they'll be setting up camp outside of town."

She paused.

"There was a huge raid last night, police brought in from all over the county. They cleared out the pillboxes, the hut down at the station, and then they turned up here at three in the morning with a warrant for the camping barns and emptied those out too."

All of which seemingly I'd slept right through.

"Anyone who wasn't actually arrested was put into a police van and driven away. Apparently, they're being dumped on the Devon side of the Tamar Bridge, with a warning that if they come back into Cornwall, there'll be a lot worse waiting for them."

"And they're looking for Paul?"

"Claudia came round first thing. She said it wasn't exactly a raid, everyone very polite but also very firm and just what did they know about him? They left eventually, but..." She gave a sigh. "Anne wants to go home straightaway and Don's pretty freaked, so we'll be setting off for London this morning."

"Well, thanks for letting me know. And for coming to say goodbye, I really appreciate..."

"Don says to ask if you want a lift?" she interrupted.

I stared at her and then nodded. There was no reason for me to get caught up in any of this, but if I did and they started checking my background...

"Shall we pick you up here?" Lee asked.

I stood up.

"I've only the one bag and it won't take me five minutes to pack it - I'll walk back with you."

* * *

Claudia was waiting by Don's Rover, its boot open and

full of suitcases.

"It was horrible," she said, giving me a hug. "They were everywhere, going through all of our things."

"They were looking for Paul?"

She nodded.

"They kept asking over and over again why we'd invited him to our home, and what we'd talked about. Aunt Anne was brilliant. Eventually she said, 'Look, my husband gave him a lift back to barracks, maybe he knows something.' 'Where is your husband?' asked one of the policemen. 'Oh, he had to return to London,' said Aunt Anne, 'would you like me to telephone him?'. The policeman looked at one of the Army officers, who nodded. Aunt Anne rang home, explained to Alex what was happening, and then handed the phone over to the policeman."

Claudia paused.

"My God, you should have seen his face when he gave the phone back to Aunt Anne," she said and then shook her head. "I think my uncle's a lot more important than he lets on."

And that would in no way surprise me, I thought, but stayed silent.

"Anyway, that was that," said Claudia. "Once he'd handed the phone back it was apologies all around for the intrusion and they left. But Aunt Anne really doesn't want to stay here, she..."

Claudia broke off as Anne came out of the house with Don, who was carrying another suitcase. He nodded at me and Anne managed a bleak smile.

"Can I give you a hand with anything?" I asked, but he shook his head.

"This is about it," he said and indicating my bag on the ground added, "If that's all you have, let's see if we can squeeze it into the boot."

* * *

Ten minutes later we were driving out of the town.

But as we came to the harbour, we had to slow down, the road partially blocked by civilian workmen unloading oil drums from a lorry. Drawing closer, we realised that a crowd had gathered and a crowd with an air of agitation about it. Winding the window down, Don asked one of the workmen, who was directing traffic, what was going on?

The previous night's raids hadn't been entirely successful, it transpired, with at least one individual managing to slip through the net. Because, the workman told us, during the night someone had swum out into the harbour and hacked through the rope links holding the oil boom sections together.

And now, not only was the entire beach inches deep in a thick, black sludge, but painted along the harbour wall in letters large enough to be read a quarter of a mile away was 'FUCK YOU'.

30. Claudia

As soon as we arrived back at Portman Square, I knew something was wrong. It wasn't just the way that Alex gave Aunt Anne a perfunctory kiss on the cheek by way of a greeting, whilst staring over her shoulder at me. It was – as Kit would put it – the whole vibe of the place. Even the air felt wrong, still but heavy, almost like a presence.

"Claudia," said Alex, moving past Aunt Anne and taking my hand. He guided me to the sofa and gently pulled me down to sit beside him. "I'm so terribly sorry, but there's been an accident. I'm afraid something dreadful has happened to your mother."

I was conscious of Aunt Anne's hand flying up to her mouth and her eyes wide with shock, but although I understood the words Alex was speaking to me, I couldn't seem to extract any meaning from them. God knows how long it took for him to explain to me what had happened, softly repeating himself under my blank eyed gaze until it finally sank in, Aunt Anne sitting on the other side of me, holding my hand and gently weeping.

The nursing staff at the sanatorium had realised that Mummy was gone from her room at about eight o'clock the previous night. She would often go for a walk in the grounds after dinner, and so they immediately started a search for her. When she wasn't found, they contacted the local police to inform them they had a patient missing and to give them her description. Next morning, at first light, the staff conducted a more thorough search but to no avail, at which point the police made an appeal for volunteers to search the surrounding area. But before that could get underway, a couple walking their dog on the beach discovered her at the foot of some sea cliffs, about half a mile away.

"No one's exactly sure yet what happened," said Alex, when I finally seemed to be able to grasp what he was saying. "She probably went for a walk, lost track of time and found herself on the cliff tops in the dark."

Even in my distressed state I realised how charitable an interpretation of the facts that scenario was, but I nodded.

"I haven't telephoned your father yet," said Alex carefully. "I was waiting until I'd spoken to you before…"

"I don't want him here!" I was on my feet almost before I knew it, staring at my aunt and uncle wild-eyed.

"Claudia…" began my aunt.

"*I don't want him here!*" I realised I was practically screaming, but I didn't care. Alex stood and wrapped his arms around me as I sobbed uncontrollably.

"This is all his fault," I remember saying repeatedly. "If it weren't for him, this never would have happened."

All I'm sure of from that point onward is Alex gently consoling me, whilst holding me tight. I recall a doctor and that he took me to my room, where he gave me something to drink from a small plastic cup and then, mercifully, came oblivion.

* * *

The ten days up to the funeral were a haze.

I assume I was being medicated, if not exactly sure how. I never discovered the nature of Alex's conversation with my father, but his only contribution to the proceedings was a wreath which, after Alex had a quiet but terse word with the funeral director, was moved to the back of the floral tributes.

There was speculation at the inquest as to Mummy's state of mind at the time of her death, but in the absence of a note and with her doctor's assurance that he had no grounds to believe that she'd wished herself harm - 'well, he would say that wouldn't he' I heard *sotto voce* from somewhere behind me - the only verdict the coroner could justifiably reach was misadventure.

It seemed an apt description.

Alex accompanied me for the reading of the will. There was just the two of us and the solicitor, kindness personified and who made it all as informal as possible, which I greatly appreciated. There were no surprises - everything left to me, but to be held in a trust administered by Alex until I reached twenty-one. I'd be able to draw on it for expenses pertaining to my education, but any other items would be at Alex's discretion.

After leaving the law firm, we found a small Italian restaurant off Fleet Street for lunch.

"Do you know yet what you're doing about University?" asked Alex.

I shook my head. I'd applied to colleges in both Oxford and Cambridge, but I wasn't optimistic about either, I told him. It was looking like Bristol.

"The reason I ask," said Alex, "is that we ought to make a decision about the apartment."

"You mean sell it?"

"Not really a good idea in the current economic climate. Also, you'll need somewhere to stay out of term time and let's not pretend you wouldn't be bored out of your mind billeted with Ann and I, out in the sticks."

I stared at him. This wasn't something I'd actually thought about.

"The thing is," he said, "I had lunch with Don Mayberry the other day."

I was surprised. I knew there'd been lots of handshaking and backslapping and 'We must get together when we're back in Town' down in Cornwall, but I hadn't really expected anything to come of it.

"Don's getting divorced," continued Alex. "His wife will have the house, and he's looking to rent somewhere for a year or two, while he sorts himself out. Financially."

"He wants to rent the apartment?"

"We were talking about a three-year lease for a joint cohabitation. You'd still have your room for when you were in London, and Don would be based in the middle of the West End, which is what he needs. Plus," with an almost sheepish smile, "you'd have the income from the tenancy to do with as you pleased, it would fall outside the trust." He shrugged. "And then at the end of the three years, you'll be twenty-one and can do as you wish."

I considered. Most of the year I'd be away at university and even in the summer holidays I planned to travel. The money was less of an incentive than Alex might have imagined, I was pretty confident that I could wheedle anything I wanted past his discretionary powers, anyway. But what it did mean was that I could put off deciding what to do for at least another three years. It wasn't until I thought Alex was talking about selling the apartment that I realised what a tremendous wrench that would be. It had been Mummy's and I couldn't bear to lose it so soon, with memories so raw.

"Okay," I nodded. "That does make sense."

"Right," he said with a smile. "I'll give Don a ring."

PART THREE

Phases of an Eclipse & Fragments of a Summer

1. Spike

Probably, reflected Spike, only cleaners spent more time in deserted offices than he did. Major upgrades like this one could only be done when the system was offline and that meant either overnight or at weekends. Given a choice he preferred nights, staff often came in on Saturdays and Sundays to catch up with work or prepare for the week ahead, but the nights he had to himself. Spike had always gotten off on that after midnight spooky *'every sound means something'* vibe, and he could usually arrange to slip out in the early hours as the clubs emptied and cruise for a while.

The thing that invariably got to him were the photo cubes and picture frames on all the desks, the cute kids and smiling spouses. When Spike first started working in offices he'd had a definitely jaundiced take on this, symbolic ball and chains keeping all these poor chumps shackled to their desks.

A couple of months ago he'd made a crack along those lines to Barry. Barry'd wanted a look at some guy's phone records, a cheating husband supposed Spike. They'd been sitting in a wine bar on Upper Street, Barry working his way through the printouts and making an occasional scribble in a small notebook. Spike thought Barry had either ignored him or was concentrating too intently to have noticed. But after he'd finished, Barry slipped the notebook into his jacket pocket, sat back in his chair, and looked across the table at Spike.

"No mate," he said, reaching for his drink, "it's a lot sadder than that. Hostages to fortune, is what they are."

He smiled as Spike stared at him quizzically.

"Consciously or not, the poor buggers are trying to humanise themselves in the face of indifferent corporate carnage. You know, like when some clown sticks up a post office with a sawn-off and the middle-aged jobsworth behind the counter shoots his arms up in the air and goes, 'Oh please, no, I've got a wife and two kids, I'm begging you.' It's the same thing. The message to anyone approaching their desk is, 'Okay, I may be an incompetent muppet, hanging onto this pathetic job by the skin of my teeth, but hey - screw me over and look who'll really suffer'."

The waitress had left the bill in a small leather folder. Barry slipped four fifty pound notes into it and pushed it across the table.

"I'll let you settle up," he said, standing. "Might have something for you at the end of the week. Call me Friday, okay?"

Spike had nodded, keeping his face expressionless. After paying the bill, he'd be left with about a third of what those phone records were worth.

"*One of these days,*" he'd thought to himself. "*One of these bloody days...*"

With a shake of the head, he brought himself back to the present and glanced at the clock. About elevenish, Barry had said. Another thirty minutes. That shouldn't take long and the database update he was running was likely to finish about one... So, he might get out for an hour and still have enough time to run a full diagnostic before finishing for the night. And be out of the building before Ms fucking Jeffreys arrived for work.

* * *

Spike had clashed with the office manager on day one, when she'd taken exception to his work attire of sweatshirt and jeans.

"It's company policy for all employees to wear a jacket and tie," she told him.

"I'm not an employee," he pointed out, "I'm an agency contractor."

"Whilst you're working on these premises," she replied tartly, "we expect you to adhere to our dress code."

Spike had considered this for a few seconds and then nodded. "Okay," he said, then picked up his bag and left.

Charlotte from the agency had rung almost immediately. "What's going on?" she asked wearily and listened while Spike relayed the details of his encounter with Ms Jeffreys. "Okay, I'll sort it out and get back to you," she said, but Spike told her not to bother.

"There's enough work out there without having to put up with shit like this," he said, and Charlotte knew he was right. They were five months away from the end of the century and millennium bug panic was rampant. Even crap software developers were charging premium rates and Spike was one of the best.

"You signed a contract," Charlotte said, testily.

"Which had no dress code clause in it," replied Spike, "and which she violated by refusing me access to my designated place of work."

Charlotte had taken a deep breath and then said okay, they weren't going to fall out over it, let her talk to the M.D.

She called back an hour later.

"Right, I've got you another twenty-five quid a day - payable as a lump sum bonus at the end of the contract - if you have it all signed off by the due date," she told him. "Now get back in there and play fucking nice."

Ms Jeffreys was nowhere to be seen when he returned to the office, but a few smiles came his direction as he set himself up at a desk in the far corner of the main office.

"Hi, I'm Mike," said a youngish-looking guy. "Want a coffee?"

Mike stopped to chat for a while after bringing it over. Ms Jeffreys, Spike learnt, was up on the fifth floor being hauled over the coals. The phone call she'd received from above had been loud enough for everyone in the room to catch the gist that - in the grand scheme of things - next year's orders not going out dated January 1st 1900 was a damn sight more important than some geek's dress sense or lack of it.

She didn't appear until the following day and they greeted each other with frosty nods. That was fine by Spike. Staying out of each other's way was probably their best working option.

But it appeared that Ms Jeffreys wasn't one to forgive or forget. The opening salvo was her disappearance from the office whenever his timesheet needed to be signed. The first occasion it happened he put it down to carelessness, the second time he realised he was in a war of attrition here.

'Okay,' shrugged Spike, metaphorically spitting on his palms and rubbing them together, *'game on'*.

* * *

"I've received no emails today and none of my own have been sent out." Spike had looked up to see Ms Jeffreys standing by his desk, arms folded and staring down at him. "Is this anything to do with the changes you're making to the system?"

"Could well be." Spike gave a nod. "It's not unusual to get knock-on effects. I'll look into it right now."

"Thank you," she said curtly and turned to walk away.

"But as you're here," Spike lifted a sheaf of blank time sheets. "If you'd go through these and sign them while I check the system, it'll save you being bothered by me in the future."

She glared at him, and then almost snatched them from his hand. While she furiously scribbled her signature, Spike made a big performance out of tapping at the keyboard and squinting at the screen as he reactivated her email account.

"Please let me have a photocopy of each one you submit," she'd said testily as she'd handed them back. Spike had smiled and told her that of course he would.

"I'd watch your back there, mate," Mike said quietly. Spike nodded and said, "Yeah", as he watched her leave the room.

And there was the rub...

Spike knew Ms Jeffreys believed that the only world which existed was the one hosting her physical presence, and that the only reality which mattered was the one in which she was the epicentre of every little drama she chose to create and manipulate.

That might have been true twenty years ago, even ten, but not any longer. The essence of everyone's life was now distilled down to the ones and zeros in multiple databanks, where finances, correspondence and lifestyle traits were raw material being churned over by algorithms growing exponentially more powerful by the year. And the identities that these created, far from being a reflection of ourselves, were, to all intents and purposes, the actuality.

This was Spike's world. And he decided to take a look.

As a child, Spike remembered watching an episode of some TV series which featured a medieval siege - *Robin Hood* or *Ivanhoe* probably. The way the hero breached the castle's defences was to wait until nightfall, tie a very thin cord to an arrow and then shoot the arrow over the corner of the battlements, so it fell back to earth looping the cord around a merlon. Then, a rope was tied to the end of the cord and pulled along the same loop until its end was secured back on the ground. The hero scrambled up the rope, over the ramparts and released the chains securing the drawbridge, which dropped open and the besieging army poured into the castle.

Spike's arrow was an email.

The system update targets were kept on a spreadsheet and every Friday afternoon he emailed a revised progress report to management, including Ms Jeffreys. This Friday he disabled her email account again and was uncharacteristically contrite at her irritation, offering to stay behind and fix it. In the meantime, he'd email the progress report to her personal account. Suitably mollified, she gave him her email address and thought no more about it.

The spreadsheet Ms Jeffreys opened later that evening at home seemed identical to the one the rest of the management team received, but it wasn't. Embedded behind the user interface was a macro, a series of pre-programmed keystrokes that executed without the user being aware of them. The macro logged onto Spike's computer from where it downloaded a keylogger, a standalone script of Spike's own design. Not being an actual program, no installation permissions were required and therefore it triggered no virus alerts. Its function was in its name, it recorded all the keystrokes typed. When the PC began its Shut Down sequence, it would save them to a text file and then send that file to Spike. Within days, Spike had all of her passwords and some interesting insights into her life.

And by the end of the next week, things had become very intriguing indeed.

* * *

My Richard was a popular topic of Ms Jeffreys' conversation in the office.

'*My Richard* said' and 'Oh, me and *My Richard*' could be the opener for observations on any subject from politics to the previous evening's TV viewing. It would have been easy to form the opinion that they were one of those couples initially united by a shared worldview and whose bond had only been forged stronger in the fires of whatever tribulations the subsequent years had brought. And indeed, a cursory examination of their finances would seem to confirm this. They shopped together, dined together and holidayed together.

But then there was Ms Jeffreys' book club.

'Well, you've got to have something to talk about,' she emailed one of her fellow readers who'd questioned, apparently yet again, why her husband couldn't be persuaded to join their little circle. 'And *My Richard's* not much of a one for books.' And so, on Tuesday nights Ms Jeffreys took along her carefully revised list of bullet points on their current novel - perhaps a recent Booker winner, unless that had proved a tad too controversial - to the room hired at the local library and left *My Richard* to his own amusements.

And amuse himself he did. How he must look forward to these Tuesday nights, thought Spike, as he ran through *My Richard's* deleted web browser history and his cache of images hidden deep in a nest of sub-folders. Most people yearned for the weekend, couldn't wait for Friday to roll around. And while Tuesday afternoon was supposedly the psychological low point of the week for the average working Joe, *My Richard* must have been counting off the minutes with bated breath. Spike would bet Ms Jeffreys hadn't fully reversed her car out of their driveway before *My Richard's* clammy fingers were pecking away at the keyboard.

Because *My Richard* liked schoolgirls.

Or more accurately, *My Richard* liked the *idea* of schoolgirls. Spike seriously doubted that the schoolgirls who were feeding *My Richard's* fantasies had actually existed in any way, shape or form outside of warped delusion, with their gymslips raised and navy-blue knickers around their ankles as they bent over in anticipation of the strap, cane or slipper with a backwards glance of saucy defiance or shy humiliation. There was almost a St Trinian's element of farce to it all, thought Spike, the too short, too tight uniforms on models obviously half a decade out of the schoolyard, but Spike knew that this represented nothing funny going on in *My Richard's* psyche, at least not in any comical sense. He also knew that should *My Richard's* browsing history come under close scrutiny, it would reveal a trail of what some people might term aberrant interests stretching back through cyberspace, probably for years.

Which, concluded Spike, would make a fork in that trail at this point all the more plausible. One thing he'd learnt from Barry was that if you wanted to construct a deception, you'd best build its foundations on the truth. As with cutting a diamond, you needed to know the exact spot to fracture to create two perfect gems rather than a handful of shards.

And his two gems, decided Spike, would be *My Richard* and *His Richard*. *My Richard* already existed, and Spike would keep an eye on him and his regular Tuesday night Bacchanalia, but otherwise let him continue unhindered.

His Richard was an altogether darker construction, lurking behind a series of aliases which were hidden but ultimately not unfathomable. *His Richard* would venture into much murkier and unsavoury areas of cyberspace, forming links and alliances whose deeply disturbing fruits would be buried far deeper than *My Richard's* collection of classroom minxes, but if subjected to forensic examination would carry exactly the same fingerprint.

His Richard is burrowing out a sinkhole inches below the ground *My Richard* walks on and Spike is a trapdoor, separating the crumbling surface under *My Richard's* footfalls and that bottomless pit. Spike can slip the bolt anytime he chooses - a careless comment in a monitored chat room, an email attachment to the wrong recipient - but he has learnt to bide his time.

'Our little secret' in a decade of children's homes and foster parents, innumerable beatings under the guise of discipline but blatantly satisfying only a sadistic bent, had mentored Spike well. Lesson one - if you want to really hurt someone don't go after them, go after who they love. Lesson two - pick your battles.

A year and a day is Spike's rule of thumb. Arseholes, he reckoned, generated petty animosities with such frequency that - like a tape loop in a CCTV camera - the grievances and rancour of twelve months ago would have been many times written over. And, as they tried to make sense of the chaos unfurling around them, not only would Spike be a memory long gone, they'd never understand in a million years that his fulfilment is not triumphant gloating, rather the satisfaction of knowing that pieces which he's set in motion are now running their inevitable course, observed or otherwise.

It doesn't matter to Spike whether *My Richard* reaches

out and drags Ms Jeffreys down through that trapdoor with him or that with a disbelieving screech she manages to pull herself back and away from his grasp.

What matters is that, either way, life will never be the same for her again...

* * *

Spike was startled back to the present by the doorbell. Crossing the room, he glanced at the clock on the wall. It had to be Barry, but he switched off the light before stepping into the Reception area. He let his eyes adjust to the dark for a few seconds. Two figures were silhouetted against the frosted glass of the front door and he slipped the catch and opened it.

"Everything okay?" asked Barry. Spike nodded and led them through to the main office. After closing the door, he switched the light on.

"This is Kit Franklyn," said Barry. "We go way back."

Spike looked at him curiously. He hadn't given it much thought, but he supposed he'd been gearing up for a different vibe, more along the lines of a bulky ex-cop being two-timed by a skanky wife and compensating with belligerence. But Franklyn gave Spike a brief nod and a small smile.

"Good to meet you," he said, "I appreciate your help."

He was careful not to offer his hand, Spike noticed - Barry must have given him a heads up on his aversion to being touched.

"No problem," he said.

Barry sat down at the nearest desk and spread himself out. Franklyn remained standing until Spike gestured at the next desk.

"Coffee?" he asked.

Barry shook his head impatiently, but Franklyn nodded.

"Thanks," he said. "Black, no sugar."

"So how did you get on?" asked Barry, as Spike poured coffee into a mug.

"I took a look at your wife's PC," said Spike to Franklyn,

"and found him pretty quickly."

"I'm impressed," said Franklyn. "I was expecting a couple of days, at least."

"Once you know who you're looking for," said Barry, "everything else is instantaneous. Right?" he added, turning to Spike.

"Right," said Spike, lifting a folder up from his desk. "Does the name Richard Hanson mean anything to you?"

"Yes." Franklyn thought for a second. "Yes, it does. He was the boyfriend of a girl who had a room at Pembridge Villas… Veronica something, worked as Lee Munro's PA for a while."

Spiked opened the folder and glanced down at the top sheet of paper.

"He married a Veronica Hewitt in September, 1970," he told Franklyn, who nodded.

"That was the summer Carin was spending time at the house," he said.

Spike handed Franklyn a photograph

"This him?"

Franklyn studied the print.

"I remember him thinner," he said eventually, "and with a beard. But, yeah, it is." He looked up at Spike. "How did you find him?"

"A Hotmail account being accessed by your wife was a huge flag. A common trick - used by criminals and terrorists - to avoid email interception is to set up an email account but only use the drafts folder to communicate."

"I don't understand?"

"Okay - your wife logs into the email account, types an email but instead of sending it, she saves it as a draft and logs out. Richard Hanson logs into the account, reads your wife's email, types a reply and saves that as a draft. Smart and simple. Nothing incriminating gets left on either of their computers."

"Right." Franklyn nodded his head. "Clever."

"Not really." Spike smiled. "It does have one major weakness."

"What's that?"

"It assumes the only people who know about it are the two who are exchanging messages." His smile widened. "And that both parties are tech savvy – which, I can tell you, your wife isn't."

"No, she's not - but how do you know that?"

"I'll get to that in a minute." Spike handed Franklyn the folder. "I got the IP addresses of the computers logging onto that Hotmail account, together with times of access from the subscriber accounts at each Internet Provider. There were only two, Carin and Richard Hanson. That gave me his address and bank details, and from there I did the rounds. Inland Revenue, Credit Card companies, DVLC, DHSS, PNC..." He nodded at the folder Franklyn was now holding. "Once you've been through that, you'll probably know more about him than he does himself."

"Thanks."

"One more thing – what I said about your wife not being tech savvy?"

"Okay?"

"I noticed she uses auto complete a lot."

Franklyn shook his head. "You've lost me."

"As you start typing something in, say an email address, the system checks to see if you've typed anything like it before - and if you have it fills it in for you. You just hit the tab key to accept it."

"Okay."

"The Hotmail account uses the dot co dot uk domain name." Spike smiled again. "I've set up a Hotmail account with the same username and password, but with the dot com domain name. And copied that into your wife's PC's history file. So, when she starts typing the username in..." He shrugged.

"Auto complete will log her into the new account," said

Barry, "while this Hanson character will still be logging into the old one."

"And you know about both accounts," said Spike to Franklyn. "You can read their messages before passing them on or replace them with messages of your own."

Barry was smiling.

"You Machiavellian little bastard," he said, admiringly.

Franklyn was shaking his head.

"Sorry," he said. "You're going to have to run this by me again."

Spike made to speak, but Barry quieted him with a dismissive gesture and turned to Franklyn. Spike thought he probably missed the flash of anger he felt cross his face, then realised that Franklyn was giving him a curious stare.

"How it works at the moment," Barry began, and Franklyn dropped the stare to focus on what Barry was saying, "is like this. Richard Hanson wants to get a message to Carin, right?"

Franklyn nodded.

"So, he logs into the Hotmail account, types an email and saves it as a draft. Doesn't send it anywhere, okay?"

"Okay."

"Carin logs into the same email account, reads Hanson's draft email, deletes it and types her reply. Also saves it as a draft and doesn't send it anywhere. Right?"

Franklyn gave another nod.

"Then Hanson logs in, reads the reply, and we start all over again."

"Okay," said Franklyn, "That bit I've got."

"What Spike has done," Barry continued, "is to create another email account with the same name and same password but on a different domain."

"Domain?" Franklyn gave a puzzled shake of his head.

"Think of it like Wheatacre Road and Wheatacre Crescent," said Barry, "on the Post Office delivery route of a dyslexic postman." He sat back in his chair. "So now Richard

Hanson types his draft email into the Hotmail dot com account. But instead of Carin reading it, you do. Then you log into the Hotmail dot co dot uk account and either type in Hanson's email, or your version of it, and then she logs into that account and reads whatever you want her to."

He shrugged.

"Or maybe you do nothing at all. Maybe you leave it exactly the way Spike's set it up, so they both think the other one's dumped them." He sighed. "Maybe you let it go."

"No." Franklyn spoke quietly. "No, that's not going to happen."

He thought for a moment before turning to Spike.

"What I'd like you to do, is send an email to this Richard Hanson, which appears to be from Carin, okay. Telling him she's in England for a few days and she wants to meet up. We'll arrange a rendezvous." He smiled. "Somewhere quiet and out of the way."

"For fuck's sake, Kit!" Barry stood up. "How well is that going to work out?"

Franklyn stared at him.

"Okay," said Barry quietly. "Let me handle it."

"Handle it how?"

"We'll set up the meet, only I'll go." He looked Franklyn straight in the eyes. "I'll put the fear of God into him. Even drag him out of his car and give him a kicking, if that's what you want. But something he'll walk away from, right? And something that can't be directly connected to you."

Spike watched the two of them stare at each other for a few seconds and then Franklyn gave a curt nod. Barry slowly exhaled.

"Where do you want it set up?" he asked.

"Let me think about it," said Franklyn.

Barry gave him a long look and turned to Spike.

"I'll give you a bell, when it's all sorted," he said. "And then you'll handle the emails?"

"Okay," said Spike.

Franklyn stood up, suddenly seeming to be in a hurry to leave.

"Thanks again for this," he said to Spike. Then hesitantly, "Shall I sort things out with Barry, for whatever I owe you?"

"Don't you worry about Spike," said Barry. "Spike always gets taken care of."

Spike felt the colour rush to his face but was aware that Franklyn's attention was on him again, as the two men walked towards the door.

"We'll let ourselves out," Barry said, pulling the office door shut behind him.

* * *

Spike gave it twenty minutes and decided to leave. The diagnostics in the progress report looked good, and he needed to get Barry Denham out of his hair. He deadlocked the front door and stepped onto the pavement.

It was nearly midnight, there'd be some drift between the late bars and the clubs, maybe he'd get lucky, slip into a well stewed stag or hen do on the move and see who he could separate out from the pack...

"Hi there."

"*Jesus!*" Spike almost jumped out of his skin. "*Jesus fucking Christ!*"

"Sorry," said Kit Franklyn, stepping out of the shadows. "I was about to ring the bell when I heard movement inside." He gave a smile. "Thought I'd better make sure it was you."

"You nearly gave me a heart attack." Spike could actually feel the pounding in his chest and he took a breath. "So, what's the problem? Did you leave something behind?"

"Can we talk?" asked Franklyn. "Privately. Somewhere quiet."

2. April 1970

Aidan

For all of his words of encouragement, when Don Mayberry dropped me off in London after the drive back from Cornwall, I expected that to be that. But a week later a note was left at the Slade asking me to call him, leading to lunch the next day at a rather grand club on Piccadilly.

"As I said, I'm really keen to take a look at your work," he told me as we waited to order, "but what I wanted to talk to you about today is this house I've bought."

He explained he was in the process of getting divorced and that the soon to be ex Mrs Mayberry planned on taking him to the cleaners. He didn't go into detail, but I had the sense there was dirt to be spilt if things got nasty and a role in a Hollywood movie, which his agent was currently finessing, was likely to go tits up if that happened.

"So, I've bought this wreck over in Notting Hill," he explained. "It's all I can afford at the moment, but the plan is to restore it to its former glory."

I knew that quite a few actors renovated houses for an income during the periods they were 'resting'. But Don was quick to point out this was a completely different proposition.

"I'll be getting builders and decorators in as and when I can afford to," he told me, "and I reckon it's going to take two to three years, if not longer. So, when I'm in London, I'll be staying at Claudia Falcone's apartment until it's completed." He smiled at my surprised expression. "She'll be away at university for most of the next three years."

"Right," I said.

"As each room is finished, I'll rent it out - a room on the

ground floor's already habitable and Lee's moving into that one. She's going to manage the house for me while I'm away - collecting the rent and investing the money back into the renovations."

All very interesting, but I didn't see what it had to do with me. As if reading my mind, he sat back in his chair and studied me.

"The place has a basement," he said. "Where the kitchen, scullery etcetera used to be, but most of it's been ripped out. It would make a great studio - probably be big enough to live in, too."

"Okay," I said slowly.

"If you want it, it's yours," he told me. "I'll get it cleaned up and habitable, before I leave for the States."

"I appreciate the offer," I said carefully, "but I'm really not sure I could afford..."

"I wouldn't want anything for it," Don broke in. "Sorry, I should have made that clear. I know how difficult - and expensive - it is to get space of your own in London these days, so I thought this might be a solution. On the understanding that I get it back when the house is finished and I want to move in." He shrugged. "It'll help tide you over until you've a large enough body of work to get yourself established, and it's probably the closest that I'll ever get to being a patron of the arts - in any meaningful sense, that is."

The bugbear of my life at that time was trying to find somewhere to work uninterrupted. It was almost impossible not to collect an audience using one of the rooms at the Slade, and although I'd converted a spare room next to the kitchen at home into a studio of sorts, it was a noisy household to say the least.

"This is incredibly generous of you," I told him. "I really don't know what to say."

"You haven't seen it yet," said Don, "but it won't take long to get it liveable."

And it hadn't - two weeks later I was whitewashing the

walls of the first place of my own that I could call home. I also drafted in a couple of the lads from one of my uncle's sites. They got a lavatory unblocked and flushing, rewired the mains so an electric heater wouldn't blow out the fuse box and - most importantly - bricked up the entrance to the basement from the stairwell. The inconvenience of having to go out of the side door and around to the front entrance to let myself back in again whenever I wanted to use the kitchen or have a bath, I felt, would be more than compensated for by the fact that it would be an equal hassle for anyone else in the house to bother me.

And I was right enough there - as the house began to fill up, the presence of the misanthrope in the basement would not go unnoticed or unremarked. But that isolation didn't prevent me from having a ringside seat to the social upheavals of the next few years.

* * *

If ever you should find yourself in a position where you need to convince someone that the late sixties counterculture was little more than kids playing with the dressing-up box, there aren't many better arguments than pointing out the speed with which things went from *All You Need Is Love* to lighting up the Molotov cocktails. One summer everyone's dressed like Afghan shepherds with flowers in their hair, and by next spring it's combat jackets in Grosvenor Square, while Paris burns. And, as someone who'd grown up with the reality of rifle butts taking down your front door, I was less than impressed.

The one exception I made to this was Wilf Brownlow.

We'd come into contact again, purely coincidentally, a few months after returning from Cornwall. Lee had met up with Kit through some radical theatre group that she was performing with and Kit was writing for, and I'd been dragged along to a less than grand opening night. It had been held at the Roundhouse, a disused railway engine shed in Camden Town which had been adapted as an arts venue by the playwright Arnold Wesker. He was a socialist and heavily involved with CND, so it was no surprise to find Wilf and Frieda in the audience. Back then, it really did seem like everyone knew everyone else.

In the pub afterwards Wilf asked me if I'd come and give a talk at the next meeting of his local SWP. Wesker was nodding along, saying that the 'Irish Struggle' needed to be better understood and leaving me thinking I didn't actually have much choice. But it wasn't really an arm twisting, I did feel that I owed him for his hospitality in Cornwall, plus I genuinely liked the man. Frieda could be hard going but once you got past the bombastic rhetoric, Wilf, I thought, was okay.

And as things turned out it was a good evening, I kept firmly to my family's experiences of the Easter Rising and subsequent Civil War. As ever, when recollections grow personal their reception becomes more respectful and by the end of the night the meeting had become more of a sombre discussion than a lecture or dialectic rant. I've no doubt at all there was a police spy or two in the room, but any baggage I might once have felt about that was aboard a ship long since set sail.

We stayed in loose touch, mainly through Emma's occasional visits to the house as it filled up with an eclectic mixture of fringe theatre performers, poets and musicians. Lee seemed to assess a potential tenant's suitability more by their 'vibe' than financial standing which, she once explained to me, wasn't so much of a problem. Anyone unemployed had their rent paid by the National Assistance Board, the state blissfully unaware it was funding a cultural hothouse.

Quite a few faces from St Hannahs also began to appear. Paul, his problems with the military seemingly resolved, had a room there for a while. Jake and Kit both moved in at some point over the next couple of years. It was difficult to keep track as people would hang out before moving in and revisit after they'd left. Loose arrangements that seemed to get even looser as Lee graduated from theatre to TV and became less and less involved in the daily running of the house.

In fact, the only ground rules she did seem to insist on were no hard drugs on the premises and no dealing. I'm not sure whether she deliberately turned a blind eye to Kit or if they had some unspoken arrangement that whatever he was up to needed to happen elsewhere, but it was obvious where his money was coming from. He certainly wasn't making anything from his contributions to the underground press or theatre 'workshops' and nor was it the NAB keeping him in leather jackets and snakeskin cowboy boots.

By the spring of 1970, the house was pretty much finished. With Don flitting back and forth between London and Hollywood we didn't get to see an awful lot of him but, as the final lick of paint went onto the walls in the stairwell, I think we all knew that informal eviction notices, friendly as I'm sure they'd be, wouldn't be long arriving.

Claudia

In retrospect, one of the oddest things about the next few years was how we all kept in touch as individuals whilst hardly ever coming together as a group. I can't think of a single occasion throughout that period that found us all actually in the same room at the same time, yet I doubt any of us lost that sense of intimacy we'd forged in St Hannahs.

I was at university in Bristol, of course, but I did come back to London a lot more frequently than I'd expected to. Not homesickness exactly, rather that there seemed lots more to do. I know it sounds dreadfully snobbish, but I quickly learnt that I really wasn't cut out for the provinces. I understood that student life was as much to broaden our social horizons as to educate us, but spending Saturday night after Saturday night in dingy pubs, trying to avoid being felt up while boorish rugby players poured pints of beer over each other's heads, had rapidly broadened them quite far enough, thank you very much.

At first, I worried how Don would react to having me around every other weekend, but it never became a problem. His initial film role in Hollywood was to have taken a month, but he'd been offered another part almost immediately and so was never really at Portman Square for the first six months. He came back to London the following year for a season at the RSC and he also played the lead role in a TV series about a London gangster, which became quite notorious for its levels of violence, although the publicity seemed to do his career no harm at all.

It was Lee who spent more time at Portman Square than anyone. Ostensibly, she was living at Don's Notting Hill slum - *'Maison Rachman'* as she referred to it - but the place really was awful. She absolutely refused to take a bath there and I didn't blame her. In truth, I'd much rather someone was actually staying in my apartment than have it stand empty and by way of a thank you she'd always arrange some treat for whenever I came back to Town.

Emma I also met up with quite often, Oxford was only an hour away and she was home most weekends too. I'd either take her out for a meal or she'd whisk me off to a demonstration against something or other. There seemed no shortage of noble causes to occupy her time.

Aidan I saw less frequently. He had his studio in the basement of Don's house and whilst not exactly discouraging visitors, you did get the sense he appreciated not feeling intruded upon. But I'd go over there occasionally with Lee, collecting the rent or solving some problem with plumbing or fuses.

Familiar faces from St Hannahs would pop up. Kit moved into Pembridge Villas, keeping himself as much to himself as he had in Cornwall - not enigmatic exactly, but you were never really sure what was going on with him. Jake also, but whereas in St Hannahs you tended to think of him as sweet but harmless - following Emma around like a little puppy dog - there was more of an edge to him now. You could be charitable and say that he'd grown in confidence, but it struck me as being more like arrogance - not an attractive trait at all.

"Perhaps he's just starting to realise how we thought of him back then," suggested Emma, "and now he's overcompensating."

She could have been right and maybe it was something which he had to go through. I just wished he was going through it somewhere else.

For a while Paul had a room there too - all the drama of his disappearance from St Hannahs seemingly water under the bridge now. He'd obviously left the army, but under exactly what circumstances I was still unclear about.

"I bought myself out," he told me on one of the rare occasions I pressed him on it, but with a smile inscrutable enough to suggest there was a lot more to it than that. He was equally reticent about his current employment.

"Security," he'd say with that same smile which, to be honest with you, could get a little irritating.

But, and in spite of Lee's cautionary warning, I still couldn't stop myself having feelings for him.

* * *

During the spring of 1970, I found myself spending most of my spare time in London. In Bristol I'd been involved in a romance with a nice enough chap but which I'd never seen outlasting the degree course. Now it was becoming obvious that he felt differently - he wanted me to meet his parents, was talking about moving to London in the summer to find a job. I'd yet to learn that in an unequal emotional relationship one side letting the other down gently is little more than wishful thinking - I seemed to be forever on the telephone listening to either angry remonstrations or anguished remorse.

So, at the beginning of the Easter break I was back in Portman Square, not exactly furtively peeking around corners when I went out but close enough. Lee had a part in a TV series that was being filmed in London but was out of town doing *'the location shoots'*. Paul did offer to *'take care of things'* for me, but Lord knows what that would have left on my conscience.

But he did mention it to Aidan, who rang to say that he was off to Dublin for a couple of weeks and that I was welcome to stay in his studio while he was away. I didn't need too much persuading.

Pembridge Villas had come on in leaps and bounds since the last time I'd been over there. I suppose that the rooms had been finished for a while, but now the common areas had been decorated - hallway, stairs and landings all restored to their previous glory.

With the keys Aidan had left a note with instructions for the boiler and also a couple of tickets for the opening of an art exhibition, curated by one of his lecturers at the Slade.

'Don't know if you're into German Expressionist art' he wrote *'but Karl Öttinger's worth a look.'*

* * *

I'd mentioned the tickets almost casually to Emma - suggesting that the two of us going off to an exhibition together would be almost like old times - so I really wasn't prepared for her reaction.

"What - *the* Karl Öttinger," she exclaimed. "The German painter."

"I suppose so," I said. "I think it's unlikely there'd be two of them."

She became quite animated.

"He's a famous anti-fascist, he had to leave Germany during the nineteen thirties."

"Because of his art?" I asked.

"He was very politically engaged," said Emma, "which was reflected in his paintings. But after the war he was able to move back to the DDR."

"Well, apparently he'll be giving a talk so…"

"What!" broke in Emma. "He'll actually be there himself?"

"That's what it says," I told her, reading the ticket. "*A short talk on German Expressionism in the Weimar Republic, followed by cheese and wine.*" That I'd be looking forward to the latter more than the former was a thought I kept to myself.

"Are there any tickets left?" she asked.

"I expect so," I said. It seemed an unlikely event to have created a thriving black market.

"I know Mum and Dad will really want to go," she said. "And probably quite a few of their friends."

I told her that if she couldn't get tickets from the Slade, then Aidan had given them out to everyone in the house and I was sure there'd be spares.

* * *

Which is how, two nights later, I found myself sitting in a pub around the corner from the exhibition not only with Emma but also Wilf and Frieda, together with half a dozen Socialist Workers Party members and all keen to engage with their anti-fascist hero.

And bizarre doesn't even begin to cover it.

To ensure that the evening started out on the right foot, we'd had a speech from Wilf before leaving the bar. It began with a collection of caveats against the feckless world we were about to enter and concluded with a caution against being seduced by the cheap baubles of *'bourgeois bohemianism'*. And, needless to say, delivered boisterously enough to treat the rest of the pub to his insights.

"It's something new," I heard one trendy looking patron tell his bemused girlfriend as we all filed out of the door. "I think it's called street theatre".

"Are we supposed to clap?" she asked.

So, in much the same manner that a Christian charity group dedicated to the welfare of fallen women might gird their loins whilst setting out for the fleshpots of Soho, we made our way along the road to the Slade.

"Hello, Emma, long time no see," said a figure, falling into step alongside the two of us.

"Hello Raymond," said Emma. "This is Claudia."

I got a frank appraisal from Raymond before he turned his full attention back to Emma, ignoring me completely.

Raymond was in his mid-twenties, with the appearance of an almost caricature Lothario. His glossy dark hair was swept back in a style he probably thought Byronesque, his beard carefully sculpted and his overcoat draped over his shoulders rather than actually worn. Complimented with a stand-offish nose in the air attitude, this all suggested a combination of affectations which I'd learnt the hard way masked the kind of vanity easily punctured by rejection and only re-inflated by refusing to take no for an answer. And on one occasion, right up to a finger poked in the eye.

I made a mental note not to find myself alone with him during the evening.

* * *

As you'd expect from political art, Karl Öttinger's work offered little by way of subtlety and he was certainly no draughtsman. But there was something about his fraught, almost cartoonish, protagonists that was surprisingly touching. You didn't really need the occasional introduction of a marionette to grasp his point that to a degree we are all puppets in dramas not of our own devising. I'd also have to say there wasn't a single piece in the entire exhibition that I would want on my living room wall.

By contrast, Öttinger himself seemed a jolly soul. He must have been in his seventies and whatever traumas and deprivations lay in his past, they certainly hadn't seemed to have spoilt his appetite. His talk on the Weimar Republic - translated from his German on the fly by a young woman introduced as *'Heidi, my right hand'* (a declaration which drew more than one ribald comment from behind us) - was short and succinct, while his gaze was repeatedly drawn to the buffet table visible through an archway at the far end of the gallery.

And he was happy to chat on any subject to just about anyone, from life in Berlin during the twenties with Wilf and Frieda to Bridget Riley's Op art with a young student. Although I started to wonder whether his views might be gaining a little in translation, Heidi's expositions invariably much longer in English than the original German.

Emma had wandered away somewhere, and I walked through into the bar looking for her. I found her sitting at a table talking to Raymond, not something I wanted to get involved in. I was wondering if it might be time to go home when a voice behind me said, "Hello Claudia."

I turned to find Kit standing there.

"Wouldn't have thought this was your kind of thing," he said with a smile. "I've always had you down as a Pre-Raphaelite kinda gal."

"Aidan left me the tickets," I told him. "I felt a bit obligated."

Before he could reply, a girl - an art student, I guessed by the predominance of black in her clothing and makeup - joined us.

"Excuse me," she said, "but she's a friend of yours, right?"

She nodded over to where Emma was sitting with Raymond.

"Yes," I said curiously.

"I thought so, I saw you walk in together." She leaned forward and lowered her voice. "I was just at the bar and that bloke she's talking to was buying drinks. One of them was a double vodka, and I saw him pour it into that cider she's drinking."

"Right," I said. "Okay, thanks."

She nodded and moved away.

"So, let's..." I began, but Kit cut me off.

"It's okay," he said. "I'll handle it."

"This isn't the place to start any trouble," I told him.

"I know," he smiled, taking a packet of cigarettes from his pocket and lighting one. "Trust me."

* * *

"But education is the key," Emma was saying to Raymond. "It's almost impossible to find capitalism acceptable when viewed in its proper historical context."

Kit walked over to their table, and I moved closer myself to overhear their conversation.

"Hi," he said to Raymond, sitting down at their table. "I'm Kit. Sorry to barge in, but I wanted to... *Oh Jesus!*"

Reaching across the table to flick the end of his cigarette into the ashtray, his arm somehow managed to catch both of their drinks, tipping them over. He grabbed Raymond's glass before it rolled off onto the floor, Emma caught hers with her knees.

"Bloody hell!" cried Raymond angrily, almost jumping to his feet.

"Really sorry!" Kit was all contrition. "So stupid of me - let me get you two more."

If not completely mollified by this, Raymond did at least nod his head.

"What are you drinking?" Kit insisted.

"A pint of Black Velvet," said Raymond and Emma asked for a cider.

They sat in silence until Kit returned with the drinks.

"So what," Emma asked as he set them down on the table, "were you going to say?"

"Forget it," said Kit, "it's not that important and I've caused enough chaos for one night."

He smiled at them both and walked back over to join me.

"Black fucking Velvet," he said softly. "Jesus, what a poseur."

"Kit, what...?" I let the sentence trail off.

"Get Emma away from him," he said. "Explain to her what's going on and if you stay here, both of you keep out of his way for the rest of the night." He stared right at me. "Got that?"

"Why, what are you going to do?" I asked.

"Me, I'm off home," he said. "But remember, stay away from him."

With a smile, he turned and left the room.

Wondering how to get Emma on her own, she eventually solved the problem for me by getting up from the table and heading over to the Ladies.

I was waiting for her as she came out of the cubicle.

"How do you feel?" I asked to her quizzical expression.

"What do you mean?"

I explained about the drinks.

"So that's why..." She stared at me. "Where's Kit now?"

"He went home - but I think he's done something to Raymond's drink." I shrugged. "Maybe we should leave too."

She looked at me and nodded.

"Will you come over with me, while I get my coat?"

Back in the bar, Raymond was staring down at the glass he was holding. As we approached, Frieda and Wilf were passing his table from the opposite direction. Raymond looked up and gave Frieda a glassy-eyed stare, to which she returned an uncertain smile.

I doubt whether anyone not within two feet of them could have heard what Raymond said to her. But the words had hardly left his mouth when Wilf grabbed him by the throat and lifting him out of his chair slammed him against the wall.

Raymond looked at him and giggled.

Within seconds they'd been surrounded by figures trying to pull them apart, but not before Wilf threw a punch to Raymond's jaw and his legs just crumpled - he looked to be out cold.

"Dad!" Emma started to move forward, but I held her by

the arm.

"Wait a second," I told her.

"What's going on here?" Someone in a dinner jacket, obviously in charge, had pushed his way to the front of the crowd.

"I wouldn't repeat what he said to my wife in a barracks room," Wilf told him, but the man shook his head.

"Even so, that's no excuse to..."

"He tried to spike that girl's drink." The art student we'd spoken to earlier broke in and pointed to Emma. "I was at the bar and saw him do it."

Every eye in the room turned to Emma, who bit her lip and then nodded. With a roar, Wilf turned back to Raymond's limp body and raised his fist, but he was quickly pulled away. Frieda held onto his arm and whispered urgently into his ear, at which he seemed to calm down.

"We'll just go," I heard her say. "Let them take care of it."

"And if he doesn't behave when he comes around," the man in the dinner jacket said to Wilf, "we'll make damn sure he gets a good hiding and a night in the cells." He shook his head in disgust. "Kids these days - a sniff of the barmaid's apron and they're all over the bloody place."

As everyone began to shuffle away, I pulled Emma to one side.

"You can't say anything," I told her. "They'd think we were involved."

"I know," she said. And then, with not a little venom, "Bloody Kit – does he think I can't take care of myself?"

Before I could react to this, I was aware that Karl Öttinger was standing alongside us, a wide smile on his face - he'd obviously been taking in the entire scene.

He said something in German and I turned to Heidi.

"That takes him back, he says."

Kit

It was the first truly spring-like evening of the year and other than Aidan and Jake, everyone else in the house had taken themselves off for the weekend to some free festival in Devon. We'd been invited, but I think it was unspoken between the three of us that we'd still had enough of the West Country to last us a good while yet.

Aidan and I had been sitting in the kitchen, mulling over whether to head into central London or just make our way down to the pub. Then Jake appeared and said that he'd heard about a party in Holloway.

"We could give it a try," I said to Aidan. "If it turns out crap, we can always go down to the West End."

We took the tube to Tottenham Court Road and out to Archway. Eventually we found the address Jake had been given, a Victorian terraced villa *a la* Charles Pooter. The party itself had all the appearance of a sixth form end of term bash but we didn't even make it through the front door, our passage blocked by a po faced middle-aged man wearing a cravat and a comb-over, demanding to know whether we were friends of Charles or Naomi.

"Definitely Naomi," said Aidan.

A teenage girl, chatting to friends in the hallway, whipped her head around at this and stared at us.

"I've never seen these people before in my life, Daddy," she said.

"Oh, hello there Naomi," Aidan called over to her, as Daddy started to bristle. "You probably don't recognise me with my clothes on."

"Fetch Gary and Russell," yelped Daddy, which I took as our cue to disappear. A pair of Neanderthal prop forwards, I guessed.

"It's okay, we're leaving," said Aidan with a smile. "Keep your hair on."

We didn't wait for a reaction to this, or the arrival of

Gary and Russell, but turned and headed off down the street.

"For fuck's sake," said Jake. "If we'd played it cool, we could have talked our way in there."

"Doubt it," I said.

"Well, we'll never know, will we?" Jake shook his head. "So much for Irish fucking charm - thanks a lot, Paddy."

The tone was jocular, but there was an edge to it. As we arrived at the junction of the Seven Sisters Road, I was noticing an uncharacteristically tense vibe from Aidan.

"I suppose we could try *Cousins*," said Jake. "The all-nighter won't be starting yet, but you can sometimes get in for the last half hour of the early session without paying."

"Who's playing?" I asked.

"Who cares?" shrugged Jake.

"I know somewhere." Aidan stopped walking and gestured to the other side of the road. "It's only around the corner."

"A club?" asked Jake.

"Well, something like that." Aidan gave him a smile. "After all, if it's me that's buggered up your evening, shouldn't it be down to me to make things right?"

Without waiting for a response, he stepped off the curb and after a second or two Jake and I followed, catching up with him as he turned into the Caledonian Road.

* * *

"And here we are," said Aidan. He pushed open the door to what from the outside you'd have taken for a pub, but instead we found ourselves standing in a small foyer. There was a double set of swing doors at the far end, while to our left a young couple sitting behind a trestle table abruptly pulled apart from each other to stare at us.

"Good evening to you both," said Aidan and Jake and I glanced at each other, as his usually indiscernible Irish lilt morphed into a full brogue. "And how much would you be asking of the three of us, seeing as the evening is already well underway?"

"You'll be paying five shillings each whatever time you choose to arrive," answered the girl, in an accent almost as thick as Aidan's.

"Well, it's the romantic in me that'll be digging his hand deeper into his pocket, rather than the skinflint spending time arguing," said Aidan, taking out his wallet, "as it's obvious to all how eager you are to get back to your canoodling."

The girl blushed as she took a pound note from him, tore three tickets from a roll and handed them over with two half crowns. Her boyfriend just continued to stare, mouth hanging slightly open, as we walked on through the swing doors and into a room about thirty feet wide and sixty feet long.

Immediately facing us was a bar. At the other end of the room - on a raised platform rather than a stage - a band was playing. The line-up was five fiddles, penny whistle and squeeze box and they were all dressed like nineteenth century tinkers - brightly coloured neck scarves under striped collarless shirts, leather waistcoats and corduroy breeches tucked into boots that laced halfway up the calf. They were making a fair old din, though.

"Bloody hell," said Jake softly.

A wooden bench ran the full length of each wall. On one side sat around forty young men and opposite them an equally long row of girls. The dance floor in between was empty, presumably before we'd arrived they'd simply been sitting there staring at each other, but now, as we made our way to the bar, every eye in the place was on us.

"Three pints of Guinness," said Aidan, "and is that a Connemara single malt I can see there on the shelf behind you?"

"It is," said the barman, eyeing Aidan cautiously.

"We'll be chasing them down then," said Aidan, "and would you care for one yourself, if that's to your taste?"

The barman's expression softened.

"Thank you, sorr."

As he poured our drinks, the band finished their number and stepped down from the stage, which really emphasised the stony silence. The girls were looking over at us with unconcealed interest, while the hostility on the other side of the room was intensifying by the second.

In the bar area were a dozen or so tables, most of them occupied by large, ruddy faced, middle-aged men with well-muscled shoulders and soft fat bellies squeezed into ill-fitting suits, which were obviously Sunday best. As we carried our glasses over to an empty table they appeared more intrigued than hostile and one of them even gave Aidan a perfunctory nod and a smile. Not that that seemed to be easing the tension any.

McAlpine's Fusiliers, I guessed, *'Down the pub to drink the sub'* but Dominic Behan's lyrical romanticism was suddenly a lot more attractive on the page than in its sweaty reality.

"Nice vibe," said Jake as we sat down, but he was careful enough to keep his voice low.

Two girls stood up and walked over to the bar, smiling as they passed us.

"Good evening ladies," said Aidan, sitting back in his chair. "I was about to explain to my friends how Irish girls are the loveliest in the world, when suddenly here you are, leaving my words redundant even before they've left my mouth."

They giggled.

"Would you join us for a drink?" he asked and without waiting for an answer stood up and moved a couple of chairs from a neighbouring table over to ours. Hesitantly, but still smiling, they sat down and Aidan collected two Babychams from the bar.

From the corner of my eye, I saw that over on the bench one of the young men had angrily risen. His friend next to him took his arm to pull him back down, but he shook him off and strode across the room towards us.

"Carmel," he barked at one of the girls. "What is it you

think that you're doing?"

"I'm having a drink, Ryan," she replied, "as if that would be any business of yours."

Four or five of his friends had now crossed the room and formed a group around him.

"Making a holy show of yourself is what you're about," he shouted. "And who do think ye are," turning his attention to us, "ye feckin pansies, coming in here with ye airs and feckin graces?"

"We're just here for a quiet drink and some pleasant company," said Aidan, softly and with a smile. "We're not looking for any trouble."

A bit late for that, I thought, and Ryan seemed to feel the same way. He turned his head back and forth to his friends.

"Well, trouble's come and found you, it surely has," he said stepping forward and around him it was all nodding heads and squared up shoulders. "It's outside with the bunch of youse and we'll settle matters there."

It was at that point I noticed that the man who'd smiled at Aidan when we'd arrived had risen and gone over to a neighbouring table. He was bent over, whispering in the ear of a bullish looking man. As he straightened up, I could see the blood literally drain from the seated man's face. Ashen, he turned towards our table.

Aidan seemed almost amused at Ryan.

"Well," he said. "If that's how..."

He broke off, as the bullish looking man came up behind Ryan, and laid a hand on his shoulder. He gave a surprised start and tried to pull away, but the man turned Ryan all the way around to face him, put his hands on both shoulders then leaned forward and spoke too softly for me to hear.

Ryan twisted his head to look at us, but the man shook him by the shoulders, before pointing him away from our table and giving him a shove. He walked slowly away with a resentful look back at us, his friends following with puzzled expressions. The man who'd sent him on his way turned to us.

"I'm sorry about that, sorr," he said to Aidan. "They're all good lads at heart, they work hard and they play hard and sometimes with the drink and high spirits an' all they can get a little carried away with themselves."

He stuck out his hand and Aidan leaned forward to shake it.

"Brendon O'Doherty, sorr," he said. "I know your uncle very well, we've worked on most of his properties here and he's always been a pleasure to deal with, unlike some. He even had us back over the water for the renovations at his daughter's house in Waterford."

"It's a pleasure to meet you, Brendon," said Aidan. "And I've been to Caitlin's home many times, it's a fine job that you made of it."

"Thank you, sorr." He hesitated. "Could I buy you gentlemen a drink?"

"Well thank you Brendon, but we're going to be on our way now." Aidan smiled. "We were passing by chance and I had the fancy for a breath of the ould country."

"Well, you'll always find that here. And I promise you - I promise all of you gentlemen - that anytime you come back here you'll get a warmer welcome than you found tonight, and that's on the word of Brendon O'Doherty."

He gave a nod and walked back to his table. Aidan finished his Guinness and picked up the glass of whiskey. Jake was already slipping his jacket on.

"Let's give it a couple of minutes," said Aidan.

Ryan and his cronies were nowhere to be seen and the two girls, unsurprisingly, had melted away too. Gradually, eyes were turning away from us and the buzz of conversation was picking up.

"I think that's our cue," said Aidan, as the band returned to the stage.

* * *

It was smiles all around as we made our way out, even from the couple in the foyer. Maybe it was the drink, but outside on the pavement the spring evening now seemed to have a bite to it that wasn't there half an hour ago. We headed toward the tube station and as we passed a darkened alley, I heard low moans and a series of muffled thuds. I came to a halt, turned, and could just about make out Ryan being held by his arms while Brendon O'Doherty worked him like a punch bag.

"Keep walking," said Aidan softly, without turning his head.

None of us spoke on the walk to the tube station. As Aidan went over to the kiosk to buy the tickets, Jake turned to stare at me.

"What the fuck," he said, "was all that about?"

"I'm not exactly sure," I told him, "but if I were you, I'd stop calling him 'Paddy'."

3. Sy Johnson

It seemed the Gulfstream was only minutes wheels up before the pilot flicked the seatbelt light on again and the nose dipped down. Heading in from the States, thought Sy, wouldn't it have made sense to touchdown at Newquay and then on to London instead of doubling back, but what the hell did he know? Wasn't like it was his dime, he and Lee were piggy-backing a corporate flight courtesy of a CEO with a long term hard-on for her. They'd dropped off a couple of Vice Presidents of Whatever for a London meeting, so maybe he should just count his blessings they weren't setting out on a seven-hour road trip down to Lee's place in Cornwall.

In the seat opposite, Lee stirred but didn't wake. Sy could never sleep on planes, wasn't that he was a nervous flier or anything, just something he could never do. But Lee had closed her eyes as they'd taxied out of the private hanger at Burbank and was gone before they reached the runway. She didn't even wake when they'd touched down to refuel at that airfield in New England. He guessed she'd taken a pill.

Sy made small talk with the two VPs for a while, who to be honest were kind of pissed they weren't getting to chat with a real-life movie star. Sy spent some time smoothing things over with a few juicy morsels of Tinsel Town gossip before intimating that Lee's schedule had been a nightmare over the last few days so, hey guys, let's not wake her. They nodded understandingly and moved to seats at the rear of the cabin, from where Sy caught occasional snippets of high-level office politics, wrapped in dark murmurs of discontent.

He'd tried reading, given up on that, there was nothing

outside of the window but cotton candy clouds, so he'd let his head fall back and his thoughts inevitably tumbled yet one more time into the swirling maelstrom of the previous week.

* * *

It wasn't that the call had been unexpected, it was that events riding in on a long-awaited inevitability can sometimes still hit harder than a bolt from the blue. For months now Sy had kept an overnight bag not just at home and the office, but also - fortunately - in the trunk of his car. Fortunately, because he'd been behind the wheel when the hospital rang his cell.

Sy had been heading to a location shoot at San Clemente - increasing friction between one of his clients and the director was finally starting to spark - and he was passing Irvine when the call came. He got through to Rachel, his PA, as he looped around the next interchange and it took her less than ten minutes to come back with the options to get him in the air to Colorado. She could charter a Lear to the small airfield outside Burlington, which was only a thirty-minute drive away, but there'd be a three, maybe four hour wait. If he went commercial, there was a flight from LAX to Denver International in seventy-five minutes and she could have a limo waiting at the other end.

Traffic was heavy and for a while it was touch and go whether Sy would make it, but he did. Rachel had gotten a cab to the airport and was waiting there as he pulled up outside Departures. She'd already collected his ticket and handed it to him, together with an envelope stuffed with hundred dollar bills - sometimes Amex just didn't cut it in the High Plains - and taking only a second to squeeze his arm, she slipped into the driver's seat and accelerated away before a uniformed security guard could take more than half a dozen irate steps towards them. Sy ignored the dirty look as he brushed passed him into the terminal.

He made the gate with minutes to spare, was the last passenger to board, and he sank down into his seat with relief. There'd been nothing left in first class and it must have been twenty years since he'd flown coach. But sitting beside a young mother and helping tend to her infant daughter did a pretty good job of locking his emotional turmoil into cold storage for the next two-and-a-half hours.

Waiting in Arrivals was a chauffeur wearing a peaked cap and holding a handwritten sign with his name on it. The limo was in reserved parking right outside and five minutes later they'd skimmed the outskirts of Denver and were heading west on 70.

Other than to ask Sy whether he'd like to listen to some music or perhaps the news - which Sy declined - the driver was silent, leaving him to his thoughts. The road signs slipped by quickly - Strasberg, Deer Trail, Arriba and then they hung a left and entered the small town that for the first eighteen years of his life had been home.

* * *

Sy had been only three years old when his Dad shipped out to Korea. He was pretty sure that the few childhood memories he had of him were probably constructs from family anecdotes that had run like tape loops through every Christmas and Thanksgiving since, but he clung to them anyway.

Mom never remarried. She'd worked all her life as a bookkeeper at the family hardware store, which for five generations had been passed down from oldest son to oldest son, until times changed and her brother finally saw sense and sold out to Builders Square. They'd let Ted go but kept Mom on until times changed again, and they'd gone to the wall a couple of years ago. Sy had tried to persuade Mom to move out to LA, he'd find her a nice little gated condo along the coast, get her away from these deep freeze winters and blast furnace summers, but Mom had other ideas. She'd lived in that house on Trinity all her life, she told him, and the only way anyone was getting her out of there would be horizontal and feet first.

Growing up hadn't been easy, not because back in the fifties a single mom wasn't the everyday thing it would later become - she was a war widow and that counted for a lot in a small town with the stars and stripes flying on most lawns - but money was tighter than people imagined. The family might own the store, but between Mom and Sy, Ted's family and their Dad in a nursing home, things could sometimes get spread a little thin.

Through Elementary and Middle School, Sy spent a lot of time with their neighbours. With Mom working, that was where he'd go after classes, until she'd arrive to collect him. 'He's no trouble at all,' they'd tell her, 'he just sits there and reads.' In return, evenings or weekends Mom would sit for them whenever occasion warranted a night out at the Roadhouse.

Which was how Sy had met Cassidy Martin.

He'd been in the last year of Middle School when the Martins moved in two houses down, recent arrivals in town from Wichita, Mr Martin being the new manager at First National. Cassidy was a year older than Sy, which would have made her unobtainable *whatever*, but her being the prettiest girl he'd ever seen and Sy now a gawky, acne riddled geek in horn-rimmed spectacles, was the universe introducing him to the notion of exquisite torture.

That she was so sweet-natured only made things a million times worse. If she'd been a spiteful little sneak - which in Sy's experience was the default setting for most pretty little girls - he could have hidden away in a corner and buried his face in a book. But Cassidy was solicitude itself to what was widely regarded as his semi orphan status and so blessed him with the worst possible outcome for the unrequited love of males at any age, sisterly affection.

At that point it would have seemed impossible to Sy that life could get any worse, but the universe wasn't through with him yet. After he started at Junior High, most days Cassidy would walk home with him and so into his life came

Richie Stevens and Buck Richmond, zeroing in on Cassidy in a frenzy of teen hormones and on Sy as a target for alpha male chest beating.

Richie wasn't too bad, things were more of a haze with him, but Buck haunted Sy's dreams for years. Every small town has its kingpin, and theirs was Jack Richmond, Buck's father. He owned a couple of car dealerships and had a finger in most of the Chamber of Commerce's plum pies, up to and including the Country Club. Went without saying that Buck was also star quarterback on the school's football team and usually had a flurry of cheerleaders around him, but it was Cassidy that he'd set his sights on.

So, when Ritchie and Cassidy started going steady, Sy felt the first delicious pangs of what he'd later learn to call *schadenfreude,* but that didn't last long. For some reason Buck got it into his head that Sy had said something to Cassidy that turned her against him - instead of accepting the obvious conclusion that she'd finally come to recognise what a total asshole he was - and from then on life became hell. Hardly a week passed without Sy's head being held in a toilet bowl as it flushed, or his pants ripped off and thrown into a tree. And because Buck was 'popular' - God, how Sy came to hate that word - it was then *carte blanche* for every other jerk in school to pin a target on his back.

Sy wasn't dumb, he understood that the classic technique for surviving school bullying is humour, to become the class clown, but he also knew that wasn't going to work for him. He wasn't naturally extrovert and he wasn't funny looking, least not that way.

So, what Sy did was to become a fixer.

It began with homework. He did math for some of the jocks, who let him hang and that kept most of his antagonists at bay. Then it was cherry bombs - dropping one down a toilet bowl in the boys' restroom created Old Faithful scale geysers for the girls next door, irresistible high jinks for his new buddies. Stocked by the dozen at the store they weren't missed, and he turned a tidy profit on them, as he did with the switchblades and handguns that he legitimately purchased through the register on the occasions he worked in the store alone. Candid conversations with some of his less reputable customers led to introductions made in Denver bars for fake driving licences, weed and pretty much anything else a High School senior in a hick town felt his world was lacking.

Even Buck came around in the end, Sy never ever got an apology but after getting Ritchie two tickets for the Denver Broncos game against the Detroit Lions - when they became the first AFL team ever to win against the NFL - Buck came up to him on the Monday morning and Sy got a slow punch to the shoulder. Before Sy could respond, Buck gave him a nod and walked away.

Sy's imagination still kept Cassidy swaddled in romantic fantasies, but she and Ritchie were a solid item now and there was talk of an engagement to be announced after graduation. But then - two weeks after school was out - for Sy everything changed forever when Janis Joplin and the Big Brother Holding Company blew into town.

It hadn't been a planned stop. The tour bus cracked an axle en route to a gig in Kansas City, but the itinerary had a few days slack in it and so the band decided to chill. They took over the school hall for a makeshift concert, more of a jam really, but most of the town showed up for it and - judging her audience perfectly - Janis ditched the West Coast psychedelia she'd been making her name with and sang old blues and country numbers way into the night. Some of the road crew were looking to score, Sy took care of it, and that was how he got to meet her.

He was never really sure why she took to him, but she did. He guessed later that she must have recognised a kindred spirit - Janis had been bullied all through high school and probably knew the signs better than most - and when the band rolled out of town Sy left with them, on the payroll as a gofer. Mom wasn't too pleased, but he told her he was only putting college back a year and hell, this was a chance to see something of the world.

One year turned into two and Sy hadn't stayed a gofer for long. Acumen for closing the deal - combined with a distaste for pretty much all drugs except alcohol - had made him someone who Janis came to rely on more and more, but even he couldn't save her from her own demons. He'd remained loyal to the end, but once she'd gone he'd struck out on his own, and in the movie business rather than the rock world. He wasn't going through that again, he told himself, but of course he did, many times over.

In the years since, he'd had his heart broken into a lot more pieces than Cassidy Martin ever managed and he'd suffered way more malignant entities than Buck Richmond, but hey, first cut is the deepest. And although the scars gradually fade from sight, tracing even the lightest touch along their length never lets you forget how deep they really run.

* * *

They say that when you go back home everything seems smaller than you remember, but to Sy every haunted recollection they passed on the way to the hospital - the football stadium, the park, Jensen's Soda Fountain, the fucking High School - loomed as large in the bright afternoon sun as it ever had in his memory.

Outside the hospital the driver took Sy's bag from the trunk, accepted the fifty dollar tip with a gracious nod and was gone. Through the automatic plate glass doors - they were new - he found the nurses' station deserted, but a candy striper pointed him to a room along the corridor away to the left.

At first he thought that after battling his way through all the chaos of this day he was too late and he stood rooted to the spot. Then her chest rose. She blinked, and he walked over to the chair by the bed.

"Mom," he said. "It's Seymour."

She seemed to be trying to speak and he took her hand. But before he could say anything a young doctor came into the room, accompanied by a nurse.

"Mr Johnson?" she asked, as the nurse moved around the bed and moistened Mom's lips.

Sy nodded.

"I think you might have only just made it here in time," said the doctor, British by the sound of her. She indicated the corridor with her hand. "May we speak?"

"Sure," said Sy.

"As you're probably aware, your mother suffered a stroke during the night." Her tone was efficient but empathetic, Sy guessed she got a lot of practice. "It was much worse than the last one which I believe was..."

She glanced down at the clipboard she was holding.

"Eight months ago," said Sy.

The doctor nodded.

"She's been receiving care at home?"

"After the last time, the doctors said that she'd be as comfortable there as in a nursing home, so long as she had around the clock care." Sy shrugged. "It's what she wanted."

"I'm sure they were right, I don't believe there's much more that could have been done for her." She hesitated. "If you have any other family who'd wish to be here, you should contact them."

Sy shook his head.

"It's only me." Someone else seemed to be saying the next two words. "How long?"

"One can never be absolutely certain but," a slight grimace, "hours rather than days, I'm afraid."

"I can stay with her?"

"Of course. She may not seem to respond, but it's often the case that patients are aware of their surroundings and do take comfort from the presence of loved ones. You should feel free to talk to her."

Sy nodded.

"Thank you."

The doctor smiled and left.

So what's your story, thought Sy, stepping back into the room, *what winding path have your feet followed from the leafy shire or smoky old mill town?*

The nurse was dabbing Mom's lips with a wet sponge. He sat down on the other side of the bed and reached out his hand.

"It's okay," he said to her, "I can do that."

She passed him the sponge and a small bowl of water.

"Can I get you a drink?" she asked. "Or maybe a snack from the commissary?"

"A coffee would be great," he said, "black no sugar. Thank you"

She nodded and left.

For the next few hours he sat and talked, told Mom what he'd been up to and the celebrity gossip she loved to listen to during his regular but could be more frequent phone calls home. He was aware the nurses had changed shift, the new ones refilling his coffee cup and continually checking the readout on whatever it was they had Mom hooked up to, but it was a presence that was never intrusive.

Then, as the twilight outside the window turned to darkness, Mom suddenly stiffened. One of the machines began emitting a persistent beeping noise and within seconds the room was full of people in scrubs and he was being escorted, politely but firmly, out into the corridor. There was a bench against the wall opposite, Sy sat and buried his face in his hands.

A few minutes later, the doctor he'd spoken to earlier came over and sat down beside him. He straightened up and turned to her.

"I'm sorry, Mr Johnson," she said. "I know it's little consolation, but there was no pain and I'm sure she knew you were with her at the end."

It was nice of her to say that, even though she couldn't

be certain.

"Would you like us to contact the Funeral Home?" she continued. "There is only the one in town, we can arrange for them to get in touch with you, to make the necessary arrangements."

"Thank you," said Sy, and she nodded and stood up.

He sat for a while, alone with his memories, then figured he'd better call a cab and go on over to the house. Deal with the Care Agency and get things finalised with them, maybe think about contacting a realtor...

His thoughts broke off as he became aware of someone standing motionless, a few feet away. He looked up to see one of the nurses who'd been bringing him coffee for the last few hours.

"Hi." He forced a smile. "Thanks for taking care of her the way you did. I'm sure..."

"I'm so sorry, Seymour," she said. "The whole town will miss her."

Sy stared as her face seemed to move in and out of focus. And then he realised that it was Cassidy Martin he was looking at.

* * *

They were in the commissary facing each other across a table, Sy still embarrassed.

"I'm sorry," he'd said as they'd sat down. "With the journey and Mom... I guess I just wasn't registering anything at all."

"That's okay." Cassidy smiled. "It's been a long time."

Looking at her Sy struggled to understand how he'd not seen it, wasn't that she'd gotten heavy or aged badly. Her hair was cut short now, but that hadn't changed the shape of her face or anything. Then again, there was something missing, and it was nothing to do with the passage of time... More like a switch had been flicked and that something inside was now turned off.

They'd chatted awhile, mainly about Sy and life in

Hollywood, until Sy asked how long she'd been a nurse.

"I started training right after Ritchie and I got married," she said, "so almost thirty years."

"Wow," said Sy. "And what does Richie do nowadays?"

"Ritchie got sick," she said quietly. "He passed last year."

"Shit! Oh God, I'm sorry, I didn't know."

"No reason you should," said Cassidy. "It was right after your Mom's stroke, so she wouldn't have known."

Sy was silent.

"But he'd been ill a long time - it was..." She shook her head. "We pretty much lost everything."

"But what about the insurance?" asked Sy. "You saying Ritchie wasn't covered?"

Cassidy was silent for a few seconds.

"You know they always say, 'You can't fight City Hall'? Well trust me, City Hall is a stroll in the park compared to one of these big insurance companies, once they've got their mind made up." She shook her head again. "We'd have been fighting two battles there, and we hardly had the stomach for one. It was easier to take out a second mortgage to cover the hospital bills and pray that we'd get a chance to start over. That things would work out for us."

Cassidy bit her lip.

"You lost your house?" asked Sy.

"That, savings, pensions - all just sucked away." She sat back in her chair. "I stayed with Mom and Dad for a while, but they moved to Boca Raton when Dad retired last year. They said they'd rent me the house, but I knew they were counting on selling to get by down there.... For a while now, I've been living in a double wide out by Cyprus Creek. The trailer park belongs to Buck Richmond. You remember Buck, right?"

Hah!

"Buck's been good to me this last year. Everyone has, really."

They sat in silence for a while.

"You know Cass," said Sy eventually, "I think there's a

way we could help each other out here."

She looked at him quizzically.

"I need to be thinking about selling the house," he said, "but there's a lot of work to be done first. Mom didn't like change, even change for the better. The driveway needs repair, the yard's a mess, and I should get someone to look at the roof." He hesitated. "I thought I'd have to spend time out here getting stuff organised, but if I had someone staying there, someone I could trust to do all of that for me," he raised his hand as Cassidy began to speak, "I'd cover living expenses of course and pay for time spent..."

He broke off as Cassidy, softly, began to cry.

* * *

Through the main doors of the Richmond Motors Sales showroom the reception desk was just off to the left, and Sy waited there until a young woman wearing a pants suit and cornrows - old man Richmond would never have gone for that - came over to ask how she could help. Sy explained he was here to see Buck. Nope, he didn't have an appointment, but his name was Seymour Johnson. She smiled, said she'd check if Mr Richmond was free and disappeared through a door marked 'Employees Only'. Sy strolled over to kick the tyres on an imported Range Rover, but almost immediately he heard the door open behind him.

It seemed to Sy that Buck hadn't so much aged as morphed into his old man - if someone had shown Sy a photograph, he would have staked his life that he was looking at Mr Richmond Senior. He even walks like his dad, thought Sy, as Buck came across the showroom towards him, a look of almost bemusement on his face.

"Seymour." They shook hands, Buck slowly shaking his head. "Jesus, how long has it been?"

"Must be twenty-five years," said Sy.

"And then some." Buck's expression saddened. "About your Mom, I'm real sorry, man. She was a nice lady."

Sy nodded.

"Molly and I would see her most Sundays after church, and she'd always be talking about you. She was real proud, you know? Shit man, we all are, someone from this pisspot of a town making something for themselves."

Sy suddenly found the words stuck in his throat, while Buck seemed to choose his own words carefully.

"I guess we really made your life hell back then, huh?" he said quietly.

Sy let the 'we' go, heard himself saying something like what the fuck, we were just kids and that's what kids do, but Buck slowly shook his head.

"No," he said. "What happened, that's the kind of shit that sticks, right?"

Sy stayed silent.

"Want to get a beer?" Buck nodded towards the door. "There's a place down the street, does a mean steak too - after your time I think."

As they walked, Buck pointed out the changes - what had gone, what was new, what was never going to change in a million years. In the bar Buck was greeted by name and, as they settled into a booth, the waitress brought over a pitcher and two glasses without being asked.

"So," said Buck, after she left, "what can I do for you?"

Sy explained about the house and what he'd agreed with Cass.

"So, there's a couple of things," concluded Sy. "I need a runabout, nothing fancy, just something to leave on the driveway for whenever I'm back here - and for Cass to use for any errands she'll need to run."

"Errands..." said Buck. "Right. Okay, that's not a problem."

"The other thing is that Cass told me she's gotten behind with the rent for the trailer - she says that she needs to talk to you about that, says she's not happy moving on still owing you."

"Okay..."

"I'd like to clear it." Sy paused. "I don't really want her worrying while she's..."

"If you were counting," Buck broke in, "which I'm not - she owes just under eight hundred. Which, coincidentally, is exactly the price of a nice little used Taurus sitting on my lot out back. So..." The smile he gave Sy was almost shy. "Guess we both carried a torch there at one time or another, right?"

Sy hesitated only slightly before returning Buck's smile.

"Okay, we gonna eat?" asked Buck, turning his head to look for the waitress.

* * *

Buck had been right about the steaks and as they washed them down with the last of the beer, Sy asked him how long he'd been running the business.

"Fifteen years now - Dad died in eighty-four."

"I'm sorry."

Buck just grunted.

"You know, if I were to close my eyes," said Sy, "I can still see him now, up there in the bleachers, arms raised, cheering you on."

"And every time we lost," said Buck quietly, "we'd get home, he'd walk me through to the garage, take his belt off and whip the shit out of me."

"*Jesus!*" Sy stared at him. "Fuck, man!"

"'There are no losers in this family!', he'd say. 'No room in this house for quitters and deadbeats!'"

Sy was genuinely lost for words.

"I'm sorry, man," was all he eventually managed.

The waitress came over to clear their dishes and Buck got up to use the Men's room.

"When did Ritchie get ill?" asked Sy when he returned.

"Ninety-two," said Buck. "Well, that's when he was diagnosed - you only had to look at him to see something was wrong. He must have lost four stone in a year."

"Nothing was picked up earlier, in his check-ups?"

Buck stared at him.

"He had AIDS."

"What?"

"Cass didn't tell you?"

Sy shook his head.

"No reason why she should, but the whole town knew." He sighed. "Story was a blood transfusion in a Mexican hospital, after falling down some steps. Not something he'd ever told me about."

"You think...?" Sy let his voice trail off.

"Who knows, man? Who knows what the fuck goes down once that front door closes and who knows what the fuck is really going on in someone else's head?" Buck shrugged. "He sure travelled a lot."

"What about Cass?"

"She's healthy - about the only silver lining to that story." He sighed. "I should get back."

They were silent walking to the showroom.

"If we don't get a chance to talk at the church," Buck told him, as they shook hands on the forecourt, "look me up the next time you're in town. Molly and I would love to have you over for dinner."

"I'll do that," said Sy, and he did mean it, but perhaps only because deep down he knew that once he'd gotten through the next few days - return here or not - this town was a chapter of his life that had finally closed.

* * *

Sy arrived at the office expecting to be buried in work for at least the next two to three days. But Rachel had made a pretty good job of covering the bases, handing him a re-arranged itinerary and prioritising the calls he needed to make.

He'd been working for about an hour when Rachel buzzed through to say that Kellie Blake was on the line and Sy grimaced. Kellie was personal assistant to Avril Ashley, one of the bigger jewels in Sy's coronet of clients, and Sy knew that if Kellie was playing go-between, then Avril had an axe to grind. Unpleasantness, like so many other distasteful necessities of a movie star's life, was always something to be farmed out.

"Kellie," greeted Sy with all the fake bonhomie he could muster. "How's it going?"

"Well, I have to say Sy, not good. Not good at all."

"I'm sorry to hear that, what can I do for you?"

"You could return my calls. That'd be a start."

"Yeah, sorry about that Kellie. I had to leave town for a few days, couldn't be avoided. But I'm back now."

"Avril's real disappointed, Sy, I gotta tell you that." Kellie left a pause. "There was stuff she needed to go through with you, you know, important stuff."

"Well here I am, Kellie, what is it you need me to do for you?" asked Sy, leaning toward placating rather than contrite, but Kellie wasn't finished yet.

"Kaden Wood from JVK." Somewhere between a question and a statement, Kellie let the sentence hang in the air. "You know Kaden?"

"Sure," said Sy. JVK was a rival agency, but he and Kaden went way back and usually tried to grab lunch together at least once a month.

"Well, Kaden's been talking to Avril, promising all kinds of things," said Kellie. "And I have tell you, Avril's starting to listen."

Sy smiled. He guessed that, like every other agent in town, Kaden spent at least one morning a week working the phones with his Rolodex. He also guessed that at the other end of the line Avril would be listening in on speaker phone.

"I'm sorry that Avril's upset." Sy tried to at least sound sincere. "What can I do to make this right?"

"Okay, well... Avril would like a book."

"A book...?" What the fuck? He was supposed to go shopping for her now. "Which book is that?"

"*Her* book." Kellie sounded on the edge of exasperation. "Avril wants to have a book out."

"A book out...?"

"Avril feels that at this stage of her career, it's time to make a unique statement. That she maybe needs to appeal to a different kind of demographic."

"Okay..."

"She saw that Connor Everett got on the bestseller list last month," said Kellie, and that's when the light bulb finally switched on over Sy's head.

Connor Everett was a young actor who'd made a name for himself in a couple of indie productions, which he'd also co-written, before hitting it big in a Warner Bros summer blockbuster two years back. Since then he'd written a barely fictionalised account of the trials and tribulations of trying to make it in Hollywood, which had sold mainly on the premise of it being a guessing game as to who his protagonists actually were. Paramount had recently optioned the novel, and now had the interesting challenge, reflected Sy, of persuading the public that the actors who'd been cast weren't, in fact, portraying themselves.

Could this town get any fucking crazier?

"Okay," said Sy slowly. "Well, if Avril puts together some notes of what she wants to write, then I'll hook her up with a couple of ghost-writers who can work with her..."

"Oh, for chrissake!" broke in Kellie. "Just fix it, okay? Get the fucking thing done, then we'll have a briefing with Avril so you can explain what the fuck it's about and what she needs to say at the launch. But that needs to be before the fifteenth of next month. She starts the shoot in Europe after that."

Sy felt his grip tightening around the phone. This is a woman, he told himself, who's won two Oscars, who sits on the board of more charities than you've fingers on both hands and who dines with princes and presidents. Who fifteen years ago had talked long into the night of Strasberg and Stanislavski, who ten years ago turned down Spielberg for an off-Broadway Samuel Beckett production.

What the fuck is it that happens to us?

And then it hit.

And it came in like a tsunami.

It wasn't only delayed grief, although that must have been part of the whole kaleidoscope vision that he suddenly seemed to be tumbling into and through - Mom, small and still and lifeless under the white hospital sheet. It was Cassidy weeping in the commissary, old man Richmond walking Buck into the garage, Ritchie wasted away to a skeleton. It was everyone who'd ever walked into this office ready to make a Faustian pact with a smile on their face. It was...

"Sy? Sy, hey, you still there?"

He carefully put the phone back down into its cradle.

Sy wasn't sure how long he sat there, was only vaguely conscious that the intercom kept buzzing, of Rachel asking if he was okay and would he like a glass of water? Should she call someone?

And then she was gone, and he became aware of another presence, less disturbing. All he could discern was quiet breathing close by but that was okay, the only thing he wanted in the whole world was to carry on sitting here with his eyes closed.

And when, eventually, he did open them, it was to see Lee Munro in the chair on the other side of his desk, studying him carefully.

"You alright now?" she asked, softly, and he nodded.

"Yeah," said Sy, "I guess so." He paused. "I'm really not sure what happened there."

"Your mum died is what's happened." She shook her head. "Jesus Sy, why didn't you call me?"

Sy stared at her.

"I had to hear it from Kaden Wood," she said, "but by that time you'd left town."

"Kaden Wood?"

"Yes, apparently that cow Kellie Blake has been stirring the shit again. Once she found out about your mum from

Rachel and that you were out of town, she started calling around the agencies, dropping hints that Avril's not happy." Lee shrugged. "She got short shrift from Kaden, but he was worried when he couldn't get hold of you and so he checked with me."

"I'm sorry." Sy felt like he was getting his bearings again. "Things happened pretty quickly. It was a rush to make it to the hospital before... before Mom passed."

"I'd have gone with you, you know that." Lee was gently reproachful. "It's not something you should have to go through on your own."

"The way things worked out," said Sy, "I wasn't." He gave a small smile. "In the end, it was all okay."

"Well, you can tell me all about it," said Lee. "On the flight."

"The flight?" Sy stared at her bemused, then gave a start. "Oh shit! The eclipse!"

"I got us onto a company flight, from Burbank."

"Lee, I..."

"What you need," said Lee, "is a sense of your relevance to the cosmos. Trust me, this'll do the trick."

"I..."

"You'll be away three days, max. I've already talked to Rachel and there's nothing she can't take care of. And," her sweetest smile, "can you think of a better FU2 for Avril Ashley?"

Sy gave a small shake of his head.

* * *

Sy opened his eyes to see Lee staring at him.

"You never sleep on planes, huh?" she said with an amused smile.

"I was resting my eyes," began Sy, but glancing out of the window saw they were on the ground and taxiing off the runway. The co-pilot stuck his head into the cabin.

"Customs will be about ten minutes," he said. "Sorry for the delay."

Waiting for them to board, Sy stood up and stretched his legs as Lee talked on her cell.

"Paul's already here," she told Sy, snapping it shut. "He'll pick us up from the plane."

Sy nodded, keeping his face impassive. Although he'd never admit it in a million years, Paul was someone he just didn't get, and he'd known him almost as long as he'd known Lee.

And at first Sy hadn't been that impressed. Security was *de rigueur* at the premieres and award ceremonies where his clients came closest to engaging with their fans, and it was part of his job to make sure that that wasn't uncomfortably close.

The bodyguards tended to be moonlighting cops or ex-military - the occasional gang-banger if someone was looking to up their street cred - and while they generally didn't have to do more than occasionally lay a restraining hand on someone's shoulder, they did come with a presence. Paul was a head shorter than most of them and while Sy got the impression that his slim frame may have been held together by a wiry strength, he wasn't sure how much stopping power was there. But Lee wanted him around, and so what the hell, that might as well be one less argument with her that he'd eventually lose.

It was backstage at the Golden Globes that John Belushi's manager came over to Sy and Lee, to ask if Paul might be available for the next couple of days. They were looking for someone to drive John around, he said, and to '*keep him out of trouble*'. Sy guessed this was down to a seriously pissed husband or bookie or probably - as it was John – dealer, that the studio was taking their own sweet time placating, hoping that if they left John to sweat for a while then maybe he'd think twice in the future.

Fat chance.

"What's the problem?" asked Sy. "Don't you have your own people."

"John's heard a few things," he shrugged, "from the guys."

"If it's okay with Paul, sure," said Lee.

"Thanks," he said. "We'll owe you."

As he walked away, Sy looked quizzically at Lee but got nothing back except an inscrutable smile.

For the rest of the night, Sy kept an eye on Paul as he shadowed Lee across town from party to party. And for the first time he noticed that whenever Paul crossed paths with another minder, there was a small exchange of nods, almost imperceptible if you weren't paying attention but definitely there. Mutual respect, assumed Sy, but on what basis? He hadn't heard about Paul running into any trouble since he'd been over here, and he was pretty sure that he would have. Perhaps it was like that thing gay guys are supposed to have, where they can spot each other without anyone else realising. Gaydar, they called it. Maybe this was some weird kind of testosterone vibe. Who the fuck knows?

* * *

As they pulled out of the airport, in the same beat-up Land Rover Lee had kept down here for the last twenty years, Sy asked how long it would take them to drive to St Hannahs.

"Usually about an hour, but it took twice that on the way here." Paul shrugged. "August, the eclipse."

Already, Sy could feel the sweat in the small of his back. 'At least get something with air conditioning,' he'd berate her every time he stayed here, but she'd just laugh.

"Has Kit arrived yet?" asked Lee, as he waited for a gap in the traffic to join the A39.

"He's due later." He hesitated, then seemed to choose his words with care. "He said to give you a heads up - that we may get a visit from the Met during the next few days."

"Met?" Lee was startled. "You mean as in Metropolitan Police?"

"They've opened a cold case on someone who disappeared back in 1970. Who stayed for a while at Pembridge

Villas."

"And they've only now gotten around to it?"

"They tracked down Kit and spoke to him the other day. They also want to talk to you - as you were managing the place."

Of course they do, thought Sy. He hadn't met a cop yet who wasn't a star fucker at heart.

"Who are they looking for?"

Paul shook his head.

"Kit didn't say, only that he'll have it sorted out within twenty-four hours. And that if they turn up before then, you should put off talking to them." He shrugged. "That'll be easy enough - jet lagged, the Gallery opening tomorrow. Nothing for you to worry about, but we thought you should know."

An odd use of the term 'we', reflected Sy, but maybe he just wasn't tuned in to the nuances of British vernacular. He couldn't see Lee's face, only the back of her head in the front passenger seat and for a second it seemed it twitched slightly towards Paul, but when she spoke her tone was casual enough.

"Okay, well, we've a few things to go through with Kit, so perhaps we'll get that done as soon as he arrives." She turned around to Sy. "Say over dinner, unless you need to crash out?"

"No," Sy told her. "I'm good."

* * *

There's little we find more disconcerting than waking from a nap we didn't intend to take, particularly in strange surroundings.

Sy blinked, swung his legs off the bed and sat upright. *Lee's place, Cornwall* - okay. He glanced at his watch, which said seven thirty, but he had no idea whether that was day or night or even if he'd remembered to set it to local time. He was about to go over to the window and pull back the heavy drapes, when a sharp knock on the door registered as an echo of something from a few seconds ago, probably the sound that woke him.

"Sy!" It was Paul's voice.

"Yeah?"

"Dinner in thirty minutes."

"Okay."

He heard footsteps moving away along the corridor outside. At least he had time to shower and collect his final thoughts on how he was going to present the project to Kit. Even though this wasn't what the guy probably had in mind, Lee said he'd go for it, but Sy had his doubts. No-one got skittish faster than a writer when you started threatening his babies.

After freshening up, Sy tried to remember his way to the dining room. Every time he came here he lost his bearings at some point - Lee had an entire wing of the place and all Sy remembered about the dining room was that it was on the first floor. *Ground floor* they called it here, the first floor being the second floor, which was what had sent him off on a fifteen-minute wild goose chase during his first visit.

It was the sound of voices at the bottom of the staircase that led him in the right direction, along a corridor and to a door left slightly ajar. But it was those same voices that suddenly caused him to pause.

"So, Barry Denham went for it, did he?" Paul's voice.

"Hook, line and sinker," said a voice that Sy didn't recognise. "It was even his suggestion to turn up for the meeting by himself. And, as a bonus, we've now got this narrative reinforced by an email trail going back years - I'll explain about that later. How did things go with Liam?"

"As soon as I started talking, he'd pieced it all together," said Paul. "He knew exactly what was happening and who it was. I gave him the place and time and told him we'll handle things from there - and he's more than grateful. These days it's beyond plausible deniability, his hands need to be completely clean."

"Well, Harry Slater's happy to take care of it," said the

other voice, "and for obvious reasons. He says it's a debt long overdue, but all the sweeter for that."

"He knows how to make it look?"

"Don't worry. But what about the Gallery? She could be down here by now and if she recognises..."

"It's already handled," Paul broke in. "We've had some Travellers working on the driveway and..."

His voice trailed off at the sound of a door opening.

"Hi Kit. So good to see you again." Lee must have entered the dining room from the other side of the house. "Has anyone given Sy a call?"

Before either of them could respond, Sy pushed the door open and stepped through.

"Hey," said Lee. "This time you found it all by yourself. Kit, this is Sy, Sy meet Kit."

* * *

"First of all," said Sy, "I want to thank you for the introduction to Powys." He lifted Kit's battered script an inch or two from the tabletop and then let it rest back down again. "Over the last few years, I've probably enjoyed him more than any other writer who I read for pleasure."

The three of them - Sy, Lee and Kit - were alone in the dining room after Paul had excused himself, citing 'business up country' whatever that meant, but likely connected to that enigmatic conversation he'd eavesdropped on earlier.

And which he figured the less he knew about the better.

"You're welcome." Kit gave him a slightly bemused nod.

"And what you've done here - it's a smart approach and nicely crafted."

"I'm guessing there's a 'but' coming," Kit smiled.

"Not really," said Sy. "Or maybe not in the way you think."

"To cut to the chase," said Lee, "we're talking to people about dramatising the original novel."

"Right," said Kit slowly, and then shook his head. "You mean as a movie?"

"We both know that's a non-starter," said Sy. "Assuming we could talk a studio into it, you'd never even scratch the surface of what Powys was aiming for in a two-hour feature."

"So...?"

"Have you heard of a TV series called *'The Sopranos'*?" asked Sy.

"A TV series?" Kit shook his head, his quizzical expression flicking back and forth between Sy and Lee. "No."

"Okay. Well, there're fundamental changes taking place in US home entertainment right now. Cable TV companies are commissioning original drama, rather than re-broadcasting network shows or Hollywood movies." He paused. "The important thing to understand is that the cable channels don't have to comply with the usual broadcasting standards. They have paid subscribers, not network viewers."

"You mean there's no censorship?"

"Other than what we could define as 'the boundaries of good taste', no. And that's a pretty fluid benchmark, these days." Sy shrugged. "There've been a few shows on cable - a prison drama called *OZ*, *Dream On* - that have pulled in solid critical acclaim, but it's *The Sopranos* that's been the real game changer. There's not only a critical buzz, it's really generating subscriptions for HBO."

"Okay," said Kit, still slightly bemused.

"What *The Sopranos* has shown," said Lee, "is there's a market for serious, adult, high-quality drama. The fly in the ointment with all of this is the perception by actors in the States that TV is a career graveyard."

"It's a hard sell," admitted Sy.

"Not a problem with English actors though," said Lee. "Remember Laurence Olivier in *Brideshead Revisited*. Alec Guinness in those BBC John le Carré adaptations."

"One production is even thinking of casting British stage actors as Baltimore cops," said Sy. "Who saw *that* coming?"

"But is this," asked Kit slowly, "what an American studio would really go for?"

And there's the rub, thought Sy.

He took a breath.

"The copy of *A Glastonbury Romance* which I read had a revised foreword, added by Powys twenty-five years later," said Sy.

"The Picador edition?"

"Yeah. In it, Powys describes the novel as an attempt to 'intermingle the sacramental and the excremental in the spirit of absolute undogmatic ignorance'."

Kit smiled.

"That *'God whispers to us in more voices than we are able to hear or understand when we do'.*"

"Exactly," said Sy. "It's obvious from Powys' notes in the various editions that he placed as much emphasis on the sensual as he did the spiritual. The morés of the time meant one had to be woven into the background, rather than take centre-stage, but if we were to reverse that dynamic, it would still be true to Powys vision."

"Reverse?"

Sy picked up his notes and began to flip through them.

"The first character introduced to us in the novel, John Crow, is obviously bisexual and he misremembers a childhood erotic encounter being with his cousin Mary - later his wife - when it was actually with his friend Tom, who subsequently comes back into both of their lives. John then befriends Owen Evans, a bookseller who becomes increasingly dominated by fantasies of sexual sadism, which ultimately leads to a murder. John's wife Mary is also the paid companion to an elderly spinster, who is in love with her. Mary's cousin, Persephone, leaves her husband, a communist agitator, to have an affair with another of their cousins, Philip Crow. She then abandons him for Angela, daughter of a local solicitor. The son of the town's vicar, Sam Dekker, fathers a child with Nell, wife of the bastard son of the Marquis of..."

"Whoa!" Kit held up his hand, laughing. "And that's how you've been pitching it, is it?"

Sy took a breath.

"Look Kit, the essence of this novel is the battle between Romance - essentially the legend of the Holy Grail in a Christian context, represented by the character John Geard - and twentieth century industrialisation as personified by Philip Crow. And for all the literary finery that comes dressed in, the selling point is classic white hat versus black hat."

Kit leaned back in his chair.

"You know," he smiled, "when Lee said, 'I'd like you to meet my Hollywood agent' this isn't exactly the way I imagined the conversation panning out."

Lee grinned.

"Sy's complicated."

Kit considered.

"I do know what you mean," he said, eventually. "If you consider that Powys was writing during the same period as D. H. Lawrence, then it's incredible what he got away with. Whether that's down to style subjugating substance - he has a way of sweeping you along with his narrative - or the naivety of a 1930s readership, I'm not sure."

"But from a late twentieth century perspective," said Lee, "this rural Somerset backwater was heaving with sublimated - and not so sublimated - eroticism."

"And so, the reworked prime resonance throughout the town," continued Sy, "would now be sensuality and the esotericism becomes the woven background."

"And so exactly how would that work?" asked Kit.

Lee smiled.

"Well, that's what you're here for," she said, uncorking a bottle of Glenmorangie single malt. "Get comfortable, we're both still on LA time so it's going to be a long night."

And Sy, hunching forward, eye finally back on the ball, felt the last week fall from him like a heavy mantle.

4. May 1970

Aidan

"Come in," said Kit, in answer to my knock.

I had the door halfway open before I realised he wasn't alone.

"Oh, hello Claudia," I said.

She gave me a smile, but it was obviously an effort.

"Look," I told her, "I can come back later."

"That's alright, Aidan," she said, "I was just leaving."

But on her way to the door, Claudia paused and turned back to Kit.

"If you hear anything at all, you'll let me know?"

Kit nodded, sombrely. I got another smile from her, this one with more life to it, and she closed the door behind her.

"Long story," said Kit, reading my curious expression.

"I've a friend of my family downstairs," I told him, "who'd like some discreet advice on a confidential matter."

"Okay," said Kit. "Lead the way."

Down in the basement, I made certain of locking the outside door before leading Kit into the studio.

"Kit, this is Liam," I said and then turned to Liam. "Kit's to be trusted, you can speak freely."

"I'm pleased to hear that," said Liam, shaking hands with him. "And also pleased to meet you."

"What can I do for you?" asked Kit.

"My associates and I," said Liam slowly, "have come into possession of certain goods, whose value we'd like some help in assessing."

"Goods?"

"Drugs," I said. "A lot of drugs."

"What do you have?" asked Kit.

"Marijuana, heroin and perhaps cocaine." Liam gave a slight shrug and a smile. "I have to be honest here, it's not exactly our field of expertise."

"I thought we'd go and take a look," I told Kit. "And that maybe you could give Liam an idea of what he's sitting on."

* * *

An hour later we were in a workshop at the back of a motor showroom in Acton, surrounded by half a dozen cars in various stages of being resprayed.

"This way," said Liam, and we followed him over to where a tool board had been fixed to the wall. Liam slid his hand behind it. There was a click and then it swung open to reveal a large alcove.

"That's the stuff." Liam indicated a bench running the width of the alcove and piled high with plastic-wrapped bundles, maybe two-thirds of them packaged in blue and the rest white. There were also a good few brick sized blocks of what even I could recognise as hashish.

Kit stepped forward and picked up one of the white packets, which I noticed had Chinese or Japanese lettering on them. He studied it for a few seconds and then put it down. Picking up one of the blue packets he made a small tear with his thumbnail, dabbed his forefinger inside and withdrew it coated with white powder. Carefully, he rubbed it into his upper gum.

"Okay," he said, turning back to Liam. "The white packets are Chinese heroin, the blue packets are cocaine. You've also got about forty pounds of hashish.

"The street value of the hash is fifteen quid an ounce which would be," Kit did a quick calculation, "around eight thousand, if you're planning on having someone sell it for you by the ounce. But to sell the lot together, a third of that."

Kit paused.

"The Chinese and the coke will depend on how much it's been cut."

"Cut?" asked Liam.

"Until recently, pretty much all the heroin and cocaine in this country came from prescriptions for registered addicts," Kit told him. "So, it was a hundred percent pure. But doctors registering addicts as patients is a thing of the past and so now, like everywhere else in the world, it's smuggled in - the heroin probably from Southeast Asia, the coke almost certainly from South America. And the more it's cut, the bigger the profit."

"How do we find out how much it's been cut."

"Find a chemist who'll test it and keep his mouth shut."

"Do you know of someone?"

Kit nodded.

Liam seemed to be thinking.

"When the tests you've spoken of have been completed, do you think you could find a single buyer for the entire shipment?"

"Yes," Kit said, cautiously. "But not at a very good price."

"I understand that," said Liam. "But as I explained, this is a business which we have little experience of and it's not one that we'd care to be thought involved with. Is that clear?"

Kit nodded.

"If we were to offer you a thousand to broker the transaction, plus any expenses, would that be acceptable to you?"

"Yes," said Kit.

"You'd handle all negotiations with prospective buyers, but I'd emphasise again that our involvement is known only to yourself and our man here," Liam indicating me with a nod of his head.

"I understand," Kit told him.

"I hope so," said Liam softly. "I really do."

He reached into the inside pocket of his jacket and took out an envelope.

"An advance of expenses," he said, handing it to Kit. "What kind of timescale would we be looking at?"

"A day or so to get the purity checked," Kit told him. "If the people I'm thinking of going to first are interested, they won't have a problem getting the money together, so…" He shrugged. "Four or five days. But longer if I have to look for another buyer. Obviously I'll need samples."

Liam handed him a packet of Chinese heroin and a packet of cocaine.

"Let Aidan know the results of the testing and the figure agreed upon. Wait for his confirmation before finalising the deal. Is that understood?"

"Understood."

Liam turned to me.

"Other than that, your grandfather is adamant that your hands remain clean here, right?"

I nodded.

"Do I have to be saying that twice to get a response from you?" said Liam sharply.

"I understand."

"I'll not be detaining you gentlemen any longer then," said Liam.

* * *

"So," I asked Kit, as we made our way to the tube station, "when are we off to meet the chemist?"

"I thought you weren't supposed to be getting involved in this," said Kit.

"You wouldn't begrudge me a touch of excitement now, would you?" I asked, and he grinned.

"Well, now's probably just as good a time as any," he said, looking at his watch.

But to be honest, I was being somewhat disingenuous in leading Kit to believe that my involvement was down to a devil-may-care penchant for an adventure. The truth of the matter was I'd expected Liam to thank him for his opinion, slip him twenty quid or thereabouts for his trouble, and for that to be the end of it. Because once he knew what he had, Liam would have enough contacts familiar with the seamier side of London life to take it from there.

But I hadn't really thought things through. On the

streets of Belfast people were getting kneecapped by Liam's people for dealing drugs, and so this wasn't something they could be seen to have an involvement with at any level. My guess was that the stash in the car showroom had come their way courtesy of either a debt paid off or - as was probably more likely - a debt not paid off.

All of which meant that when this deal was done and dusted, Kit could be regarded as something of a loose end. I was confident that if all went smoothly, Kit's safety would be guaranteed by being a friend of mine. But if things did start to unravel, there would be only one link Liam would need to sever to be detached from the affair and sever would probably be an appropriate term. Entangling myself in this would, hopefully, make that scenario rather more complicated.

* * *

It was my naivety in such matters that led me to imagine our visit to 'The Chemist' would likely involve a labyrinthine journey through a disused warehouse or suchlike, to reach a clandestine laboratory where we'd find a sinister, white-coated figure presiding over a Heath Robinson construction of distillation flasks, condensers and test tubes.

A 1930s semi-detached, suburban house in Harlesden was the reality, with the door answered by a middle-aged housewife complete with starched apron, who greeted Kit by name and with a smile.

"Hello Mrs Bailey," said Kit. "Is Grenville around?"

"He's not home from school yet," said Mrs Bailey, "but he shouldn't be long - would you like a cup of tea?"

We sat in the kitchen chatting for ten minutes - the weather, the upcoming World Cup in Mexico, would the Beatles ever get back together.

"I wasn't expecting him to be late home today," said Mrs Bailey eventually. "Is it urgent?"

"I've a friend who needs some assay work," Kit told her. "I could get it done elsewhere, but I'd prefer the money went to Grenville."

"I know Kit and I really appreciate that," said Mrs Bailey, nodding her head. "Since his Dad…" Registering me, she gave a slight shrug and broke off. "Every little helps, you know?"

Before Kit could respond, the door opened and Grenville came in. Even without the school uniform and NHS specs, he wouldn't have looked much over fourteen, but I guessed he must have been a sixth former. If it surprised him to see us he didn't show it. He simply said 'Hi' to Kit and gave me a nod before bending down to give his mother a peck on the cheek.

"Hello Mum," he said.

"Kit has something he needs you to take a look at," said Mrs Bailey and then turned to Kit. "Did you say it was jewellery?"

Kit simply smiled.

"It shouldn't take long," he said.

"Right," said Grenville, "let's go out to the shed."

"Dinner will be ready in half an hour," said Mrs Bailey.

"Okay, Mum."

Security was pretty tight for a garden shed, a Chubb deadlock on the door, and I noticed that the windows also had locks on them. And once we were inside, Grenville locked the door behind us.

"What have you got?" he asked.

"H and coke," said Kit. He handed over the two plastic bags. "We need to find out how much they've been cut."

Grenville opened a cupboard door and took out a couple of test tubes.

"Be about ten minutes," he said, unlocking the door, "if you wanted a smoke while you waited?"

There were two garden chairs in the middle of the lawn, where Kit and I settled ourselves down.

"Hard as it might be to believe," he said, "probably half the acid sold in London this year came out of that shed."

"Right - chemistry homework, was it?"

"If you were looking for the perfect cover for this kind

of operation, you'd be pushed to do better than a schoolboy swot."

I stared at him.

"You're serious."

"He's a genius chemist - we met a couple of years ago when he was selling at the Roundhouse, which wasn't too cool." Kit drew on his cigarette. "So, I set him up with someone who could take over the distribution. That's who'll we be going to see once we've an idea of what we've got."

The shed door opened, Grenville came over to the table and sat down.

"The coke's a hundred percent pure," he said. "The H is around ninety."

"Okay," said Kit slowly. "Wow."

"If you're interested," said Grenville, "I've some Owsley White Lightning." He shrugged. "Took it as a trade, mainly to run an analysis."

"How much?"

"Let's call it twenty quid for five blotters and running the tests."

"Okay." Kit got out his wallet and handed two tens over.

"Back in a sec." Grenville headed over to the shed.

"White Lightning?" I stared at Kit.

"Think of it as Connemara single malt," he said, with a smile.

Kit

The Builders Arms had never paid much attention to licensing laws. There were usually a couple of plainclothes drinking gratis at the bar who'd have a word with any jobsworth from the local council who might come around poking their nose in. And sharing a street door with the boxing gym upstairs gave it a good alibi, although the irony was that it was a damn sight easier to get into the public bar out of hours than to get into the gym at any time.

Aidan and I arrived mid-morning to find the place busy enough. It didn't do much in the way of food beyond pork scratchings and crisps, but most of its clientele were in the habit of setting themselves up for the day with liquid calories.

The barmaid served Aidan two Whisky Macs - when in Rome - while I tried to catch the landlord's eye, over by the till with a folded newspaper and engrossed in today's form. When eventually he came over, I had a quiet word. He nodded and disappeared into the back, while Aidan and I took our drinks over to a table. No-one gave us a second glance, it was the sort of place where other people's business wasn't your concern.

After a few minutes, the landlord reappeared and gave an upward nod of the head. We finished our drinks and left the bar, but instead of turning right and out into the street, I led Aidan down a shabby corridor in the opposite direction and then up a flight of bare wooden stairs. At the top was a set of closed double doors and I rang an old push bell set in the wall beside them.

They were opened by a bruiser in a hundred guinea suit, who gave me a nod and, after closing them carefully behind us, indicated to the other side of the room.

"In the office," he said.

The centrepiece of the gym was a full-size boxing ring, where a teenager in shorts and singlet sparred with an older man wearing a tracksuit. Around the gym was an assortment of punch bags and barbells, all utilised by young hopefuls being coached by seasoned elders.

"It's going to look pretty low rent," I'd told Aidan on the way over, "but half a dozen British champions have come out of there and a couple of those were world title contenders."

The 'office' was a makeshift room constructed along the length of the far wall by chipboard panelling, and if you didn't know it was there, it was hard to spot at first. The door was made from the same material and set flush at one end. Two punch bags were hung in front of what appeared to be large mirrors but were actually one-way glass and afforded a panoramic view of the gym to anyone inside.

The door opened before we reached it, and the figure that emerged smiled and extended his hand.

"Hi Kit," he said. "Good to see you."

"You too."

I indicated Aidan with a nod of my head.

"This is Aidan," I told him. "Aidan, this is Coochie."

* * *

"It's really that pure?" he asked.

We were sitting in the office, Coochie behind the desk scribbling figures on a notepad.

"According to Grenville," I told him.

"Okay." Coochie hesitated. "So, where's it from?"

"It's the settlement of a debt to some associates of mine," said Aidan, before I could reply. "Accepted in lieu of cash."

The scenario that should have come to mind before now was that the stash could have been lifted from a London outfit, one that Coochie's own associates had ties to. Why the hell hadn't I pressed further on that with Liam?

But the answer seemed to satisfy him. At least there didn't seem to be a light bulb suddenly clicking on over his head about a hundred grand street value's worth of gear gone missing.

He gave a slow nod.

"What are you asking?"

Then the door opened, and my heart sank as Chas Slater walked into the room.

After the Kray twins had been sent down, there'd been any number of turf wars in London's East End trying to establish who'd be taking over from where they'd left off. So far there were no outright victors but, as I'd explained to Aidan on the journey over, the Slater brothers were very much front runners.

"Well, family does tend to prevail in enterprises established beyond the boundaries of law and order," he'd reflected.

"Blood thicker than water?" I'd asked, and he'd given a slight grimace.

"It's where weaknesses are understood and more readily forgiven," he'd said quietly. "And the price of betrayal usually considered too high to pay."

I was tempted to quip something along the lines that Christmases must be a real hoot at the McShane household, but thought better of it.

"This friend of yours, this...?"

"Coochie."

"Right - this Coochie. How does he fit into things?"

"He grew up in the East End playing truant with Chas and Harry Slater, when both of them were gofers for the Twins."

"I meant, how did *you* meet him?"

"He was a hustler around the West End three or four years ago." I shrugged. "It was a small scene."

"Drugs?"

"Among other things." I paused. "Ten, maybe even five years ago you wouldn't find a genuine London villain who'd touch drugs with a barge pole. Hash was for the West Indians in Notting Hill and Brixton, opium was lascar sailors or the Chinese over in Limehouse. And like I said to Liam - heroin, coke and speed were actually legal if you registered yourself as an addict."

"But that's all changed now?"

"With the realisation that not only is it easy money, it's also a soft business to muscle your way into. When your only competition are tripped out hippies, it's not exactly going to be tommy guns on the streets of Chicago, is it? You just need someone who's been on the scene and who knows what's what."

"Your man Coochie?"

My man Coochie indeed, prodigal son of the East End underworld. We'd reconnected when I'd been after a bulk buyer for the quantity of high-grade acid which Grenville could supply, and another dealer had arranged a meet with *some really heavy cats, man, but they do have that kind of bread to lay on you*. His contact had been Coochie, fronting for the Slater brothers.

"Good to see you again, Kit," Coochie had said, as our mutual acquaintance made his exit after facilitating the introductions we'd both pretended were necessary. "To tell you the truth, I was half expecting yet another twat dressed up as Abdul the Bulbul."

So, for the last eighteen months I'd been a conduit between Grenville and the Slater organisation, with Coochie my cut-off point at the sharper end of things. But now, with Chas Slater slowly looking me up and down, I was reminded of one of those Chinese 'terrible blessings' - *May you come to the attention of those in high places.*

"What the bleedin' 'ell's going on 'ere then?"

"Just a bit of business, Chas."

Chas was looking dubious.

"Would you give us a minute, Kit?" said Coochie, standing.

Aidan and I went out into the gym and had time to smoke a Woodbine each before Chas stepped out of the office. He studied us both carefully, as if making sure we knew we were being committed to memory, and then, giving an ostentatious shake of the head, moved away to where a young blond youth was working a punch ball. He dropped a hand onto the kid's shoulder and began a litany of soft encouraging words, kneading the shoulder with his fingers.

Coochie appeared at the office door.

"Okay," he said, and we went back inside.

"Sorry about that." He sat down behind the desk. "Some other business that needed taking care of."

"No problem," I told him.

"So how much?"

"I was thinking thirty," I said.

"Naw." He shook his head. "Might go to twenty."

We eventually finished at twenty-five, as we both knew that we would.

"Do you want us to deliver here?" I asked.

"Best not," he said. "Too many prying eyes". He tore the sheet from the notepad he'd been using to work out his figures for the deal, lit it with a desk lighter and dropped it into a large glass ashtray. Then he started scribbling on a fresh page.

"I've got a lock-up," he said, handing me the sheet of paper. "Do you know where this is?"

"I can find it," I said. "When were you thinking of?"

"It'll take a few days to put that much cash together, without people getting curious that is." He shrugged. "Say Monday night, about tennish."

"Sure," I told him. "See you then."

Out on the street, Aidan seemed unusually thoughtful.

"You okay?" I asked. I was feeling jittery myself, after our encounter with Chas Slater.

"Crazy eyes," he said, with a slight smile.

I hadn't really noticed, but I gave a shrug.

"Chas?" I shook my head. "Yeah, well - you should have met Ronnie."

Still smiling, he turned his head toward me.

"I meant your friend Coochie."

Claudia

"We had this huge argument," said Frieda. "She was talking about not taking her finals at all. Just leaving."

I'd always had the feeling I was someone Frieda disapproved of. That everything from my accent to my background was designed to set her teeth on edge, and so I'd never really found myself able to warm to her. But here, sitting on my sofa sipping tea, she seemed such a frail figure that my heart went out to her.

"Do you have any idea why?" I asked. "Something must have happened?"

"I don't." Frieda gave a shake of her head. "She only said that she couldn't do this anymore, that there were more important things in the world which she couldn't keep on ignoring."

"And this was...?"

"Two weeks ago."

"And nothing since?"

Frieda shook her head again.

"Apparently she left her rooms in Oxford the same day that she rang us. No-one there has heard from her either." She looked around the room. "I hoped that perhaps she'd come to stay with you, I know what good friends you are."

She probably didn't intend for that to sound almost an accusation.

"I'm sorry," I told her. "I haven't seen Emma in weeks."

Frieda nodded, put her cup and saucer back down on the coffee table and began to rise.

"If she gets in touch," she asked, "would you call me? Even if she doesn't want to see us, just so we'll know she's alright?"

"Of course," I said, taking her hand and squeezing it. "And I'll ask around the places she'd be likely to go if she were in London."

"Thank you, Claudia." She managed a thin smile.

But no one had seen her, not for a month at least, and no one had any idea where she might be. I'd done the usual rounds, the college meeting rooms, the grubby North London coffee bars, the magazines that came and went but always from the same dingy offices. The shabby bookshops that stacked revolution and poetry side by side, preached anarchy from posters in the window and had *'Shoplifters will be Prosecuted'* stickers on the till.

The day after I'd been over to Pembridge Villas, Kit rang to ask if I'd found her.

"No," I told him.

"I was thinking," he said. "There's a big anti-Vietnam War demo tomorrow. If she's in London, that's where she'll be."

"In Trafalgar Square?"

"That's usually where it begins, then a march up to Grosvenor Square."

"Will you come with me?"

He hesitated.

"I've got a lot on at the moment," he said.

"Kit, please!"

Eventually he agreed to meet at Trafalgar Square tube station the next day.

There were a few more places to try - a pub off the Holloway Road where the local CP went after their meetings, a folk club in Camden, but it was the same story everywhere. It was as if she'd completely fallen out of the life she'd been leading.

And now I was getting worried too.

* * *

This was the first demonstration I'd been to since the ones that Emma had taken me on, and the changes were noticeable. Violence in the early days had been flashpoints, spontaneous anger suddenly boiling over, but the day had usually started out with good-humoured banter between the crowd and the police. There was none of that here, placard carrying demonstrators and helmeted police were eyeing each other warily, seasoned campaigners squaring up against each other yet one more time.

A bad vibe was how Kit described it as we moved through the crowd and I took his arm and squeezed it, glad he was with me.

A stage had been erected in the centre of the Square

and the familiar collection of left-wing politicians, bumptious thespians, bad poets and sanctimonious clergy all took their turn to use the microphone. The one thing that hadn't changed over the years was the loudspeaker system. They could have been reciting their shopping lists for all the sense I could make of them through the hisses and whistling feedback.

We circled the Square and Kit suggested we walk up to the balustrade in front of the National Gallery, where we could look down on the crowd. We waited until the speeches began to taper out, but there was no sign of Emma.

Kit passed me a flyer that we'd been handed when we arrived.

"The march is going up Charing Cross Road onto Oxford Street," he said, "and then off into Grosvenor Square. Why don't we walk up to Tottenham Court Road and watch it go by?" He shrugged. "If Emma is in this crowd, it'll be a lot easier to spot her when it's stretched out."

We strolled up by the theatres and bookshops and waited outside the tube station. It took about an hour for the march to pass by and still with no sight of her.

"Maybe," said Kit, "she went straight to Grosvenor Square. The police use the marches for surveillance." He indicated a second-story window above a record store across the road. It was open, but with the curtains drawn almost shut. A gust of wind blew the material back for a second and I glimpsed a kneeling figure, pointing a camera downward.

"You get a much clearer shot in a slow-moving procession than a melee," he said. "And anyone they have pegged as a troublemaker gets pulled out of the crowd before they get a chance to start anything."

"Alright," I said, and we walked west along Oxford Street. The march was being carefully marshalled, we were moving twice as quickly along the pavement as the procession was in the road. By the time we reached Oxford Circus we were probably back up to halfway along its length. The crowds were being directed towards Grosvenor Square via a street off to the left, and we turned the corner with them.

It was narrower here, people spilling sideways onto the pavement. Then ahead of us came the sudden sound of shouting and the procession in front stopped, but the marchers behind us were still coming forward. Kit grabbed my arm.

"Claudia," he said tersely, "move over to the wall."

And then the police charged.

They came out of a side street on horseback, three abreast and wielding long batons. The panic was instantaneous. A young woman with a child in a pushchair was screaming as she tried to get out of their path. The crowd surged, forcing Kit and I apart. I'd managed to press my back against a wall, but Kit had been carried out into the middle of the road, directly in front of the horses. The movement of the crowd halted, those behind now realising what was happening. But as the pressure suddenly eased people lost their balance. I saw Kit stumble, but a girl next to him lost her footing completely and tumbled over, seemingly right under the horses' hooves.

"*She's dead,*" was the horrified thought that flashed in my mind. Then I gasped as Kit dived out of sight down after her. "*Jesus Kit, no!*"

The horses surged ahead, the crowd confused eddies in their wake. I had a vision of trampled broken bodies underneath, but Kit's head and shoulders suddenly appeared like a swimmer breaking the surface. He had both arms wrapped tightly around the girl, she was wide-eyed and openedmouthed with shock, blood was running down over one eye from a cut on her forehead.

Kit said something to her, but she stared at him blankly. He unwrapped his arms from around her and then taking her by the hand began to lead her back up the street. Occasionally he looked behind him, each time I waved but he couldn't see me and so I moved along the pavement, following him as best as I could and praying I wouldn't lose him in the chaos that was now everywhere.

I passed a young policeman laying on the ground unconscious, his helmet beside him and bleeding from the back of his head. A middle-aged man in a duffle coat, kneeling down to help him, was set upon by two truncheon wielding policemen. Smashed windows of parked cars had carpeted the street with tiny fragments of broken glass that crunched under my feet. Everyone seemed to be screaming, more than a few stumbling around holding their heads.

'*How has this all happened so quickly?*' I remember thinking to myself. In my mind, it was barely seconds ago that we'd turned into this street. Had I blanked out, had my brain shut down - time was supposed to stretch out in a crisis, seconds becoming minutes, catastrophe unfolding in slow motion, not the reverse..."

"*Claudia!*"

Kit was on the other side of the street, by the entrance to a narrow alley. I nodded and as he guided the girl into it, I picked my way across to the opposite pavement and followed him. After the bright sunshine my eyes couldn't adjust, so I just stumbled forward behind the dark shadowy figures in front until we burst out into the sunlight again, on Oxford Street.

And a normal everyday Oxford Street, afternoon shoppers with not a care in the world ambling along, gazing into store windows.

It was almost dreamlike in its serenity.

The girl was still dazed. She rubbed her forehead with her hand and then gasped when she saw that it had come away with blood on it.

"It's okay." Kit took her hand and squeezed it. "It's not as bad as it looks." He nodded at an *Egg & i*, about twenty yards along across Oxford Street. "Let's go for a coffee and get you cleaned up."

The staff gave us a few funny looks as we entered, but

no-one said anything. I led the girl straight into the Ladies, while Kit found a table away from the window.

"No, it's alright, she just slipped," I heard him say to a waitress, as I pushed the door open. "She'll be fine."

* * *

I took out my handkerchief and held it under the cold tap. Once the blood was wiped away, the cut didn't seem that bad, and I studied her carefully as I dabbed around it.

Once you broke through the initial tomboyish effect of a brown leather jacket, T-shirt and jeans rolled up over a pair of Doc Martins, it came as a bit of a surprise that she was actually very pretty. But she had deep wide-apart eyes, set in a heart-shaped face framed by a mop of short tight curls, and if she'd bothered with makeup she could have been beautiful. She didn't look English, and I guessed Scandinavian - there's something about those Nordic girls.

"It's stopped bleeding and I don't think you'll need stitches," I told her, passing her my handkerchief. "But you should keep that pressed against it for a few minutes."

"Thank you," she said, still dazed. And then burst into tears.

I hugged her for a minute or two, while she pulled herself together.

"I'm so sorry." She shook her head, admonishing herself. "How silly you must think of me."

Dutch, from her accent.

"Of course not."

"I was really frightened."

"It's alright."

"I was down on the ground," she said. "The horse's feet were coming right at me and I thought they would break my head open." For a second it seemed she would start crying again, but she just gave a sniff and stared at me. "And then your boyfriend threw himself over me. He saved me."

"He's not my boyfriend," I told her. "Well, we're friends, good friends, but not a couple."

"Oh," she said, perhaps a little more perky with that piece of information than I might have wished.

"I'm Claudia, by the way," I told her.

"Carin."

"Okay Karen, shall we...?"

"*Carin*." She interrupted. "C-A-R-I-N."

"I'm sorry."

"It's okay." She smiled for the first time, God, she really was pretty. "I'm used to it. In England no-one knows of the Dutch name."

"Shall we have a coffee?" I raised my palm. "If you'd like a little longer to collect yourself, that's alright, there's no hurry."

She shook her head, and we went back out into the restaurant.

"This is Carin," I told Kit, as we sat down at the table. "And Carin, this is Kit."

She looked at him, smiling shyly and with a coy, slight tilt of her head. *Hmmm, she might not be much for war paint and frills,* I thought, *but she knows how to get the big guns out when she wants to.*

"So, you are my knight in armour. Isn't that what you say?"

"Knight in shining armour," Kit smiled back at her.

"Are you on holiday here, Carin?" I asked, trying to cool things down before I'd have to throw a bucket of water over them.

"I'm a student," she said. "I am studying History of Art at the Central London Polytechnic."

"Oh, over the road here," said Kit.

"Yes." She shrugged. "I came in today to use the Library. Leaving I see the March, see it is against the Americans in Vietnam. I joined in. We turn off Oxford Street and then..." She broke off. "Why would the police do that? There was no violence."

"It's unofficial policy to keep political demonstrations

as violent as possible." Kit shrugged. "Back in the fifties, CND demonstrations attracted a broad cross-section and so…"

"Broad cross-section?"

"People from lots of different backgrounds."

"I understand."

"The Government didn't like the appearance of unified opposition," said Kit. "So, the police got the nod to put the boot in." He sipped his coffee. "What happens is that on the next demo the women with pushchairs and kids don't come back but the blokes do, looking for payback. And whatever's being protested about gets buried under accusations of mindless thugs attacking the police."

"You seem to know a lot about it," said Carin, and Kit gave another shrug.

She finished her coffee.

"Where do you live, Carin?" I asked. "Will you be okay getting home?"

"The Halls of Residence are only around the corner, I'll be fine." She stared at Kit again. "You really did save my life, you know?"

She reached into her bag, pulled out a pen and a small spiral notebook.

"I've arranged to meet some friends," she said, "and with all of this trouble, I think it might worry them if I am late."

"That's okay," said Kit. "It was good to meet you, Carin."

"But I would like to thank you properly," she told him, flipping the notebook open, "and the least I could do would be to buy you dinner." She gave Kit that same shy smile again. "If you would like that?"

"Yes." Kit returned her smile. "I'd like that very much."

She began to scribble.

"This is the phone number, ask for Carin in room twenty-three if I don't answer." She tore the page out and passed it across the table. "The best time to call is between six and seven."

Carin stood up.

"Thank you again," she said to him and then flashed me a smile.

"Bye bye, Claudia."

And she was gone.

Kit held the torn scrap of paper, staring at it.

"What are you going to do?" I asked him. "About Emma," I added, as he raised his eyes to meet mine.

"Even if she's in Grosvenor Square, we won't be able to get anywhere near it now," he said. "But I don't think she is."

"Neither do I." I stared at him. "I'm really worried, Kit."

He said nothing.

"And this Carin?" I asked. "After all, the *least* she can do to thank you is to take you out for dinner."

He smiled, glanced again at the paper in his hand, then folded it in half and slipped it into his pocket.

"But seriously Kit," I told him, "that was an incredibly brave and an incredibly stupid thing to do."

"Actually, it was neither." He gave me a smile. "I didn't know she was down there until I landed on top of her."

"What?"

"Horses instinctively will never trample a human, especially trained police mounts, even in a skirmish. The safest place is on the ground in front of them, they'll always rear away to one side. A lot safer than getting crushed between two of them or having your head broken open with a baton." He grinned. "As soon as I realised that I couldn't get out of their way, I dropped onto the ground. They went right around us."

"*You frightened the life out of me*," I almost yelled at him.

Kit

The lock-up was a railway arch, with a steel roller shutter door fully open. As we approached, Coochie came out to wave us in. We parked alongside a Ford Zodiac saloon with the boot lid already raised.

The blond kid who'd been at the gym pulled on the chain to lower the shutters, but Coochie motioned him to stop.

"We'll only be a few minutes," he said. "We don't want that racket drawing attention."

He turned to us.

"Everything okay?"

I nodded and opened the rear door of the van. The gear was in two suitcases, I took one and Aidan the other. We carried them over to the Zodiac, putting them down on the ground as Coochie lifted a holdall out of the boot.

"You want this in the back?" he asked, and I nodded again. As he put the bag in the van he was obscured for a moment by the open door and when he stepped back into view he was holding a sawn-off shotgun.

For a few seconds, everything seemed to freeze.

"Step away from the car," he said. "No-one's going to get hurt if you do what I say."

"I wouldn't be too sure about that," said Aidan softly.

Coochie motioned with the shotgun, and we moved over to the side of the garage. The kid took the holdall from the van and put it into the boot of the Zodiac, then packed the suitcases in there too.

"Back it out, the keys are in the ignition," said Coochie, stepping away from us and standing next to the kid. "I'll keep them covered."

The closest thing I've ever experienced to what happened next was when I once stood too close to the edge of the platform at Reading railway station and a nonstop Intercity 125 came barrelling through. It felt like I was being lifted off my feet and about to be sucked into some terrifying vortex, and this was exactly the same sensation. Except Coochie actually was flying upside down through the air, before slamming into the brick wall at the back of the garage and with a thud that was still audible through the thunder in my ears. Then the blond kid's head, separate from his body, bounced onto him as he fell to the floor.

I must have blacked out at that point, for how long I'm not sure, but the next thing I remembered was sitting in a chair and Paul was asking me if I was okay. I nodded, even though I had no idea whatsoever about that.

Aidan appeared in my field of vision, shaking his head.

"They're both gone," he was saying, in a weird, echoey kind of voice. *'Well, there's a surprise'* went through my mind, *'you mean no-one's stuck his head back on yet?'* Then, almost as if someone had flicked a switch, there was a moment of decompression in my ears and normal service was resumed.

"You alright?" asked Paul again, and I nodded.

"What...?" I began, but Aidan broke in.

"I didn't have a particularly good feeling about your man there," he said, "so I asked Paul to ride shotgun for us."

"Shotgun?" I shook my head. "Jesus, you don't mess around, do you?"

"The thing is," said Aidan, "what do we do now?"

"That depends," said Paul, "on whether your friend here was going freelance or carrying out orders."

They were both staring at me.

"If the Slater Brothers were planning to rip us off for twenty-five grands' worth of gear," I said, "I can't see them leaving it all down to Coochie and his boyfriend to handle."

"Let's have a look in the car," said Paul.

I started to rise, but my legs almost immediately gave way underneath me.

"Stay there," said Aidan.

They were gone less than a minute.

"Two packed bags in the back," said Paul. "Someone was planning on going away."

"I'll ring Harry Slater," I told them. Neither brother was going to be over the moon about this, but Harry you could at least talk to. "Because we either let him know what's happened straightaway or he'll think we've ripped him off and come gunning for us."

"Do you have a number for him," asked Paul.

"Yeah." I sighed. "We passed a phone box along the road, not too far away. I'll take a walk down there and call him."

"Best to leave this place exactly as it is," said Paul. "We don't want it looking like it's been tampered with. I'll come with you, just in case."

I nodded and stood up. This time I made it.

Aidan

The phone box must have been a lot further away than Kit remembered, because he'd only been back a few minutes when there was a squeal of brakes outside. A couple of heavies piled out of the rear of a Rover and positioned themselves with their backs to the lock-up in a classic stance of belligerent immobility. The man who emerged from the front passenger door of the car was smaller and slimmer, dapper in a camel hair overcoat but no less menacing for that. From the driver's side a taller, bulkier figure stepped out, his eyes skipping around the scene before him, taking everything in.

"Mr Slater," said Kit respectfully, moving forward. I hung back, Paul was sitting on an oil drum, his pose casual but watchful, hands pushed deep into his jacket pockets. Harry Slater was staring with an expression of incredulity at the crumpled bodies against the far wall.

"What in God's bloody name," shaking his head, "has happened here?"

Kit began to explain, although the scene pretty much told its own story - the cash and the drugs in the boot of Coochie's car and the sawn-off lying across his body. As Kit finished speaking, another car pulled up and the driver hurried inside. Slater and his minder turned toward him and listened as he spoke softly and urgently.

When he'd done, Slater gave a nod and turned back to us.

"The little shit's cleared his gaff out - no doubt he was about to do a runner."

"There's one other thing," I said, and all eyes swung towards me. I looked at Slater. "How much did he tell you the deal was for?"

"Forty thousand," said Slater, and Kit's head whipped round to stare at me.

"And that's what's in the bag," I said, "but the deal we made was for twenty-five." I met Kit's stare. "I counted it while you were at the phone box." I shrugged. "I thought it strange he didn't haggle a little harder."

There was a silence.

"Alright, let's sort this bloody mess out," said Slater. He turned to his minder. "Tony, start by checking the gear."

As Tony went over to the car, Slater gave a half apologetic shrug.

"No offence, but the way this has gone down so far you'll pardon my caution."

Tony finished rummaging around in the boot, straightened up and gave Slater a nod.

"Right," said Slater to him. "Bring the cash over here."

Tony carried over the holdall and dropped it down on the car's bonnet.

"Twenty-five was the original deal you said?" Slater asked Kit, who nodded.

Slater began pulling bundles of notes from the bag and counting them out onto the bonnet.

"Twenty-five grand," he said eventually. "Plus," he dropped down three more bundles, "a grand each for your trouble."

He stared at us.

"We all happy with that?"

Paul and I nodded.

"Thank you, Mr Slater," said Kit.

Slater seemed to reflect.

"So, what's the score here?" he asked. "You lads setting yourselves up as an outfit or...?"

"No," said Paul. "Kit and Aidan are old friends and wanted me to watch their backs tonight."

"I see." Slater reflected. "Well, speaking of watching your backs, for the next few weeks you might want to keep an eye out for Chas." He looked at Kit. "You know, my brother?"

Kit nodded, and Slater continued.

"Because he is not going to be happy about tonight, whatever the reasons. He and David were, well, friends..."

He broke off as Tony guffawed and turned his glare full on him. Tony gave a shake of his head and walked over to speak to the heavies still stationed outside the garage.

"I will have a word with Chas," continued Slater, "and I will make him understand he has to behave himself... But he can be impetuous."

"We'll be careful," said Kit.

Slater nodded.

"We'll finish up here," he said, which I took as clear an invitation to be on our way as we were likely to get. We shut the back doors of the van but before we got inside Tony came over.

"How exactly," nodding his head towards the bodies, "did that happen?"

There was no undercurrent to the question, it genuinely seemed one of simple professional curiosity.

"An improvised shaped charge," said Paul quietly. He opened the passenger door of the van, rummaged inside and pulled out the bottom half of a wine bottle, neatly severed and packed with what looked like plasticine.

"Tie a petrol-soaked cord around the middle of a wine bottle, then light it to get a clean break. Pack it with *plastique*, stick a remote detonator in and place it in position. When it fires," he turned the bottle upside down and tapped the indentation on the bottom, "it blows out through the punt."

"You're army?" asked Tony.

Paul gave a half smile

"Was."

"What mob?"

"South Yorkshires."

"You with them when they was in Aden?"

Paul nodded.

"I know how rough that was," said Tony. "My cousin was out there."

"Who was he with?"

"The Argylls," said Tony quietly. "He bought it at Crater."

"I'm sorry to hear that." Paul shook his head. "A lot of good blokes who should have made it back didn't."

"Look mate," said Tony, "what Harry was telling you about Chas - he wasn't bullshitting. I don't think he's going to let this go." He hesitated. "If I hear anything, is there any way I can get in touch?"

Paul took a small notebook out of his pocket and a ballpoint. He scribbled on a page, then tore it out and handed it to Tony.

"Thanks," he said. "Hopefully you won't be hearing from me."

Kit backed the van out of the garage, Paul and I climbed in and we drove away into the darkness.

5. Amanda Palmer

Travelling to the West Country always reignited childhood memories for Amanda. To avoid the horrendous traffic jams they would journey overnight, in a big unmarked Jaguar that dad 'borrowed' from the motor pool while everyone turned a blind eye. A lot of blind eyes were turned in those days...

Memories both fragmented and vivid. The sleek silver cat stretched on the front of the bonnet, glittering yellow under the sodium streetlights. A walnut dashboard filled with flickering dials and a miasma of leather, polish and octane stirring the senses in a way that even the most upmarket of today's marques failed to evoke.

And reading the road signs as they sped by, almost impossible to imagine distances back then - a hundred miles to Exeter, ninety miles to Truro... Distances which today she'd swallowed effortlessly. Even now, on the last leg across Bodmin Moor, she was in a stream of traffic making a steady fifty or sixty and expected to be in St Hannahs before lunch.

But that was then, she told herself, and now is now. She let the past slip away - with little regret - although before focusing on the job immediately to hand, she cast her mind back to her last encounter with Chief Superintendent Kendall.

Just what, she mused, had he really been trying to tell her?

* * *

The meeting had broken up quickly, Venables escorting Sir Richard out of the room while Kendall took Shravasti to one side. After a brief word, she nodded and hurriedly departed.

Amanda liked the young DS. She'd only known her for the few days they'd been together on this case, but she was bright and had that rare gift of being able to process detail whilst not losing sight of the bigger picture. But what impressed Amanda the most was that once she believed she was on the right track, she remained unfazed by criticism. Even from senior officers, a rarity in a profession where standing your ground was more likely to generate antipathy than respect. What that also told Amanda was that she knew Kendall would always have her back, and Amanda envied her that - her own career path had been over far rockier territory.

Amanda fastened her briefcase and headed for the lift. The sooner she was on her way down to Cornwall, she thought as the doors opened, the sooner they were likely to have some answers. She pressed the button for the ground floor and the doors had almost closed when a hand shot between them and they sprang open again.

"Sorry," said Amanda to Kendall, "I didn't see you there."

"That's okay." Kendall gave her a smile and then hesitated. "Do you have an hour or so, DI Palmer?" he asked. "There's something I'd like to go through with you."

Amanda was rather taken aback.

"Well, I was going to get myself sorted out for heading down to St Hannahs."

"Did you drive over - if not, can I give you a lift?"

"Alright." Amanda was still dubious but felt she had little choice.

Kendall reached out and pressed the lowest button.

"I'm in the basement," he said.

"So, what was it you...?" began Amanda as the lift descended, but Kendall simply smiled and raised a finger to his lips.

"Shravasti is quite taken with you," he said conversationally. "You should feel complimented. She's inclined to be… brittle, when it comes to relationships. Work or otherwise."

"I've noticed," said Amanda, then smiled. "I like her too."

"See something of your younger self, do you?" asked Kendall and Amanda gave him a sharp look, expecting an edge there. But she saw no hint of that in his face.

"Perhaps," she said eventually, as the lift doors opened.

"I'm just here," said Kendall, indicating a powder blue Mercedes Coupe.

"Belongs to the wife," he added, catching Amanda's expression. "Mine's in for a service."

"Well, that's a relief," said Amanda, and he gave a short laugh.

"The things we are judged upon," Kendall said softly, shaking his head.

"How did Shravasti come to work for you?" asked Amanda as they strapped themselves in. "I assume she was a graduate entry."

"Not at all." Kendall shook his head. "I came across her working a case."

"Really?" Amanda turned to him in surprise. "That sounds like a story."

"It is." At the exit to the garage, Kendall waited for a break in the traffic and then slipped out into the Pentonville Road. "A while ago, one of our teams had a target who they were certain was the kingpin of a multi-million pound cocaine syndicate. So, they raided his place, didn't come up with anything tangible, but they got their hands on his Psion Organiser. Except, they couldn't get through the password screen." He inclined his head towards her slightly. "You know what they are, right?"

Amanda nodded.

"Pocket computers. PDAs, I think they're called."

"That's right. So, we contacted Psion to see if they could help and they lent us Shravasti for a week."

"She cracked the password?"

"It was more bypassing it, from what I understand - which isn't much - but the result was the same. And it was pure gold - not only was he keeping all his current contacts and deals on there, he also believed that when he deleted something it was actually gone forever. Shravasti pulled around two years' worth of data off it. From that, three international networks were rolled up and around fifty big players in half a dozen countries went down with double digit sentences. Additionally, we got our hands on over thirty million in cash and assets, through proceeds of crime orders."

"Impressive," said Amanda.

"We thought so. Enough to make her an offer - she ummed and ahhed at first, so we guaranteed fast-track promotion and that swung it for her to come on board."

They'd pulled up at a set of lights, and he turned to face her.

"So Amanda, what would it take to get you on board?"

"I'm sorry?" His question genuinely startled her. "What?"

"To join us at NCIS - what would persuade you?"

"You're aware that Keith Venables has made me an offer," she said, carefully.

"I am," nodded Kendall. "I'm also aware that ex police officers rarely do well in the intelligence community."

Amanda forced a smile.

"Isn't that a bit of a generalisation?"

"If you're looking for job satisfaction, to acquire a sense of worth or accomplishment, then implanting a binary mindset - a black and white rationale - into a 'shades of grey' world is not the route to take, I can assure you."

"Yes, well, I didn't find an awful lot of self-worth during fifteen years with the Met." Amanda savoured the terseness that had crept into her tone.

"Would you mind if we took a slight diversion?" Kendall asked. "I'd like you to see something that might change your mind."

Again, Amanda didn't feel she was able to argue. Equally, she felt little obligation to fill the silence as they drove eastwards across the city.

"And here we are," said Kendall, pulling up opposite a police station in Hackney, one that Amanda knew well from her time on the beat.

"What exactly...?" she began, but Kendall raised a hand to silence her. Then almost immediately a black cab pulled up in front of them and Shravasti climbed out, a large leather satchel slung over one shoulder.

"She had to stop off to pick something up," said Kendall. "After you're done here, she'll drop you back home."

"Done here?" asked Amanda.

Kendall gave an enigmatic smile.

* * *

Amanda and Shravasti entered the building as Kendall drove away. Amanda was led through a series of corridors into a large squad room, where it was obvious that a briefing was about to begin. At the far end of the room two chairs had been placed behind a couple of desks pushed together. Another twenty or so chairs were arranged in rows facing the desk but Amanda knew that the more seasoned detectives would stand against the walls at the back and sides of the room, where they could slip out for a quick smoke if - when - things started to flag.

Amanda recognised John Hammond, who she knew from the Robbery Squad. She guessed he'd be leading the briefing. The other chair would be for any officer called on to update their aspect of the investigation.

Hammond suddenly noticed Amanda, acknowledging her with a slow nod and a slightly quizzical smile. After a few seconds of hesitation he moved to come over to her, but Shravasti stepped forward and extended her hand.

"Superintendent Hammond?"

"Er, yes," said Hammond, taken aback.

"DS Sule, sir," she said. "NCIS."

Hammond shook her hand cautiously.

"You met my boss, Chief Superintendent Kendall, at the annual review last week. If you recall, you discussed this case, and he offered to get one of his people to have a look at it for you." She let the silence continue just long enough for it to actually register as a silence and added, "That would be me, sir."

"Yes. Right." He glanced around the room. "This really isn't the best time to get you up to speed on..."

"Oh, no sir," she interrupted. "I've already run an analysis. And it's generated some data which I think you need to examine quite urgently."

Amanda sensed Hammond stiffening. A DS - a female DS at that - did not go around telling Superintendents what they needed to do.

"Oh really," said Hammond, with an edge that Amanda recognised and didn't like. "Well, we're about to begin here, but when the officers who have actually been working this case have finished their reports, perhaps you'd be good enough to share your insights with us all."

"Sir," she said. Hammond gave a shake of his head before walking away, and Amanda turned to Shravasti. Her first instinct was that it had been an uncharacteristic misstep from her and a huge one, because Amanda had no doubt that Hammond intended to put her up in front of everyone and inflict a death of a thousand cuts. Yet Shravasti's placid expression suggested that Amanda just might be missing something...

The briefing was an update on a gang of armed robbers who'd been operating in a random pattern around the country for the last three months. It went very much the way these briefings always did. Witness statements were being followed up, informants had leads worth looking into, none of the banknotes had turned up yet, regional police forces were cooperating...

As the last officer returned to his seat, Hammond leaned back in his chair.

"And finally, we're fortunate enough today to have someone here from the NCIS, who've been taking a look at what we've been up to." He paused and let his gaze rest on Shravasti. "Who are you again, love?"

"DS Sule, sir."

Hammond's smile tightened. "So why don't you come up here, DS Sule, and take us through the finer points of where we've been going wrong?"

As Shravasti walked over to the table, the low-level laughter morphed into fractured, hushed conversations around the room and Hammond left his seat to talk to a couple of detectives. She opened her case to reveal a laptop computer, which she connected to a small box with a lens on the front. She tapped on the keyboard and the box threw a large square of light onto the wall behind her. She adjusted the lens until it brought into focus the NCIS logo.

"Could someone get the blinds, please?" she asked. At first no-one moved, then a young constable rose from his seat and walked over to the window. Comments like 'Is it a bluey?' and 'Pass the popcorn' drifted around the room.

"Right," said Shravasti, turning away from the screen and facing them. "As Chief Superintendent Hammond explained, I work as a data analyst at the NCIS and I've been asked to examine the information gathered so far by this investigation. Essentially, to see if the techniques used by our organisation could bring fresh light to bear on your case."

Hammond was still talking with the other officers, his back turned to the screen and a half a dozen murmured conversations were also continuing. Two plain-clothed officers were leaving the room.

"So, I started with the Securicor van in Leeds on the fourth of May, which you've assumed - incorrectly, as will soon become obvious - was the first robbery carried out by this gang."

The conversational drone disappeared as if someone had thrown a switch. One of the detectives froze in the doorway and slowly turned to stare at her. Hammond also turned, his mouth slightly open, which gave him an almost stupefied air.

Shravasti pressed a key on the laptop. The screen divided into four smaller squares and sequences of numbers began scrolling through the top left one.

"Cellular telephones are a relatively new technology as far as the general public are concerned. So, it's still a little-known fact that, whether they're being used or not, they will always log on to the nearest tower. Those," she indicated the numbers scrolling on the screen, "are the mobile phones that connected during a two-hour window to the closest tower to the Leeds Securicor robbery. An hour on each side."

She pressed the keyboard again. Numbers began scrolling down the upper right-hand section. "Gloucester, the 25th May." She pressed again and the bottom left of the screen began scrolling. "Oxford, 10th June." One final key press and the last square filled up and began to scroll. "Leicester, the 5th July."

She turned to face them and smiled.

"I'm sure you can see where I'm going with this."

A blank square appeared in the centre of the screen. A telephone number wrote itself across the top of the square. Then underneath that another. Then another. And one last one.

"These numbers logged onto the cell tower closest to where each of these robberies took place, within an hour of them happening. Which stretches coincidence well beyond the limits of credibility, I'm sure you'd agree."

You could have heard a pin drop. Amanda was sure that quite a few in the room were holding their breath.

"Now these numbers - for convenience let's call them Red, Green, Yellow and Blue," and as she spoke each number coloured itself in, *how on earth did she do that* thought

Amanda, "are 'burner phones' - mobiles bought with cash and topped up anonymously. So, we can't trace who they belong to."

There was a collective expulsion of breath in the room, the disappointment almost tangible.

"But what we can trace," said Shravasti, "is where they've been." She smiled. "We know every cell tower that these phones have logged into, and we know the date and time that happened."

The squares on the screen vanished, and now a map of England appeared. Coloured lines matching the numbers drew themselves around the map.

"We're pretty sure," said Shravasti, "that Red lives in Shepherd's Bush, Green lives in Balham, and that Yellow and Blue are based in Walthamstow. Not exactly narrowing things down but bear with me."

The map zoomed into the Gloucester area. Coloured lines cleared, reappeared, and again began to creep around the map.

"This pattern follows the cell towers along the armoured van's collection route," she said. "But what's interesting is that this schematic is seven days before the actual robbery took place."

"They're casing the job," said a voice from the darkness.

"In every instance," said Shravasti, nodding. "Including," the map zoomed out, moved north and zoomed in to a suburb of Manchester, where the now familiar coloured lines reappeared, "April the seventh. Not an armoured van, which is probably why you missed it, but an armed robbery at a building society. Perhaps they gave that a try and decided it wasn't their thing, or maybe it was done to finance the weapons, cutting equipment and the rest of the gear they needed for the vans. But where it gets really interesting..."

The map zoomed out again, slid south and zoomed in on the town of Alton in Hampshire. Again, coloured lines began creeping around the map.

"So what's this?" asked Hammond, his voice strained. "Another one we're supposed to have missed?"

"No sir," said Shravasti brightly. "This is from last Friday morning."

There was a moment of silence as that sunk in, and then everyone seemed to be talking at once.

"Jesus Christ!" said a voice loudly. "They're putting another one together."

Shravasti had switched the projector off and was disconnecting the lead to the laptop.

"Get on to Hampshire police now," said Hammond. He turned to Shravasti and began to falter. "DS…?"

"Sule, sir," she told him. Amanda had a feeling that name would be burned into his mind for a long time to come.

"Is there no way," he asked her, "that we can identify who those phones belong to? Before Friday?"

Amanda knew what he was thinking. If you're going to have a dozen coppers lying in wait for an armed robbery to go down, let's find out first if these are four villains who'll be putting their hands up or a bunch of nutters.

"Possibly." She stared at him and the room had gone silent again. "When I showed this to my boss, I suggested correlating the postcode addresses covered by the home cell towers with known armed robbers and filter the results by matching patterns of association - joint enterprise criminality, shared prison cells or overlapping sentences at the same gaol etcetera. Then analyse financial records for purchases in the robbery areas, petrol stations and…"

"What did Kendall say?" broke in Hammond.

"He vetoed it." She shook her head. "He said that you could well have someone in the frame for this already, in which case the information I'd correlated would merely be confirmation." She shrugged. "Essentially, that I'd spent the best part of a morning on this and that I needed to get back to my priority cases."

"Priority cases!" Hammond looked fit to burst. "What

the fuck is more of a priority than putting these bastards away?"

"With respect sir," Shravasti's smile had vanished and now she was fixing him with a chilly stare, "there's no one in this room with a high enough security clearance for me to discuss that with."

Hammond stared at her incredulously, while she finished zipping up her laptop.

Lifting the bag onto her shoulder, the smile came back again. "But I'm sure that if you contact Chief Superintendent Kendall, he'll do everything he can to help you out here. Sir."

The hundreds of man hours thought Amanda, the thousands spent, and this slip of a girl taps on a keyboard and...

She was aware of Shravasti standing in front of her, an expectant look on her face.

"Ready?" she asked, and through a gauntlet of stares Amanda followed her out of the room.

"The boss says," Shravasti told her, as they walked down the steps of the building and onto the pavement, "that if you liked what you just saw, then call him when this Irish business is sorted. That there's plenty more where this came from."

* * *

Even the local nick looked like a holiday cottage, thought Amanda as she waited at the front desk for her contact, a Sergeant Vanner, to make an appearance. She guessed he wouldn't be best pleased having to be nursemaiding her on what was most likely his busiest day of the year, but she also knew that the request - to have St Hannahs' longest serving police officer available to assist her enquiries - had been channelled down directly from the Chief Constable of Devon and Cornwall Constabulary and so didn't expect too much in the way of bother.

"DI Palmer."

It was a reassuring start. His welcoming smile seemed

genuine enough and his handshake, while firm, wasn't one of those bone-crushers that junior officers - more often than you'd think - would try to intimidate her with.

"Sergeant Vanner - it's good to meet you. And thanks for your time, I appreciate how busy you must be today. If it had been possible to put this off for a few days, I would have."

When showing up on someone's patch - with an unknown agenda - a lot of lines were drawn in the sand by initial impressions, and so Amanda always attempted to start out with a show of respect. If you had to use the big stick from the off things rarely went well, but Vanner simply acknowledged her thanks with a brief nod.

"Anything we can do to help. Would you like a drink - tea, coffee?"

"Coffee would be great. White, no sugar."

She studied him as he turned and spoke to the constable at the desk. In his early to mid-fifties, he must have his thirty in by now, so if he was still here it was because he wanted to be. He was big, but most of his bulk looked solid and she guessed his ruddy complexion was more down to gingers never tanning than a fondness for the bottle.

He led her into a small office and sat down behind a battered old wooden desk.

"Not very comfortable, I'm afraid," he said, indicating her chair. "This doubles up as an interview room."

"That's okay."

"So - you're down here for a *historical* investigation, I understand." Vanner let just an edge of puzzlement enter his voice and Amanda understood why - if this is a cold case then what's with the rush?

"Well, that's how it started out - but a few stones got kicked over on the way and now..."

She shrugged.

"Things have crawled out?"

Amanda gave a nod.

"And you need to interview Susan Marshall?"

"Do you know her?"

"She taught my kids." Vanner's expression was quizzical. "I have to say, I find this a very strange request."

Amanda kept silent.

"You also want to speak to Lee Munro?" Vanner leaned back, studying her. "Assuming that she's actually up at the Grange - she doesn't spend that much time here."

"She flew into Newquay yesterday, by private jet," said Amanda quietly. "My understanding is that she'll be here at least until tomorrow."

"Well, you seem better informed than I am." Vanner continued to stare at her. "And both are related to your case? I ask," breaking into Amanda's slight hesitation, "because in a place like this everybody may know everyone else, but I've never had reason to put those two together in my head."

Country cop or not, he had a look in his eye which said he was nobody's fool. So don't get too clever here, Amanda told herself. Stick with the basics until you've spoken to both women and let's see what shakes down out of that.

The door opened, and the constable brought in a tray with two coffees, giving her an opportunity to appear to be considering. After he'd closed the door behind him, she gave a small nod.

"In 1971, Susan Marshall reported her brother missing." She paused. "Were you in the job then?"

"I was, but not here. I joined in sixty-six as a cadet but stationed in Truro. I'd be over here occasionally during the summer, to make the numbers up when things got busy, but I didn't move to St Hannahs until seventy-seven."

"At your own request?"

"I'd passed my sergeants exam the year before and this was the next promotion to come up. The wife had fallen pregnant with our first and we needed the money."

"So you never knew Peter Marshall - Susan Marshall's brother?"

Vanner slowly shook his head.

"I didn't even know she had a brother - which for St Hannahs is odd in itself, believe me."

"We've compelling evidence," she said, picking up her cup, "that he was murdered in the summer of 1970."

Vanner stared at her.

"Bloody hell," he said softly. "And that's what you're here to tell her?"

Amanda nodded.

"And to find out what she knows about her brother in the months leading up to his disappearance." She hesitated. "But Lee Munro - I'd like to see her first."

"You think there's a connection between them?" Vanner seemed to be struggling with his thoughts.

"Peter Marshall was living in the same West London house as Lee Munro when he vanished. And we know she was staying in St Hannahs in 1967, so it's a good bet that's when they originally met. Which is why I'd like to hear what she has to say, before speaking to Ms Marshall."

"How are you so sure that she was here then?"

Amanda smiled.

"The Aidan McShane exhibition, which opens here this week..."?

Vanner looked at her inquisitively.

"All the initial artwork was created in St Hannahs, around Easter 1967. Lee Munro was the model for quite a few of the paintings."

"Well, we'd better have a word with her then," said Vanner.

* * *

"Sorry again about all of this," said Amanda, more by way of conversation than genuine regret. "You must be really busy today?"

They were stuck in traffic, trying to cross the square in the centre of St Hannahs. She guessed *'Park and Ride'* hadn't made it down here yet, but it wouldn't be a bad idea for a place with a road layout that probably predated the stagecoach.

"Nothing too urgent," said Vanner. "We've been having a few problems with Travellers this week."

"Is that a big issue in Cornwall?" asked Amanda.

"Not much more than trespass usually," Vanner shook his head. "But a group of them have set up in a field just outside of town. A local businessman, friend of the owner, went over there to talk to them about it and ended up in hospital."

"What happened?"

"That's what we're trying to find out. He was found collapsed by his car in a Viewing Area, about half a mile away."

"Badly hurt?"

"Well, he's in an induced coma with a lump on his head the size of a golf ball. He could have blacked out and whacked it on the way down - tests do show evidence of a pre-existing medical condition - but that still doesn't rule out him being attacked. There's a lot of bad feelings around at the moment, on both sides."

"No witnesses?"

"Oh, plenty of witnesses - who all say he was fine when he drove away." Vanner sighed. "Anyway, they started screaming persecution and then last night one of them broke into the new art gallery and attacked a painting."

"Jesus - was it badly damaged?"

"Well, I'd been intending to go and find out about that today."

"Sorry again," said Amanda.

"I'm guessing it's some sort of protest gesture," continued Vanner. "He won't talk until he's got a solicitor, and that's fine by me. He can sweat in the cells until I've had a chance to see about the damage."

They sat in silence for a while.

"You must have seen a lot of changes down here, over the last thirty years?" suggested Amanda. "In the job, I mean."

"Back then it was mostly domestics," said Vanner.

"Fishing and the tourist trade kept the town's economy ticking over, at least to the extent that anyone who wanted a job had one. The downside of that was that it was the women working in the hotels and the men away at sea. 'Flashpoints of temptation and retribution', my old sergeant used to call them and that was all too true, in a place small enough for everyone to know each other's business.

"The fishing went in the late seventies, early eighties, a combination of EU quotas and Health and Safety regs. And that's when you felt the demographic really shift, young folk moving away to the cities looking for work and houses being snapped up by retirees and Londoners after a holiday home. I know you can still see boats in the harbour, but these days they're only putting out to sea for tourist trips along the coast."

Amanda nodded towards the crowds, overspilling the pavement.

"The tourist industry looks healthy enough, though."

"Day trippers mostly," said Vanner. "All the large hotels have been taken over by big chains, and with managers regularly being moved around the country there're no roots going down here. They might recruit bar and kitchen staff locally, but at the height of the season they prefer students. Who are a lot cheaper and less likely to kick off about pay and conditions - all they're here for is a three month piss-up and shagging spree."

He slipped into first gear as the traffic inched forward.

"Most of the smaller places have been bought by people from up country. You can buy a guest house in St Hannahs for what you'd sell a semi for in Wimbledon, and a lot of them think retirement into the bed-and-breakfast trade is easy pickings. Which it can be if you know what you're doing, but most of them can't grasp that it has to be a business and not a hobby."

He shook his head.

"So, the only people making real money are the ones

whose families have ruled the roost since the year dot. They hold the ground rents on just about the entire town - if they're not actually on the council, then they've a hand up the arse of whoever is and ditto working the planning and licensing committees."

"You sound a shade cynical."

"Show me a small-town copper who isn't. Same setup the country over I'd imagine, give or take a little local flavour."

"You keep busy here all year round?"

"Police work, like just about everything in Cornwall," said Vanner, "is seasonal. The summer's almost exactly what you'd expect, alcohol and testosterone in all its rich pageantry, from pub brawls to taking on a rip current after a liquid lunch. You can pretty much cut and paste the paperwork from the previous year."

Amanda smiled.

"It must quieten down after the summer, though?"

"Winter's the slow burning stuff." Vanner gave a slight grimace. "Most people here work like buggery for six months of the year and then spend the winter living off - depending on how the summer went - profits or benefits. A bad season in either farming or tourism can have the bank knocking on the door and there's nothing like the threat of bankruptcy to put relationships under a terminal strain."

Amanda stared at him.

"Literally?"

There was that grimace again.

"Most will ride it out, obviously, but it's unusual to get through to the spring without having to deal with at least one case of someone who's decided enough is enough." There was a slight smile on his lips, but there was nothing humorous about it. "You always hope it's not going to be a farm."

Amanda gave him a quizzical stare.

"They have guns," he said quietly.

* * *

As they reached the outskirts of the town, Vanner slowed to make a left turn, coming to a stop at a set of large, wrought-iron gates. He opened the door to climb out, but they silently swung open.

"Well, someone's home," he said. "And watching."

They continued along the driveway, and after a sharp corner the Grange came into view.

"Impressive," said Amanda.

The house was on the crest of a wooded hillside, only a few hundred feet away as the crow flies - or by the steps cut into the slope over to their left - but Amanda guessed the driveway would loop back on itself more than once to create a drivable gradient and she was right.

There was definitely something Gothic about it. At least one turret was visible, but painted brilliant white against its wooded background and silhouetted against a blue sky suggested something of the Alps too.

"It's not as old as you might imagine," said Vanner, dropping back down a gear for the last stretch of the climb. "It was built in the twenties, as a retreat for a London businessman."

"He must have done alright for himself," said Amanda.

"He shot himself just before D-Day," said Vanner. "After being charged with fiddling petrol coupons."

"Wasn't everybody at it back then?"

"He'd been awarded the VC in World War One," said Vanner. "So who knows what was going through his head." He shrugged. "It was empty after that until the fifties, when it became an," he adopted an upper-class accent, "Academy for Young Ladies." He smiled. "That didn't last long. Then it was owned by someone in the music business, who managed pop groups. They still talk about the parties he threw."

"What happens in St Hannahs, stays in St Hannahs?" smiled Amanda and Vanner chuckled.

"It was a hotel for a while after that," he said, "and then this lot took it over about five years ago."

"Do you have much to do with 'this lot'?" asked Palmer as they pulled into a courtyard in front of the house.

Vanner shook his head.

"But one thing I will tell you," he began, but broke off as the large oak door opened and two figures walked down the stone steps toward them.

* * *

"Detective Inspector Palmer," smiled Christopher Franklyn. "I had a feeling we'd be bumping into each other down here."

"Mr Franklyn," acknowledged Amanda with a nod.

"Sergeant Vanner." The man accompanying Franklyn stepped forward and held out his hand. "Good to see you again."

They shook, and Vanner turned to Amanda.

"This is Paul Chapman, who's the managing director of *Executive Action*." As Chapman shook hands with her, Vanner turned back to him. "Although it's Ms Munro that we were hoping to speak to."

"Yeah, so I hear." Chapman smiled at Amanda. "Apparently you have a mystery to solve?"

"Which we hoped Ms Munro might cast some light on."

"I told Lee about our meeting in London," said Franklyn, and at the periphery of her vision Amanda caught Vanner's surprised glance at her. "And she's more than happy to answer your questions."

"Okay, that's great," said Amanda. "Well, what we'd like is…"

"Unfortunately, it won't be today," Chapman broke in. "She's sleeping."

"I'm sorry?"

"She arrived yesterday on a flight from California, spent most of the night on LA time wide-awake and went to bed straight after the eclipse. She took a pill, so she'll be under for at least six hours, and we've a reception tonight at the Gallery which she's flown eight thousand miles to attend." He gave a conciliatory shrug. "Tomorrow morning, say tennish, wouldn't be a problem."

Amanda hesitated. She'd half expected to be brushed off completely, and there would have been nothing she could have done about it. Not unless Susan Marshall came up with something game changing. So, on balance, this she could live with.

"It's longer than I planned to stay," she said, "but okay - let's say tomorrow at ten, shall we?"

Chapman gave her a brief nod. He and Franklyn turned to climb the steps. She and Vanner slowly walked to the car.

"Understandable, I suppose," said Amanda. "I know what I'm like the day after I fly back from the States."

"Except," said Vanner softly, "there was someone watching us from behind a curtain on the second floor and while I wouldn't *swear* it was Lee Munro..."

He gave a shrug as Amanda turned her head to stare at him.

* * *

"You were saying," prompted Amanda, as Vanner started the engine, "when I asked if you had much to do with them."

"During the normal course of things, no." Vanner shook his head. "Some of the... *guests* I suppose you'd call them can get a bit rowdy, but no worse than your typical stag party. We've had the occasional shout when someone gets lost on the moor or takes a fall, but in all the time they've been here there's been nothing more serious than a broken leg."

"But...?"

"Whenever somebody new sets themselves up on my patch, I check them out. Right?" he turned his head to look at Amanda. "You want an idea of who - or what - you're likely to be dealing with."

Amanda nodded but stayed silent.

"I did a CRO check on Paul Chapman about a week after they moved into the Grange. Nothing out of the ordinary came back, he'd been in the army - which you'd expect - worked in personal security - again no surprise - and was a director of a couple of companies, one of which was *Executive Action*. No real criminal record to speak of, a few Causing an Affray and ABH charges from his late teens and early twenties but again, a bunch of squaddies out on the town pissed would probably be a safe bet there. Since then, only parking tickets and a few speeding fines. So, I tucked it away in a filing cabinet, thinking no more about it."

He slowed as they approached the gates and waited as they swung open.

"Until this week, the Chief Constable had only contacted me directly on one occasion and that was the day after I ran that CRO check. And he was *rattled*. What was it I was looking into, he wanted to know? So, I explained it was only a routine query. The bloke had moved into town and set up a business - I didn't want any surprises. That seemed to smooth things over, but someone had definitely gotten to him."

"You were warned off?"

"No, that was the end of it. Once he'd heard me out it was how's the job, how's the missus, how're the kids, my door's always open and he was gone. And, as much as my interest was piqued, I decided to - other than keeping a weather eye open - leave well alone."

"Right," said Amanda slowly.

"The reason I mention it," said Vanner, "is that..."

He broke off and seemed to reflect for a few seconds.

"My old man," he said, "was an engineer. A centre lathe turner, if that means anything to you, at a factory in Redruth. And he always used to say that in this country, if you put a pair of overalls on to do your job people think that you're thick." He gave a slight shake of his head. "Sometimes, I believe you could say the same thing about a uniform."

"Look," began Amanda, "I really..."

"I understand about chain of command and need to

know," broke in Vanner quietly, "and I think 'above your pay grade' is the current vernacular. But if I've got a shitstorm building on my doorstep, I want to see it coming."

"No." Amanda shook her head. "I didn't know about Chapman. But I will tell you - although I shouldn't - that this concerns matters of national security, most of which are as much above my pay grade as they are yours. I'm here to ask questions of people about something that happened - or might have happened - a long time ago and hundreds of miles from here. Then to report back what they've told me. And that's it."

Vanner seemed to consider and then nodded.

"Alright," he said. "Let's find out what Sue Marshall has to say."

* * *

Vanner switched his radio off.

"So, we'll call round to her house at four o'clock," he said, although he knew Amanda had overhead the conversation. "They'll get back to us if there's a problem."

"What time does school finish?"

"Well, it's actually the holidays, but they're having an 'Eclipse Day' there, for the kids. Which should finish about three."

"What do you think of her?" asked Amanda.

The hesitation was slight, but definitely there.

"She taught both of my girls and they adored her," he said. "And you'd be hard pressed to find anyone in this town with a bad word to say about her."

Amanda let the silence play out.

"I've always found her heavy going, I have to admit."

"In what way?"

Vanner shook his head.

"Nothing you could put your finger on, really. The wife says I'm imagining it. And who knows, maybe she's right."

"But you don't think so?"

"She's never anything but polite. Always a smile. But

you do get the feeling that..."

"Something's not right?" suggested Amanda.

Vanner nodded.

"Anyway," he said, "that does give us some time to kill - do you mind if we stop off at the art gallery? I want to take a look at the damage that little bastard did."

"No, of course not - in fact, I was hoping for a chance to pay a visit while I was down here."

"Not my thing, I'm afraid - modern art. I like a face with all of its parts in the right places."

* * *

"So, these paintings," asked Vanner slowly, "would be scenes from the Bible but set in Ireland?"

In appearance, Ruth Weinstock was almost a caricature of an art gallery curator. In her late fifties, Amanda guessed, tall and spindly with greying hair pulled tightly back into a bun. More bracelets and bangles than it seemed her thin arms would be capable of lifting and wearing the skirt and blouse of a Romany Gypsy. But the eyes peering over the inevitable pince-nez were bright and clear, and her smile was mischievous.

Amanda had liked her from the off.

"Indeed, Sergeant, the Ireland of the Troubles."

"And all the models he used," queried Amanda, "were local to St Hannahs?"

"Famously so. Or at least people who were staying here that Easter." She nodded towards a painting over to the left of them - the back view of a bedraggled and handcuffed man standing before a military tribunal - and indicated the centre figure on the bench, wearing a colonel's insignia. "This representation of Pontius Pilate is based on the actor Donald Mayberry, who was holidaying in St Hannahs. Over here, Lee Munro is a very disturbed Mary Magdalen in the *Gethsemane Céilí* piece - more than apt casting, from what one gathers," she added dryly.

"This collection must have been quite controversial at

the time," reflected Amanda.

"Oh absolutely, back then the religious themes alone simply screamed sacrilege - and then stirring in a huge dollop of Sixties promiscuity, in the guise of a Pre-Raphaelite *homage*, left very few people who would not be offended, one way or the other." She gave an approving nod. "That's how you kick-start a career."

"The painting that was damaged." Vanner was giving the appearance of being a bit painting'd out by all of this. "How bad is it?"

"Yes, '*The Woman at the Well*'," said Ruth. "Yet one more of the wayward girls of the Bible, if you're not up on your scripture, Sergeant."

Amanda suppressed a smile.

"Not too bad actually," Ruth told him. "Washable ink on oil isn't going to do that much damage, as long as you're careful not to smear it. Luckily for us, it seems he didn't really know what he was doing." She gave a sad shake of her head. "Any ideas why, Sergeant?"

"This specifically, no," said Vanner. "Once he's got a solicitor sorted, we'll hopefully find out when we interview him. Mind if I take a look at it?"

"It's off to London, I'm afraid. We were confident we could manage the restoration ourselves, but the insurance company was insistent." She paused. "Oh dear, how silly of me – it's evidence of course. Does that present a problem, Sergeant?"

Depends whether or not he pleads guilty or if he even gets charged, thought Amanda. As there didn't seem to be any major damage, if she'd been Vanner she'd possibly try to persuade the gallery to let it go. She could see this becoming exactly the kind of trial which the media loves to turn into a circus.

"Probably not," said Vanner, and Amanda guessed he was thinking along the same lines that she was. "But I'll need to take a statement."

"Of course, come on through to the office." Ruth turned to Amanda with a smile and gestured to the artwork with a wave of her hand. "Please – enjoy."

Left to herself, Amanda slowly walked through the Gallery. She wasn't familiar with the paintings but soon found herself - surprisingly - quite emotionally drawn to them. Well acquainted scenarios from childhood Sunday School, but now infused with a new resonance.

And was that the artist's sleight of hand, thought Amanda as she moved from canvas to canvas? That the past is so full of pitfalls, but our strongest comforts nestle there too?

6. July 1970

Aidan

For most of my time at Pembridge Villas, I'd been aware of the polyamorous normality unfolding around me without really becoming embroiled in it. This was swinging London after all - if you believed the press - but maybe that reserve was down to the Catholic country boy in me. Once you've had the Church seeded into your soul the roots do grow deep, however close to the ground you may later wield the scythe.

But perhaps what stuck most in my craw was a sense that the lip service of liberated women and enlightened men, rather than shining a light into our darkest natures had merely established more complex ways for those murky undercurrents to manifest themselves.

I recall one morning, Jake sitting in the kitchen with a girl he'd met at a party the previous evening and who'd spent the night at Pembridge Villas. She finished her coffee and before leaving scribbled her phone number on a piece of paper for him. He waited until the door closed behind her and the sound of her footsteps had ceased echoing on the stairs, before picking it up, crumpling it into a ball and tossing it across the room into a waste bin.

"You know," he said. "No matter how bright a chick might be, they're all fucking twats when it actually comes to their twats."

Needless to say, there wasn't one of those 'fucking twats' in the room when he said that, and what wouldn't I have given for Lee Munro or Emma Brownlow to have been standing behind him as he shot his mouth off. But I guessed I wasn't the only one of us adding that little homily to an increasingly lengthy list of transgressions stacking up for a day of reckoning that, hopefully, wouldn't be long coming.

When all's said and done, late teens are a vicious age for relationships. Our romantic expectations are still very much based on those courtship rituals which we saw enacted throughout childhood – either portrayals on the page and screen or at a very superficial level between the adults in our lives. And so, unless you were unfortunate enough to have been subjected to the kind of childhood that few of us could imagine experiencing, it's not until you've been around the block a few times that those hidden voids of the opposite sex open themselves up to you. To realise what beasts men can make of themselves with such little pricking of conscience or the low cunning and vindictiveness that can break the placid surface of any woman who, for whatever reason, has come to regard herself as a victim.

After a while the continual flow of arrivals, matings, dissolutions and departures at Pembridge Villas simply became the normal background clutter of the house. You were aware of the occasional upset - playing musical beds, there's always going to be someone left with nowhere to go when the music stops. Always someone left abruptly alone, baffled by the realisation they're neither the person they'd wanted to be or had been persuaded that they were.

And so, to encounter a girl sitting sobbing at the bottom of the stairs was not as unusual an occurrence that a popular press - seemingly obsessed by the permissive society - might have led one to believe.

* * *

"Are you okay?" The ultimate stupid question, which we all ask in the face of obvious distress.

She gave a little nod and wiped her eyes with a small lace handkerchief. I recognised her as the Dutch student Kit had met at some demo and who had seemingly fallen hard for him - in Pembridge Villas this kind of knowledge was absorbed by osmosis.

"What's happened?" I asked, as gently as I could. That

tiny handkerchief would never be up to the job, I thought, as I sat down on the stairs beside her.

Piecemeal and confused and doubtless losing a lot in translation, the story came out. In Kit's room she'd come across a cache of letters written to him by Emma, dated from three years ago until just recently. As we'd all suspected there was quite a bit going on there, a veritable saga of passion and recrimination, *amour fou* as the French would have it. But of course, it was nothing to do with love but obsession, usually dark and twisted and - as this poor kid had discovered - always damaging.

Because when she'd confronted him, he'd found little to offer in the way of comfort – no, he wasn't still seeing her but was silent when she asked if he was still in love with Emma. And so she had stormed out.

"You need to let this settle down," I told her. "Wait until tomorrow and then come back and talk to him. You'll both have had time to think and things might look different then."

She gave a small nod and almost managed a smile but was obviously taking little consolation from my platitudes.

"Why don't you go home?" I asked her. "I'll go and get a taxi. It's okay," as she started to protest, "I'll cover it."

There was usually a black cab passing along outside every few minutes but today, typically, there was neither hide nor hair of one and so I had to cut through to the Portobello Road to flag one down.

But when we got back to the house, she was gone.

Veronica came out of the kitchen.

"Did you see the girl who was sitting here," I asked her.

"Carin? Yes," giving a nod, "she just left with Jake."

I thought about taking a cab to try to find her. They couldn't have gotten far. But to tell her what? To watch out for Jake, that he's a total S-H-One-T as Claudia so elegantly put it. But she was probably feeling that about all men right now and who knows, maybe Jake was about to bite off more than he could chew.

Or maybe not. Maybe she was stepping out of the frying pan and into the fire.

But I had no idea where they'd gone or even which direction they'd taken. In the end, I simply gave the cabby his fare and went back inside.

Claudia

And all of a sudden it was as though you couldn't open a newspaper without Lee's face leaping right back out at you. The detective series which she'd been working on for the past few months began showing on TV and to everyone's surprise - well, mine at least - had not only proved a hit, but Lee's role seemed to be most people's favourite character.

She played the superficially scatty - but actually extremely astute - English daughter come secretary of an American private eye, based in London. It was a London where everyone lived in a cobbled mews in Chelsea and any journey by car involved passing the Houses of Parliament once and crossing Tower Bridge twice. But the fact that no-one took it very seriously, except the ageing Hollywood actor in the lead role, lent it a certain quirky charm that had been one of the biggest factors in its success.

But showbiz whispers of an antipathy between Lee and her leading man began to circulate, and a story had appeared in the tabloids that he'd told the producers it was either him or her. When, according to the rumour mill, they'd said in effect *'we'll think about it'* this created both a surge of public warmth for a supposed underdog and the impression that here were two careers crossing paths, one on the way down but the other very much on its way up.

To escape this flurry of attention, Lee had moved back into Portman Square on a permanent basis. On the one hand, I was rather flattered she'd chosen my home as a bolt-hole and on the other, how much of a bolt-hole was it when the phone never stopped ringing? But most evenings there was someone around for drinks whom I'd previously only seen on a cinema or TV screen, and that was a novelty yet to wear off.

Lee, to her credit, was a lot more blasé about it.

"Like they say, today's headlines wrap up tomorrow's fish and chips," she shrugged. "It's what I do next that's important."

* * *

Lee was in the bathroom when there was a knock at the door, unusual because most visitors had to use the entry phone. Supposing it was a neighbour, I strolled over and opened it. But the two people standing there I'd never seen before, and I assumed they must have arrived at the lobby entrance as someone else was leaving.

The couple were striking in their similarity. Neither was tall, a man in his fifties who was obviously the father of the girl beside him, but their shared delicate features - rosebud lips and small pert nose - that gave her a doll-like prettiness, had aged into an almost dissolute mask for him.

"Hello," I said. "Can I help you?"

"We're here to see Lee Munro," said the girl. Her father just stared at me, a disquieting experience.

"Is she expecting you?" I asked.

"At some point, I'd imagine," she replied, rather tartly.

I hesitated only slightly before stepping back and gesturing with my hand.

"Please, come in."

Leading them through into the living room, I indicated the sofa.

"Have a seat. Lee's taking a shower at the moment, but she shouldn't be long. Can I get you a coffee or perhaps a...?"

"Are you her secretary?" interrupted the girl, sitting down.

"I'm sorry?"

She rolled her eyes, as if exasperated with having to deal with someone so incredibly dense.

"Do you work for her? If so, would you please just go and tell her that...?"

She broke off as the door opened and Lee walked into the room, dressed in a bathrobe with a towel wrapped around her head. When she saw the two figures on the sofa she stopped, frozen.

"Dad. Helen..."

Her father nodded.

"Hello Eileen."

* * *

Helen turned to me.

"You were saying something about a coffee, I believe," she said imperiously. "Mine's white with one sugar. Dad?"

"Tea with milk."

I stared at her for just the fraction of a second before rising to my feet.

"Of course." I looked at Lee. "Darjeeling, Miss Munro?"

"Thank you, Claudia," she said, seemingly not trusting herself to meet my eye.

In the kitchen I took my time assembling the tea tray, wondering if I should make some excuse and depart but yet equally reluctant to leave Lee alone with them. And to be honest, the scene was not lacking a certain morbid fascination...

"Obviously, Larry would help out if he could," her father was saying as I carried the tray back into the living room, "but his hands are tied."

I put the tray down on the coffee table and began to pour the drinks.

"Anyway, the Playhouse are definitely going ahead with the Shaw season this year - and Helen will be taking the role of Violet in *Superman*."

It was so tempting to ask who'd be playing Lois Lane, but I bit my lip.

"Of course, what would really benefit your sister's career right now, would be a TV credit or two - and I have to say, Eileen, we're very surprised that you haven't offered your help there. Surely you could use your influence to find something for her in," he made an almost dismissive gesture with his hand, "this show of yours."

But Lee, I noticed, after her initial shock seemed to have recovered most, if not all, of her composure.

"If you've been reading the papers," she told him, "you'd have seen that I might not have a role myself in the next series - so this wouldn't exactly be a good time to start throwing my weight around as to who plays who."

"Which makes all this," he indicated my apartment with a sweep of his hand, "all rather extravagant, don't you think? Under the circumstances, it might well be a sensible idea to consider living a little more frugally."

"I'd have thought," said Helen, "that the money might better be spent employing staff who could competently manage your correspondence. I've written to you several times over the past few months and I've yet to receive a reply."

"Oh dear." Lee looked over at me and this time did meet my eye. "It seems I have reason to chastise you yet again, Claudia."

I lowered my head in supplication.

"I'm very sorry, Miss Munro," I said meekly.

"And now we're being pestered by Arnold Manning," said her father. "Apparently he's had none of your receipts for the past year. There's a tax return to file and any delay..."

"That's because I've changed accountants," Lee interrupted.

"What?" Her father's head whipped up.

She shrugged.

"I know Arnold's a good friend of yours, but I live in London now and it makes sense to have someone here, rather than a hundred miles away."

"But you can't." He was shaking his head.

"Really? Why's that, Dad?"

Lee was smiling, but her eyes were suddenly very cold.

"Your... Your affairs are very complicated, Eileen." He wasn't exactly stumbling, but close. "The trust fund, the fact that you're a child."

"Not anymore, I'm not," said Lee. "In case you missed it, as of this year anyone over eighteen is now an adult."

"Even so, asking new people to come along and try to..."

"Actually, I'm surprised that Arnold hasn't already heard from Sydney Barrett," interrupted Lee.

"Sydney Barrett?"

"My accountant," Lee told him and then turned to me.

"Claudia, you did supply Sydney with all the information he asked for?" she questioned.

"Yes, Miss Munro," taking my cue. "And he wrote back to say that he was enumerating a list of queries for both your father and your previous accountant to clarify." I paused. "As Mr Munro is actually here now, should I give Mr Barrett a call - they could perhaps speak together?"

"I'm afraid we're not going to have time for that today." Helen was staring daggers at me. "I've a casting call in thirty minutes and we're meeting a producer for lunch."

"That's okay," said Lee easily. "There's no real hurry."

She turned to me.

"Ask Sydney to put his concerns in the post and," turning back to her father, "the next time Dad drops by we can go through them all, item by item."

He nodded and started to rise.

"Of course."

"I do hope the audition goes well," Lee said to Helen, as she walked them to the door. "What's it for?"

Helen hesitated only slightly.

"It's a commercial," she said.

"Well, break a leg," smiled Lee, closing the door behind them.

She turned, and we faced each other.

"*Syd Barrett!!!*" I said, with not entirely mock incredulity.

She walked across the room, put her arms around me and buried her head in my shoulder. Lee began to softly shake, I had no idea whether she was laughing, sobbing or manifesting some weird fusion of both.

Family, the soft underbelly of everyone's psyche.

Kit

I arrived back at Pembridge Villas after a day at the Roundhouse which had not gone well, the gulf between West End productions and street theatre considerably widened by the addition of a couple of acid blotters to the communal teapot. Luckily, the stuff wasn't strong enough - or had been diluted too much - to completely freak anyone out, but actors are the last people in the world who'll allow an opportunity for drama to go begging. Between dealing with resurfaced and relived childhood angst and threats to get the police involved, not a lot got done.

I was in the kitchen, making a coffee and thinking of heading out for something stronger when Veronica, one of the girls with an attic room, popped her head around the door.

"Someone's here for you, Kit," she said. "Waiting in your room."

"Who?" I asked. I really needed to get that lock fixed.

She turned to someone I couldn't see.

"Did she say who she was?"

Her boyfriend, Richard, stepped into view and shook his head.

"No. Only that it was important - even when we told her we weren't sure when you'd be back, she still wanted to wait."

These days, a 'she' waiting in my room didn't exactly narrow things down.

"Okay," I said. "Thanks."

I finished making my coffee and climbed the stairs. On

the landing I hesitated for a few seconds, looking at my door in the same way that you'll sometimes just stare at a letter in your hand instead of opening it. Then I turned the handle and stepped inside.

Sitting on the edge of my bed was Frieda Brownlow.

"Hello Kit," she said. "Was it you who tried to phone me last night?"

"Phone you?"

"I wasn't home, but someone left a message about Emma."

"No." I shook my head. "I haven't seen her for weeks. What did they say?"

"Kushal - an Indian seaman who's lodging with us - took the call and his English isn't that good. But whoever called told him they were a friend of Emma's, and that if we wanted to find her she was staying with Dave and Anna, in Camden Town." Frieda hesitated. "I rang Claudia, who said they were friends of yours but she didn't know their address."

God knows how many times over the years I've run that moment through my mind, when I could have shaken my head and told her Claudia must have been mistaken, that I'd never heard of them. And then waited until the next morning to go over to Camden and check it out by myself.

But I didn't.

"Yes, they are," I said. "Do you want me to take you over there?"

Nodding, she stood up.

"Thank you, Kit."

* * *

Most of Emma's political friends she'd met through meetings, workshops, demos and the like, but Dave and Anna she knew through me.

Dave worked as a typesetter for the company who'd printed *International Times,* until the CID suggested they might find themselves falling foul of the Obscene Publications Act, a local variant on the Al Capone getting busted for income tax routine.

He'd become an unlikely fan of *IT* and was helpful in finding an alternative publisher, a Jewish émigré to Britain from Nazi Germany who - having experienced Gestapo tactics literally at first hand - wasn't the pushover his predecessor had been. When word got back to the Old Bill of Dave's role in this, his reward was to be accosted one night by a couple of hefty DCs. Leaving his local a bit worse for wear, he found himself being frogmarched into the nearest alley for a 'good kicking', as they termed it.

It was almost a classic example of how to politicise the indifferent. Up to that point, Dave had regarded his weekly union subs as little more than a necessary evil of employment and had never attended a print union branch meeting in his life. But post 'good kicking' - and with careful coaching from Emma, who also arranged support from one of the more radical union officials - within three months he'd taken over as shop steward and extracted payback from his employer in spades.

So far not too exceptional a tale, but it was Anna who'd led him out to the far reaches of political extremism. She'd been a Maoist firebrand when Emma first met her, and I'd lost count of how many times at the kitchen table at Pembridge Villas I'd heard them argue the finer points of Marxist theory.

Dave had gone head over heels, hanging onto her every word and following her around with such devotion that you really couldn't help but wonder what she might be doing to him once the lights went out.

But it was a friendship that if not exactly turned sour had waned, in the way that people will sometimes slip out of your life with you being hardly aware of it. I recalled the arguments had certainly become more intense, Anna insisting that direct action was the only answer, that all this political theorising would get them nowhere.

Bad blood over dialectic nitpicking wasn't exactly unknown in these circles and so at the time I didn't think too much of it. But in retrospect, it occurred to me that there might be more to Dave and Anna also dropping off the radar than simple coincidence.

I was having less and less of a good feeling about our journey over there.

* * *

A feeling which I still hadn't shifted by the time we arrived in the narrow side road off Camden High Street.

"It's the last house on the right," I told Frieda as she pulled over. Noticing a small newsagents on the corner of the street, I added, "But let me go and buy a packet of ciggies first."

She nodded, four decades immersed in clandestine political activism had left her needing no lessons in caution. But things seemed quiet enough. A cream Mercedes was parked in front of Frieda's car, but that didn't worry me. Back then the cops - even undercover ones - only used British cars and certainly nothing as flashy as that. As I reached the newsagents, a scruffy white builder's van turned the corner.

I was the only customer and pocketing the cigarettes I stepped out into the street. As I did so, the passenger door of the Mercedes swung open and out climbed Chas Slater.

In his right hand was an automatic pistol.

* * *

The cliché is that in moments of crisis perception slows down, events unfold in slow motion.

Not that day they didn't.

I only froze for a second and then stepped sharply backwards into the shop, thinking only of rear exits and cover. As Slater moved forward, drawing level with Frieda's car, a loud shout came from across the street and he turned sideways.

Uniformed police were tumbling out of the back of the white van that I'd noticed moments before, but the driver's door was also open and a figure stood there, dressed in jeans and a combat jacket, pointing a revolver at Chas Slater.

There was a lot of yelling, none of it coherent, and Slater hesitated. The newsagent had come from behind the counter and was standing alongside me, watching the scene unfold.

Whether Slater thought the undercover cop facing him was the only armed officer there and he fancied his chances or if he just didn't care anymore, no-one will ever know. But as he raised the gun, a volley of shots rang out from around the van.

Slater fell backward. One last shot sounded and the window of Frieda's car exploded. I stared disbelievingly, the newsagent grabbed the sleeve of my coat and was pulling me back away from the door.

"Is best we saw nothing," he said, shaking his head, his accent mid-European, maybe Polish. He gestured with his free hand toward the street. "Big trouble coming."

I looked at him and nodded.

"Then it's probably best," I suggested, "that I was never here at all."

He considered for a moment.

"Come with me."

I followed him through the counter flap and into a large stockroom. Crossing the room, he unbolted a steel-lined door at the back and opening it gestured me through.

"Okay," he said. "You not here, I not see."

"Right," I said, but the door had already closed behind me. I was in a small yard, I let myself out through a wooden gate into an alleyway which led me out onto Camden High Street.

* * *

Every instinct I possessed told me to get as far away from there as fast as possible, but I just couldn't.

The sound of sirens drew closer and a crowd was gathering at the entrance to the road where Frieda and I had parked. I slowly walked along the High Street to join them, where two panda cars had pulled up nose to nose, creating a makeshift barrier. Dave and Anna's front door was hanging half off its hinges. There was much shouting and at least one piercing scream came from inside.

But the crowd's focus wasn't on the house. By the open driver's door of Frieda's car, the shape of a body prone on the ground could be clearly made out despite a couple of police tunics laid over it.

And seeping out from underneath was a large, still spreading pool of blood.

I turned and began to walk, the image seared into my brain. An ambulance arrived and I just hoped that Frieda would have been taken away before Emma was brought out of the house.

7. Reverend Warwick

"I'm afraid Sergeant Vanner's not here at the moment," the constable behind the desk told her. "And without the Sergeant's say so, the only person entitled to see him would be his solicitor."

"What time are you expecting him back?" asked Jenny Warwick.

"Why don't you try again this afternoon?" he suggested.

She knew better than to argue. Her work in the inner cities had brought Jenny into close enough contact with the police force to be aware of the disdain with which the clergy were regarded by them. Or more specifically, members of the clergy who actively engaged with those elements of society in most need of support, rather than dutifully performing a decorative role at weddings or a sombre one at funerals.

To the officers she regularly encountered on a day-to-day basis - the ones on the ground that is, not senior officials trotted out to spout the usual, well versed lines about community spirit and strength in diversity - she was a 'Do Gooder' and as such was held in far less esteem than the criminal element whose exploits, she suspected, if not secretly envied then at least provided motivation to which they could relate.

To this mindset, 'Do Gooders' were simply useful idiots, their naivety seized upon by feckless deadbeats to exploit disadvantages in their background which those of a more robust character would use as a spur to escape.

And any hopes that rural Cornwall would prove different to Toxteth or St Annes were swiftly discounted. She'd had her first run-in with the local constabulary - in the form of Sergeant Vanner - almost before she'd finished unpacking.

Four years previously, a child on holiday with her family in St Hannahs had been swept out to sea and drowned. Only six years old and unsupervised - her parents at their campsite were sleeping off a lunch which consisted of little more than potato crisps and bottles of cheap cider - she'd carried a blow-up rubber duck down to the beach and then into the surf, where she'd been caught by a rip current. Her dilemma had been spotted almost immediately, but even in the few minutes taken to launch a RNLI inflatable she had vanished from sight.

An hour later the inshore rescue craft returned with her body.

The tragedy was initially reported in the local news with as much sympathy as would be expected. But when the sequence of events became clearer, and her family subjected to the kind of journalism based on handing out ten-pound notes to neighbours in exchange for gossip, the mood quickly changed. Within days the story found its way onto the front pages of the tabloid press and it had been like shooting fish in a barrel.

Living on benefits, seven kids, demanding payment for interviews and as the weeks dragged on it didn't get any better. They tried to sue the local council for not providing adequate safety warnings - the flying of a red flag over the beach not signifying anything to them other than decoration - and received withering condemnation from the coroner.

Just about the only support they found locally was from Jenny. Overhearing a crack between a local TV reporter and Sergeant Vanner, along the lines that the most effective way of preventing a repetition of the tragedy would be to lace Chicken McNuggets with oestrogen, she'd rounded on them.

Just because the poor girl's parents didn't know how to articulate their grief, she told them, didn't mean it was any less real.

"Oh, so it's society's fault, is it?" was Sergeant Vanner's response and something in Jenny had snapped.

"No," she'd retorted, "not its fault. But if society refuses to make it its responsibility, then let's not pretend to be surprised when we eventually find ourselves living in a shithole of a country."

Vanner's jaw had dropped at that. She saw the reporter turn toward the cameraman, who gave a slight grimace and shook his head. The only good thing about the incident, reflected Jenny as she'd walked away, but it had set the shape of all their subsequent encounters – undertones of antipathy tempered with superficial civility - and Jenny knew she had to find a way to break that pattern before something ended badly.

* * *

For Jenny, St Hannahs had been a thunderbolt. She'd expected the East End of London, perhaps back to inner city Liverpool or Glasgow. Ministering to the homeless was how she'd seen herself, bringing comfort to the forlorn.

She'd even queried the appointment with the Bishop, wondering if some mistake had been made, but his response was uncharacteristically curt.

"It is not the business of the Church to give you what you want," he told her. "Or even necessarily what you need. The Church's first duty is to its parishioners, and it has been decided that this is how they would best be served."

The congregation of the Holy Trinity Church in St Hannahs were equally stunned. That one of only thirty-two newly ordained female Church of England priests should be assigned to their parish was, mostly, regarded as less a blessing than an anathema. There was a definite sense that 'political correctness' was the thin end of a wedge about to be driven between themselves and the traditions which they held so dear. As much as Jenny understood this - and to a degree empathised with it - the exodus of most of her congregation to the neighbouring parish on her first Sunday had stung.

They could at least have given her a chance.

The next day had brought a visit from the Reverend Clarkson, cleric of said parish, who handed her a plastic shopping bag, heavy with coin.

"Hello, I'm Simon," he said. "This is half of yesterday's swag."

Smiling, she led him through to the sitting room, still packed with cardboard boxes.

"It will get better," he told her. "People expect the church to be a bastion of stability, particularly out here in the sticks, so any change would have been problematic."

He nodded as she pulled a bottle of red wine out of a box and looked at him questioningly.

"The one thing that you do have going for you is that Leonard died, rather than retired."

He grinned at her half shocked, half quizzical expression - Leonard Samson had been her predecessor.

"The Reverend Samson definitely leant toward a vengeful, rather than loving, God - trust me, you wouldn't have wanted him egging things on from the sidelines."

"One tip," he told her, before departing a slightly tipsy couple of hours later. "Win over the ladies - they're the ones who really matter when it comes to getting things done here. Get the WI on your side and you'll be home and dry."

Sound advice, but easier said than done. Jam, Jerusalem and passive aggression reflected Jenny a month later.

Margaret Carstairs, the local Women's Institute chairwoman, had managed to politely and skilfully derail any suggestions Jenny made, particularly that of utilising the Parish Hall as a local 'Sure Start' morning for first-time mothers. Jenny'd been quite taken aback by the number of young single mums in the town and who seemed to receive nothing from the community at large other than sour looks. Pensive silence was Mrs Carstairs' default setting, but at this prospect her outrage could hardly have been greater if Jenny'd proposed commandeering the hall as an occasional bordello for bored husbands.

Something needed to give.

And a few months later, it did.

* * *

Songs of Praise was a weekly programme from the BBC Religious Affairs Department, a well-worn format of intercutting a Sunday service with short profiles of members of the local community. Jenny understood the attraction of St Hannahs, female clergy - *'vicars in knickers'* the unfortunate catchphrase coined by one of the redtop tabloids - were still very much a novelty and even more so in a rural setting.

The producer who'd contacted her had explained that he was aware of her previous life as a city highflier which naturally would be of great interest to their viewers - forks in the path of life etcetera. Jenny guessed that he'd had his card marked by the Bishop on her reticence regarding that subject, and so was sounding her out before reaching a conclusion as to exactly how much good TV the entire package would represent.

"Yes, I can appreciate that," she'd told him, thinking *What the hell!* After months of growing a rhino hide simply to get by on a daily basis, what was the point in getting all coy at this stage.

The thing that had been nagging at Jenny the most - an empty church - proved to be the least of her worries. Confiding that *'the congregation's dropped off a bit'* the producer quickly brushed her concerns aside.

"As a rule, we invite the neighbouring churches to the service," he told her, "if that's okay with you?"

"Of course," she said.

"And everyone," he continued, "wants to see themselves on the telly. Trust me, it'll be standing room only."

So, who else in the village, she'd asked him, were they thinking of profiling?

"Entirely up to you," he said. "We normally try to strike a balance - people who've lived there all their lives talking about the changes they've seen and people who've moved there explaining why they did so. All local worthies, obviously, but we need to see how they come over on camera before making any final decisions." He paused. "We'll be sending a couple of researchers down a week before shooting, to scout out points of interest that we can use as backdrops for the interviews - it would help if you had a list by then."

"Right," she said. "Who's presenting it?"

"Simon Miller."

The show had recently moved from the format of being fronted by a regular host to having a different guest presenter each week. Simon Miller was a TV newsreader and occasional talking head for BBC documentaries. A safe pair of hands, reflected Jenny.

"He'll sit down and have a long chat with you the day before," he told her, "then go away and format a list of questions designed to bring out the most salient points of what you've discussed."

"Right," said Jenny slowly, probably sounding a little dubious because the producer had been quick to reassure her.

"Don't worry," he told her. "Simon's bloody good at this - he'll look after you."

* * *

The following few weeks were actually the most fun part of the whole thing - a quiet word placed in one or two carefully chosen ears and the impending visit by the BBC had become the talk of the town.

Jenny's next move was to invite the Mayor - whose family could trace their presence in St Hannahs back to the time of the Crusades - up to the Rectory, to ask if he'd like to appear in the program. He was a lovely man but a notorious gossip, and as her invitations were extended to the coxswain of the lifeboat crew and the chairwoman of the local historical society, she took almost a vicious satisfaction in the sudden and massive growth of her Sunday congregation.

She took an equally unchristian pleasure in keeping Margaret Carstairs dangling. And even more so in resurrecting her Sure Start project.

"I think it would be such a wonderful opportunity," Jenny told her, "for the Women's Institute to show the nation their relevance to the changing nature of rural communities." As a backup strategy, Jenny had justified to herself a fib about the program's producer already contacting the WI's national committee about this, but she hadn't needed to. Mrs Carstairs surrender was immediate and absolute.

The power of television reflected Jenny.

And with that done and dusted, Jenny concentrated on her own role.

* * *

"So exactly," asked Simon Miller, "how did all this begin for you?"

A good question and it wasn't like she'd even had much of a religious upbringing - Sunday School as a child and then the church choir as a teenager was about it. Jenny'd been an academic high-flyer, which - combined with a talent on the tennis court that saw her through to the finals of the Junior County Championships - made her a shoo-in for Head Girl at her grammar school, where she'd won a scholarship to Oxford.

A first in Economics took her to the City and her rise in corporate banking had been rapid, one of the first female hedge fund managers. There'd been a marriage along the way, all enveloping at the time and yet almost irrelevant in retrospect. Graham had wanted children, there were arguments about careers but when she finally conceded it all proved a complete abstraction, nature seemingly sharing her view that she wasn't cut out for motherhood. The divorce was quick and simple, Graham trading her in for a fully functioning model and Jenny genuinely surprised that her overriding emotion was relief rather than pain.

But other things were disturbing her too, not least the almost obscene amounts of money washing around the City of London, in stark contrast to the huddled figures sleeping in the doorways she passed by on her way to the office.

Jenny started to keep loose change in her pockets.

"You're only encouraging them, you know," a colleague told her one morning, after observing her drop a pound coin into a beggar's cup.

"To do what?" she'd replied. "Sleep in a piss-soaked doorway?"

Mostly they were transient figures, but across the paved courtyard of her office building a bearded middle-aged man was there in all weathers. His coat, though threadbare, was of good quality and his accent refined as he politely thanked her when she dropped a few coins into his cup every morning. He also had a companion, a collie cross which always appeared well groomed, had a leather collar and leash rather than the almost mandatory piece of string, and wagged its tail enthusiastically at everyone who stopped.

From her office window Jenny could observe him all day long. Unlike the other beggars who occasionally turned up in the courtyard, the police didn't move him along. She saw them stop and chat now and again, guessing they cut him some slack because of his demeanour, used to a more confrontational and belligerent response to their presence.

It had been a cold, frosty December morning, she'd been late for a meeting and so dropped the coins into his cup and hurried on without exchanging their customary few words. Returning to her office after her meeting, she noticed a commotion down in the courtyard - an ambulance was parked there and two paramedics were attending to a figure prone on the flagstones alongside it. Jenny couldn't make out who it was, but she didn't need to. The clearly distressed collie a uniformed policeman held by its leash was unmistakable.

By the time she'd made her way down there, the ambulance was gone and so was the dog. A solitary policeman was talking on his radio and Jenny approached him.

"What happened?" she asked, and to his flicker of interest said, "I'd see him most mornings."

"Cardiac arrest the paramedics reckon, but they won't know for sure until the autopsy."

Jenny's heart sank.

"What about his dog?" she asked.

"Battersea Dogs Home probably," he told her, and then in response to the expression of dismay which must have passed over her face added, almost kindly, "I wouldn't worry too much, love - a dog like that will find a good home easily enough."

"How...? How long had he been there?"

"Two, maybe three hours they reckon."

Jenny had nodded, turned and walked back to her building.

* * *

"And that had been it?" asked Simon.

"I'd love to tell you," said Jenny, "that I went to his funeral, discovered his history, adopted his dog... But no, I returned to the office and worried about the meeting I'd had that morning, of which now I can't recall a single detail." She hesitated. "But yes. It..."

She gestured with her hand.

"It primed the pump?" suggested Simon.

Jenny nodded.

"Took about a year," she said. "But I think I knew from that moment on my life needed to change."

"What was the reaction of your family and friends?"

Jenny considered.

As far as family went, only mum was left and she was gaga in a nursing home, not knowing which day of the week it was, let alone what her daughter might be doing with her life.

But friends had been another matter.

She'd lost a lot of them, including people she'd been

really close to. Their bafflement she'd expected and could understand, what she'd been totally blindsided by was their fury. There'd been a dinner party before she left London that was little more than a thinly veiled intervention. It had started with the assumption that anyone who believed in God was *de facto* stupid and become quite vicious.

"I can't understand how you can swallow this superstitious claptrap," said Tony, who she'd known since university, "when we're living in a world where science can provide a rational premise for any observed phenomena."

"Can it really?" asked Jenny. "Gosh, I didn't know that."

Tony had leaned back in his chair, with almost a sneer on his face.

"Obviously," he'd said. "That's because your reason d'etre is faith and faith is belief without evidence."

"Right," said Jenny, placing her elbows on the table and settling her chin on her interlinked fingers. She gave him a quizzical smile. "So, how does dowsing work, then?"

"What?" The sneer slowly froze.

"Dowsing," said Jenny brightly. "Holding a twig in your hands, walking across a field and the twig starts to twitch when there's water under…"

"That's just old folklore," broke in Tony. "Nobody…"

Jenny burst into laughter.

"*Old folklore!*" She shook her head. "My grandparents were told there was no water on their farm by both a surveyor and a geologist. It took a dowser fifteen minutes to show them where to sink a well." She smiled at him. "You need to be careful - you're sounding like those priests who refused to look through Galileo's telescope to see the craters on the moon."

Tony had thumped the table with his fist.

"Whether it's real or whether it isn't, one thing I can tell you is that if it is, there'll be a scientific explanation for it and not fairies at the bottom of the bloody garden." His face had gone quite red.

"Well, there're two points there," Jenny told him calmly. "The first is until we do have an explanation for dowsing, you can only have *faith* it's not fairies at the bottom of the garden. Because, as you say, faith is belief without evidence.

"Secondly," she raised a hand to quieten Tony who was now looking fit to burst, "if science were this noble quest for truth you'd like to think it is, then dowsing would be absolutely top of its to-do list." She sat back in her chair. "Unknown forces creating involuntarily reactions in live organic matter to the remote presence of water. There's a Nobel Prize there for someone, surely?"

"You have no..."

"Unless," she continued, steamrollering over his reply, "there was an unspoken, universal suspicion that this was a loose thread which if given a firm tug might leave them with one huge, unravelled mess at their feet."

Tony had stormed off and she'd never seen him again.

And a lot of her friends had fallen away but probably would have, she consoled herself, if she'd moved from London to take-up any other job.

Probably.

Simon, she was aware, was staring at her.

"Some found it difficult," she said. "But most were supportive."

* * *

It had indeed been standing room only.

She'd stuck firmly to *Hymns Ancient and Modern*, a succession of rousing choruses to lift the Christian spirit and unlikely to upset anybody although, rather mischievously, she'd chosen the theme of 'Change and Renewal' for her short sermon, concluding with 2 Corinthians 5:17 - *And for anyone who is in Christ there is a new creation, the old creation has gone and the new is here.*

And here to stay, she'd thought, closing shut the large, gilded bible on the lectern.

The interviews had all gone well, including her own -

the death of the beggar had been edited to give it more of a *Little Match Girl* slant than she was entirely comfortable with, but in fairness it wasn't too mawkish.

And it had certainly been a revelation to most of her flock that she'd carved such a chunk for herself out of a man's world before taking the cloth. Day-to-day dealings with her parishioners now came with a tinge of respect and if some of that was grudging, well, so be it - as far as she was concerned that simply meant it was well earned.

Finally, it began to feel like she'd arrived.

* * *

"Jenny!" Lee Munro beamed as she walked across the terrace towards her. "I was beginning to think you weren't going to make it."

Then leaning forward to peck Jenny on the cheek, added *sotto voce*, "And in civvies too - I'd been counting on you to keep my guests on their best behaviour."

"I've long observed," replied Jenny, "that people on their best behaviour are rarely at their best."

Lee grinned as she slipped her arm through Jenny's and led her over to a trestle table, the remnants of a buffet breakfast at one end and a collection of champagne flutes at the other.

The introductions were a whirl.

'You know Paul, of course' - 'This is my agent Sy' - 'Kit and I go back so far I'm scared to even think about it' and found herself introduced as 'Jenny and I are involved in a project together'.

After leaving the Police Station, Jenny'd returned home and changed into jeans and a blouse before making her way over here. Lee had said - as she'd be glad-handing the Gallery opening tonight - she was keeping this one for close friends and Jenny, whilst flattered at the invitation, took a rare opportunity to bypass the preconceptions of strangers.

"A busy day here for you?" asked Lee, handing her a glass of champagne, "or has the town taken the secular route in celebrating the majesty of the heavens?"

"Indeed," said Jenny and indicating the cloudy skies with a nod of her head added, "Something they may now start to regret."

Lee laughed and the man she'd introduced as Kit joined them.

"Any idea how long we've got?" she asked him, and he glanced at his watch.

"A couple of minutes," he said.

"Okay, back in a sec," said Lee, putting her glass down. "This stuff always goes straight through me."

"Have you come far to be here today?" Jenny asked Kit.

"I live in Amsterdam, so yes," he told her, then nodding his head at the group of people chatting at the other end of the terrace, "but not as far as some people."

"Lee said that you two have known each other for a long time?"

"Over thirty years," he nodded. "We were both involved with a street theatre group in London, back in the sixties."

"Are you an actor too?"

"No," shaking his head but rather than clarifying that any further asked, "And you - how did you meet Lee?"

* * *

One of the things Jenny had inherited from Leonard Samson was the Church Roof Repair Appeal, launched six years previously and still less than halfway to meeting its target. In the aftermath of the *Songs of Praise* visit, Jenny decided to strike while the iron was hot and began canvassing local businesses.

Quickly abandoning her original idea of telephoning for an appointment - *'So busy at the moment, can I get back to you in a month or so'* - she'd taken to turning up and politely but firmly planting herself on their premises until a cheque was forthcoming. It may only have been twenty quid here and thirty quid there, but it was mounting up and she figured she'd have a sizable sum before she'd need to start the merry-go-round again.

'Executive Action' had not been high on her list. All that militaristic ethos - running around on the moor in combat gear, jeeps with camouflage paint jobs - definitely rubbed her up the wrong way but she knew that it was one of the more successful commercial ventures in the area and so, eventually, decided to go knocking.

The Grange seemed deserted when Jenny'd arrived, everyone probably off somewhere 'team building' or whatever, she'd thought. But then Jenny heard movement in the house and, trying the front door, found that it swung open.

"Is anyone home?" she called out.

Again, no response, and so she stepped through into a hallway. Uncertain whether to venture further inside or call it a day, she was suddenly startled to hear a voice behind her.

"Hello?"

She turned to find herself being scrutinised by a middle-aged woman, silk scarf around her head turban fashion and a man's shirt tucked into jeans, the sleeves rolled up over elbow length marigolds. She was carrying a plastic bucket with a plunger in it.

"Hello there - I'm Jenny Warwick." The thing about a dog collar was that you rarely had to embark on lengthy introductions. "I was looking for Paul Chapman?"

"He's out at the moment," said the woman, studying her carefully. Then she gave a small smile. "You look a bit flushed," she said. "Fancy a cuppa?"

"Wouldn't say no," said Jenny, following her into a large kitchen. "It's a steeper climb than you'd think."

The woman indicated the sink. "Stick the kettle on, while I have a scrub." She raised her arms. "Blocked soil pipe, out back."

Jenny filled the kettle and lit a gas ring. She washed out a teapot and two mugs while waiting for - she'd thought cleaning lady at first but a little too self-assured for that, perhaps housekeeper - to return.

"That's better." She'd changed into a plain shift dress

and her short blond hair was brushed back. Sitting down at the table while Jenny made the tea, she gave her a quizzical look. "So, you're looking for Paul? Was he expecting you?"

Handing her a mug, Jenny shook her head.

"No," she said, and finding herself under a frank but friendly gaze decided to put her hands up. "I'm here with my begging bowl, actually. And I've learnt that a heads up isn't a smart way to play that."

The woman smiled.

"Steeple fund?"

"Close enough - roof repairs."

"It really is a lovely church you have there - magnificent aspects in the evening." She sipped at her tea. "We get the sunrise here, but after midday it's gone from the terrace. Since I was a little girl, I've watched sunsets from that bench by the Lych Gate." She smiled. "Whatever kind of day you've had, watching a sunset always seems an apt conclusion."

"You've lived in St Hannahs all your life?"

She shook her head.

"As a child, my family came here most summers. Then holidays with friends."

Jenny still couldn't decide whether this was an employee or a visitor she was chatting to. Or possibly a spouse?

"This is a beautiful house," she said.

"I just wish I got to spend more time down here." She shrugged. "But you know, we all have to work."

Okay, that clears that up.

"So, whereabouts is it you work?" asked Jenny, taking another sip of her tea.

The woman seemed to consider her with quiet amusement before replying and then finally - maybe the light falling a certain way onto her face, triggering some image deep in the recesses of memory - the penny dropped.

"Oh, bloody hell," said Jenny, staring back at her across the table. "You must think I'm a complete muppet."

Lee Munro laughed.

"Actually," she said, "It's quite refreshing."

They'd chatted for twenty minutes or so, mainly about *Songs of Praise* which Lee had seen a VCR recording of and Jenny's Sure Start program. It was an easy conversation, with not even a hint of the *'But enough about me, what did you think of my last performance'* she thought would have been inevitable from a Hollywood star. Then Jenny caught her glancing at her watch.

"Sorry, you probably have things to do," she said, "that I'm keeping you from."

"About the church roof," said Lee. She fixed Jenny with a steady gaze. "I'm not going to make a donation - my view is that the church is an incredibly wealthy organisation and is more than capable of maintaining its own assets." She gave a shrug. "This isn't anything to do with you, it's about principles."

"Of course." Jenny made to rise. "I do understand and thank you for..."

"But what you're trying to do for young mums is something different." She reached over for a large leather handbag on the sideboard and took out a chequebook. "Will five thousand get you up and running?"

Well, the shocks were coming thick and fast this morning.

"That's... incredibly generous," Jenny eventually managed. "Yes, it will."

"I'm normally insistent about anonymity when I give to charity," Lee said slowly and before Jenny could say *Yes, of course,* went on, "less through altruism than being thought an easy mark, but let's make an exception here."

Jenny looked at her quizzically.

"When you've got the centre off the ground, I'll come back and officially open it. All false modesty aside, I can pull a crowd and I'm more than adept at twisting arms for good causes. In fact," she tore out the cheque and handed it over to Jenny, "let's set this up as a charitable trust, with me as its patron. I'd imagine that any problems of logistics - or attitude - you might have locally would get smoothed over pretty quickly at the prospect of me sounding off in the media about them."

"I really don't know what to say..."

"You could give me a tour of that church of yours sometime."

"You've never been inside?"

"Years and years ago." She grinned. "Your predecessor made it very clear that I was definitely *persona non grata* as far as he was concerned - in fact, he once denounced me from the pulpit."

"What!!?"

"He had it in his head that I'd been in Ken Russell's *The Devils* - I hadn't but I did a screen test for it, which is probably where the story got its legs - and he practically called for hellfire to be rained down on me."

"I'm so sorry..."

"Thought it best to keep out of his way after that." Lee stood up. "Pity I wasn't around for his funeral, though. I'd have gone as a nun."

* * *

"Lee's the patron of a charity which I help set up," Jenny told him. "We only met a couple of years ago."

"Is that local or... *Wow!*" Kit broke off, staring up at the sky.

Jenny followed his gaze. The clouds were still unbroken but now seemed to have taken on an almost translucent property, behind which could be discerned the globe of the sun, a sun that was not golden but a bright silver. And *behind* the clouds was a misnomer. Whatever trick of the light was in play also created the illusion that the sun was actually at the forefront of the clouds and shimmering, as if projected there.

"Have you ever," Kit sounded awestruck, "seen anything like that?"

Jenny shook her head.

From the lower left this apparition had been almost entirely eaten away, and in the distance Jenny could hear the rumble of a loud cheer - from the beach, she guessed, the site of the town's official celebrations.

"Bloody hell," said Lee from behind them, "what did I miss?"

The light, noticed Jenny, was starting to change. Not yet darker, more... brittle was the word that came to mind, as if it were taking on the quality of something easily shattered. That lasted only a few seconds - or at least only *seemed* to last for a few seconds - and then darkness did begin to settle over them.

She was startled by a great flapping of wings, birds heading back to their nests, she realised, panicked by this unexpected early onset of night.

The sun, now barely a crescent, gave a sudden blinding flash to one side- *'The diamond ring effect,'* thought Jenny, and the darkness was complete, more intense for the suddenness of the transition, giving the eye little chance to adjust.

Jenny felt Lee's hand find hers and she gave it a squeeze. It wasn't just the darkness that was so eerie, it was the silence - humans and animals alike - as if the world for a moment was holding its collective breath.

And then there was a flash of light.

The cheers rose again from the beach and Jenny imagined it echoing down the ages to the dawn of man. Terror turned to thanksgiving as the source of all life reignited once more in the heavens above.

They watched until the silver disk, as suddenly as it had appeared, seemed to fade away into the thickening cloud.

"I'm sure," said Lee softly, "there's a completely plausible scientific explanation for what just happened here, but right now, at this very moment, I'm totally with you on this."

She gave Jenny's hand a last squeeze and let it go.

Lee's agent - Jenny couldn't remember his name - was

walking over towards them. There was a tear, Jenny noticed, in the corner of his eye.

"See," said Lee to him, with a smile. "Told ya."

* * *

"I'm going to have to get some sleep," Lee said to her. "It's not just the jet lag - Sy, Kit and I were up most of the night working, but you're welcome to stay. Help yourself to coffee."

With a wave of her hand, she indicated the buffet table, but Jenny shook her head.

"Thanks, I'm afraid I need to get back into town."

"Will you be at the Gallery opening tonight?" asked Lee, as she walked Jenny over to the steps leading down to the driveway.

"Actually, Ruth invited me to take a look at the exhibition this afternoon," said Jenny, hesitantly. "Privately. She thought it might be a little less..."

She shrugged, and Lee gave a smile.

"A little less controversial than a photograph in the local rag of our vicar beaming benevolently against a background of blasphemous artwork?" she suggested.

"I want to see them," said Jenny. "If only because it's such a landmark occasion for the town. I just don't want to become a distraction to that."

"It's okay, believe me, I get it."

"And if after seeing them I don't think that will be a problem then I'll probably come along tonight - you know me, anybody's for a glass of white wine."

Lee gave her a hug.

"If I don't see you tonight, I'll give you a ring in the morning," she told her. "You can bring me up to date on the Foundation."

"Okay," said Jenny. "And sleep well."

She'd hardly reached the bottom of the steps when her mobile phone began with its invidious bleeps and she inwardly groaned. Of all the devices the devil might have created to torment mankind...

"Hello," she answered brightly. "Jenny Warwick."

* * *

She spent the afternoon dealing with a succession of calls. Being bounced between dispensing spiritual comfort and arranging practical help for those members of her flock to whom she was regarded as a last resort, was pretty much par for the course of any day.

But one phone call - a message left on her voicemail while sitting with a young mother at the local children's hospice - had intrigued her enough, with its combination of importunity and vagueness, to skip a coffee break at the Rectory which she'd promised herself and be knocking on Sue Marshall's door.

"Thank you so much for this," said Sue, showing Jenny into her living room.

"I'm not exactly sure," said Jenny, "what you're thanking me for."

"I had a call at the school earlier, from Tina Farlow," said Sue, sitting down on the sofa. Tina was a civilian clerk at the Police Station. Jenny had spoken to her on a couple of occasions, but they'd never met. "She said that Sergeant Vanner would like a word with me and would it be okay if he called round later this afternoon." Sue hesitated. "She also told me - although I got the feeling that she wasn't supposed to - that he was spending today with a high-ranking detective from London."

"Okay..." said Jenny slowly.

"She also asked - but I took it to be more of a suggestion - if I had a member of my family, or a close friend who'd be able to be here. I couldn't really get hold of anybody at such short notice, so I was hoping..."

"Of course," said Jenny, reaching out and taking Sue's hand.

"I'd appreciate you not mentioning what Tina told me to anyone else. I don't want her to get into trouble."

"This is just between us," Jenny reassured her.

"Thanks."

"Do you have any idea what it might be about?" Jenny asked.

Sue seemed to consider.

"If it's what..." she began, but then the doorbell rang.

"It looks as though we're about to find out," she said, standing up.

As Sue led the two police officers into the living room, Jenny was struck by how Sue's manner had suddenly shifted. Not waspish exactly, but she was definitely wary. Jenny couldn't say she knew Sue that well, only through the school really, but this was a side of her she hadn't seen before.

"You know Reverend Warwick, Sergeant," she said, and Vanner seemed nonplussed for a second to see her there. "And this is, sorry...?"

"Detective Inspector Amanda Palmer." She extended her hand, which Jenny shook. "I run a Cold Case Unit in the London Metropolitan Police Force."

"Have a seat," said Sue, indicating two armchairs facing the sofa. "Can I get you something to drink - tea, coffee?"

"I'm fine thanks," said DI Palmer, and Vanner shook his head.

"Well, a Cold Case Unit," said Sue, eyeing the detective carefully. "So, obviously I haven't been up to anything lately."

DI Palmer let a smile flicker briefly across her lips and then took a cardboard folder out of her briefcase, resting it on her knees.

"The reason for our visit concerns a missing person report that you filed in October 1971. About your brother, Peter."

"Peter?"

"Yes. You filed it in Exeter, at Heavitree Road Police Station on Monday the 5th October."

"That's right - I was about to start University there."

DI Palmer took a photograph from the file and passed it

over to Sue.

"Is this your brother?" she asked.

Jenny leaned over to look, as Sue studied the print. It was a head and shoulders shot of a young man in his late teens, good looking with longish curly hair.

"Yes," said Sue. "And this is the photograph I gave to the Salvation Army, after it became obvious that the police had no interest in looking for him. So how come you have it?"

DI Palmer seemed a little taken aback.

"Ah, well, the Salvation Army are cooperating with our enquiries."

"Really? Well, better late than never, I suppose." She fixed DI Palmer with a tight smile. "And exactly what enquiries might they be?"

"I'm sorry to have to tell you this," said DI Palmer, "but - and I imagine this isn't going to be entirely unexpected news after all these years - we have compelling evidence that your brother died in the summer of 1970."

Jenny had been present with a lot of people as they received bad news, and if you'd have asked her she'd have told you that she'd seen just about every reaction possible. But Sue Marshall was a first. She didn't so much as blink as she continued to stare at DI Palmer. For a second Jenny considered reaching over to take her hand. Sometimes shock made people shut down completely, but then Sue simply gave a shrug.

"And exactly what evidence would that be?"

"I will go through all the details with you, but I need to ask some questions first - there are facts we need to verify and blanks which we need to fill in."

"Verify away," said Sue, tonelessly.

"Well, firstly the chronology seems a little strange. In September 1971 you tell the police you hadn't heard from him in over a year - why did you wait so long to report him missing?"

"I didn't - I went to the Police Station, here in St Hannahs, six months before then."

"There's no record of that in the files."

"I know," said Sue. "They told me to fuck off."

"*What!!?*" DI Palmer's head jerked up in surprise.

"Or to be precise, *'Fuck off, slag'*."

DI Palmer stared at her speechlessly but Sergeant Vanner, Jenny noticed, had gone white as a sheet.

Sue sat back in her chair, her eyes fixed on DI Palmer.

"Why don't I give you a little background to all of this?" she said.

* * *

The ramshackle wooden building had originally been constructed over a hundred years ago, temporary housing for both the craftsmen who had built the railway station and the labourers who had laid the branch line. But now, although still British Rail property, it stood outside the neat brick boundaries of St Hannahs station itself and it had been decades since it had served any official purpose. Its outer walls were covered with moss and lichen, making it less of an eyesore than its years of neglect might suggest, blending it in to the wooded hill which served as a backdrop and was probably a factor in deferring the expense of demolishing it.

The four vehicles that arrived in the station car park took advantage of the slight incline down from the road to switch their engines off and silently coast the final hundred yards. A clear sky also gave them enough moonlight to kill their headlights. Three of the vehicles were Land Rovers belonging to the local constabulary, the fourth was a covered Military Police jeep. For the moment, two Transit vans carrying backup stayed parked up on the road, as did the dog handlers - their Alsatians were trained to silence but there was no point risking them getting spooked.

Everyone checked their watches. They were ready, but the operation wasn't due to begin until two thirty and the Superintendent in charge wanted to impress the army with his force's military precision. And so they sat twiddling their thumbs for five minutes, risking discovery if one of the dossers stepped outside for a piss.

Dead on two thirty, the Super came on the radio and gave them the go. The Redcaps stayed in their jeep while ten uniformed officers carrying heavy flashlights - their go-to piece of kit for both illumination and assault - stepped over the car park's low wall and made their way across to the building. They knew that the only entrance - or from the operation's objective – exit, was a rotted wooden door at the side, the two windows at the front were long broken and boarded up but one of the officers was stationed by each of them, just in case.

The filed report would state that the sergeant leading the team knocked on the door, identified himself as a police officer and stated that he had reason to believe that illegal drugs were on the property and that he was in possession of a search warrant. The reality was that the first the inhabitants knew about the raid was a boot to the door, that not only kicked it wide open but left it hanging askew from a single hinge.

The cops piled in quickly. As they'd expected most people inside were asleep, a dozen or so sleeping bags scattered around the room but one figure, a long-haired youth was sitting at a table reading a magazine by candlelight. Startled, he jumped to his feet.

"What the..." he began, but then a flashlight crashed down onto his skull and he crumpled to the floor.

The sleeping figures started to wake, but before they could extract themselves they found their sleeping bags being jerked up off the ground. As they slid down inside them, the tops were twisted shut over their heads and fastened tight with plastic ties. Dropped back down onto the floor, they writhed helplessly, much to the amusement of the reinforcements from the Transit vans who were now pouring in through the door.

The bodies began to be unceremoniously dragged outside, any struggles subdued with a hefty kick. The Transits and the dog van had been driven into the car park, and together with the three police Landrovers were training their headlights onto the building. The army jeep still sat in darkness.

Standard procedure would have been to either take them down to the Police Station for processing or ship them off to Truro, but tonight - with an unspoken acquiescence from above of a blind eye being turned - was intended to be more expeditious than that.

And to send a message.

The officers not involved with the sleeping bags were gathering together all the possessions in the building, carrying them outside and dumping them onto the ground. Once it had been emptied, all twenty uniformed officers formed a circle around the prone bodies, drawing their truncheons.

Two detectives had set up a trestle table in the car park, where a live radio link had been established to the records office in Bristol. The procedure was to release the detainees one at a time, let them get dressed and gather their things before taking them over to CID, who'd try to establish their identity. They'd use the radio to see if there was a card on them at Bristol, if so they'd go straight into custody. As would anyone else they didn't like the look of - or gave them any lip - charged with the possession of a lump of cannabis resin which would find its way into their pocket or possessions back at the station. The rest of them would be bundled into a fleet of Transits, driven to the Devon side of the Tamar Bridge and told that if they ever showed their faces in Cornwall again, all that would be waiting for them was a good hiding and a fit-up.

As each figure crawled out under the collective glare of a score of cops - tapping their truncheons into their palms - any sense of belligerence evaporated. But the fourth bag they released held a surprise. Not one person inside, but a skinny youth of about eighteen and a young girl.

"Well, what have we here?" smiled the sergeant. "A pair of lovebirds, it seems."

At that there was general laughter, but which quickly developed into an unmistakable air of salaciousness as one of the cops grabbed the bottom of the sleeping bag and pulled it free of them, *revealing they were both naked. The girl squealed, at first using her hands as she squirmed to try to cover herself, but then she suddenly bolted for a break in the circle. She was easily caught and frogmarched back, tears streaming down her face.*

"For fuck's sake, give her a coat," *said the boy she'd been with. The cop standing next to him turned and head-butted him in the face. Blood poured from his nose as he dropped down onto one knee.*

The sergeant walked over to the table and spoke into the radio for a couple of minutes. Coming back, he gestured to the next bag.

"What about her?" *asked the cop holding the girl's arms behind her.*

"Oh, she's fine where she is," *smiled the sergeant.* "Aren't you, love?"

Tears still rolling down her cheeks, she was pleading with her eyes, but he turned away.

Another three had been released before they heard a high revving car approach. The sergeant turned to one cop in the circle, a young cadet.

"You," *he said.* "Give her your coat."

As he slipped the tunic over her shoulders, a Rover saloon screeched to a halt in the car park. The middle-aged man who got out was in so much of a hurry that the driver's door was left hanging open. As he approached, his expression was a mask of rage.

"Look, dad..." *began the girl as he came to a stop in front of her, but he raised his hand and slapped her viciously, twice across the face.*

"Get in the car," *he hissed, then hesitated and looked at the sergeant. Who, staring straight back at him, seemed to consider for a few seconds and then nodded.*

"Take her to the car," *he said to the cadet.*

Still crying and with livid red marks now appearing on both of her cheeks, the girl let him lead her over to the passenger door of the car.

"Which one was it?" *the father said to the sergeant, who with a nod of his head indicated the boy still on the ground.*

He walked over, stared down at him, and then launched a kick into the side of his ribs. The boy howled and fell sideways. The father drew back his foot for another kick.

"No more of that," *said the sergeant sharply, and as the father turned to stare at him, he gestured at the two nearest uniformed officers.* "Get him onto his feet and hold him."

He turned to the father.

"Just your fists, Frank."

Over by the car, the girl cried out at what she was seeing. The cadet placed his hands on her shoulders, turning her away from the scene but the sounds they could hear were sickening enough.

"That's all, Frank," *the sergeant told him, and then the only sound was the father's heavy breathing and his footsteps coming towards them.*

The cadet closed the passenger door for her, as gently as he could. Her father slammed his door shut behind him and then, with a squeal of tyres and a last impression of the girl's terrified face, they were gone into the night.

Vanner couldn't remember whether he'd got his tunic back or not.

* * *

"And of course, that wasn't the end of it," said Sue, in the same flat, matter-of-fact tone she'd spoken all the way through her recollection of that night's events. "The next morning, I was taken down to the Police Station and questioned - they were interested in drugs mainly, not just the Beats but any locals who were involved with them. I was told if I didn't make a full confession - a confession mind, not a statement, that was the expression they used - they would charge me as an accessory and I'd be sent to jail. Even as a naïve little sixteen-year-old I knew what rubbish that was and so I told them to go ahead and charge me."

She paused.

"Which really got their backs up. So, at that point they decided to give me an examination."

"I'm sorry," said DI Palmer. "What?"

"A physical examination. With my stepfather's consent, of course. Supposedly to determine if I'd suffered any physical abuse, but it was to all intents and purposes a virginity test."

"You mean they actually brought in a doctor and…"

"A doctor?" Sue cut DI Palmer off with a harsh little laugh. "Jesus, no! I was taken into another room and told to strip off. After a few minutes, a policewoman came in, had me bend over and then she had a good poke around down there. Once she'd finished, they let me get dressed and said I could go home."

For the first time since she'd started speaking, there was a catch in Sue's voice. Jenny raised her arm and slipped it around her shoulders.

"Do you want to take a break?" she said. "Go into the garden for some fresh air, while I make a cup of tea?"

"No." Sue shook her head resolutely. "Let's get this over with." She gave DI Palmer a tight smile. "So, next question."

"I am so sorry, Ms Marshall." DI Palmer was genuinely shocked. "I… I just really don't know what to say."

Sue remained silent.

"Was Peter one of those arrested that night?" eventually asked DI Palmer.

"No, he was off with some girl."

She paused.

"He and my stepfather had never gotten on. The first time things blew up was after Pete did O'levels. He wanted to stay on for the sixth form and then go to university, but Frank - my stepfather - said he had to leave school and get a job. *'Start bringing some money in rather than wasting your bloody time and mine'* was how he put it".

"What happened?"

"Pete vanished. We got up one morning to find a note

for Frank on the kitchen table. *'You're right,'* he'd written, *'time to stop wasting your bloody time and mine'*. And that was that."

"He just disappeared?"

"We heard nothing from him for well over a year, until he turned eighteen. I think up to that point he'd worried that, as a minor, Frank could have him brought back. In the sixties, although you weren't an adult until you were twenty-one, you could legally leave home at eighteen."

She paused.

"He wrote to me at a girlfriend of mine's address, to let me know he was all right."

"Where was he during that period?"

"He didn't say, but his letter had a London postmark." She sighed. "I told my mum he'd been in touch, I had to, she'd been worried sick."

"But he came back down that Easter?"

"Showed up completely out of the blue. He met with me and mum but refused to have anything to do with Frank. Mum was hoping for a reconciliation – is there anything worse than having two of the people you love most in the world at each other's throats? She was trying to persuade Pete to come back home and Frank to let him do A'levels at a Further Education college.

"And then that dreadful night…" She shook her head. "When Pete found out what had happened to me, he turned up at the house and it was terrifying. Frank didn't even get a chance to open his mouth before Pete laid into him with his fists. My mother was screaming, I was crying. He had Frank down on the ground and was pounding him, over and over. Then he stood up and before he left told Frank that if he ever touched me again, he'd kill him."

Sue gave a shake of her head.

"I know that's what a lot of people say in anger or the heat of the moment but… Jesus, you should have been there - we all knew he meant it."

"Did your stepfather go to the police?"

She shook her head again.

"No - Frank had something of a reputation as a local hard man and he knew he'd never live that down in people's minds. In fact, he didn't leave the house for a fortnight, not until the bruises had vanished. But he never touched me again."

DI Palmer seemed to consider.

"One thing I'm not clear about was the Army's role in all of this - what were they doing there?"

"They were looking for a deserter." All eyes turned to Sergeant Vanner, who studiously avoided meeting any of them. "He'd been down here with the South Yorkshires, cleaning up the beaches, and then he went AWOL. There was talk he was wanted for something serious that had happened when they'd been posted out in Aden, but there were never any details."

He raised his eyes to meet Sue Marshall's, who held his gaze for a few seconds and then gave him a small nod.

"Okay." DI Palmer considered. "Peter leaves again, moves back to London – do you have any idea of where he was living during that period?"

"His letters usually had a West London postmark, but..." She shrugged. "And after about six months they stopped completely."

"In those letters, did he ever mention Lee Munro?"

"The actress?" Bemused, Sue shook her head. "No, why would he?"

"They were living in the same house, in Notting Hill." DI Palmer paused for a second. "She was also in St Hannahs at Easter 1967, where we think they probably met."

"Are you sure?" Sue seemed amused. "He's never mentioned it - and that does seem like something which would have come up at some point."

"Well..." began DI Palmer, before the meaning of Sue's words registered with her. "I'm sorry - *'come up at some point'*?"

"Hobnobbing with movie stars - it wouldn't be like Pete to keep that quiet."

DI Palmer was staring at Sue.

"Ms Marshall, when did you last see your brother?"

"Oh, it must have been..." Sue appeared to consider, before giving a small nod. "A couple of months ago."

"Your brother is alive?"

"Oh, yes."

"But..." DI Palmer seemed to be really struggling. "For how long have you known this?"

Sue shrugged.

"I remember it was around the time of the Munich Olympics that he got back in touch. You know, the terrorist attack on the Israeli..."

"How did he contact you?" broke in DI Palmer.

"He turned up at my Hall of Residence."

"And you didn't see fit to inform the police?"

"*Are you bloody serious?*" Sue Marshall's laugh was ringing. "Why would I assume they'd be the least bit interested in my finding him, when they didn't give a damn about his disappearance?" She gave a dismissive shake of her head. "You people...! *Jesus Christ!*"

DI Palmer sat back in her chair.

"I have to tell you there's no record of your brother in this country from 1970 onward," she said. "No income tax returns, no passport, no..."

"He'd changed his identity." Sue gave another dismissive shrug. "He told me he'd had to disappear a couple of years earlier, that he'd stumbled across something which had put his life in danger. He's never gone into detail, but I've always had the impression police corruption was somehow involved." A short laugh. "You'll understand I had no problem believing that."

"Ms ..." began DI Palmer, but Sue cut her off.

"And I'm guessing that's what all this is about, isn't

it?" She stared at the policewoman. "Something's crawled out from under some fetid little stone, something you people thought was long buried, and now you're all scrambling around trying to get it covered up again."

"No." DI Palmer was shaking her head. "Facts have come to light recently, but we're working to get to the bottom of what happened back then." She hesitated. "If what you say is true - and I don't doubt you - we really need to speak to Peter. We need the name he's using."

"Go to hell!" said Sue Marshall.

"Ms Marshall. Sue." DI Palmer's tone was almost gentle. "I understand you had an appalling experience - but hampering a police investigation is a criminal offence."

"So, arrest me," said Sue. "Because I'd love to go into the witness box with this. Believe me, you don't know the half of it."

"That's alright." Sergeant Vanner had risen to his feet. "Thank you for your cooperation, Ms Marshall. We're done here."

DI Palmer turned to stare at him.

"As you explained it to me," said Vanner, returning her stare, "you were here to inform Ms Marshall you believed her brother to be deceased. As that's clearly not the case, I don't think we need to take up any more of her time."

"But..."

"Any other matters discussed were done without informing her of her rights. If you want to pursue this further, you're obviously free to do so. But not before Ms Marshall's had the benefit of legal counsel and in a formal setting."

DI Palmer slowly rose.

"As you say, Sergeant." She nodded toward Sue. "Thank you for your time, Ms Marshall."

Sue simply sat there, staring at her woodenly.

"Why don't I show you both out?" said Jenny.

* * *

"Are you alright?" asked Jenny, coming back into the

room.

Sue nodded and gave an almost sheepish smile.

"God, I can't believe I just did that."

Jenny knelt alongside her chair and took her hand in hers.

"But it's the first time I've ever talked about it, you know?" She squeezed Jenny's hand. "Completely, I mean - I've told my brother bits and pieces but never the entire story, I was too scared. But," she shook her head, "now I have, it feels so..."

"Cathartic?" suggested Jenny. "As if a weight's been lifted?"

Sue nodded.

"Do you really think that's it? That they won't be back?"

"I don't know." Jenny considered. "Here, probably not if Sergeant Vanner has anything to do with it. I don't know about your brother, though."

"Hmmm." Sue's expression was inscrutable.

"It's likely I'll be seeing the Sergeant later," said Jenny, after a short silence. "I need to visit someone being held in the cells. Do you want me to have a word?"

"I'm not sure - perhaps. If that woman's not there, maybe you could find out exactly what all this is about?"

"Okay," Jenny stood up. "I'll play it by ear. Are you going to be alright - is there anything you'd like me to do before I leave?"

"I'll be fine," said Sue, with a smile that now didn't seem forced. "A couple of stiff drinks and I'll be right as rain."

"If I do discover anything, I'll pop back," Jenny told her. "Otherwise, I'll give you a ring later, to check you're okay."

Sue nodded.

* * *

"I'm afraid he's not available," said the constable at the front desk.

"Not... What is this, Groundhog Day?" Jenny felt fit to explode. "I know he's here, I saw him arrive."

Getting out of his car with that detective from London, she almost added, but then thought better of it. No point in admitting she knew he had reason to be otherwise engaged.

The constable studied her.

"Is this about chummy who you wanted to see earlier - in the cells?"

"He has a name," said Jenny. "Camlo Sterescu."

"Right," said the constable. "Well, you're a bit late, Vicar. He's gone."

"Gone?"

He sighed.

"The lady from the Gallery obviously decided pressing charges would be more trouble than it was worth. It's not likely she'll be getting much in the way of compensation, is it? So, Sergeant Vanner had a word with him and said if they were all gone by tonight that would be the end of it."

Jenny raised an eyebrow.

"Seriously! *'Get out of town by sundown'*?"

The constable smiled.

"That's how we do things out West," he drawled.

Jenny couldn't help but smile back at him.

"Okay," she said. "But I was on the phone a couple of minutes ago to his wife and she knew nothing about it - I should…"

Jenny had taken her phone out and was staring at it.

"You won't get a signal in here," he told her. "It's a dead spot." With a slow shake of his head, he pointed to a door on the left. "If it's local, you can use the phone in the Interview Room."

"Thanks."

Once inside Jenny sat down at the desk, lifted the phone from its cradle and was about to press down on the keypad when she realised someone was already on the line. She hesitated before placing it closer to her ear.

"… so I think we can be sure that - despite what he was telling us - he was in deep with this, probably from the beginning." She didn't recognise the speaker, a male with an authoritative tone and there's a surprise in a police station. "The techs have found some damning stuff on Denham's computer, it seems they kept in touch using an email account but not actually sending emails, however the hell that's possible. Anyway, McKelvey arranged a meet with Barry Denham last night, but when he turned up, there was somebody else waiting, someone who didn't want either of them talking. No prizes for guessing who that might be, given the M.O."

"What exactly happened?" said a voice Jenny immediately recognised as DI Palmer.

"Not on an open line, Amanda." The voice hesitated. "So how did you get on? Have you spoken to that Marshall woman yet - do we have a positive ID for her brother?"

"It's definitely her brother," said DI Palmer slowly, "but she says he's still alive."

"What!!?"

"She claims he stumbled across something in 1970, which forced him to change his identity. He must have got a fake ID from somewhere and has been using it ever since."

"What name is he using?"

"She won't tell me... It's a long story - and not a very pleasant one. So..." She let her voice trail off.

"Do you believe her?"

"Yes." DI Palmer sounded almost contrite. "Yes, I do."

"So, we've been played for bloody fools all along." There was a snort which could have been either exasperation or disgust. "It would seem our Mr Franklyn was right after all, with his little Johnny Walker homily."

"I haven't spoken to Lee Munro yet. I'm seeing her in the morning."

"Just get back up to London."

"The thing is, the one person I don't trust in all of this is Christopher Franklyn - I don't believe a word he's told us." She paused. "If I were to put pressure on Lee Munro, then we might..."

"Coppers instinct?" he interrupted.

She was silent.

"Amanda, we're not coppers." He softened his voice. "We're not in the justice business. We're in the containment business. We had a major problem. That problem has disappeared and so now we move onto the next problem and there will always be a next problem. We leave the detritus behind - it's no longer our concern."

DI Palmer still said nothing.

"Please don't think I'm doubting your instincts," he told her. "I'm not, you may well be right, in fact you probably are. So, let's be clear here - what I'm doing is disregarding them, for expediency's sake. And if that's something which doesn't sit right with you, then perhaps you should consider Chief Superintendent Kendall's offer."

"I'm sorry?"

"Oh, please..." His sigh was audible. "You've a lengthy drive ahead of you Amanda, regard it as an opportunity for some serious thinking."

The line went dead.

Jenny took the receiver from her ear and slowly placed it back onto its cradle.

What on earth had she just heard?

* * *

'We're not coppers' the voice on the phone had said. Then who, puzzled Jenny as she walked through the town, were they? Agents of the state of some kind and didn't that absolutely justify Sue Marshall's accusations of a cover-up. And what did Lee have to do with it?

It seemed it was her feet rather than her head which had led her to the Gallery, suddenly finding herself surprised to be standing outside the main entrance.

'Come around the back' Ruth had said, but before she could decide if she now wanted to be here at all, the door was opened for her by a burly uniformed security guard.

"Ms Weinstock said you might be along, Vicar," he told

her with a smile and Jenny recognised him as the son of a local fisherman, Understandably, they were taking every precaution against any possible further vandalism.

Thanking him, she moved through the lobby and into the main exhibition space, lit but deserted.

"Hello," she called out.

A door at the far end opened and a woman in her late forties, early fifties appeared and strode toward her.

"I'm Fiona," she said. "Ruth's partner - she's back home at the moment getting ready for tonight." She gave a shrug and a smile. "She was expecting you, but our schedule got a bit knocked for six today - you heard about what happened?"

She gestured with her hand at the artwork on the wall.

"Yes, of course," said Jenny.

"Why don't I make you a coffee while you look around - how do you take it?"

"Oh, thank you. Milk, no sugar would be great."

Jenny turned her attention to the walls.

* * *

Jenny hadn't expected to be so... well, *touched* was the word, she supposed. She knew *of* the paintings of course but had never actually seen them and for that she was now grateful. Scaled down to coffee-table book size or magazine page dimensions, they would probably have confirmed her initial assumption that it was nothing more than a gimmick. She'd once attended a production of Shakespeare's Richard III set in thirties Germany, and it had irritated her beyond belief, she'd had to leave halfway through the second act.

But this was different.

The artist's intention, she supposed, was to show that the story of mankind is forever interspersed with the same themes, endlessly repeated under various guises but here, in the scriptures, is where they form their first impression. In Jenny's case, and for many people of her age, that would have been Sunday School but Faith or not, who didn't know of the Good Samaritan, Prodigal Son, Pilate washing his hands or thirty pieces of silver. These parables echoed throughout all our lives and with a resonance that belied their seeming simplicity.

In a way, Jenny was glad that Ruth wasn't there to take her through the exhibition herself, giving her the background to each painting as she'd offered to. Jenny would be happy to receive that information at some point, in fact a couple of the paintings posed some intriguing questions. But for the same reasons she never used an audio guide or joined a tour when visiting a gallery or exhibition for the first time - shoehorning initial impressions into accepted convention always seemed to diminish rather than enhance what she was standing in front of - she was content simply to be there.

"You alright?"

Jenny hadn't been aware of Fiona's return and turned to find her standing alongside. She gave a small nod.

"They really draw you in, don't they?"

"At college, my first boyfriend - and, as things turned out, my last - was into Peter Ouspensky. Ever heard of him?"

Jenny shook her head.

"Early twentieth century Russian philosopher, one of those intellectuals who got sidelined into mysticism when he ran out of rational explanations for the woes of the world - no shortage of those, hey?"

Jenny smiled.

"But an expression he came up with was *'objective art'* and that's something which has always stuck."

"I'm not sure what that means."

"According to Ouspensky it was anything produced by a creative process that defied subjectivity." Fiona shook her head. "I know, but what I understand it to mean is... Let's say you receive some terrible news - the death of a parent or something equally traumatic. And on the radio, at that very moment, a piece of pop music is playing. From then onward you'll never be able to disassociate that piece of music from the event, right? You'll probably never want to listen to it again?"

"I suppose," nodded Jenny.

"Now, if the music playing at that moment were, say Beethoven's Ninth or a piece by Bach, it might remind you of the event, but it will overcome the emotional subjectivity you feel towards it by the power it possesses in itself."

"It's an interesting perspective," Jenny acknowledged.

"Well, Jeremy turned out to be a complete dork," said Fiona. "So, I suppose the lesson is that one finds nuggets of gold in the strangest of places."

Jenny smiled.

"Any word on the damaged painting," she asked.

"It's not as bad as we'd originally thought," Fiona told her. "The effect was more dramatic than damaging, which leads us to suspect that always was the intent."

"What do you mean?"

"Soluble ink is actually a lot harder to get hold of than waterproof. Usually, you only find it in art supply stores, but you can pick up a bottle of Quink at the nearest W H Smith." She shook her head. "And why ink? If he'd wanted to do some real damage, why not black gloss or even paint thinner?"

"You think it was only about publicity?"

"Who knows?" Fiona sighed. "There's a lot of bad feeling at the moment between the Travellers and the townsfolk, but I don't see why he should have picked on us." She shrugged. "Maybe because we were a soft target... Anyway, your coffee's out back. Food and drink aren't allowed in here, I'm afraid."

'Out back' proved to be a large studio, artworks stacked against the walls and a couple of works in progress on easels.

"Are you repairing the painting here?" asked Jenny.

Fiona shook her head.

"We probably could but the insurance company's insisting on a professional restoration, so it's gone off to London - should have it back in about a week. Here, let me show you."

She flipped open a laptop computer and pressed a few

keys. It was obviously connected to a projector behind them, because a large bright square lit up on the wall opposite. Fiona continued tapping at the keyboard and then an image appeared, blurry at first before suddenly snapping into focus.

"For the insurance company," she said.

Blue splashes obscured the bottom half of the painting, but that's not what caught Jenny's attention.

And she froze.

"This is..." she began and then stopped.

"The Woman at the Well," nodded Fiona.

"No, I meant..." She shook her head slowly. "I recognise..."

Her voice trailed off as she tried to gather her thoughts.

"Lee Munro – yes, she's in most of the paintings. Although you perhaps wouldn't see that at first glance, would you?"

But that's not who Jenny was staring at. The young British soldier being handed a drink of water by the girl was - other than the curly hair cut short - the same young man in the photograph DI Palmer had given Sue to identify.

She was looking at Sue Marshall's brother, Peter.

And also, she realised, there was now something terribly familiar about him, something she just couldn't put her finger on.

"The boy in the picture," she said. "The soldier."

Fiona picked up a catalogue.

"Models," she read out, "Lee Munro and Christopher Franklyn."

Jenny gave a start.

'The one person I don't trust in all of this is Christopher Franklyn - I don't believe a word he's told us.'

Amanda Palmer's words echoed in her head as she stared at the painting.

Christopher Franklyn. And the longer she stared at it, the stronger grew the sense of familiarity.

"We've decided not to press charges," Fiona continued.

"The Travellers are going to be moving on anyway, it seems they've finished the work they were doing here."

Jenny turned to her.

"The work they were doing here?"

Fiona nodded.

"Yes - they'd been re-tarmacking the driveway over at *The Grange*."

And then as crisply as the image on the wall had snapped into focus, so did the nebulous sense of familiarity in her mind.

The face was older but now given the context, it was unmistakable.

'Kit and I go back so far together,' Lee Munro had said, *'that it frightens me.'*

* * *

A sparkling golden causeway ran from where the sun was touching the edge of the ocean all the way into the rocky cove below. And, although the evening was still warm, on the bench by the Lych Gate Jenny Warwick shivered.

What was it Lee said to her, back on that afternoon when they'd first met? 'Whatever kind of day you've had, watching a sunset always seems an apt conclusion.'

Sitting there, it seemed to her that she held all the pieces of a puzzle whose solution should be simplicity itself, yet however she arranged them they refused to fit together.

But did it matter? The woman who'd claimed to be a detective - with the connivance of the local police force - was heading back to London and Sue Marshall, it was safe to assume, was no longer of any interest. So what was any of it to her now, really?

Because for all that Jenny believed in worlds beyond this one - perhaps even intertwined with this one - she didn't think of herself as being given to flights of fancy. But she did trust her instincts, and she took seriously the sense of foreboding which had been growing steadily stronger since she'd left the Gallery. Wheels within wheels, she'd thought to herself, the machinations of man.

It wasn't only the night that held terrors, Jenny reflected. The human instinct was to fear all that hid in the shadows, but perhaps more chilling were the secrets of a bright noonday - teeth and tentacles inches below the tranquil surface of still waters or glistening eyes and sharp claws crouched in the long grass of an open savanna.

Let go and walk on. The voice in her head was as clear as if it had been spoken beside her.

The ring of her mobile phone snapped her back to reality.

"Hello," she said.

It was Tina Farlow, from the Police Station.

"Sergeant Vanner thought you should know," she said. "There's been a case of food poisoning at a barbecue." Tina hesitated. "It's bad, at least one death and several others seriously ill." There was a catch in her voice. "Apparently the fatality is a child."

Jenny stood up.

"They're at the Cottage Hospital?"

"No, Treliske. The Sergeant said he'd send a car if you needed one."

"It's okay, I'm on my way."

Jenny almost ran toward the Rectory. Her thoughts of a few seconds ago already seemed little more than fanciful musings, scattering in the face of an oncoming storm.

8. August 1970

Claudia

In the aftermath of Frieda's death, Kit came to stay with me. There was no obvious reason for the police to connect Emma to either himself or Pembridge Villas, he told me, but better safe than sorry.

And I was glad of the company.

The previous week, I'd arrived back at the apartment to find Lee fuming.

"What's happened?" I asked.

Silently she handed me a tabloid newspaper, folded open halfway through.

TV Star Terror Ordeal As A Child screamed the headline. And in smaller but no less lurid type below, *Trauma may have scarred her for life, reveals sister.*

I lifted my eyes from the paper and stared at her.

"Go on," she said. "All of it."

I started reading.

TV star Lee Munro has never spoken publicly of the childhood ordeal she spent at the hands of an intruder at her family home, her sister has told this newspaper.

"It was horrific," says actress Helen Munro. "My mother, father and I had gone out for the evening, but Lee hadn't been feeling very well and so stayed at home. When we returned, I went up to her room to see if she was any better. But when I pushed her door open, she was lying on the bed wearing just her nightgown, with a masked figure standing over her. I screamed and ran out of the room - he looked really terrifying - and by the time my parents rushed upstairs he'd escaped out of the window. The police said that he'd probably used the drainpipe to climb up and down the outside wall.

> "My sister told us she couldn't remember anything that happened until she heard my scream, but that's often what happens with severe shock, isn't it? The mind blanks out all the horrendous details that it can't bear to face.
>
> "But the police never discovered who it was, which must have been horrific for her, not knowing if he might try to return."

Lee's relationship with her family was never the same after that, a saddened Helen discloses.

> "Before that terrible night we were as close as two sisters could possibly be. I can only think in some subconscious way she blames us for what happened. That if we'd all been at home together, she would never have been scarred by those dreadful events."

The article continued in much the same vein for another half page, before feeding its readership the tantalising titbit that Helen Munroe was currently touring in a production of George Bernard Shaw's *Man and Superman*, check your local press for details. Two photographs of Lee accompanied the piece. I recognised the smaller one at the bottom as a publicity still from her TV series. But the larger image, taking up almost a quarter of the page, was of Lee as a child, perhaps not ten years old and smiling uncertainly into the camera.

The article concluded with *'Lee Munro has been contacted for a comment but has yet to respond'*.

"Can you fucking believe it?" She shook her head as I handed the newspaper back to her, the only time I've ever heard her use profanity that wasn't in a script.

"Oh Lee," I said, really not knowing how to comfort her.

"*'The mind blanks out...'*" still shaking her head. "I was fast asleep until she started shrieking - that's enough to scar someone for life."

"It'll all blow over soon," I told her, but she shook her head again.

"There's plenty of mileage in this yet, believe me - after six years in *The Hendersons* one thing I learnt never to underestimate is the unspoken perv factor and this has it in spades."

I didn't know what to say.

"And it's not something I can bring to your doorstep." She gave a slight nod, as if arriving at a decision. "I should disappear for a while." And then shrugged. "Who knows, maybe you are right - taking the oxygen out of the story might kill it. If I'm not around then…"

She broke off as I walked over to the bureau, opened a drawer and then tossed her a bunch of keys.

"*Cam Ryr*," I told her. "St Hannahs, remember? Alex and Aunt Anne will be down in October, to close it up for the winter, but it's empty until then. There'll be no-one looking for you there."

"Oh, Claudia!" She came over and hugged me with a strength I thought her tiny frame could never possess. "You're such a good friend."

* * *

Kit and I working through our options together did at least give us the sense that we were doing something, however dark things might have looked.

There was no point Emma requesting a Visiting Order for us, her solicitor had said. Judith had been recommended by a member of the legal team at the Claims Union Emma had worked for, an earnest, ridiculously young woman, but with an impressive track record defending politically motivated criminal prosecutions. They wouldn't refuse one outright, she told us, but we'd most likely find the request becoming bogged down in a quagmire of bureaucracy, achieving little other than bringing ourselves to the notice of the authorities. Attention we could well do without.

But then we had a visitor.

"It's Aidan," announced the voice on the entry phone. Kit and I exchanged looks. From his expression, he wasn't expecting good news.

"Nice place," said Aidan, looking around appreciatively as I led him into the living room.

"Is everything okay?" asked Kit.

Aidan took a breath.

"For the past week there's been a GPO tent on the pavement opposite the house and I have to say that I've never seen such well-groomed telephone repairmen."

"Shit!" said Kit and then hesitated. "Are you sure you…?"

"A bus, two tube trains and a taxi," said Aidan dryly. "No one followed me."

"Okay."

Aidan paused.

"And your little Dutch girl's off and away with Jake since the beginning of the month, I've heard," he said carefully.

Kit stared at him.

"Carin?"

"He's been a tower of strength in these trying times, it would seem. They've gone to the Isle of Wight together. Apparently, he's found himself a job at the Festival site there."

Kit was silent, his expression inscrutable.

"Anyway," said Aidan, "I just thought you should know. The actual reason for my visit," he reached inside his jacket and pulled out a folded sheet of paper, handing it to Kit, "is this."

Kit unfolded it and stared.

"It's a Visiting Order for Emma," he said.

"For this afternoon," said Aidan, "so you'd better get your skates on."

"How did you get that?" I asked.

"My family has connections," he said. "This is not unfamiliar territory for us."

"But this," Kit looked up from the Visiting Order at Aidan, "is made out for Andrew Barclay."

He must have caught the puzzled expression on my face.

"Jake, in the actual world," he said to me, dryly.

"Indeed." Aidan gave a shrug. "As you'd imagine, Special Branch will be all over anyone visiting Emma like flies on a cowpat. So, I took the view that an MI5 file opened in his name might bring a few chickens home to roost in later life. When youthful indiscretions are done and dusted and he's after a career in the Civil Service or applying for a visa to the United States."

Kit slowly shook his head.

"Remind me never to get on your bad side."

"As I said, not unfamiliar territory." Aidan looked at his watch. "You'd better get going."

* * *

I don't know what I expected prison to be, but Holloway certainly wasn't it, a Gothic monstrosity that simply couldn't have been more out of place in North London. Even Kit seemed intimidated as we walked towards the giant gates.

"I feel like an extra in a Hammer horror film," he said, as a door in the gate opened and we were shepherded into a room with twenty other people, all queueing at a glass partition. Kit indicated a row of wooden benches at the back.

"See you out here," he said.

It took about ten minutes for him to reach the window, where it was immediately obvious that something was wrong. The prison officer unfolded the Visiting Order Kit handed him, stared at it for a few seconds, then stood up and disappeared out of view.

He returned a minute later, shaking his head. I couldn't hear the conversation, but the officer seemed almost apologetic, shaking his head again and giving the occasional shrug against Kit's quiet persistence. Finally, he picked up a pen and scribbled on the Visiting Order before handing it back through the window.

Kit gave him one last stare, took it from him and walked over to me.

"What's happened?" I asked.

"Emma's visiting rights have been rescinded for today, he says."

"What... Why?"

"He doesn't know, but he says that it is temporary - today only." He lifted the paper in his hand. "He's amended this for tomorrow and told me to come back then." Kit made a gesture halfway between a shrug and a sigh. "There didn't seem any point in creating a fuss."

"Of course not."

"Come on." He managed a smile. "Let's go and get something to eat."

With much locking and unlocking of doors we finally found ourselves outside, the fresh air at least dispelling emanations imagined or not of body odour and cheap perfume. Walking toward the road, I had no inclination to look behind me and I'd already decided that I wasn't going to return here with Kit tomorrow. There was something just too...

With a screech of tyres, a car pulled up alongside us and the doors flew open. The driver stayed behind the wheel as two heavyset men in their forties climbed out of the back. Although they didn't seem to be rushing, they were moving with a speed that belied their bulk.

"What..." began Kit, before one of the men jabbed his fingers into Kit's midriff. He gasped and doubled up as the other man grabbed him from behind, at first for support and then to bundle him into the back of the car. I started to scream, but the man who'd hit Kit turned to point his finger at me and slowly shake his head. The sound died in my throat and I found myself backing away from him. Not taking his eyes from me, he made his way around the car and with a last malevolent smile lowered himself inside. The car accelerated from the curb before the door had pulled shut.

Seconds later it had turned the corner and was gone.

* * *

"Okay," said Aidan. "Let's go through it again."

I'd taken a taxi home, but I really didn't know what to do or where to go after that. My initial thought was to contact Emma's solicitor, but I realised that her first question would have been where had the Visiting Order come from and I had no intention of opening that can of worms.

So, despite Aidan's warning about Pembridge Villas being under surveillance, it didn't seem I had any choice. He needed to know what had happened. And in all probability there were already photographs aplenty of my visits there.

But when I arrived at the house, there was no sign of the GPO tent across the road that Aidan had described. Nor of any vans parked nearby, or indeed any vehicles that weren't obviously empty.

"They packed themselves up and left about an hour ago," said Aidan as he let me in and then, staring at my face, "Claudia, what's happened?"

He poured me a stiff whisky and listened without interruption as I stumbled through it all. That's when he took me through it again, this time questioning and clarifying as I sipped at my drink, which was definitely taking the raw edge off.

"And you're sure they were policeman?" he asked me when I'd finished, which seemed a strange question.

"Well, yes," I said. "Who else were they likely to be?"

He stared at me for a second and nodded.

"Yes, of course."

There were a few seconds of silence.

"I just stood there," I said eventually. "I let them take Kit away without doing a damn thing. If I'd screamed or made a fuss, people might have seen what was happening and…"

My voice trailed off as Aidan reached out and squeezed my hand.

"You did exactly the right thing, Claudia," he told me. "You'd could have been hurt or taken as well - and at least now we know what's happened, so don't go beating yourself up over it."

"But what would they want him for?"

Aidan shook his head.

"I don't know."

"What are we going to do?"

"You go back home and stay there," he said. "I'll make some phone calls - I should be able to find out where he's being held and why. When I've sorted that out, I'll come over."

"Okay," I told him. "Thank you."

Kit

Squeezed between the two of them on the back seat of the car, I couldn't be sure at first who'd grabbed me, cops or East End villains. Superficially, there was never that much to choose between them - the same arrogance in the same shitty pubs and clubs where they cheated on the same dowdy hausfraus with the same brassy tarts. But in practical terms, it would probably mean the difference between finishing the day in a cell or under a car park.

When I demanded to know what was going on, the one on my left dropped his hand between my legs, grabbed my balls and squeezed.

"Unless you want more of this, shut your fucking mouth," he said as I tried to stifle a scream, but I knew then that they were cops, vicious bastards who hurt without leaving a mark. Gangsters liked to leave their handiwork on display.

We drove down the Holloway Road to Highbury Corner, onto Upper Street and then into the Angel. After the City Road I started to lose my bearings, this part of London I wasn't familiar with, but when we finally pulled up to the kerb, I reckoned we were in Hoxton. And - I wasn't sure whether to be worried or not - we weren't at a police station.

We were outside a school.

* * *

They took an arm each and frogmarched me in through the main entrance. In the foyer, a uniformed constable was talking to a caretaker. They broke off their conversation as we approached.

"Third room on the left," said the caretaker, with a nod towards a corridor.

The building was being decorated, we passed ladders leaning against the walls and the smell of fresh paint was everywhere. The corridors were deserted, school holidays I remembered.

One of the cops opened the door to a classroom and went inside. After a few seconds he stepped back out, grabbed my arm again and between the two of them they bundled me in through the door.

It must have been an infant year classroom. The chairs and desks were tiny, and there was a giant picture of Donald Duck on one wall. A youngish guy, maybe a couple of years older than me, was sitting on the edge of the teacher's desk and as we came closer, he stood up and stared at me. Despite the longish hair, leather jacket and flared jeans, he still managed to have cop written all over him.

"It's okay," he told the two detectives, "I'll handle it from here."

He waited until they'd closed the door behind them and then extended his hand out to me.

"Hello Christopher," he said as we slowly shook hands. "Sorry about the rough stuff."

Christopher!!?

"My name is Brian Maddox," he continued. "Detective Sergeant Brian Maddox. I'm with Special Branch." He paused. "I believe your dad mentioned me to you - gave you my contact details in case you couldn't get through to him in an emergency?"

He reached into his pocket, took out a handkerchief and offered it to me. As I stared blankly back at him, he pointed at my nose. I touched it and my fingers came away sticky with blood. Must have happened when they were getting me into the car. I took it from him and buried my face in it, furiously trying to think.

What was happening here?

* * *

"We've been trying to find you for a while now," the cop was saying. "Chief Superintendent Franklyn had told us you were going to be away with your girlfriend, but he wasn't sure where."

I finished wiping my nose and - keeping my expression as neutral as possible - made to hand it back to him. He motioned for me to keep it. He pulled the teacher's chair out from behind the desk.

"I think you'd better sit down," he said.

As I sat down, he leaned forward and put his hand on my shoulder.

"I'm afraid I have some really bad news." The cop - *Maddox, remember names* - seemed to be struggling to find the right words.

"Your father had a heart attack at the beginning of August," said Maddox softly. "He hung on for two days but then suffered a second one, which proved fatal. I'm very sorry."

Aware that my bewilderment was now most likely to be mistaken for shock, I slowly shook my head. Maddox had a briefcase on the desk and from it he pulled out a newspaper folded open. He passed it over to me. It was some North London rag.

'*Senior Detective Mourned by Friends and Colleagues*' ran the headline.

'*The funeral took place last Tuesday of Detective Chief Superintendent Jack Franklyn,*' it read, '*whose unexpected death from cardiac arrest, came as a shock to friends and colleagues alike*'. The rest was just a blur, other than the last paragraph. '*Chief Superintendent Franklyn's only family is his son Christopher, who is spending the summer travelling in the United States and is believed not yet to be aware of his father's death.*'

"We put a story out about you being abroad," said Maddox, "to explain why you weren't at the funeral. We've been doing everything we can to find you, but we couldn't risk blowing your cover." He paused. "In the end we issued a warrant for your arrest and Holloway got back to us on the Visiting Order, which is why we staked it out. Sorry," he said, "if it got a bit rough, but we had to make it look good. The two DCs who brought you here have no idea who you really are."

I was shaking my head slowly, trying to put all this together.

"I know you and your father didn't have much chance to talk about what happened over at Camden Town," Maddox went on, "but he wanted you to know you did the right thing. There's absolutely no doubt they were behind the attacks and finding the *plastique* there will put them away where they belong for the rest of their lives." He paused. "Your father said you'd used old takeaway boxes out of the rubbish for the fingerprints, that was really smart, Christopher."

Jake planted the explosives!

It was Jake who'd put Emma behind bars.

"I'm so sorry that you had to find out this way." Maddox shook his head. "But the thing is, we need your help again."

I stared at him, not trusting myself to speak.

"It's not been in the news," he continued, "because we've a D-Notice on it. But last night the London Police Commissioner's house was bombed. Have you heard anything about that?"

I shook my head.

"We're pretty sure it's not the Paddies, which means it's probably the Angry Brigade again," he said, "and the only link we've got to them is you."

All I wanted was to get out of there - at some point this Maddox was going to discover what a colossal blunder he'd just made and - *Jesus Christ!!!* - Special Branch conspiring to pervert the course of justice wasn't something I'd be walking away from unscathed when he did.

"You want me to find out what I can?" I don't think my mouth had ever felt so dry.

He nodded, then reached into his pocket and took out a

card.

"Use this number from now on," said Maddox, handing it to me. "It will find me day or night." He hesitated. "Best if you memorise it and throw it away."

"Okay."

From his briefcase, he took out a set of keys.

"I don't know if you still have a set of house keys," he said, passing them over. "Everything's left to you, obviously - I gather there's no other family?"

I stayed silent.

"There's a lot to sort out," he said. "Probate, the will. It would be better if you kept your head down right now, so we'll take care of all of that for you... But as ever, we'll keep contact to an absolute minimum."

"I need to get back," I told him, lifting my eyes to meet his with what I hoped would be taken for stoic resolve rather than loathing.

"Are you going to be alright?" he asked. "I do realise how much of a shock this must be for you."

That's true enough, I thought but just nodded my head.

"If you need to talk," he said, "we have people who can help. The next few weeks aren't going to be easy for you..."

I shrugged.

"Do you need a lift anywhere?" he asked.

"No." I shook my head. "It's safer if I make my own way over to Notting Hill." I forced a smile and stood up. "And it'll give me a chance to come up with an explanation for this afternoon."

We shook hands.

"It's good to finally meet you, Chris," he said. "I'm only sorry it's under such terrible circumstances."

Not, I thought to myself as I closed the door behind me, *as terrible as they're about to become.*

Aidan

Claudia couldn't have been gone more than ten minutes when there was another knock on the door, soft but insistent.

"Kit!"

I stared at him as he brushed past me into the studio.

"You're okay?"

"You heard?"

"Claudia's just left, she was worried sick about you." I closed the door. "So was I, but for different reasons. I thought it might have been Slater's mob, with a score to settle."

Kit shook his head.

"No, it was the cops." He hesitated. "Jake - any idea when he's due back?"

"The festival finishes today, so later this week I'd guess."

"Okay." Kit seemed to consider. "So that gives us a few days, at least."

"A few days for what?"

Kit indicated the whiskey bottle that I'd opened for Claudia.

"Pour a couple of stiff ones," he said, "and make yourself comfortable."

* * *

"Bloody hell!" I was sure the incredulity I could hear in my voice was mirrored by my expression. "That's unbelievable."

"I've had an hour or so for it to sink in," said Kit, "and I'm still having problems getting my head around it."

"So?" I tried to order my thoughts. "This cop actually thinks that you're Jake?"

"Thanks to your Visiting Order." Kit gave a wry smile. "AKA Andrew Barclay but real name Christopher Franklin - who's not only been feeding Special Branch every titbit of information he's come across since he's been here, but who also planted the explosives at Camden Town. Which got everyone in the house arrested - including Emma."

"Kit..."

"This Maddox," he continued, "wants me to find out about a bomb attack on the Police Commissioner's house last..."

"*Kit!!*"

This time my voice was sharp enough to cut him off.

"You do realise," I tried to keep my voice slow and even, "what will happen if this cop finds out who you really are. After he's told you that Camden Town, where two people died, was down to a fit-up by a police informant?"

"From what he was saying, no-one other than Jake's old man ever dealt with him."

"Okay, so what do you have in mind? To get him on tape admitting it and go to the press?"

"Well, that had been my first thought."

"No national paper would touch it. And even if they did, what about D-notices? Or the Defence of the Realm Act?"

"I said that was my first thought." He smiled, lifted the whiskey bottle and topped up our glasses. "I've had time for a few more."

He pushed the cork back into the bottle and set it down on the table.

"I know how to use this to get Emma out," he said.

* * *

"It's a hell of a risk," I told him when he'd finished.

"From what this Maddox was saying, we'd have the whip hand here. Jake is the only inside man they have, so they'll be pretty desperate to keep him on board."

"And when the real Jake turns up?"

"I can get Emma out of gaol," he said. "Can you get her out of the country - maybe to America, with somewhere safe to stay and a new identity?"

"If I could," I conceded, "it would take longer than a few days to make those kinds of arrangements."

"Okay, then when Jake gets back we snatch him and

stash him away in a basement someplace." Kit shrugged. "Paul would help."

"'Stash him away in a basement someplace'! Jesus, you're mister secret bloody agent man all of a sudden, aren't you?" I paused. "How can you be sure no-one else knows his face? What if he has a passport, his photo would be on file?"

Kit pulled a set of house keys from his pocket.

"The family home," he said. "Maddox gave them to me. It shouldn't be too hard to get the address, might even find it in his room upstairs. We go there, root around, see what we can dig up?"

"Look," I said, "let's give Paul a ring. Get his take on it."

"And if he's in, are you?"

I gave him a reluctant nod.

Kit

Next morning, I phoned the number on the card Maddox had given me and was told to be on the corner of Moscow Road and Bayswater Road at ten to twelve. I hadn't been sure what to expect, so when an empty black London taxi pulled over, I hesitated. The driver indicated the back of the cab with a nod of his head, so I opened the door and climbed in.

"I'm Barry," said the driver, sliding the glass panel between us open. "From now on, I'll be your main contact."

"Okay."

"I'll give you a phone number to use whenever you want a meet, and the procedure will be the same as today. You'll get a time and a place where I'll pick you up. Nothing suspicious about that, right, lone figure in the back of a cab?"

"Right," I agreed.

"We'll drive around, chat, and then I'll drop you off." He half turned his head backward toward me. "Sorry, about your Dad," he said. "I didn't know him that well, but the couple of times I picked him up from home he was always okay with me - not like some of those arseholes with pips on their shoulders."

A thought came to me.

"Actually," I said, "when we're done, could you drop me off at home?"

"Sorry?"

"I don't mean Pembridge Villas, obviously," I told him. "Dad's place - I've not had a chance to get back there since... Well, since I found out. There're a few things I need to do."

"Okay, yeah, of course." He paused. "So, did you hear anything?"

"About the other night?" I shook my head. "No, but I'm seeing some people later."

"Okay."

I took a breath.

"There might be a problem with Emma Brownlow, though."

"Problem?"

"So, do you have anything definite on her - fingerprints or forensics?"

"Nothing to tie her to the explosives, but plenty of form. Probably enough to get her sent down if we're lucky with the judge." He gave me a puzzled look. "Why?"

"Someone I know was talking to her boyfriend. He says that there're witnesses to the shooting."

"Witnesses?" He turned his head back to me. "There were no bloody witnesses."

"It looks like there are - solid ones. Citizens. Who say the police gave no warning before opening fire and Slater never fired a shot. That he was just gunned down."

"That's bollocks. And so why haven't they come forward?"

"They're waiting for the trial. Apparently, they know that there were no spent bullets from Slater's gun recovered at the scene and that the forensic test on it showed it hadn't been fired."

"Yeah, well, good luck with them proving that."

"I'm sure that little detail's been rectified by now. But I think they've got a copy of the original report."

Barry was silent.

"They also say that the shot which killed Frieda Brownlow was fired after Slater was down on the ground. By an undercover officer wearing jeans and a combat jacket. Definitely not by Slater."

With a squeal of brakes, Barry brought the cab to a halt by the side of the road and turned to face me full on.

"Just who the fuck," he hissed, "are these witnesses?"

"I don't know," I said, shaking my head.

"Well, you need to bloody well find out."

I returned his stony stare, although I was feeling nowhere near as confident as I was trying to sound. That last item I'd made up on the fly, after recognising Barry as the officer in the combat jacket who'd fired the shot through Frieda Brownlow's car window.

"The thing is," I told him, "they're keeping all of this under wraps until the trial. Emma Brownlow's defence is going to be that it's a police fit up. Normally that'd get tossed out of court on its ear, but if you've two solid joe citizens saying they saw the cops blazing away like they were at the OK Corral *plus* an original police forensic report contradicting prosecution evidence - and if they have that then what else do they have - the defence will get listened to."

Barry was silent.

"So, I can't afford for Emma Brownlow to stand trial," I told him. "If they start digging, they're going to find things. And then we're all fucked."

Barry considered.

"How is releasing her going to make this go away?"

"Her boyfriend told the guy I was talking to that if they could get her out on bail, they'd do a runner. Disappear abroad somewhere. If she were released for lack of evidence, but then word got to them that the cops had turned her loose only for the chance to fit her up properly, they'd be gone within days."

"That still leaves the witnesses."

"The driving force behind all this seems to be Emma's boyfriend - they might not be so eager to come forward if he's not around. The other thing is that while Emma Brownlow isn't actually guilty, everyone else is. She'd never cop a plea, but with her gone, there's a good chance the others would. If the right kind of pressure were applied."

Barry slowly nodded his head.

"Yeah... I see your point."

"Obviously, it's your call," I told him, "but if Emma Brownlow goes to trial, I disappear."

Aidan

The house had little to distinguish it from its neighbours, a gravel driveway led from wrought-iron gates up to a mock Tudor facade. The gardens and shrubbery had the look of being professionally cared for, the paint on the windows and doors glistened and the brickwork had a sheen suggesting a recent scrub. I'd have guessed a stockbroker but obviously a career spent as a bulwark between a capital city and the temptations it has to offer comes with its rewards too.

"Hi." Kit opened the front door, and after I'd passed through closed it quickly behind me.

"How did you find the place?" I asked.

As he led me through the hallway and into a large living room, he explained about his meeting with the undercover Special Branch cop.

"Nicely done," I said. The previous night we hadn't come across anything of use in Jake's room and all the telephone directory revealed was that he must have been ex-directory. "What have you found?"

On a sofa there was a holdall half opened, I could see

picture frames and a couple of cardboard files in it.

"There are no photos with Jake in them looking older than about ten or eleven," said Kit, "but let's clear them out, anyway. There's a study along the hall with a locked filing cabinet I can't find a key for. But upstairs in the bedroom..."

I followed him back out into the hallway and up the stairs.

"I went through some paperwork and letters in the study," Kit said as we walked, "and I found the copy of a will dated six months ago. There's provision for an aunt - there're monthly bills from a care home in Solihull in his desk - but the only other beneficiary is his son, so it's a good bet that will be the only family."

We stepped into a bedroom where, like every other room we'd been in, the air hung heavy with furniture polish. Then, looking around, I realised there was not a speck of dust on any of the surfaces.

"The photographs," I told him. "You need to put them back."

Kit turned to me with a puzzled expression on his face.

"There's still a cleaner coming in," I said. "She'll notice."

"Shit."

"It's not like he's recognisable in them," I said as Kit, shaking his head, opened the door of a built-in wardrobe.

"Anyway," he said, "there was a key for this."

Half a dozen suits were hanging on a rail. He slid them across to one side to reveal a small standalone safe sitting on a sturdy wooden shelf that looked purpose built to support it. He took a keyring from his pocket, inserted the key and swung the door open.

Kit reached inside and took out a two-inch-thick block of five pound notes, tightly bound with a bank wrapper. Then another one. And another.

"Doubt the cleaning lady will miss this," he said dryly, stacking them on the bedside table. "Or these," he said, reaching back in and then handing me a bulging leather pouch about ten inches long and six inches wide.

It was surprisingly heavy, unzipping it along the top revealed it was full of coins.

"Sovereigns," said Kit.

Next, he pulled out a small black notebook.

"I've no idea what this is," he said. "It's just names, dates and numbers. But probably enough to put the wind up somebody if we could figure it out."

Taking the notebook from him and quickly flicking through it I saw he was right. The pages were filled with small, neat handwriting, detailing what were obviously financial transactions.

"And finally." He took out a silver key, the number 587 printed on the head but the shaft rather than being notched held a series of irregular circular ridges.

"I'm guessing a safe deposit box." He shrugged. "And if there's more of the same as here," he nodded toward the open safe, "it's probably worth finding out where that is."

I nodded.

"Okay," I said. "What else?"

"Paperwork mainly, what looks like the deeds for a property in Spain, solicitors' letters, bank statements..."

"Okay," I told him. "Go downstairs and put the photos back where they were. I'll go through the paperwork and see if I can find out where that safe deposit box is." I paused. "We'll take the cash and the sovereigns - that'll get Emma well on her way, but the rest we'll put back."

"There's nothing," said Kit slowly, "that I think we need to worry about. If anyone has been looking around here, they wouldn't have found anything to make them suspicious. If they hadn't met Jake before, that is."

"Right," I said. "So, what's next?"

* * *

Emma was deathly pale and had lost weight, but no surprise there. I'd grown up watching friends of my grandfather vanish from our lives - questions not encouraged - and reappear months later as wraiths of their former selves.

"Hello Aidan." She gave a weak smile. "Long time no see."

Emma's solicitor had collected her from Holloway and they'd taken a taxi back to her office, a shabby building in a warren of streets behind Paddington Station. It was thought best Kit stayed well out of sight until we were as certain as we could be that she wasn't under surveillance and he'd slipped out of the car as soon as we'd seen her being released.

I don't know where Paul got the sleek Jaguar saloon from and I didn't ask questions. I concentrated on jotting down in a notepad the last three digits of license plates around us as we headed west across London, Paul holding the cab in sight without getting too close.

"Well," he said, as we pulled over, "if they are keeping tabs on her they're being pretty elaborate about it."

My thoughts too. No single car had stayed with us for the entire journey and no repetition of the license plates suggested that if they were dipping in and out en route, they were putting a lot of manpower into it.

We parked well back from the solicitor's office. Given Judith's clientele, it was to be expected that anyone hanging around her front door would be of more than passing interest to the authorities. We sat watching for twenty minutes until the door opened and Emma stepped out onto the street. As she began to walk in the opposite direction, Paul started the engine.

He let her reach the end of the road before pulling out and so we were alongside her almost immediately she'd turned the corner. She registered the car and - understandably edgy - stopped walking and backed away.

Paul wound the window down.

"It's okay, Emma," he said. "Get in."

With a simultaneous exhalation of breath and a shake of the head, she opened the rear door and climbed inside.

"For a second," she said, after greeting me, "I thought I

was going straight back to where I'd just left."

"Sorry," said Paul.

She shifted in her seat, as if trying to get more comfortable.

"So," perhaps a little too brightly. "No Kit in the welcoming party?"

"A couple of things he had to take care of," said Paul.

Giving an indifferent shrug, she turned her head to look out of the window. More to mask her expression, I guessed, than from an interest in what the world was up to.

"How did you know I was out?" she asked, after a few moments' silence. "Judith said they only decided to drop the charges a couple of hours ago and that she hadn't had a chance to contact anyone. As soon as she heard, she shot over to Holloway."

"It's a little more complicated than that," said Paul.

"Complicated how?" Her expression was unchanged, but a note of wariness had found its way into her voice.

"We're heading over to Claudia's place," I told her. "You'll be staying there for the next couple of nights."

She leaned forward and opened her mouth as if about to speak, but I raised the palm of my hand to silence her.

"But before we get there," I said, "there are some things we need to tell you and we don't have a lot of time."

Claudia

One unexpected consequence - although on reflection it shouldn't have been - of having Lee Munro as a house guest for a while, was the necessity of installing a telephone answering machine. Within weeks of her moving in, most of London apparently had acquired my number and weren't shy about using it. Lee, doubtless pulling a few strings, arranged for the prompt installation of an ungainly plastic box connected between the cable coming out of the wall and the telephone.

Lee insisted it was best that I recorded the greeting, which instructed callers how to proceed.

"You never know, they might think they've dialled the wrong number and hang up," she said.

On listening to my first attempt being played back, I realised I had never heard my voice before.

I was appalled.

"Good grief, I sound like Princess Anne!"

"Yes, you do rather," smiled Lee. "Would you like to try again for something less regal?"

It actually took four attempts before I stopped sounding as though I were addressing the nation. But whenever I telephoned the apartment to leave a message for Lee, I still cringed whilst listening to myself.

Since her departure I'd virtually ignored it and after a while it seemed to have passed into a state of limbo. Rather than being greeted by a variety of flashing lights whenever I returned home, there was now just one consistent dull amber one. I remembered the engineer warning us that if the machine were allowed to fill up, it would simply disconnect any caller who tried to leave a message, and that was absolutely fine by me. If I wasn't in then try again later, just like the rest of the world.

Which is why, I imagine, Kit was so full of ire when I opened the door to him.

* * *

"Emma's been released?" I found myself shaking my head, hardly daring to believe it.

"It looks as if the evidence against her is pretty flawed," said Kit. "And they're worried that might taint the case they're building against Dave and Anna."

"But that's wonderful news," I said and then quickly corrected myself. "Not about Dave and Anna, I meant…"

"I know what you meant," broke in Kit. "But the thing is, she needs a place to stay."

"What about her family," I asked. "She's more than welcome, of course. But I would have thought..."

I let my voice trail off.

"I didn't say anything before," said Kit, seeming to pick his words carefully, "because I wasn't sure how things were going to work out. But just after Emma was remanded in Holloway, Judith told me she'd managed to get a Visiting Order for Wilf." He paused for a second, careful to meet my eyes. "Wilf sent it back."

"Sent it back...?" I shook my head. "I don't understand." Then comprehension dawned. "You mean he blames Emma? For what happened to Freida."

Kit shrugged.

"I think that whatever's going down there, it's going to need some time to settle," he said. "But according to Judith, Emma took that really badly."

We looked at each other in silence for a few seconds.

"So," continued Kit, "given the circumstances..."

"Of course," I told him and - not wishing to make assumptions about the sleeping arrangements - added, "We've obviously plenty of room here."

"It's probably best if I move back to Pembridge Villas," said Kit.

Before I could respond to this, the entry phone buzzed.

"That'll be her," said Kit. "Give her some space. And," he added, "don't stare."

* * *

She looked dreadful. More than just the lost weight, there was a haunted quality about her, almost as if she weren't here, her body no more than a placeholder for a wandering spirit.

"I'm so sorry," I said, giving her a hug, but not too tightly. "About your mother."

She managed a weak smile and moved across the room to sit on the sofa. From the corner of my eye, I saw Kit and Aidan exchange nods.

"If everything's alright here," said Aidan, "we should be on our way. Paul's circling the block and we wouldn't want to be drawing attention."

Emma reached out and squeezed Kit's hand.

"You need to get back to the house," she told him. "I'll be okay."

"I'll call later," said Kit. And then gave me a look.

"I'll sort the machine out," I told him contritely. "Promise."

After they left, Emma took a bath while I changed the sheets in the room where Kit had been staying. My mind was buzzing with questions and I was trying to get them in some kind of order, whilst still remembering Kit's *'give her some space'*.

It was probably best to steer clear of the subject of Holloway unless she brought it up, but wouldn't the question of where had she vanished to during those past months be something of an elephant in the room, if not raised?

"I was abroad," she told me as she settled down on the sofa in my fluffiest dressing gown, both hands around a mug of cocoa. "Working with refugees."

"Abroad?"

"The Middle East." She shrugged. "Well, mainly."

"Right," I said slowly. "You mean like the Peace Corps?"

"Yes," she said. "Something like that."

9. Declan Mckelvey

While the whore got herself dressed Declan lay back and lit a cigarette, pulling the sheet across to cover himself. She didn't take long, no buttons or clasps he noticed, just a zip here, a strip of Velcro there and she was good to go. Styled for expediency, thought Declan, a professional through and through.

Well, he had no complaints, although during his telephone conversation with the woman at the agency he'd begun to wonder. Oh, for the simplicity of a brazen stare under a streetlight he'd reflected, waiting for her to bring to an end her litany of oral, Thai, anal, ATM *et al*, concluding with 'And for an extra twenty we can make it a GFE for you', which was a new one on him.

"A girlfriend experience," was the explanation. Declan was tempted to ask whether that meant she'd only give him a blow job if it was his birthday, but previous encounters within the sex industry had taught that irony was seldom well received. So now it appeared the contempt the girls held for the men who paid to fuck them had become a marketable commodity in itself, commanding premium rates for its concealment.

"I'll tell you what, sweetheart," he'd said, "put me down for a hundred and fifty and surprise me."

She'd arrived at the hotel an hour later, a trim blond with as little penchant for small talk as himself. She'd counted the notes and slipped them into her bag while he'd undressed, then stepped out of everything and followed him onto the bed. With no *faux* pantomimes of passion or desire, she'd used her hands and her mouth to bring him to the edge and then ridden him right over it. A good job well done.

Finished, she'd collected her bag and given him a nod and a smile before letting herself out of the room. Declan stubbed out his cigarette and checked his watch - there was an hour before the meet, and he couldn't decide whether to catch some shuteye or maybe go for a walk. It was a long day, he'd been up at five for the first Aer Lingus flight out of Belfast and an evening with Liam in the West End was more than likely to stretch into the early hours. The girl had taken his nerves off the boil, that you could always count on, but it still rankled that Liam hadn't said why he'd wanted him in London at such short notice.

"Can't talk on the phone," he'd told him. Which was fair enough, and Declan was certain that if this had all fallen apart, and Liam knew everything, he wouldn't have been flown to London for retribution. That would have been delivered in Belfast, home turf, where things could be managed.

But there was definitely a nagging in the back of his mind which he just couldn't shake.

* * *

It had been almost thirty years since Declan first set foot in England, sixteen years old and working the lump in North London. Four to a room in a boarding house that perpetually stank of sweat and piss and cats, although there never was a cat to be seen the whole time he lodged there. Outside the *Black Horse* at seven in the morning, standing with the other two dozen or so, as the filthy white Transit vans pulled up at the curb. A subbie at the wheel would wind down the window to point at the ones to climb in the back for a day's work and a fistful of pound notes at the close of it.

At first Declan had been amongst the last to be picked, but as the wiry strength his slight frame belied and a tendency - rare as hen's teeth in an Irishman - to say little and buckle down to the task in hand, came to be noted he gradually climbed the pecking order. After a few months Mr O'Doherty, who had gangs on most building sites across North

London, asked if he'd like to come to work for him full time, paying the stamp and all.

"I'll bump the pay up, so you'll still have the same in your pocket at the end of the week," Mr O'Doherty told him, "but if hard times come around, you'll have the dole to draw. And we'll find somewhere better for you to stay than that shithole you're in now."

Declan thanked him and moved into a small flat with Ryan, another of Mr O'Doherty's on the books navvies who was as voluble as Declan was taciturn and, mistaking silence for shyness, seemed determined to take Declan under his wing.

"We'll head down to Kildare's," he told him the first weekend. "It's a great night out - once you're inside you'd swear you were back home."

Well, that was true enough if nostalgia was staring across an empty dance floor at a row of girls staring right back at you.

"That Carmel Conley's sweet on me, she is," said Ryan, indicating a pretty brunette with a nod of his head. "And she has a friend. I'll get her to let us walk them home afterwards, just see if I don't."

It was a relief when Fergus, Mr O'Doherty's right-hand man, came over and said the boss would like a word. Declan joined them at a table near the bar and Mr O'Doherty ordered him a chaser.

"I've a job for you," he told him. "Fergus is driving up to Birmingham tomorrow to meet some people and I want you to go with him."

"Alright, Mr O'Doherty."

Mr O'Doherty smiled and turned to Fergus.

"You see," he said, "that's why I like him. No 'Oh, why is that Mr O'Doherty?' or any other tomfool questions. He does what he's asked and..."

He broke off as a man came over from the bar and whispered into his ear, indicating a table by the wall where there was an altercation going on. Looking over Declan realised it was Ryan, having an argument with three fellas who couldn't have been more out-of-place in here if they'd been paid a hundred pounds to try. And Carmel Conley and her friend were sitting with them.

Mr O'Doherty stood up and Declan followed him over to the table. Two of the fellas were English no doubt and looking as if they wished the ground would just swallow them up. But the other one was Irish, Dublin by the sound of him and wasn't he just as cool as a cucumber.

"It's okay Kit," he was saying to one of the English fellas and then he smiled at Ryan. "Like I said, we're not looking for any trouble."

Mr O'Doherty grabbed Ryan by the shoulders, spun him around and leaned forward.

"I want you outside now."

Ryan bristled at this.

"Are we just going to let them come in here and…"

Mr O'Doherty shook him.

"Would you just shut the feck up and…?"

Lost for words, he turned to Declan.

"Get him outside - now!"

Declan nodded and took Ryan by the arm.

"I'm sorry about that, sorr," he heard Mr O'Doherty saying, as he led Ryan away.

Out on the street, Ryan seemed to have calmed down. He took his cigarettes out and lit up.

"All I wanted to do…" he started to say as the door opened and Mr O'Doherty came out with Fergus. He strode over to them and with no preamble punched Ryan right in the stomach.

"Take an arm each and get him in here," said Mr O'Doherty. Ryan was doubled over and so they dragged him on his feet into the alley next to the pub.

"Have you any idea who you were mouthing off to in there?" asked Mr O'Doherty and without waiting for an answer - which would have been a while coming - sank another right hander into Ryan's solar plexus. "Were you trying to get yourself killed and my legs broken, were you?"

He stood back as a stream of vomit poured out of Ryan's mouth and then threw two more punches to each side of Ryan's midriff. Declan heard the ribs crack with each blow.

"Aidan McShane, that's who your man is. Grandson of Conell McShane and nephew of Shaun McShane and so you'll understand that this is a favour that I'm doing you here." Ryan tried to scream as another rib went but he couldn't find the air. "When word of your broken body being found in this alley gets back to them, you might be lucky enough for that to be considered adequate atonement for your disrespect. But don't think you'll ever work on one of my sites again. Or any other site in London, for that matter."

He moved forward, bringing his knee up sharply between Ryan's legs who arched and twisted while still silently gasping for air and then, as Mr O'Doherty nodded at Declan and Fergus to let go of his arms, crumpled down onto the ground. No-one looked behind them as they left the alley.

When Declan returned from Birmingham the next evening, Ryan's things were gone from the flat and another of Mr O'Doherty's men, Ronan, had been installed.

* * *

There were more jobs over the next few months and none of them seemingly of consequence - packages delivered, car journeys made with Fergus. Occasionally, Fergus would let him take the wheel on the motorways to 'get the feel of it' and as Declan grew more confident he was allowed to navigate through the cities they visited too. Declan guessed he was being tested here - would he do what he was told and then keep his mouth shut about it afterwards - and he'd a pretty good idea of what for. He knew he was doing alright when Mr O'Doherty handed him a driving licence, full not provisional and if it were a fake Declan couldn't spot it and doubted anyone else would either.

The final test came during the first week of September. Declan was sure of the date because it had been his Mam's birthday. His sister Bridget said in her last letter that the whole family would be coming to theirs and it would be grand if Declan could telephone. So, on the Thursday evening he'd gone down to the *Black Horse* with Ronan and given Felan behind the bar a ten-shilling note, with Bridget's telephone number scribbled on it. Felan spoke to the operator and after a few seconds he handed the phone to Declan.

"Five minutes only," said Felan, "and I'll be timing you."

Mam cried to hear his voice and perhaps a month or two earlier Declan might have felt the tears welling himself, as the singing and laughter he heard in the background made it feel like there was a lot more than just a few hundred miles between them. But something about him had toughened up since crossing the water, and not only his muscles from the labouring, something inside. So, it wasn't too much of a wrench when Felan pointed to his wristwatch. Declan said, "Goodbye Mam, I'll be seeing you at Christmas," and hung up.

Ronan had got them both a pint in and Declan had barely sat himself down at the table when Mr O'Doherty came over, accompanied by a smallish man who Declan had never seen before. He was dressed as a navvy, like everyone else in there, but Declan saw that his hands were smooth and his nails were clean.

"We've a bit of a job for you lads," said Mr O'Doherty, "so be finishing your drinks and out to the van."

As Mr O'Doherty moved away Declan and Ronan stared at each other and then Ronan shrugged, downed his pint in one and stood up. Declan did the same and followed Ronan outside and into the back of a Transit. It was the same as any other Transit Declan had ever been in, a wooden bench running along each side where eight navvies could squash together and stare at eight more sitting opposite, with the shovels, pickaxes and sledgehammers piled on the floor between them. But this one was empty but for the pair of them.

And two shovels.

The door slammed shut behind them, and a moment later they pulled away. Declan wasn't wearing a watch but he guessed that they drove for about thirty minutes, Ronan betraying his nervousness with an endless stream of chatter. Eventually, he got his baccy out and made a roll up which he offered to share, but Declan shook his head.

Both avoided looking at the shovels.

* * *

The van came to a stop, but they were sitting there for a while before Mr O'Doherty opened one of the back doors.

"Just be a couple of minutes more, lads," he said. He pushed the door closed, but maybe the catch was faulty because as he turned away it opened again. Only a fraction, but sufficient for Declan to see out into the street.

The small man had his back to the van, but Declan recognised who he was talking with right enough. It was the lad from the dance hall, the one who had cost Ryan that dreadful beating. Aidan McShane was who Mr O'Doherty had said he was. They were speaking softly, but Declan could make out every word.

"It's your very own man on the inside," Aidan McShane was saying. "But that's only possible if this gets taken care of." He paused. "I'll handle things this end, clean up his room and such."

Declan still couldn't see the small man's expression, but after a few seconds he gave a brief nod.

Aidan McShane turned and walked back to the house. He stood in the doorway and gestured to someone inside. Two figures came out, carrying a rolled-up rug. Declan recognised one of them as being with Aidan McShane that night at the dance hall. Chris? Keith? No, Kit. Like the cowboy. The other fella he'd never seen before.

They lay the rug down on the pavement by the van. Kit and the other man went back into the house and Aidan

McShane followed, after shaking hands with the small man. Declan leaned forward and pulled the door shut with a soft click.

A few seconds later Mr O'Doherty opened both doors.

"We'll need a bit of a hand here."

They climbed out and walked around to the pavement. Declan took the front of the rug, Ronan the rear, and they manoeuvred it into the Transit. Sticking slightly out of Ronan's end was a shoe-clad foot.

Ronan stared at it and then turned to Mr O'Doherty.

"You know that I'll do anything that you ask me to do, Mr O'Doherty," he said, "but I'm asking you not to ask me to get in there with that."

Mr O'Doherty thought for a few seconds and then nodded.

"Sit yourself up front," he said. He looked at Declan. "And you? Are you alright with this?"

Declan shrugged.

"It's you who'll be the ones breathing in Ronan's evil smoke," he told him. "And at least this one'll be quiet."

The small man gave him a smile.

"He will that," he said.

As the van waited to turn at the end of the road, Declan moved to the back windows and looked out. He saw a street sign lit by moonlight.

Pembridge Villas W2.

With Mr O'Doherty careful to keep to the speed limits it had taken about forty minutes to reach the site they'd been working, a new office block for a warehouse in Kilburn. They were no further along than digging the foundations, a maze of empty trenches waiting for the concrete to be poured.

Declan and Ronan took a shovel each, and Mr O'Doherty directed them to a trench in the centre.

"Go down another four feet," he told them.

With the two of them, it had been quick work. When they finished, they carried the rug over from the van and rolled it into the hole they'd dug. Declan picked up his shovel and began to cover it.

"Just a minute," said the small man. For one crazy second Declan thought he was going to say something over the body, but he was looking around the site. "We'll need a concrete slab or suchlike on top," he pointed down into the trench, "or a dog could have him out by morning."

Well, you learnt something new every day, thought Declan, as he and Ronan carried back three paving stones each from the site store. And at least the next time he found himself putting a body into the ground during the dead of night, he'd have the benefit of past experience as had, he was pretty sure, your man here.

They shovelled two feet of earth into the hole, lay the slabs down, and then put another couple of feet over them until it was flush with the rest of the trench. They patted down the soil with the flat of their shovels and climbed out.

"In the morning we'll pour here first," Mr O'Doherty said, "and it'll be hard by lunchtime."

The small man nodded and reached into his pocket. As Declan threw the shovels into the back of the Transit, the small man passed Ronan a roll of notes, fastened tight with a rubber band.

"Thank you, sorr." Ronan took the notes with a respectful nod, climbed up into the passenger seat and shut the door. Declan looked down at the roll of notes now offered to him and shook his head.

"You're welcome to my time and efforts tonight," he said, "as you'll be welcome to them again, should they ever be needed in the future."

The small man stared at him and then pushed the notes into Declan's shirt pocket. "Well spoken, but I'm sure you've family back home finding themselves more needy and less principled."

He turned to Mr O'Doherty.

"I'll see the lad back," he told him. "And we'll talk later."

Mr O'Doherty nodded and climbed into the Transit.

"It's Declan, isn't it?" asked the small man, as they watched the van drive away. "My name's Liam."

* * *

Declan never returned to the sites, at least not with a shovel in his hands. For a year or two he 'minded' Liam, becoming known as someone with a presence. Stood behind his chair at clandestine peace brokerings with government ministers, impressed only by their shabby unimpressiveness. And as that came to nothing and the battle lines were drawn, Liam had him step back from the front line turmoils of the Troubles and learn how to create the facades needed to finance them. To channel the funds coming from Boston and New York into a commercial infrastructure that the Belfast business community could be persuaded to interact with on more than favourable terms. And to deal with the occasional maverick entrepreneur who had a different slant on reality.

Bridget hadn't been part of the plan, a receptionist at one of the hotels which he'd taken over. They'd seen each other only a few times when she'd told him she was late, but when he'd offered her the airfare to London and the address of a clinic, she'd burst into tears and ran from his office. Her father appeared the next day, quietly insisting that Declan do the right thing. He knew who Declan was alright, knew full well the likely consequences of what he was getting into here, and that had impressed Declan enormously. He could do a lot worse, he'd decided, with both bride and father-in-law.

Patrick had been born long enough after the wedding for any tongue wagging to seem little more than malicious gossip, and it was easy to settle into the role of a successful businessman behind a mock Tudor facade in Antrim. But the business trips away were more often than not to isolated farmhouses south of the border, where implicitness in the dispensation of summary justice was regarded as a guarantor of loyalty. The actual business deals themselves frequently took place in a Libyan wadi.

These were two worlds which Declan kept well apart and he never got sloppy - over the years he was careful not to take anything for granted. And, as the peace process finally started to coalesce and the Good Friday Agreement became a reality, it really began to feel that one day he might actually be able to slip out of this life, like a snake shedding its skin.

But then Patrick had arrived home twenty-four hours early from a business trip, heard his wife in bed with her lover and gone down into the basement to unlock his gun cabinet.

* * *

Go through to the back bar, Liam had told him, it's never busy and we'll be able to talk there. Declan had to ask at Reception for directions. It was at the end of a long, unmarked passageway. Liam hadn't arrived yet. There was another man sitting at a table by an open fireplace and speaking into a mobile phone.

He broke off as Liam entered the room.

Declan gave him an affable nod and as the man resumed his conversation, he walked over to the bar and pressed a bell which had a laminated *'Please ring for service'* card attached.

A barman appeared almost immediately, and Declan asked for a half of Guinness - it would be a long night and best to start off slowly. There was an evening newspaper laying on the bar, Declan gestured toward it as the barman poured his drink.

"Sure," said the barman, taking his money. Declan put the newspaper under his arm, told the barman to keep the change, and took his drink over to a table adjacent to the door. From where he could see anyone entering the room, but they'd have to turn a hundred and eighty degrees to see him.

Old habits.

The other man in the bar was still speaking into his phone, softly enough to be considered polite in company but as inevitably irritating as all one-sided conversations are.

"No, not yet," he was saying, "but it's still early."

He paused, whether because the person on the end of the line – could you still say *line* thought Declan, now everything was all cell phone waves and whatnot – was speaking or just for effect.

"You know, the thing I don't get," the man said after a while, "is why wait until now? To do something about it, I mean?"

He paused again.

"Because Spike mentioned that one of the first things he discovered when he started checking Carin out, was that Belinda Carlisle died two years ago - which means that answerphone recording, of Carin asking about her scans, has to be at least three years old. Not that it makes any difference, I'm just curious."

He paused again and then frowned. Declan was conscious of the man turning his head in his direction.

And felt the hair on the back of his neck stand up.

"Yeah, there is, but it's not…" He hesitated and there was uncertainty in his voice.

"What's going on, Kit?"

And all the years just tumbled away.

Declan's first instinct was to rise, but his body refused to move, as if it knew better than his mind what a futile gesture that would be.

'And Death shall come like a thief in the night'.

The priests of Declan's childhood could evoke any number of spectres to gnaw at the soul of a young boy, but of all the grotesques conjured from sin and redemption in the shadows of the small church where he'd served as an altar boy, this one, a skeletal figure cowled in a hooded robe with bony fingers pushing at a half-opened door where a child lay sleeping on a bed, had found a grip on something at the very core of his being.

But it had been so long now since he'd believed death would arrive in his sleep, even longer than his last confession. And whether that final curtain would fall to an avenging angel or a zero-sum cold equation, the only real mystery remaining was would he see it coming? A few ounces of *plastique* wired to a car's ignition and he'd be away before he knew anything about it. But he'd always doubted he'd be that lucky - anyone coming for Declan McKelvey would most likely have points to labour.

And now here it was.

He knew before turning his head that the barman would be holding a gun on him and Jesus, it was a huge fucking thing, a forty-five revolver with a long suppressor screwed onto the barrel, the whole bloody contraption the length again of his forearm.

"Keep still," said the barman softly, "and let's have those hands where I can see them."

The fella at the other table was now standing, staring wildly as he turned his head from the barman to the phone in his hand and then uncomprehendingly at Declan.

His mistake, thought Declan, had been thinking he was the only piece in play here. That and the certainty he was too valuable to the CIA for the Brits to be double dealing. Because the only thing which made any sense was that the information he'd traded them was information no-one could ever know about. No-one at all.

So they'd sold him out to Liam and - given that the expression on the other fella's face showed he hadn't a clue what was happening here - were putting a tableau together to somehow tidy a mutual mess. Because that's how things are managed, in a world of deceit constructed from plausible narratives.

The barman moved his weapon onto the other man.

"Harry Slater says," he told him softly, "to say hello to Chas."

The two shots barely made a sound. That silencer was really good, thought Declan. It had to be military issue. And the shooter knew what he was about - the first to the fella's heart put him back down in the chair and the second in the centre of his forehead threw a red mist across half the room.

Declan couldn't believe how calm he felt as the gunman turned the revolver back on him. There'll be no pain, he told himself, there'd only be pain coming back from this and that wasn't a journey he'd be making.

"It's alright," he nodded to the gunman, raising his hands from the table in a gesture of capitulation. "But I'd take it as a kindness if you'd spare my family a closed casket."

He didn't hear the shot, only a sense he'd been slammed in the chest with a sledgehammer. And he was right, there was no pain, just an incredible weight bearing down on him, so heavy he knew he would never again rise up and then only darkness and silence.

10. September 1970

Aidan

It was two days after Emma's release that Paul stuck his head around my studio door and said softly, "He's back".

"Where is he?" I asked.

"He made a coffee and then went up to his room."

"Any sign that he knows?"

"We chatted a few minutes about nothing in particular." Paul gave a shrug. "If he does, then he's playing it bloody cool."

"Okay," I said, "let's pay a visit."

Jake's door was slightly ajar as we reached the second landing. With his foot Paul pushed it far enough open to reveal him sitting on the bed, turned away from us as he emptied dirty washing from a holdall into a laundry bag. I motioned for Paul to stay out of sight and he moved over to one side. I gave a cursory knock and stepped inside.

"Hello there," I said. "You're back?"

"Yeah," he said, not quite rolling his eyes. "Obviously."

"Have a good time?"

"Sure," he nodded. "Bit of a hassle getting off the island after it finished, and we spent most of yesterday queueing for a train, but it was worth it."

"Carin's back too?"

"No." A shake of his head. "She's gone to Holland, to see her folks before term starts."

Well, there was a convenience.

"Is there something I can do for you?" he asked, as I continued to stare at him.

"I was hoping for a bit of a chat," I said. "Something's come up."

He rose from the bed and lifted the laundry bag from the floor.

"Afraid it'll have to wait," he said, moving towards the door. "I need to get down the laundrette and I've a couple of phone calls to make."

"Oh," I said, turning towards him as he moved past me into the doorway, "I think we can hang fire on that for a while."

Before he had a chance to respond to this, Paul appeared in front of him. Startled, Jake took a step backwards, but neither far nor fast enough to avoid Paul's solid right hook to the jaw.

He went down like a sack of potatoes. Glancing around to make sure there were no witnesses, I lifted him by the arms and half carried, half dragged him in through the doorway. After closing the door behind us, Paul took a sturdy looking wooden chair from where it had been pushed under a table serving as a desk and carefully placed it squarely in the centre of the room.

I dropped Jake down onto the chair and held him in place as Paul rummaged around in the laundry bag. Pulling out a cotton T-shirt, he ripped it into strips, binding Jake's wrists and elbows to the arms of the chair, his knees and ankles to the legs. He pulled the belt from a pair of jeans, looped it around Jake's neck and fastened it to the back of the chair, holding him upright and immobile. After he'd checked the knots, he reached down into the bag again and took out a pair of underpants. Bunching them up in one hand, he pinched Jake's nose with the fingers of the other. As Jake's mouth opened gasping for air, he forced the underwear into it. Then taking a sweatshirt out from the bag, he knotted the sleeves together at the top and pulled it down over Jake's head, an effective hood.

Stepping back from the chair, we stared at each other before Paul indicated the door with a nod of his head.

"Go and phone Emma," he said.

* * *

Judging by the struggles – and muffled sounds from under the hood - Jake had been awake for half an hour or so before Kit and Emma arrived. Paul waited for them downstairs, explaining how we intended to handle this and also that we weren't likely to be interrupted by Carin returning.

When everyone was in the room, Paul removed the hood. Jake was breathing heavily, twisting his head around more in anger than fear until he caught sight of Emma - for a second he couldn't control his surprise at seeing her there. He began trying to wrench himself free again, but his agitation now owed as much to confusion as rage.

Emma grimaced.

"Is this really necessary?" she asked.

"He packed *plastique* into empty takeaway boxes with Anna and Dave's fingerprints on them, planted them in their shed and then tipped off Special Branch." Kit was speaking softly but there was nothing casual about the expression that was now holding Jake's full attention. "So I'd say that 'necessary' covers everything up to and including slicing off his balls with a rusty razor."

Jake began frantically shaking his head from side to side and trying to speak, but then froze as Paul removed a pair of pliers from his pocket and squatted down on the floor in front of him.

"Everyone's a bit upset," he said, "as you might imagine. But don't worry," a reassuring smile as he rested a hand on Jake's shoulder, "this isn't anything you shouldn't be able to talk your way out of." He gave a shrug. "Probably."

"That's right," said Kit. "Because we know quite a lot about you. About your father, what you've been up to with Special Branch. And so, what we're going to do is stash you away in a cellar for a few weeks, where you can't do anymore damage. Then, we're going to use what you tell us to completely screw over the prosecution's case."

"What you have to bear in mind," Paul told him, "is that

there are things we know and things that we don't know, but you can't really be sure which is which. And we're going to be asking you questions about both. If you lie to us about something which we know is true, we're not only going to break a finger when that happens," he lifted the pliers and snapped them shut, "we're also going to break a finger - or toe if we run out of them - for every other question you answered that we didn't know the answer to, on the assumption you've lied about those as well."

"And you really don't want to know where we'll be going if we run out of toes," said Kit.

I reached into my jacket, took out and unfolded his father's newspaper obituary and held it out at arm's length for him to read.

"Sorry for your loss," said Kit dryly.

"So don't think you can count on your friends in Special Branch anymore," I told him as he stared at it wild-eyed. "You've already been gone long enough for that backup contact your father gave you the details of - DS Brian Maddox - to have pretty much given up on you."

"You weren't at the funeral," said Kit. "There're bombs going off all over London and just zilch from you. So, they figure you've gone rogue - shit, you wouldn't be the first undercover cop to get turned around." Kit shrugged. "The head gets really screwed after a while - between all those drugs you need to be doing to keep your cover up and a constant stream of spaced out chicks, up for stuff your straight, suburban girlfriends couldn't even *imagine*."

Jake was shaking his head wildly.

"I'm going to take the gag out now," Paul told him. "If you yell or make any kind of fuss at all, I'll knock you cold, right? And we'll start all over again when you come to."

Jake stared at him and then nodded.

"You only speak to answer a question," said Paul. "Got that?"

Jake gave another nod and Paul pulled the gag free of his

mouth.

"Look," said Jake, "you've got completely the wrong end..."

He broke off as Paul raised a finger to his lips and with his other hand snapped the pliers shut.

"Maybe," he told Jake, "it might be an idea to pop a few fingers from the off. Help convince you that we mean exactly what we say."

Jake shook his head almost frantically.

"Okay," said Kit. "We can start getting into detail in a while - what you've said about who - but first I want to talk about Chas Slater."

I turned to Kit, trying to conceal my surprise - this wasn't something he'd brought up when we were running through how to play this.

"You see," continued Kit, "when Frieda and I got to Camden Town, Chas Slater was *waiting* there. At first I assumed that he'd found out where I lived and had been following me but - and God knows how many times I've played that scene over in my head since then - I'm certain now that his car was already parked in that street when we arrived."

We were all staring at Kit now.

"Which really begs the question of how he knew I'd be there." He paused. "And that's really down to that mysterious phone call to Frieda the night before - telling her where Emma was staying but not the address. Pretty much guaranteeing I'd be the one taking her over there. And if Chas Slater also got a whisper of where I'd be, then you'd have the prospect of him going full blown psycho in front of a dozen armed cops waiting to raid the place - because they'd be waiting until Frieda went into the house to scoop her up along with the others. All of which absolutely reeks of classic Old Bill fit up, doesn't it?"

Every eye in the room was on Jake, who remained silent.

"Except that wasn't how things went down, was it?" Kit

sighed. "So let's start there, shall we?" He looked Jake directly in the eyes. "Was it you who made that phone call to Frieda?"

Jake hesitated.

"Yes," he said slowly. "But you've got it all totally..."

"My mother's dead because of you," screamed Emma, lunging forward. "You've destroyed my family."

Before anyone could stop her, she was pounding him around the head with her fists.

Paul and Kit took an arm each and pulled her away before stopping to stare - Jake was now slumped sideways in the chair with blood streaming down his face and neck. Emma slowly unclenched her fist and a brass figurine of Buddha, that she must have snatched up from the desk, fell to the floor.

A single blow would probably have been enough. Its design was the classic one of palms and fingers pressed together above the head, which formed a more than effective bradawl...

I let out my breath. The Jake problem had either been solved or just become infinitely more complicated.

Kit

Emma and I had been in my room for about ten minutes when there was a perfunctory knock at the door and Aidan stepped inside. We both looked up at him and he shook his head - Emma sobbed and turned away.

I gave her hand a squeeze.

"Would you come upstairs?" Aidan said to me. "We need to talk."

"Will you be okay?" I asked Emma, and she nodded.

I followed Aidan back up to Jake's room. I'd expected to find him still tied to the chair, but it was empty. I had to look around the room twice before I realised that the large rug which covered most of the floor was now rolled up against the far wall.

For some reason, I found the sight of that more unsettling than the actual body.

Aidan took a deep breath.

"This isn't anything we can't fix," he said, "but you're going to have to become Christopher Franklyn for a lot longer than just a few weeks."

* * *

"The first thing," said Aidan, "is to get Emma out of the country. It was a good idea when she only had the trumped-up Camden Town charges against her, but it's bloody essential now."

"I'm not sure she'll go for that," I told him.

"How long do you think she'd stand up to any sustained questioning about what happened here?" asked Paul gently, and I took his point. I also realised - although I never expected either of them to make it an issue - that while Emma's actions might have been her own, the rolled-up carpet on the other side of the room had made all of us accessories after the fact.

"It can never be known Christopher Franklyn has disappeared," said Aidan, as if reading my mind.

"And that actually is going to be the easiest part of all this," said Paul. "The only people interested in him anymore are the police and they've no reason to be concerned while you're around."

"What about Carin?" I asked.

"She comes back to find him gone." Aidan shrugged. "He had his fun for a while and now he's run out on her. Who'd have guessed it, what a bastard, no surprise."

"And if he's told her something?"

"Oh right, you mean like one night when they were in the sack together, he thought it would really turn her on if he whispered into her ear that he was a nark for Special Branch?"

"For fuck's sake, Aidan! He could have said anything."

"And I'm sure that if she's overly concerned by his absence, you'd be more than up to the task of consoling her."

I gestured at the rolled-up carpet.

"And what about that?"

Aidan turned to look at it and then back to me.

"It will be no surprise for you to learn that I've connections capable of... *resolving* a situation such as this." He hesitated. "And also arranging a safe haven for a while in say New York or Boston - but it would come at a price."

"There's the money from Jake's father's house," I reminded him.

"The thing is," said Aidan, "is that it would be less of a financial matter and more of a *quid pro quo*."

"I'm not sure I understand," I said, although I was pretty sure I did.

"A deep cover contact within the Metropolitan Police Special Branch would be an offer difficult to resist."

I tried to order my thoughts.

"So, what you're suggesting is that I not only carry on pretending to be a murdered police informant, but simultaneously go undercover for the bloody IRA."

"Look," said Paul, exchanging a glance with Aidan which suggested this was ground they'd gone over while I'd been downstairs, "it's not as if these are roles you'd have to keep up over long periods and under close scrutiny." Aidan was nodding. "You - or rather 'Jake' - were under such deep cover with Special Branch that nobody even knew what he looked like. It wouldn't be unreasonable to insist that arrangement continues." He shrugged. "You could act equally paranoid with the Irish, in fact they might find it suspicious if you weren't. Tell them the only contact you'll agree to is Aidan, you're already sharing a house with him."

"There'll always be some risk to it," said Aidan, "but what it comes down to is how much of a risk Emma is worth."

I found myself slowly nodding.

"But whatever we need to do," said Paul, "needs doing quickly."

"I'll go and make a phone call," said Aidan. "And see if we can get this," he nodded at the carpet, "out of here tonight."

Claudia

"A scholarship?"

Emma nodded her head.

"Boston University," she said. "A PhD in Political Science."

"That's brilliant," I told her. "When do you start?"

"Term begins next week."

"Next week!!?"

She nodded again. For such exciting news, she didn't seem exactly overwhelmed.

"Where are you staying?"

"On campus - it's all been sorted out as part of the scholarship."

"Right." I hesitated. "So, you'll be leaving straightaway?"

"This afternoon." Putting her cup down, she stood up. "I've already packed. But could I ask you a favour?"

"Of course."

She took an envelope out of her bag.

"Would you give this to Kit?"

"He does know you're going away?"

I took it from her.

"Yes, of course." She shrugged and then gave a nod toward the envelope. "It's that… There were some things I wanted to say to him. And for him to have a chance to think about, before needing to respond."

"Alright," I said.

"Would you wait until after I've left?" she asked, before

quickly adding, "And hand it to him yourself? Don't just leave it for him. If that's okay?"

"I'll go over to Pembridge Villas in the morning," I told her and hesitated. "When will we see you again? Are you coming home for Christmas?"

"I'm not sure," shaking her head. "It would be the first one without mum and I don't know if I'm ready for that yet."

"I understand." I had no wish to pry into whatever her current family circumstances might be.

"You could always come over and visit," she smiled. "These days, flying to America isn't the big deal it used to be."

"Maybe I will," I said, hoping that my smile didn't seem as forced as hers did.

* * *

There was no answer to my knock at Kit's door, and so I made my way down to the basement to check that he wasn't in Aidan's studio. But that was also locked and so I decided to go up to the kitchen and have a coffee, while I thought about what to do next.

The boyfriend of one of the girls renting an attic room was in there, making a sandwich. When I asked if Kit was around, he shook his head.

"Haven't seen him today," he told me.

Richard, I remembered, was his name.

"What about Aidan?"

Another shake of the head.

"I heard he was visiting family."

"Any idea how long he'll be away for?"

"Probably a while," he said, as the kettle began to whistle. "He's gone to Boston. The one in the States. Would you like a coffee?"

Before I could answer, the kitchen door opened and there stood Carin.

"Where's Andrew," she asked, "and why are someone else's things in his room?"

* * *

"Moved where?"

She was staring at me very disconcertingly.

"I've no idea," I told her. "When I was around here last week, Kit and Aidan were cleaning up his room. They said they were getting it ready to let out again because he'd done a runner."

I refrained from adding *'And no surprise there'*.

"What is a runner?"

"To leave without telling anyone what you're doing or where you're going. And usually owing rent."

"Andrew owed rent?"

I wasn't sure if he did or not, but I gave a dismissive shrug.

"We assumed you knew about it," I said. "That he'd have let you know where he'd..."

"I'm going to have a baby," she broke in. "I'm pregnant."

We stared at each other, equally speechless with the realisation now running through both our minds.

"The bastard," I said softly, and then she burst into tears.

As I put my arm around her shoulder and guided her down onto a chair, I realised that Richard had been looking on wide eyed and wordless as our little drama unfurled. With a sharp nod of my head, I indicated the door. He needed little encouragement, one last look before he bolted and the door clicked shut behind him.

"How long is it since you've seen him?" I asked.

"When we returned from the festival," she said, reaching into her bag for a tissue. "He came with me to Heathrow for my flight home." She dabbed at her eyes. "Yesterday, he was supposed to meet me at the airport. I stayed a full hour in case he had been delayed but eventually gave up and returned to the Halls of Residence, expecting for there to be word from him waiting for me, but there was nothing."

"You've asked around? All the other girls on your floor? None of them have taken a message?"

"I asked everyone," she said, and began sobbing again. "Nothing."

The door opened and Kit walked in. We must have made a strange tableau, my arm still around Carin's shoulders and her face streaked with tears. Hearing the door open she looked up to see him standing in the doorway, stared for a second and then burst into tears again, turning her head and burying it against me as if the sight of him were too much to bear.

As he stood there, his expression flicking between bewilderment and concern, I nodded with my head to the chair on the other side of her. Slowly, he moved around the table and sat down.

"What's happened?" he asked softly.

Still pressed against me, she shook her head, not turning to face him.

"It's Jake," I said.

"Jake?" he asked, giving me a strange look.

"Yes - have you any idea where he is?"

"No." Kit shrugged. "He cleared his room out and disappeared a week ago." He gave a shrug. "I'm the last person he'd tell where he was going."

"Well, he won't get away with it." Carin lifted her head. "I'll go to the police, I'll make them find him."

"*What!!?*" Kit shook his head in puzzlement rather than denial. "Why would you want to do that?"

"Because I am pregnant," she said, straightening up and turning to stare at him. "And now he has disappeared. Because that's what men do, right? They have their fun and then they walk away."

"Oh Carin." Kit reached down and took her hand.

"But I won't let him get away with it," she repeated. "I'll make the police find him."

"The police won't get involved over something like this," said Kit carefully. "He may be an arsehole, but what he's done isn't a crime."

"Well, I'll report him as a missing person." Carin was shaking her head. "They'll have to do something about that if I tell them I'm worried. Or if not, I'll hire private detectives to find him."

"Carin," I said quietly, "if he's such a bastard, would you really want him back? Think yourself lucky that you found out..."

"Lucky! You think I am fucking *lucky!!?*"

She almost tore my arm from around her shoulders and began to rise from her chair.

"No, God, sorry, it's just an expression." I took her hand and gently pulled her back down. "What I meant was, is this someone you really want to spend the rest of your life with?"

"Perhaps not." She gave a shrug. "But my baby will have a father, or at least will know who that father is."

"Look, Carin," trying to pick my words carefully, "this isn't something you definitely have to go through with, right? Because whatever happens, things will not be easy for you."

"I know," she said nodding and for a second I thought she was about to start crying again. Then she pulled herself together. "But that I couldn't do. To take the life of a child - how would I live with myself?"

Seemingly having composed herself, she let go of Kit's hand and rose from the chair.

"If you want to go to the police, then I'll come with you," I told her. "I do think Kit's right, I can't see them doing anything other than filing a report, but they might take you more seriously if there's two of us."

"Shouldn't we try to find him first?" Kit reached out and took her hand again. "Because we're jumping to all kinds of conclusions here, aren't we - who knows what's happened?" He stared at her. "Maybe some emergency came up - did he ever talk about his family?"

She shook her head.

"Not really. Only that his mother died five years ago,

and that he has a complicated relationship with his father."

"No brothers or sisters?" I asked.

She shook her head.

"No, he's an only child."

Kit slowly nodded.

"I'll go with you," he said.

Carin stared at him uncomprehendingly.

"If it wasn't for me, this never would have happened." He reached out and put his arm around her shoulders. "You'd never have come here, never have met him, never gotten into this mess."

Jesus, Kit!!! I felt like screaming at him. *There's a time and place for everything, but this isn't helping - do you know nothing about women? This girl's still in love with you, for heaven's sake!*

Carin's lip started to tremble again.

Kit looked over at me.

"It's okay - I'll take care of her."

"Kit..." I began hesitantly, but over her shoulder he fixed his eyes on mine and gave me a smile, before nodding towards the door.

I stood up, hoping that for once he knew what he was doing.

"Call me," I said, "if you need anything. Anything at all."

"Thanks, Claudia."

Uncertain as I was about leaving the two of them together like that, stepping out of the room brought an enormous sense of relief - this really wasn't something that I wanted to be caught in the middle of.

And I was halfway to the tube station before I realised that Emma's letter was still in my bag.

Aidan

I don't recall whether it was a comedian or a philosopher - and were ever two professions less mutually exclusive - who said that if you want to hear God's laughter then start making plans. But they'd have felt pretty smug with themselves around Pembridge Villas that first week of September.

Liam was in my studio, finalising the arrangements for Emma's journey to Boston and waiting for Kit - who'd had a meeting with his Special Branch handler that morning - eager to learn how it had gone.

But when Kit arrived, he was grim faced.

"They want me to do it again," he told us. "Plant evidence."

"On who?" I asked.

He stared at me.

"On you," he said. "The thinking behind it is to get leverage on your family."

Liam slowly nodded.

"It would make sense for them to do that while they have such a good opportunity," he said to me, and turned back to Kit. "How and when is this supposed to happen?"

"As soon as possible - they've asked me for ideas on how to create a scenario that ties both you and Emma together. It really pisses them off that she's out."

"Jesus!" I couldn't believe this.

"You need to go," said Kit. "Both of you - not at the end of the week, today. Because who knows what else they might come up with in the meantime, that sidesteps me. They need to preserve my cover above anything else so if they find an opportunity to get the pair of you inside, with no connection to me, they'll jump at it."

"Kit's right," said Liam. "This has to happen straightaway."

"But what about you?" I said to Kit. "I mean, if we're on the subject of preserving cover you don't think they'll find this a tad suspicious - them asking you to fit me up in the morning and here's me falling off the face of the earth the very same evening."

"Remember when I talked them into dropping the

charges against Emma?" said Kit. "I told them I'd heard that she and her boyfriend were planning to disappear if she got out." He shrugged. "I never told them who that boyfriend was."

Liam gave a smile.

"That would work," he said, and stood up. "You should start to pack," he told me and then turned to Kit. "Emma needs to know that she'll be leaving tonight. I've fresh arrangements to make, but I'll be back in a few hours. Meanwhile, it would be best if you're not seen with either of them."

Kit nodded, and then Liam took him by the arm and led him across the room. Their conversation was too low for me to catch, but I saw Liam take an envelope from his inside jacket pocket and hand it to Kit.

* * *

The original plan for Emma had been a plane ticket to Boston from Heathrow on an Irish passport. But that evening we left London in the windowless back of a battered old Transit van, heading the opposite direction into Essex. As per Liam's instructions, there'd been no farewell meeting between Kit and Emma. She was upset, but she understood.

We arrived at Felixstowe just after midnight. The container ship was due to sail on the first tide. The Captain was Irish and cautiously genial. I guessed he didn't know exactly what he had in the way of supercargo and I daresay he didn't want to. He showed us to a cabin with two bunks and a compact shower room with a lavatory.

"Most of the crew are Asian," he told us before leaving, "and don't speak English but all the same, best to be cautious around them." He gave a shrug. "Other than at mealtimes, you'll be left to your own devices."

At eight o'clock the next morning we slipped out into the English Channel and headed south. I was standing on deck as we passed the white cliffs of Dover and, even as an Irishman, I felt a poignancy as I watched them slowly dissolve into the horizon, a real sense that here was something gone for good.

"Emotive, aren't they?" said a quiet voice.

I turned to see Emma alongside me.

"I don't imagine either of us has much by way of British patriotism," she continued, "but it hurts watching them go."

I nodded.

"I've asked Kit to come and join me in Boston," she said, just as quietly. "When he's got things straightened out."

I nodded again, thinking that by articulating her thoughts she was simply reassuring herself in the face of an uncertain future.

It wasn't until the middle of the night, when she slipped into my bed and said, *'I can't bear to be alone – please, hold me'*, that I realised what she'd been doing was making sure that there'd be no misconceptions over what was happening here.

11. Sandy Beaumont

"I think we've given them long enough," said the Director General, picking up a thin folder from his desk, "don't you?"

Sandy nodded and placed his cup down onto the saucer. Bone china, he noted and wondered if things had changed so little since he'd been the one on the other side of this desk or whether they were simply trying to make him feel more at home - his visits to Thames House these days were a rarity.

He rose and followed the DG out of his office and along the corridor to the conference room. The oval table that was the centrepiece of the room could sit over a dozen people, but at the moment was occupied by only two. The editor of one of the nation's largest circulation Sunday newspapers and a well-known TV 'investigative journalist' - muckraker was the term in Sandy's day - and to Sandy's satisfaction he saw that neither of them looked happy.

On the table was a school exercise book with a flimsy cardboard cover, once green but now faded with age. And also a leather-bound desk diary, its corners trimmed with chrome edging which, while leaving it better preserved than the schoolbook, suggested a similar age. Thin strips of different coloured plastic had been inserted at intervals in the exercise book and were matched by strips of corresponding colour in the desk diary.

Both men looked up as Sandy and the DG entered the room.

"You've examined them?" asked the DG. The editor nodded. The journalist turned his head away and adopted a blank expression with which to stare at the wall.

The DG laid the folder on the table and opened it to reveal a single typewritten sheet of paper.

"If we take the most serious allegations," he said, "the occasions when - in effect - special measures were supposedly employed-"

"Special measures!" The journalist turned back to him derisively. "Torture is what you mean."

The DG seemed to ignore him.

"You will have seen," he continued, "through references yellow and blue that the officer accused had been transferred from Latchmere House two months before the supposed author of this journal arrived there. Also, a week after these incidents were alleged to have taken place, he was admitted to hospital suffering from pneumonia. Whilst there he was given a full medical examination and none of the injuries one would expect to be present - if there were any truth in these accusations - were recorded."

"So you say." The journalist indicated the desk diary with a dismissive gesture. "How can we be sure that's not a fake?"

"Well, one of them certainly is," said Sandy softly, "and I know which it is, because I kept this log." He tapped the leather-bound volume with his fingers. "And I'm happy to answer any questions that you might have about it."

The journalist seemed about to speak, but the DG silenced him with a raised hand.

"If I may - just for a moment."

He walked over to a cupboard on the far wall and slid back a panel. Half a dozen hard backed books had been stacked lengthwise and the DG carried them over to the table. Lifting the top one, he opened it to a page marked with a yellow post-it note.

"There," he said, indicating a paragraph halfway down the right-hand page. "Presumably the origin of the error in your so-called record."

"And this is?" asked the editor.

"An unauthorised history of Latchmere House," the DG told him, "as are these." He indicated the other volumes. "We've had our people go through them with reference to the diary – and there's nothing in it that couldn't have been found in these published works. Including," he raised his hand as the reporter seemed about to interrupt, "the reproduction of some not insignificant errors."

"You say you have the medical records?" asked the editor slowly.

The DG nodded.

"And we can examine them?"

"They may not be reproduced or allowed to leave the building. If you accept that criteria, I'll allow examination by a suitably qualified independent expert witness."

Both men were silent.

"I'm afraid that you've been had, gentleman." The DG picked up the exercise book and turned it over to reveal that on the back cover were printed the multiplication tables.

"Six times seven is forty-two," he said softly, "and I'd imagine this is the only page on which you'd find even a grain of truth."

* * *

Back in the DG's office, Sandy accepted the glass of sherry. Usually, he wasn't one to imbibe before lunch but sherry hardly counted.

"Any idea where the damn thing came from?" he asked. His role had been to simply provide provenance and while he felt he'd accomplished that admirably, he knew better than most people it didn't warrant an explanation. Still, his curiosity would seem natural enough, he supposed.

The DG gave a slight shrug.

"We're not sure - did it ring any bells with you?"

"I meant who passed it on to Grub Street." Sandy knew exactly who the author of the manuscript they'd just so thoroughly discredited was because he'd overseen the latter's interrogations himself, after being given authorisation for special measures.

"It's the kind of thing that could sit in someone's kitchen drawer for decades." The DG shook his head. "Dare say it did, was probably only unearthed as part of the damned fellow's effects."

"Yes, most likely family - the fact it's in German." Sandy hesitated. "It might be an idea to check for any other surprises likely from that source."

"Possibly."

"That reporter has the air of a man with his teeth into something," suggested Sandy. "Eventually he will come across someone willing to talk… The closer one draws to one's demise, the greater becomes the need to unburden oneself."

"But not you, eh, Sandy?" smiled the DG.

"No, not me." Sandy told him. "But only because some of us wouldn't know where to start."

They sat in silence for a while. Eventually Sandy placed his glass down on the desk and made as if to rise.

"If you have a minute," said the DG, and Sandy sank back into his chair. "We're winding down an operation and as you were here, we were wondering if you'd give us your take on it?"

"My take?"

The DG nodded.

"One or two voices," he said carefully, "believe that we're missing something. I've suggested that you may be able to offer some unique insight."

"Of course," said Sandy. "I'd be happy to help in any way I could."

The DG smiled and rose from his desk.

"Please bear with me," he said. "I'll only be two ticks."

* * *

Sandy Beaumont had an ear for the truth.

Even as a schoolboy he'd instinctively known when a classmate was trying to put one over or a master's explanations or motives harboured an undercurrent. At that age he'd simply put it down to being good with his hunches, but as a young Lieutenant in 1941 he'd proved skilful enough interrogating captured POWs in the North Africa campaign for his talents to become the subject of an exchange of signals between his Commanding Officer and Military Intelligence in London.

He was flown home via Lisbon and on arrival immediately sent to the Royal Victoria Patriotic School in Wandsworth, whose premises had been requisitioned as a clearing centre for refugees and aliens from friendly countries. The London Reception Centre - more informally referred to as Trinity Road - also housed an interrogation unit, which was to be Sandy's new billet.

The purpose of the Centre was threefold, to glean any useful military information that civilian refugees might - knowingly or not - have acquired, to assess the suitability of others to be returned to their countries of origin as Allied operatives, and to identify enemy agents using refugee status as a subterfuge to enter the country.

It would be no understatement to say that the latter was probably the most successful intelligence operation ever mounted by a government agency in the history of espionage. A post-war investigation of German military records showed that 115 enemy agents had attempted infiltration into England using this method, and all but one had been identified as such by MI5. Each was offered a choice - trial and execution or to become double agents, feeding false information back to the Abwehr, the German Secret Service. In later years, Sandy often felt aggrieved that whilst the codebreakers at Bletchley Park - although quite rightly - received plaudits for their work which had changed the course of the war, the directions those changes took were down to the misinformation fed to German High Command by MI5.

After a few months at Trinity Road, Sandy was transferred to Latchmere House in Richmond, an interrogation and detention centre for both captured enemy spies and civilian detainees, the latter mostly members of the British Union of Fascists. Unlike the rather more infamous London Cage, a conurbation of houses in a salubrious part of London's Knightsbridge where a more brutal approach to the gleaning of intelligence was taken, Latchmere House - or Camp 020 as it was referred to in internal communications - employed a stealthier but no less determined methodology.

* * *

Camp 020 served two roles during its existence - initially to extract information from enemy combatants to further the Allied war effort and secondly to gather evidence, after the Axis capitulation, for war crime prosecutions. It was spectacularly successful at both, but only a few were aware of the methods used and how they were later developed during the Cold War.

Bletchley Park may have long since received its deserved recognition, but the few who knew about Camp 020 held their silence. Prisoners who'd been returned to Germany still lived under the shadow of the Allied Powers Act, and it was made clear to them that should they feel the need to share their experiences it would not only be themselves facing re-internment without due process of law, but also their families and loved ones.

Those who'd been on the other side of the wire had their own reasons for remaining silent. What may have seemed justifiable at the time - with Europe ablaze and the Nazis assembling an invasion fleet only twenty miles away across the Channel - can take on a different slant decades later. Particularly in a *weltanschauung* in which the inevitability of an Allied victory was now taken for granted.

The prisoner who'd penned the memoir which they'd just so thoroughly discredited, Sandy remembered clearly. He'd been an Obersturmführer in a Wehrmacht unit stationed in Normandy immediately after D-Day and had found his way to Camp 020 via the Commando Order.

The Commando Order was a directive personally issued by Hitler, after a British commando force - together with Norwegian resistance fighters - had sabotaged the Heavy Water Plant at Bergen in Norway, effectively terminating Germany's atomic bomb project. The directive stated that any commandos taken prisoner should be immediately executed or, if believed to be in possession of useful intelligence, sent to a concentration camp. The order was a clear and blatant breach of the Geneva Convention, but it put front line Commanding Officers in an invidious position - either disobey a direct order from the Fuehrer or commit a war crime. The defence of *'I was only obeying orders'* became a familiar one at military tribunals after the war, but international law states that only lawful commands must be obeyed and the Allies were unswerving in applying that judgement.

Prisoners suspected of executing British servicemen were sent to the London Cage for interrogation. Mostly these were men not long on guile or deceit and their short, brutish experiences there were usually enough to establish guilt or innocence. But occasionally one would be marked out as 'Special Interest' and transferred to Camp 020.

That term was carefully chosen, if queried at a later date it could imply that the prisoner was suspected of withholding information. But closer scrutiny of the selection list would have revealed interesting common traits - they were fit, healthy, of average to high intelligence and possessed a powerful sense of patriotism.

They were guinea pigs.

By 1944 the interrogators at Camp 020 knew that in a matter of months they would be receiving a stream of high-ranking Nazi officials, prior to a war crimes tribunal. The techniques which they developed - along with their American OSS colleagues at their own establishment in Dorset - had proven effective but were still in their infancy. And more to the point, while it may be expedient to break a man in body and spirit to extract information that would avert an impending military disaster, those same techniques could not be employed if you subsequently had to present him as a competent and credible figure in a courtroom.

They needed to understand how different psychological traits responded to different pressures - drugs, humiliation, deprivation, degradation - and what permutations of these measures could be applied to maximum effect in breaking a man. And then how to put him back together again, or at least create a plausible facsimile of what he had once been.

Inevitably there were casualties.

The Obersturmführer was anticipated to be more resilient than most, recalled Sandy, and so from his arrival was kept chained and naked in his cell, with sporadic recordings of extreme interrogation sessions as a background soundscape. They'd learnt that allowing a subject to mentally prepare for one form of abuse and then submitting him to another could prove highly effective. After a week of this they'd let the Turk have him for an hour or two, first lacing his food with small doses of benzedrine and hashish which, combined with the Turk's expert manipulations, always brought matters to an inevitable conclusion - the body's betrayal while being treated as a vassal the ultimate humiliation.

And then stronger drugs, hallucinogens that blurred the sensations of pleasure and pain together in scenarios beyond bizarre and were combined with relentless suggestion and questioning. All as white-coated technicians scribbled on clipboards, clicked stop watches, modified dosages...

After a month, the Obersturmführer would have told them not just what they wanted to hear - that's what the Cage was for - but everything that he needed for absolution. And whatever other secrets he may have harboured were small beer indeed compared to that and would come tumbling out piecemeal.

No real chance of putting him back together, though.

Stage two of the project, although promising, was at that point still embryonic. So, they'd marked his file 'Combat Stress' and put him back in the system, via Kempton Park internment camp, to wait out the war as a POW.

Sandy doubted that until this week the man had crossed his mind more than two or three times in the intervening years. There'd been so many - *so very many*, he heard in his head - but Sandy being Sandy, everything he'd needed was there when he'd reached for it.

Had any of us escaped unscathed from those years, he reflected, from those parasites which had unknowingly and inexorably burrowed down into the depths of our very souls? Nascent over the decades, fretful and needy and demanding satisfaction in ways we thought we'd never succumb to. And then the naive belief they'd be cast aside at the end of those dark days, only for them to prove more resilient than we ever could have imagined.

Did we really expect to break free of chains that were of our own making…?

* * *

"Sir Alexander? No, please don't get up."

Actually, Sandy had started to doze at his recollections and then been half startled back to awareness by the sound of the door opening behind him. Not to leave himself at a perceived disadvantage, he'd carried the movement of his body forward into rising from his chair and turning.

The figure that entered the room struck Sandy as yet one more aspect of the Service that he'd come to feel alienated from - the chap looked more like the successful CEO of a brokerage firm. But Sandy extended his hand with what he hoped was a pleasant enough expression, and they shook.

"Keith Venables, Sir Alexander." His smile seemed both winning and well-practised. "We met many years ago, during the first Scargill operation."

"Ah, yes." Sandy gave him a smile and as he remembered began to revise his opinion. Sandy hadn't recognised him because not only had Venables been much younger but also bearded and long-haired - infiltrating the more militant of the striking miners' union branches and reporting back from the picket lines. Sandy always had time for those who'd been at the sharp end. "Good to see you again."

"Actually, Sir Alexander, I was intending to contact you, but when I heard you'd be here today, I hoped we might kill two birds with one stone. That is, if I could have a few minutes of your time?"

"Of course - how may I help?"

"There's a current operation of ours - well, I say current but, as I think the DG explained, it's in the process of being wound down - that has its origins back in the late sixties. In events which I believe you're familiar with." Venables hesitated slightly. "I'm aware this is an unorthodox approach, but I really would appreciate your viewpoint."

"If you think I could help, then of course." He paused. "What is it you wish to know?"

"Probably best discussed in my office, Sir Alexander." He gestured with his hand. "If we could just..."

"Certainly."

Sandy followed him out of the room and along the corridor.

* * *

"So, according to this Susan...?"

"Susan Marshall," said Venables.

"Her brother's still alive?"

"Yes."

"Which rather gives the lie to the Aidan McShane strand of this story?"

"Indeed."

"And so now your assumption is that this murdered police officer..." Sandy mused.

"Ex-police officer," Venables interrupted.

"Quite. This ex-police officer is now believed to have been an informant for the Provisional IRA."

"Well, he was definitely on the take. We're still going through his computer, but it's looking as though he and McKelvey had been thick as thieves for decades. Which also ties in with Susan Marshall's story, that her brother changed his name and disappeared because he'd fallen foul of some form of police corruption in those circles."

"And you believe the Irish got wind of McKelvey's arrangement with our friends at Langley."

"It would fit the facts."

"I don't imagine the Americans are particularly happy about this."

"No, but it's odds on that's where the leak came from - only a handful of people on this side of the Atlantic knew about it."

Sandy nodded.

"In my day, half the intelligence community one dealt with in Washington still had romantic notions of them as freedom fighters, rather than terrorists - can't imagine that's changed much." He paused. "And this Durham...?"

"Denham," said Venables. "Barry Denham."

"He'd been involved in the operation at Camden Town? Which," he added, "was a complete shambles, as I recall. Two people dead and the collapse of the subsequent trial."

"Special Branch kept you in the loop on that?"

Sandy nodded.

"Purely as a courtesy, because of my niece. I attended a couple of briefings, post mortem as it were. But we had no operational involvement."

"Probably just as well the way things turned out," said Venables and paused before adding, "Your niece had been at school with Emma Brownlow?"

"That's right."

"Who, according to the files, you first met in Cornwall - St Hannahs to be precise - in 1967. Together with Aidan McShane."

"Which was the reason I filed that report," said Sandy.

"This encounter," Venables sat back in his chair. "Did you believe it was purely coincidental?"

"Yes." Sandy gave a sharp nod. "And still do. McShane had been in St Hannahs that Easter as the result of an arrangement between the artist Frank Bishop - who was his tutor at the Slade - and Joyce Kelly, who'd had a studio in the town since the forties. Neither of them had previously given cause for concern - the term 'bolshie' might have aptly been used to describe either of them but not in any political sense."

"And it was your niece Claudia who made the introduction - she'd become friends with him?"

"Claudia had bumped into Emma Brownlow, who was on a family holiday down there and staying at the same campsite as McShane." Sandy paused. "All of this was looked into very discreetly but extremely thoroughly at the time, and the notion that these events were the result of some nefarious plot was quickly dismissed." Sandy allowed himself a brief smile. "As much as we may be in a business in which there is no such thing as coincidence, it was accepted that this in fact was."

"What were you told about the Special Branch operation at Pembridge Villas in 1970?"

"Very little - we knew that there'd been sporadic attacks on political and commercial targets, claimed in a series of communiques published in fringe magazines to have been carried out by 'The Angry Brigade'."

"What was your view on that?"

"Initially that it was a false flag. The explosives used were of a type we knew had been acquired by Basque Separatists, recently run out of Spain by the Franco regime. There was little pattern to the attacks and the consensus at the time was that it was in the interest of Special Branch to use the emergence of left-wing radical terror groups on the continent to over-egg the domestic threat."

"Is that still your view?"

Sandy hesitated.

"There's no doubt that a tangible threat developed between 1970 and 1972," he said, "but one far outweighed by the re-emergence of the IRA and nowhere near the scale of the Baader Meinhof or Red Army factions in Europe. And there was also the sense that the informant Special Branch had in place was very much an *agent provocateur*. That was greatly played on at the trial, but it wasn't the reason for the collapse."

"Did you know that the Special Branch informant was the son of the officer overseeing the operation?"

Sandy stared at him and slowly shook his head.

"No," he said. "No, I didn't."

"He and Emma Brownlow met again recently," Venables told him, "during our current operation, in fact."

He pressed a button on a small box sitting on his desk.

"I wonder, Sir Alexander," he asked, "if you'd mind listening to this and sharing your thoughts?"

* * *

The first sound was a door buzzer. After a few seconds there was the click of a latch and then a male voice.

"Hello?"

"Good afternoon, Mr Franklyn. DS Diane James, I'm with Special Branch Section Two."

Female, brisk and efficient.

"I have the Secretary of State for Northern Ireland waiting downstairs, but I'll need to check the room before I can give clearance for her to enter."

A few seconds' pause.

"So - may I come in?"

"Sorry, yes of course - just rather taken aback."

"It's okay Mr Franklyn, I get that a lot."

Followed by the sense of movement you sometimes had when listening to a recording, without ever really being able to define the cause of it.

"Only the one room?"

"Yes, and the bathroom's over to the left there."

"Mind if I take a look?"

"Help yourself."

A few moments' silence and then a short burst of static.

"All clear for her to come up."

Fifteen seconds of further silence followed by a brisk *"Minister"* and the sound of a door closing.

"Hello Kit," said a voice Sandy instantly recognised. He wondered if the bug had been surreptitiously planted in the room by 'Diane James' but considered it more likely to now be on the Minister herself, a switched cellular phone or favourite pen.

"I knew we'd be seeing each other later in the week, down in St Hannahs," said Emma Brownlow hesitantly, *"so I thought it best to have a word first."*

Emma and Kit... Sandy immediately knew that should mean something to him, the so familiar frustrating sense of meaning escaping one until... He forced it out of his mind, knowing to pursue it on a conscious level would only drive it deeper - better to come at it from an unexpected angle.

"Please, take a seat," said Kit.

"Thanks." Again, that sense of motion. *"You're looking well."*

"Thanks, you too. Although even in the Netherlands we do occasionally see you on TV, so I shouldn't really feign surprise at that."

She gave a soft laugh.

"I was sorry to hear about Aidan," said Kit. *"I always liked him."*

"He liked you too," said Emma.

"Did you know he was ill?" asked Kit.

"No, it was completely out of the blue. One minute we were at the breakfast table making plans for the day, the next he just keeled over."

The sorrow in her voice was unmistakable but there was strength in it too, thought Sandy, tragedy endured and learnt from.

"*A brain aneurysm, there was some family history I found out later, but he'd never mentioned it - probably felt I had enough to worry about.*"

Sandy sat with eyes half closed - and how many hours over the decades had he spent doing that, perfectly still and waiting for just a word or the slightest nuance out of place to reveal all?

Because to the casual listener, and perhaps a trained one, this conversation they were listening to might have sounded natural enough, but Sandy knew that it wasn't. Something had happened during their initial exchange, a coded signal which could have been a certain glance or gesture that even down the years would still be pregnant with meaning.

Ask Sandy how he could be sure of his instincts - and plenty had, years before in draughty Nissen huts and damp basement cells when lives depended on it - and you'd get nothing more than a steady stare or slow shake of the head.

And when people were aware they were being listened to, Sandy would always drill into his staff, you needed to pay as much attention to what they weren't saying to each other as what they were.

"Can I ask," Emma's voice was hesitant, "*why you never replied to my letter?*"

"Letter?"

"*That day I left, I went to see Claudia Falcone. I asked her to deliver a letter from me.*"

There was silence for a few moments before Emma spoke again.

"*Asking you to come over to Boston - to live with me out there. Once you'd got ... things straightened out. To give us a second chance, away from everything - and everyone - that had happened.*"

Again, a short silence.

"*So, she never gave it you?*" Although Emma kept her voice steady, Sandy could taste the bitterness there. "*I sup-*

posed I guessed as much."

"The day after you and Aidan left," Kit was speaking carefully, "Carin came over to Pembridge Villas. If you remember, she'd been away for a while to see her family. I found her in the kitchen with Claudia, crying – she told me she was pregnant."

"Oh... Right," said Emma.

"Carin was in quite a state that day. She really believed that she'd been abandoned – and it was obvious she wasn't going to take that lying down."

"I... I understand," said Emma quietly.

"At which point Claudia must have felt discretion was the better part of valour and disappeared, leaving us together."

Emma remained silent.

"And with everything that had happened," continued Kit, "it seemed to me..."

"Of course," Emma interrupted. "Actions and consequences – right? It's okay Kit, I get it."

"Anyway, the next time I saw Claudia, Carin and I were... a couple again. So, I guess she decided whatever might be in your letter would only complicate matters."

"Probably more than a guess," said Emma dryly. "Given the situation, I'd be amazed if there wasn't a boiling kettle involved somewhere in that calculation."

She paused.

"And you're still together... After all these years. Have to say, I wouldn't have put money on that. Not," she added quickly, "that's anything against Carin, just ... circumstances... Well, you know?"

"It's okay, Emma. I know what you meant."

Kit, Emma, Emma, Kit... What was he missing here?

Then, as almost always happens, for no logical reason whatsoever, the last piece dropped into place.

And Sandy had it.

* * *

"Uncle Alex, Aunt Anne," Claudia said, leading the three figures into the sitting room at Cam Ryr. "This is Aidan

McShane, who's been working with Joyce Kelly and you remember me telling you about Emma, when we were at St Catherine's?"

At the ringing of the doorbell, he'd broken off his conversation with the young soldier who Emma and her friends had fallen in with and crossed the room to switch on the TV. It was an old set and to receive the BBC2 signal it needed a small metal box - connected between the aerial cable and its socket at the back of the TV, some tuning device he supposed - to be switched on as well. Checking that everything was functioning correctly and that for once it wasn't a half bad picture, he'd turned around to greet his guests.

"And this is Peter Marshall," Claudia continued. "He's also staying at Petroc."

All three of them had that dishevelled appearance which young people seemed to carefully cultivate these days, he'd thought, but at least they looked clean.

"Please to meet you all," he said, striding across the room with his hand extended. "I'm Alex."

"Hi Aidan, Hi Kit," Lee Munro smiled, after giving Emma a kiss on the cheek.

"I think we'll have to get another couple of chairs," Anne said.

"Do you need a hand?" asked the young man Claudia introduced as Peter, but who Lee had called Kit.

"Thanks," he said, and the young man followed him down to the kitchen. "It's Peter, isn't it?"

"On my birth certificate," the young man smiled. "Most people call me Kit."

"Isn't that usually a sobriquet for Christopher?" he asked.

"Marshall is my stepfather's name," said Kit. "We took it when my mother remarried, but my surname used to be Carson."

"Ah, I see," he said. "Like the cowboy."

"Yes," Kit grinned. "Like the cowboy."

* * *

They offered him a car which he politely declined, expressing a wish to stretch his legs.

"I'm only in Pimlico," he told them, "and I do enjoy the walk by the river."

That was true enough, twenty minutes along Millbank and done perhaps hundreds of times. He'd had the Dolphin Square flat for almost sixty years now, seen the Blitz through there and lived out the Cold War. Battles won which never felt like victories.

He'd sat through the rest of the recording, half an hour reminiscing about that Easter in St Hannah's, with little said about their summer in London. *Listen to what they're not saying to each other!* But he'd reassured Venables that there wasn't anything on the tape which struck a false note with his recollections. And Venables - whilst disappointed - had thanked him for his time and escorted him to the discreet doorway which led out into Thorney Street.

He crossed over onto Lambeth Bridge and looked down at the murky waters.

My God, Special Branch had blundered colossally back then! Sandy understood everything, or at least as much of it that mattered.

With the death of the informant's father, they'd somehow created an instance of mistaken identity with enormous significance and where revealing their hand had set in motion this dreadful sequence of events.

That a police informant - the Special Branch officer's son - died, he had no doubt. Under what circumstances seemed irrelevant, but from the conversation overheard by McKelvey – who Sandy now believed implicitly – it had created an ongoing *quid pro quo,* giving the IRA direct access to the inner workings of the Metropolitan Police Special Branch which had lasted for God knows how long.

The issue as to whose hand the crime could be laid at would also prove a moot point, accessory before and after the fact would draw little legal distinction. But from the nuances of the conversation he'd just listened to, there was no doubt in his mind that the list of conspirators would include a member of the British Cabinet.

And Claudia.

He found it too incredible to believe his niece had been directly involved, but he also knew it would prove impossible to disentangle her from any investigation. Emma Brownlow had stayed at her apartment on her release from Holloway, and Claudia was a frequent visitor to that house in Notting Hill. But most significant of all, during his career he'd trampled on enough toes of the Great and the Good for Claudia to be seen as his Achilles' heel by any who might still harbour a grudge.

And most had long memories.

Id optimum nobis militat. It could almost be the motto of the Service, thought Sandy, at least during his time. *'What serves us best.'* Sometimes, one simply had to stand back from notions of justice and probity and consider what purpose this would serve.

Well, he reflected, turning away from the parapet and slowly making his way down the steps to the Victoria Tower Gardens, if his silence ensured that this whole mess was about to be interred yet again under the stone where it had lain for all these years, then so be it.

Let it rot there.

12. Kit

In keeping so many balls in the air at once, it had begun to feel inevitable that sooner or later I'd fumble one of them. Emma's imminent departure for Boston - as much as it tugged at my heartstrings - at least meant one less that I had to worry about. But, ironically, the ball which did eventually tumble out of control was one which I didn't even realise I was juggling.

A few days after Jake's death, Liam came over to Pembridge Villas.

"Is everything still on course with Emma?" I asked him.

"Actually," he told me, "I'm here to see you about that."

"Is there a problem?"

"Not as such." He shook his head. "But there is a favour we'd like to ask of you." He hesitated. "Concerning Aidan."

"A favour?"

Liam nodded.

"His grandfather is greatly concerned by the extent to which he's become embroiled in this," he said. "It's not a path the family envisaged for him."

I stayed silent.

"So, what we'd like you to do," Liam continued, "would be to concoct a story in which the authorities have asked you to plant evidence on him. To make it appear he's deeply involved in our affairs."

"You want him out of the country?"

"Oh, I think both of us would sleep a little easier in our beds if Aidan and that girl of yours were on the other side of the Atlantic." Liam shrugged. "Safely out of harm's way for a while, don't you think?"

"Okay," I told him.

"We'll get it taken care of then. And in the meantime," he added, "we've come across something that should do wonders for your credibility."

* * *

I arranged a meeting with Barry the evening Emma and Aidan left. As the taxi pulled away from the curb, I passed the envelope Liam had given me through the open glass partition.

"It's an IRA safe house in Canning Town," I said to Barry's inquisitive stare. "There's a weapons and explosives cache buried in an old Anderson shelter at the bottom of the garden."

"Jesus!" said Barry. "How did you get this?"

It was probably old scores being settled, I thought, but the least I knew about it the better. I'd already spent most of the day concocting a plausible cover story and then poking it for holes.

"There's a Maoist fringe cell planning to raid it," I told him. "They aim to get themselves seriously tooled up - it would probably be best to pre-empt that," I added dryly.

"Any idea when this is happening?" asked Barry.

"No." Shaking my head. "But I'd guess soon."

"You're being careful, right?" He was staring hard at me. "You're not taking any risks here?"

"The reason I know about this," I said, "was that someone spiked the drinks at a party I was at."

"LSD?"

I nodded.

"It's not only that everyone gets loose lipped when they're high," I told him. "You have to understand that drugs are the way into the very heart of the counterculture. Because if you're dealing, you've carte blanche to anything that's happening - the assumption being if you're outside the law, then you can be trusted."

He was silent.

"Believe me, it would open an awful lot of doors," I insisted.

"I'll talk to the boss," said Barry cautiously. "Only be careful, alright?"

"As long as it's the Paddies that go down for this and not the Maoists," I told him, "I'll be okay."

"Sure, we can save them for another day." He gave me a nod and then a wide grin. "Great work."

"Thanks."

"We're going to get you an NUJ card," said Barry. "Set you up as a freelance journalist, which gives you a legitimate source of income and plausible reasons for asking questions, without alienating you from your lower-level contacts."

"Okay," I said. "Did you get the info I asked for?"

"Yes." He gave a slight shake of his head. "The Met weren't happy about this, so when you've gone through it make sure it all goes up in flames. Not out with the rubbish. Burn it, right?"

"Sure," I lied. "As soon as I've finished with it."

* * *

It was Paul who set the meeting up, in the back bar of a pub on the Seven Sisters Road, about an hour before lunchtime opening. He and I sat on one side of the table, Harry Slater and Tony, his minder, on the other.

"Firstly," said Harry, "I want you to know that I had nothing to do with that nonsense over in Camden Town - that was Chas being totally out of order all by himself." He took a breath. "And he paid for it. Secondly, what's done is done - I'm not out for payback of any kind over what happened. You don't need to be looking over your shoulder."

I nodded and reached into my briefcase, taking out a cardboard folder and placing it on the table.

"These are Flying Squad surveillance photographs," I said to him. "They should give you a heads up on which of your interests has their current attention."

"Bloody hell!" Tony had flipped the folder open and was staring at it wide eyed. "Where did these come from?"

"We've access to quite a bit of interesting information."

That wasn't strictly true. Barry Denham got me those photographs because I'd told him I'd heard a rumour that the Slater organisation was asking questions about Chief Superintendent Franklyn's role in Chas Slater's death. A useful heads up would be able to recognise any of their henchmen. *'You see any of those faces hanging around,'* Barry had warned me as I got out the cab, *'you get on the blower, pronto'*.

"And what," asked Slater, with a raised eyebrow, "would be expected in return?"

"With Coochie gone," I told him, "there's a gap in the market. We'd like to fill it."

"And you're looking for...?"

"Finance and protection." I indicated the photos on the table. "We've contacts in the Old Bill who'll keep an eye out for us on that side of things, it's the competition that could be a problem."

"As I recall, you seemed more than able to take care of yourselves."

"Isn't it better for business if it doesn't have to come to that?" I shrugged. "If it's known who's behind us."

"What sort of money are we talking about here," asked Harry Slater carefully, "and how are you planning on going about this?"

* * *

"You reckon five years?" said Paul as we walked along the Holloway Road, looking for a cab.

"You don't last forever in this game," I told him. "We should get legit as quickly as possible, but I'm guessing it'll be at least that long before the Irish are going to let me walk away. So, in the meantime, we might as well take what we can out of it."

Barry Denham and Brian Maddox hadn't been wild about my dealing but for expediency's sake they'd gone along with it, bar a few caveats. No hard narcotics - heroin and coke were getting a lot of attention now that registration had ended. *'And definitely no involvement in trafficking of any kind,'* warned Maddox. *'If Customs and Excise were to get involved, there'd be nothing we could do, you'd be fucked.'*

That suited me - let Harry Slater bring the stuff in.

"We should start looking for something to sink the profits into," I told Paul. "The deposit on a hotel or pub maybe and monthly loan payments – no flash cash attracting attention. And well away from London – perhaps the West Country."

Paul nodded.

"I've an idea in mind," he said.

Which, I thought to myself as a black cab pulled over to the curb, ties everything up quite nicely.

And then, that very afternoon, I walked into the kitchen at Pembridge Villas to find a sobbing Carin being comforted by Claudia and that the one ball I'd taken my eye off was spiralling away almost beyond reach.

13. Tracey De Keyser

"Today's subscriptions," said Jaclyn, arms full of cellophane wrapped magazines. "Where shall I put them?"

"Thanks." Tracey indicated the worktop alongside her PC. "There's fine."

"I'm making coffee," Jaclyn told her. "Want one?"

"Hmmm, please." Tracey began absently sorting through the titles. "Have you heard from Carin or Kit?"

"There was an email from Kit last night. They're leaving Los Angeles for New York today and should be home on Friday."

"Any idea how it went?"

"He was pretty non-committal." Jaclyn shrugged. "But then, isn't he always?"

Tracey laughed.

"You mentioned the meeting next week to them - at the university?"

"Yes, a couple of days ago. Carin says it's okay, they'll be back in plenty of time."

"Okay," said Tracey, peeling the wrapping off the first magazine. "Thanks."

* * *

It was Jan who highlighted the problem, and he'd always take credit for the solution, but it was Carin and Kit who got the entire thing up and running.

Jan had been in the university library, looking for a colleague's article in the latest issue of a psychology journal. He couldn't find it on the shelves, but eventually an assistant discovered it in the stockroom, midway through a stack of several impressive towers of unopened subscription magazines.

"We just don't have the resources to sort them during term time," she'd told him, half apologetic but also half defiant. "It's one of those jobs that gets left for term breaks, when things quieten down. Unless," that defiant flash again, "you can persuade Admin to give us someone part time to tackle it on a daily basis."

That night, Jan brought it up over drinks with Carin and Kit.

"It would have been perfect for you," Jan told Tracey. "Couple of hours a day and it's a role which can lead on to other things." He'd shrugged. "But Admin won't shift on it, they say that the budget's already stretched to the absolute limit."

"But what if it wasn't down to Admin?" suggested Carin. "What if it was down to Subscriptions?"

Jan stared at her.

"What if," continued Carin, "they were offered a service where they could hand all of their subscription details over to an agency who would manage them? And not just the renewals and payments, but also to print out a cover label showing the shelf number and sequence they should be ordered by."

"That would be possible?" asked Jan.

"Sure - and it would reduce Subscriptions down to a single person, checking issues received and managing cancellations. That wouldn't be such a hard sell to Admin if it were priced right."

Kit nodded.

"Probably not financially viable for just one library, but I'd bet this isn't a unique problem." He shrugged. "We could give them a competitive price while we got the kinks ironed out and then offer it on to other universities."

"Throughout the Netherlands, you mean?"

"Why not throughout Europe?" said Carin. "It would all

be managed by email and post."

"And you'd be able to set that up yourselves?" asked Jan.

"We know a computer whizz kid," said Carin, and Kit smiled. "I think if we were to spend a couple of days explaining how it needed to work, it would be a piece of cake for him." She paused. "If that's what Tracey wants to do, of course."

"Yes." Tracey's enthusiasm had been genuine, something of her own at last.

"We've a storage room out back which we could turn into an office for this," said Kit and shifted his gaze from Jan to Carin. "Why don't you sound them out?"

It had taken off almost immediately. Tracey had been nervous about working with the *'computer whizz kid'*, which had sounded a bit intimidating, but he turned out to be Jaclyn's boyfriend Mirko and a real pussycat. Between them they'd had the bones of a system up in a few days and the first magazines began arriving within a week.

Initially, the university had given them only half a dozen subscriptions. They liked the idea but wanted to see how it worked out in practice. But the feedback from the library had been positive. Tracey figured it would be, she and Mirko had taken those cellophane wrapped tower blocks off their hands to use as a test run for the cover label printing. And Jan told her he'd heard a whisper that Admin were asking for a meeting when Kit got back from the States, to talk about a complete handover.

And for the first time in quite a while, Tracey was happy.

* * *

Europe had been a real struggle, but not in the ways she'd expected. Language would be a problem, she'd thought, and the day before leaving home had even bought a Pimsleur Dutch course on CD. But on arrival she'd discovered most people here under fifty spoke English almost as well as she did.

"We know we are a tiny country," said Willem, Jan's friend who she'd been helping in his bookshop until something better came along, "and that our language is very difficult. So, English has become our international language and we are happy with that. But if a Frenchman should come to our country," he added, "who expects us to speak French, then we say to him 'Fuck off'."

And that was another struggle, the constant cursing. The reason the Dutch spoke such good English seemed to be because all the foreign movies and TV shows were subtitled rather than dubbed. She guessed that was because the cost of the process was prohibitive for such a potentially small audience, compared to the tens of millions of German or French speakers throughout the world. So right from childhood, the English language was background chatter in most homes, absorbed by osmosis and refined by lessons in school from year one.

But the downside of this almost complete immersion in the North American vernacular was a vocabulary which could make Tracey blush, and she was no prude. You might expect the casual use of *'motherfucker'* or *'cocksucker'* from a teenager, but even a respectable history professor on a TV quiz show wouldn't raise an eyebrow letting slip a 'fuck' or 'shit', after giving a wrong answer. Her very first afternoon here, Tracey had been walking through de Bijenkorf - the closest thing Amsterdam had to Bloomingdales - when an expensively dressed and well coiffured mother had swept towards her, practically dragging along a sulky looking ten-year-old girl to whom she suddenly turned and snapped, *'Oh Annemieke, ik ben zo pissed off'*.

But perhaps what had gotten to her the most was what she'd least expected, a questioning of her own identity. It started on the broadest of terms, that of nationality, and she understood it wasn't uncommon for expatriates to view their fellow countrymen through native eyes.

And that tourists aren't necessarily natural ambassadors.

Almost a year after arriving here - her wardrobe now entirely European and with the air of someone settled into their surroundings - Tracey found herself becoming privy to the rolled eyeballs of salesclerks and dismissive expressions of fellow shoppers. And totally sympathetic to the angry residents who continually had to chase away backpackers settling down for a picnic on the carefully tendered lawns in the sanctuary of Begijnhof.

The last sense of anything even feeling like betrayal had come at the Rijksmuseum, standing at the back of the crowd collected in front of *The Night Watch*. There wasn't exactly reverent silence to begin with but when a female voice suddenly screeched *'So Harvey, ya gonna tell ya pupils ya seen a famous painting?'* her instinctive reaction was to head for the nearest exit. A young couple moved aside to let her pass. From snatches of their conversation she'd overheard moments before, she'd gathered the girl was Dutch and her partner a Brit. *'Apparently only five percent of Americans hold passports,'* she caught his soft but clipped English tones as she passed by, *'and the general consensus is that's four percent too many.'* His girlfriend's laughter seemed to ring in her ears all the way down to the street.

Was that how people thought of her, she wondered, at the bakers or the bookshop when she opened her mouth and her identity ceased to be a lie of omission?

Did she even know who she was anymore?

* * *

And that night at the restaurant had brought matters to a head. The conversation was just so damned smart and sophisticated. Anything that ran through her mind sounded banal beyond belief... And of course, the longer she stayed silent, the harder it became to find a point to interject.

As they rose from the table and moved to the bar, she'd fled to the restroom and locked herself in a stall, trying to collect herself. Maybe she should say to Jan that she wasn't feeling too good, that maybe they should head home.

Time to get yourself together, she thought, time to...

"God, I'm ready for this," a male voice said from behind her and a female voice said, "Me too."

Startled, she glanced up and over her left shoulder, to where the small window set high in the wall was half open. Then the striking of a match reassured her.

Staff out back on a cigarette break.

"How's it going?" the female asked. Tracey recognised her voice as belonging to the pretty little Vietnamese waitress who'd served them their wine.

"Okay," the male told her, and from his accent he must be their Irish waiter. "But I'll be glad when the night's over." He hesitated. "How are you getting on with the party in the side room?"

Them, realised Tracey.

"Okay," said the waitress.

"They're often in here," the waiter told her, "and they're good tippers, but I'd be a bit careful if I were you."

"What do you mean?"

"Well," he said, "they call themselves the Share Club. And..."

He lowered his voice to confidential tones. *What on earth was the point of that*, thought Tracey irritably as she strained to hear, *if he assumed that she was the only one listening to him?*

"*Oh my God!*" said the waitress, as his low murmuring ceased. "*Seriously!!?* You mean like keys thrown into a bowl at the end of the night and then they all go off with each other?"

Tracey froze. It literally felt like the blood was running cold through her veins.

"Well," he said, "not from here, obviously. But let me tell you something - last year I was seeing a student at Leiden and that woman in the silk top and suede skirt..."

Carin, thought Tracey.

"... is a professor there. And she has quite a reputation, if you know what I mean."

"But... She must be at least fifty."

"Well." Tracey imagined the waiter shrugging. "All I can tell you is word on the campus was that nothing in trousers was safe when she was around." He paused. "And from the way I caught her looking at you a few times earlier this evening, I'd be guessing perhaps not much in a skirt either."

There was silence.

"Thanks for the heads up," she said eventually.

"Just keep a smile on your face and pick up your tips," he told her. "That's what this job's all about in the end - but it pays to know what's what."

"Right..."

"Come on," he said. "We'd better go back inside."

Numbly, Tracey stood up and left the stall. She wouldn't make a scene, she told herself as she ran water from the faucet over her hands, an upset stomach she'd say, feeling faint also - anything to get out of here.

And she'd wait until they were home to demand just what the hell Jan had known about all of this.

* * *

"*Tracey!*"

It had been the start of her lunch break from Willem's bookstore. Most days she took her sandwiches into Vondelpark and ate them by the lake, but today it was raining so instead she'd decided to walk over to the Rijksmuseum - there were usually classical music buskers in the tunnel by the entrance. Shelter and culture for free, she told herself, but almost always dropped a couple of guilders into the hat.

Closing the bookstore door behind her, she turned, startled at hearing her name.

Carin Franklin was walking toward her.

"Hello," she said softly and with a smile. "I thought the two of us should have a chat."

Tracey stared at her.

When she and Jan had arrived home after that night at

the restaurant, Tracey had laid into him with everything that she'd overheard in the restroom. He'd looked at her blankly as she'd related the conversation, before declaring it to be *'total bullshit'*.

"Is it - how do you know what went on after we left?" she'd demanded.

"Because..." he'd begun and then broke off, shaking his head. "Because no one said anything to me beforehand and do you really think this would be something to spring on someone out of the blue? *'Oh, pass the port and guess what's up next?'*"

"No one said anything to you? You mean that Carin didn't say anything to you, don't you?" She'd stared at him. "What that waiter said about her - are you telling me you've heard no rumours at the university."

Jan had dropped his eyes.

"There are always rumours about everyone," he'd said quietly. "Do you think there aren't rumours about us - why we had to leave Harvard? And believe me, the speculation is a lot more torrid than the reality."

"But we did have to leave Harvard," she'd said, softening her tone but steadying her gaze, "didn't we?"

"Carin's private life is her own," he'd said, "and not anything to do with us."

They'd let the conversation drop at that point, but both knew it wasn't finished with.

"Carin," she said uncertainly. "Hi there."

"There's a bar just around the corner," Carin told her, "where they won't mind you eating your lunch while we have a drink."

* * *

You'd have passed by on the sidewalk without even knowing it was there, but that was probably the idea, thought Tracey. Every city has its refuges from tourism where the locals can hideaway for a while. Carin was greeted by name as they entered and, after she had a few short words in Dutch with the smiling bartender, they were shown through into a small but comfortable room out back.

"One of my father's old haunts," Carin told her as they sat down at a table. "He did a lot of business here and occasionally he'd bring me along."

Tracey started to speak, but Carin raised her hand, silencing her. There was the sound of footsteps and a young woman entered the room carrying a tray. She smiled at them both as she placed a bottle of wine and two glasses onto the table and closed the door after she left. Tracey, already uncomfortable, inwardly winced at the thought that the girl might wonder if this was some form of *assignation*.

"I wanted to talk," said Carin, "because it appears several strands have tangled themselves up into a ball here and I think we need to separate them back out again."

She filled the glasses with wine.

"The Share Club really is only about good food, convivial company, and blowing off steam at the world. The only excitement we've ever had about car keys was a couple of years ago, when Clémence lost hers and we had the whole restaurant scouring the floor for them before they turned up in the Ladies. And I can't tell you how appalled she'd be if she knew there was a story like that going around."

"Look," said Tracey, "I haven't said anything to…"

"It's okay," broke in Carin. "I was talking about that waiter you overheard - bringing a touch of excitement to the mundane, I'd imagine, and probably with a view to banging that cute little waitress." She took a sip of her wine. "But no smoke without fire."

Tracey shook her head

"I don't believe that," she said.

"Oh, it wasn't a question." Carin put her glass down on the table. "It was a statement of fact."

"I'm sorry?"

"Kit and I - our lifestyle is no secret to anyone, for the most part at least, and will always be grist for the rumour mill. Which is almost certainly how this innuendo about the Share Club got started."

"Carin," Tracey felt herself beginning to redden, "this isn't any of my business and…"

Carin raised her hand again, silencing her.

"If it's coming between you and Jan, then it most definitely is your business," she said. "So, I felt that the record needed to be set straight. I like Jan as a colleague and I was hoping that we'd be friends, but if that's a problem for you, then I understand."

"No." Tracey was shaking her head. "It's not - it's that…"

Then it all came pouring out - everything that had bottled itself up over the last year just erupted. She barely registered herself lighting up the cigarette that Carin offered her or of her glass being refilled.

And eventually she seemed to run out of steam.

"I wasn't being judgemental," she finished, "at least I don't think I was. It was just one more thing I - that I couldn't understand." She looked Carin in the eye. "Maybe it's not being European or something, but I still can't… If two people love each other, then…"

She shrugged and shook her head.

Carin considered her and then seemed to reach a decision.

"Coming to live in a foreign country is never easy," she said softly. "I know, I was younger than you are now when I moved to London."

"But that's different, isn't it?" Tracey felt a terseness creeping into her voice. "I mean, I guess at college you were with a bunch of people your own age, who were away from home for the first time too."

"It became a nightmare," said Carin quietly. "And Kit saved me."

"Saved you how?" asked Tracey.

"When Kit and I first met, he was caught up with another woman," she said. "It was one of those permanently on off things that drag out for years, you know?"

Tracey nodded.

"And so, even though I was in love with him, I became involved with someone else who was living in the same house. If I was trying to make him jealous or whether I simply needed to be wanted, I don't know. It just happened."

"The house you were talking about before? Where Lee Munro lived?"

"Yes." Carin drew on her cigarette and then exhaled slowly. "And it was a disaster. I became pregnant, so the guy disappeared. One day he was there, the next he was gone."

"Jesus!" said Tracey.

"Yes, but not too unusual a story." Carin shrugged. "Anyway, the day I discovered that he'd vanished, Kit found me in the kitchen, sitting at the table and not just crying but utterly broken. I didn't know which way to turn, I had no close friends in England, how was I going to tell my family...?"

Carin shook her head slowly before giving Tracey a small smile.

"And he took care of me. At first, he helped me try to find the guy who'd disappeared. We visited the places where he used to hang out and talked to his friends. And when that came to nothing, and I was thinking of reporting him missing - I was determined not to let him get away with this, you understand, I felt like I'd been taken for a fool – he said that he'd go to the police with me if that's what I wanted. But by then ..." Carin shrugged.

"You were back together?"

"Well, we were back in bed together."

"What about the other girl he was seeing?"

"He told me that she'd left to go and live in America. And that it was over."

"And you believed him?"

"Not at first, but I didn't care. I think he was still a bit in love with her and I think that perhaps he still is. But maybe after a while you get to realise that some things are just never going to work out and that you have to walk away from them."

"And you were okay with that?"

"As much as Kit was okay with raising another man's child. Look Tracey, no one's pretending that this was a thunderstruck love match - we were both hurting and taking comfort where we could find it. And you know, in many ways that's as much of something to build on as most star-crossed lovers have."

"And then you got married?"

"Kit began working as a journalist - mainly undercover exposé work, dealing with some really unsavoury people. Often he was away for weeks at a time, living a role not compatible with that of a happily married family man."

"He was involved with other women, you mean?"

"Like I said, we did not come into this relationship as childhood sweethearts - fidelity was a vessel long set sail."

"But still - weren't you hurt?"

"For Kit and I, people are not Swiss army knives. That the best father for your child is not necessarily your best lover, who is not necessarily your best life companion, and that none of it is any big deal. There is great strength in a relationship that doesn't ask of a partner that which is not there." Carin shrugged. "But this is not a lifestyle we feel the need to be emissaries for."

"So, if you meet someone...?" began Tracey and then let her voice trail off, still disconcerted but inescapably curious.

"There are no rules," said Carin, "other than honesty. We're both more than adept at weighing up whether an *affaire* is likely to prove complicated or not. Most relationships tend to be short and intense, on the other hand I've a friend in London I've known for years and who I see whenever I'm over there, travelling with Kit or not."

"That really doesn't bother him?"

"No, and in fact I'll be meeting up with him later this

month, I'm in London for a college reunion." Carin hesitated. "Actually, that is one of the few situations where discretion does prevail – getting together with old friends."

"In what way?"

"When we meet new people, we're all pretty much taken at face value. But when it comes to discovering that you didn't really know someone who you thought you did - there's no-one quite as sanctimonious as the friend who thinks they have you nicely wrapped up inside a little box and then learns otherwise. Jan could explain the psychology of that to you a lot better than I can... But sometimes, playing to the expectations of people who don't have a large role in your life seems more expedient than hypocritical."

"Look..." began Tracey, but Carin interrupted.

"I'd like us to be friends, Tracey," she said. "But if that's not going to be possible, I'm okay with that too. I just needed you to know how things stood."

"I'd like to be friends," Tracey said softly.

"Good," said Carin. "Because if you and Jan want to join our little circle, we've all decided that you'd be more than welcome."

"I'd like that too," smiled Tracey.

"I'll email you the details of this Saturday's rendezvous," Carin told her, adding dryly, "I thought we might try somewhere different this week."

As they stood up to leave, Carin moved forward to embrace her. Just at that moment the door opened and the girl who'd brought the wine appeared. Taking in the scene, she discreetly dropped her eyes and with a slight smile slowly closed the door.

'Oh, just great!' thought Tracey.

* * *

Her reverie was broken into by the arrival of the postman – usually there wasn't much by way of regular post. The magazines arrived via a special courier service and so most mornings it was only bills, orders and junk mail. But today's delivery included a heavy, thick envelope, and curiosity getting the better of her, she set the rest of the post to one side to examine it.

It was addressed to Kit by name rather than the Gallery, but as there was nothing on the envelope saying *'Private'* or *'Confidential'* she placed it flat on the desk and slit the flap open with her thumbnail. As Tracey tipped it forward, a hardback book slid out - lifting the envelope and peering inside confirmed that was all it contained.

She turned the book over and studied the cover.

Relentless Pursuit was the title and opening it she began to read the flyleaf. It was about submarines in World War 2, how someone in the British Navy called Captain Walker had destroyed lots of German U-boats in the Atlantic. She flipped the page over and a folded press clipping fell out.

It was an article from a newspaper - *The Liverpool Echo* - dated the previous year, about this same Captain Walker. A statue of him by a renowned sculptor had been unveiled at the Pier Head, which she guessed must be the docks. Turning her attention back to the book, she noticed that an inscription in blue ink had been written opposite the title page.

'Nicely played Mr Franklyn, but a lesson well learnt.' it read. *'I'm sure that our paths will cross again, and sooner rather than later. Amanda Palmer.'*

Wow, how enigmatic was that? Well, it was none of her business but a bit odd, she reflected, as she refolded the clipping, closed the cover on it and then slid the book back into the envelope. Maybe Kit and this Amanda Palmer were interested in submarines.

Still, it seemed a funny sort of hobby for a woman...

PART FOUR

Epilogue

Claudia

The decision to sell *Cam Ryr* didn't come easily, but by the turn of the Millennium the happy memories it once held were far outweighed by darker ones. Not least of these were of a husband whose passing was ambiguous enough to warrant an inquest by the local coroner but - other than to emphasise the wish to sever all ties with St Hannahs - let's keep that a story for another day.

Alex came to Cornwall with me on that last visit - Aunt Anne had passed away the previous year and I imagine he had his own goodbyes to say. We took our time journeying down, making two overnight stops en route - there'd been no hurry and he was now of an age when sitting continuously for more than a few hours becomes uncomfortable.

I spent a few days dealing with estate agents and solicitors and also arranging for the pieces of furniture and bric-à-brac I wished to keep to be delivered to London. And then for a house clearance company to deal with the rest after our departure, not something I felt the need to be present for.

Our journey back was equally slow paced. I planned to take the old coast road up to join the motorway in Somerset, mainly out of nostalgia for that first trip down to Cornwall all those very many years ago, but not entirely.

"I've made a reservation for lunch here," I told Alex as we pulled into the car park of a hotel on the outskirts of Barnstaple. The building itself was further up a wooded hillside, along a driveway signposted *'Residents Cars Only'*. Our walk being a steeper climb than I'd expected I offered to go back for the car, but Alex shook his head.

"It's giving me an appetite," he said.

Eventually we reached the hotel and stopped to collect our breath, looking out across the lush Devon valley. It wasn't only a reputation for excellent food that had brought me here. The hotel incorporated both an art gallery and a Sculpture Garden, and the latter I could see falling away immediately before us, down a slope to the river below.

When I turned back to Alex, he was staring at the building with an expression I couldn't quite discern, somewhere between recognition and bemusement, perhaps.

"Are you alright?" I asked.

"Yes," he nodded and then gave me a smile. "Let's eat."

The food lived up to its reputation, and I looked on with envy as Alex effortlessly polished off a bottle of Chablis with his meal.

We took a walk through the gallery section after lunch, a mixture of both local and nationally renowned artists, and then I sat Alex down at a table outside and ordered him a pot of tea.

"There's something I'd like to see in the Sculpture Garden," I told him, "but I think it might be a little steep for you."

"Don't worry," he said, picking up a copy of the *Telegraph* which someone had left behind on a chair. "You take your time."

I had a quick word at Reception and following their directions made my way down the hillside. It was an eclectic collection. Formal stone pieces blending into their surroundings were contrasted by constructions of elongated sharp metal and wires which, on turning a corner, created a sense of almost being ambushed.

Eventually, at the bottom of the hill by the river, I found the piece I'd been looking for.

'*Tranquillity* by Aidan McShane' read the inscription.

* * *

I never did travel to the United States whilst Emma lived there, in correspondence which grew more infrequent with the passage of time the invitation was never again extended. Sometimes relationships simply run their course, I reflected, and perhaps this was one of those. After three or four years the exchange of letters ceased completely, although I don't recall at whose instigation.

Around ten years after her departure from England I had been making a rare visit to London, staying at Alex's Pimlico flat. My Portman Square apartment was now let through an agency, as furnished accommodation for visiting businessmen who required a West End base, and Alex had taken Aunt Anne to Paris for which anniversary I don't remember - once past a certain age they arrive fast and frequently.

Usually in London I took either a cab or the underground, but it had been such a gorgeous April morning that I'd decided to walk along by the river for a while. Cutting through between the Tate and the Chelsea College of Art to reach Millbank, I noticed a large banner hanging from the Art College entrance.

'*Spring Exhibition*', it said in letters six feet high. '*Aidan McShane*'.

Which stopped me in my tracks - I must have stood motionless, staring at it for a good thirty seconds before slowly approaching the building. Inexplicably, I found myself almost shaking - what was the matter with me? On being ambushed by the past the mind often reacts like a startled hare – instinctively it knows things can go either way. But all I remember thinking about was the likelihood of Aidan being there? And if so, did I need to gather my thoughts a little before going in? There was a cafe on the street across the courtyard where I could collect myself.

'*Oh Claudia, pull yourself together!*' Grasping the nettle, I strode in through the main doors and following a series of arrows on pedestals climbed a flight of stairs and entered a small gallery.

A girl in her late teens was sitting at a desk. There were

perhaps a dozen people clustered in ones and twos in front of the paintings.

"Hello," she smiled at me. "Would you like a catalogue?"

"Thank you," I said, extracting my purse from my handbag and gazing round as she counted out the change. I could see there were probably fifty or sixty exhibits, mainly oils, a few watercolours and some charcoal sketches.

I made my way slowly around. Some paintings I recognised, remembered seeing them in his studio at Pembridge Villas. None of the *Cradle of Thorns* series were here, I noticed, I assumed they were all now in private collections. But on reaching the far wall - and for the second time that morning - I found myself stopped in my tracks.

It was an oil painting, a head and shoulders portrait against a seascape and which must have had a sunset going on out of the picture, given the tricks of light and shadow being played across the subject's face.

But it was eminently recognisable.

I stood there unmoving, not really registering time passing until I was aware of someone alongside me, the girl who'd sold me my ticket.

"I couldn't help notice you engrossed in it," she said. "It's one of my favourites too. It's like he captured something from deep inside, isn't it?"

"Yes," I nodded, turning to her, "it is."

She smiled, but then as she looked at me her expression became one of uncertainty. Her gaze flicked backward and forwards between my face and the portrait, and then her eyes widened.

"Oh, goodness," she said.

* * *

"He's away for the week," the girl who'd introduced herself as Debbie told me. "I'm sure he'll be sorry he missed you."

Perhaps, then again, perhaps not. While she'd been making us coffee, I'd begun thumbing through the catalogue where there were surprises aplenty. That I hadn't realised half a dozen of the paintings were of Emma could have been put down to artistic license, but I wouldn't have recognised her from the photograph on the inside cover either. She was still attractive, but what had been prettiness had taken on a brittle quality. Emma had not regained the weight she'd lost a decade ago, but - rather than gauntness - her features were now all sharp angles and tight lines. Also, there was something about her expression, a sense that the combativeness - never far from the surface - had finally risen to the fore.

"So how did you know Aidan?" asked Debbie brightly, and I chose my words carefully before replying.

'Aidan and Emma first met in the United States,' I'd gleaned from a quick scan of the Introduction in the catalogue. 'Emma had been a student at Boston University and Aidan, originally from Dublin, was staying with relatives in the city.'

Oh, really? I wasn't sure what narrative was being created here - or why - but anyone from the actual past clodhopping through it would doubtless, I assumed, find themselves shy of a welcome.

So, I simply smiled.

"My family had a holiday home in Cornwall," I told her, "when Aidan spent some time at Joyce Kelly's studio. We met by way of mutual friends."

I took a sip of my coffee.

"Do you know him through the college?" I asked.

She nodded.

"Since I started last September." She smiled. "I babysit for them too - Brianna's adorable."

"What's Emma up to these days?"

"Well, she's on the local council, which takes up most of her time," Debbie said. "She's also the Labour Parliamentary candidate for Hackney, the current MP's standing down at the next election. So, fingers crossed."

Not too tightly, I thought. In Hackney they probably weigh the Labour vote rather than count it.

"Would you like to leave your address or phone number?" she asked.

"Actually," I said, "that painting - how much is it?"

She told me and inwardly I winced, but I knew I was going to have it. And would doubtless have to lie about it when I arrived home but was becoming accustomed to that as the *de facto* state of affairs.

I took out my chequebook and pen.

"Were you thinking of taking it with you?" she asked, a little nervously.

"No, it's alright," I told her. "I won't be leaving you with a space to fill. I assume there's no problem delivering it once the exhibition's over?"

"Delivery on the UK mainland is included in the price."

"The address is The Grange, St Hannahs, Cornwall," I said and gave her the postcode.

"That sounds rather nice," she smiled, making out a receipt.

"It's a hotel - in fact, you could say to Aidan that I'm in partnership there with... Eileen." I allowed myself a small smile. "Another old friend from those days."

"Eileen," scribbling on a notepad. "Right, I'll tell him."

I walked back over to the painting with Debbie and studied it again as she stuck a red dot onto the frame.

"You won't regret this," she said.

* * *

I was startled back to the present by a young couple walking along the path. We exchanged smiles and I stepped aside to let them examine the sculpture.

"They say he'd have shared the Nobel Peace Prize, if he'd lived," the man said to the young woman. "Apparently Clinton had him talking to all kinds of people in the background and his wife was in the British Government. Still is, I think."

"I like his paintings better," she said staring at it and they continued their walk.

Me too, I thought as I moved back close enough to touch

the piece, but I never did buy the whole Nobel Peace Prize story. They didn't give it to Emma, and she was as involved as anyone in putting the Good Friday Agreement together.

The painting arrived a month after I'd bought it, unheralded and unaccompanied by nothing other than an invoice, which I should have had the presence of mind to have asked to be sent separately. But there'd been no phone call in the intervening weeks or letter or even a note. The feeling I'd had at the gallery, of history if not being rewritten then of being carefully edited, seemed confirmed and I made no further effort to communicate.

Time passed.

I'd come across an occasional piece in the newspapers or on TV - Hackney's rising star MP hosting a Women's Rights conference, an arty farty analysis on the ambivalence between the YBA and *'our more conventional artists'*. Two very different strands that began to draw together, a mural on a wall built to divide Protestant and Catholic areas in Belfast, workshops in North London where victims of domestic violence found catharsis through oil paints. Emma in the Shadow Cabinet, a major exhibition at the Tate, late night TV discussions on the role of art as political commentary or the scandal of its removal from Secondary School curricula. And then a Labour landslide, standing either side of the President's envoy to the Peace Talks, the Secretary of State for Northern Ireland and a husband whose family embodied a century-long struggle of conflict and sorrow.

* * *

The phone call had come in the middle of the night and you just know that means trouble. Instinctively, you never reach for the phone straightaway. However startled from sleep you may be, there's always a moment taken to collect yourself.

"Claudia." It was Lee, and for a second I relaxed. She did have this habit of calling from wherever in the world she might be, with little regard for time zones. Then I remembered she was staying at *The Grange*, was aware that a silence was lengthening.

"Lee - what's the matter?"

"I didn't want you to hear it on the news," she said. "Aidan McShane died yesterday."

I was silent.

"Would you like to come over?" she asked. "We've no-one here at the moment."

"Yes," I told her.

I'd sold my share in the hotel to Paul four years earlier, he and Lee now ran it as a glorified Duke of Edinburgh Outward Bound Scheme for business executives with more money than sense. But I still had a front door key and so letting myself in, I followed the aroma of fresh coffee to the kitchen.

We embraced.

"I start filming at Universal next week," she said, "and I've been getting myself back on LA time. I switched on the news and…"

She shrugged and indicated my coffee.

"Perhaps something a little stronger in that?"

I nodded.

"When did you last see him?" I asked her.

"Probably the last time you did," she said, reaching for a bottle of Jameson's and pouring a generous measure into each of the mugs. "We'll make it an Irish, shall we?"

I took the mug from her.

"August, nineteen seventy," she said. "But that doesn't really matter, does it? *'Any man's death diminishes me and therefore never send to know for whom the bell tolls, it tolls for thee'*. Old Johnny Donne knew where it was at, didn't he just?"

I guessed this wasn't her first Irish coffee of the night.

The early morning news was full of tributes, switching from channel to channel brought famous faces generous with platitudes, but in the end it took a flickering old black and white clip of an art student in a Cornish studio to break us.

"I'm done with this shit," said Lee, flicking the TV off with the remote control and picking up the bottle of Jameson's. "Let's go and watch a sunrise."

And so we'd made our way down to the beach, shoes in hand, arm in arm, striding barefoot through the surf over to the Burrows.

* * *

I returned to the hotel to find Alex had finished the newspaper and appeared to be dozing, sitting back in his chair soaking up the early afternoon sun. But as I approached, his eyes opened, and he smiled.

"Shall I bring the car up for you?" I asked, but he shook his head.

"Be good to stretch my legs before we set off," he said. "Where are we staying tonight?"

"Salisbury," I reminded him. "You said you'd like to visit the Cathedral."

"Ah yes. They have Magna Carta there, you know?"

I did, he'd mentioned it several times regarding our journey home, and I was starting to wonder if Alex was... Well, not beginning to get a bit dotty, but perhaps *slowing*, as they used to say.

For a few minutes we walked down the leafy driveway in silence.

"Are you alright, Claudia?" As we came to a sharp bend, he stopped and turned to stare at me. "You seem a little down."

I was aware that I hadn't been able to shake my sombre mood from the visit to the Sculpture Garden, but I gave him a reassuring smile.

"I'm fine," I told him. "It's just that sometimes..." I shook my head. "You begin to wonder about the decisions you've made. How things might have worked out if you'd taken that other fork in the road." I shrugged. "And if maybe you should have."

He gave a slow nod, and we walked on for a while.

"This wasn't always a hotel, you know?" Raising his hand, he indicated up to where the building could just be seen through the trees, now high above us. "Back in the sixties, this was a private house."

"Really?"

"Yes, it was owned by a lady very much involved in local politics, a staunch supporter of the Liberal Party, as it then was. So much so, that she allowed the local Parliamentary Candidate - who subsequently succeeded in becoming the MP - to lodge here on his visits to the constituency. Together with any companion he'd chosen to bring." Alex turned toward me. "Do you remember Jeremy Thorpe?"

"Yes, of course." It had been a huge scandal, twenty or so years ago - Jeremy Thorpe had been an MP who'd had a homosexual affair with a male model. Later he'd been arrested and put on trial, accused of being involved in a conspiracy to murder his ex-lover, who was threatening to go public about it. It was quite a sensation at the time. Thorpe was eventually acquitted, but many suspected an establishment cover-up.

"Well," said Alex, "this was certainly the scene of at least one of those trysts."

I didn't ask how he knew this or where it might be leading. After many years I'd finally learnt that with Alex you let things go at their own pace.

"You know," he said eventually, "we always tend to think it's the major events that determine the course of history - battles won or lost and great statesmen coming together to decide the fate of nations. But of course, it's not."

He stopped and stared up at the house.

"Thorpe's proclivities were well known around Westminster during the sixties," he said, "and particularly the Scott affair. But it was a different time back then and with a less feral press. By the seventies he'd become leader of the Liberal Party and established himself as a significant figure in national politics. Not a potential Prime Minister perhaps but possibly a kingmaker."

There was a small wooden bench by the side of the drive and we sat down.

"And then came the 1973 General Election. The three-day week had forced the Prime Minister, Edward Heath, to seek a mandate from the country, but in that he failed. Harold Wilson's Labour Party secured a majority but a very slight one. So rather than resigning from office, Heath decided to try and establish a coalition government with Thorpe's Liberal Party, which would have given him an overall majority in the House of Commons.

"Immediately after the election Heath held a meeting with Thorpe, outlining his proposal and offering him the cabinet position of Home Secretary, if he accepted it. Which in principle Thorpe did, give or take a degree of the kind of political horse-trading one would expect around a deal like that.

"But when Wilson got wind of this, he called Thorpe into his office and told him that if this arrangement went ahead, he'd make sure that the Scott affair would be headlines in the national press before the week was out. In effect destroying both his political career and personal life. Thorpe was married and with children."

"So...?"

"So, the proposed coalition collapsed, Heath was forced from office and Wilson became Prime Minister. But," Alex turned to me, "let's speculate, without becoming too fanciful, on the course of events had Wilson not held that leverage.

"Margaret Thatcher won the leadership of the Conservative Party as a result of Heath losing that 1974 election and became Prime Minister in 1979, after the disastrous and chaotic events of the late seventies - economic collapse and almost permanent industrial unrest. But under our alternative scenario, Heath would remain Prime Minister until

1979 and Labour almost certainly would come to power that year, given that the same social turmoil would have taken place regardless of who was in Government. Even assuming Margaret Thatcher would still become the Tory Party leader, she wouldn't have had a chance of becoming Prime Minister until 1984."

Alex shook his head.

"Which would have been after the Falklands War, after the miners' strike - everything that's thought of as her legacy. And probably too late to forge the special relationship with Ronald Reagan, which was far more crucial to the demise of the Soviet Union than has ever been made public. Late twentieth century politics - internationally as well as nationally - would have been changed beyond recognition." He paused. "We'd be living in a far different world now and all because," with the same gesture of his hand he indicated the hotel again, "of some sordid little itch being scratched in a North Devon attic room."

The last half of that sentence was delivered with such genuine bitterness that I wasn't exactly sure how to react. Alex slowly stood and continued down the drive, while silently I followed.

"You know," he said softly, "I sometimes think that much the same could be said of ourselves. Reliving the seismic events of our lives, it's inevitable that we regard them as major turning points and it becomes easy to point the finger at those we hold accountable. But should we wonder if these are not simply roles that we've chosen to cast in scenarios we've been led into by processes of which we understand little and experience almost as bystanders? That the real decisions in our lives have been taken so far beneath our cognisance that it's perhaps futile - if not self-indulgent - to admonish ourselves for them?"

We weren't a family much given to physical displays of affection, but he looked so disconsolate that I reached forward and embraced him. And at his touch I felt my own blue mood begin to fade, as if he were soaking it up together with all the other troubles of the world.

"I really don't deserve you, my dear," he said, and when I began to dissent, he shook his head firmly. "No, I really don't."

I'm not sure who was the first to break the embrace, but it was done with ease rather than awkwardness. We continued to walk down to the car in silence, but a comfortable one.

* * *

"How long do you think?" asked Alex, as we turned onto the A39 and headed toward Blackmoor Gate and Exmoor.

"Oh, three, maybe four hours," I said. "Unless you'd like to stop somewhere on the way?"

"What about Porlock - that's where the *Rime of the Ancient Mariner* was written, you know? And goodness me, yet one more fraught tale desperate in its need to be told."

"Alright," I nodded. "I'll probably be ready for a cup of tea by then."

"But only if we have time," he said.

"Alex," I told him, "there's time."

Afterword

We hope that you enjoyed *Amanuensis*, the first novel in the St Hannahs series.

Like most independently published novels, its success is dependent on word-of-mouth recommendation rather than mainstream marketing. If you did enjoy it, a rating or review on Amazon or any of the online review sites would be greatly appreciated.

Felo de Se, the second St Hannahs novel is available from Amazon in both eBook and paperback formats.

ABOUT THE AUTHOR

Phil Egner

Phil was born in Nottingham in 1949.

During the late 1960s he was involved with a number of projects that had their genesis in the London counterculture and was a regular contributor to the underground press.

A career in software development followed, primarily as an IT contractor working in both the public and private sectors throughout the UK, mainland Europe and United States.

Home is now a Devon village where his time is increasingly occupied with the St Hannahs series of novels. Amanuensis and Felo de Se are currently available from Amazon, Belladonna will be published during the summer of 2022.

Printed in Great Britain
by Amazon